Road Home

Jules Nelson

The author can be contacted at jules.nelson@ymail.com

For additional information visit Jules Nelson's website at julesnelson.net

This book is a work of fiction and does not represent any individual, living or dead. All places, names, characters, and incidents either are products of the author's imagination or are used fictionally.

Cover design & Interior design by Julie Christine Nelson
Author photo by Jen Gusey Photography
Interior Editing by Cheree Castellanos

Summary: Sometimes the road home is a twisted, tumultuous path. Emma and Thane thought their first year of marriage would be a time of establishing a home. However, rumors cast a shadow of disapproval over Thane, threatening the peace the young couple so desperately seek. Being left behind to care for their farm in a community eager to be rid of them, Emma seeks God's guidance to light their path home.

[1. Historical Fiction 2. Young Adult – Fiction 3. Christian – Fiction 4. Michigan history-fiction 5. Family – fiction 6. Life in 1850 – fiction 7. Pioneer Life – Fiction]

ISBN: 978-1-7341355-0-3 (sc)
ISBN: 978-1-7341355-1-0 (eb)
ISBN: 978-1-7341355-2-7 (hc)

Library of Congress Control
Number: 2019916603

~for~

My Parents

Who never told us marriage
would be easy,
But showed us for 47 years
that it is worth it...

Therefore a man shall

leave his father and mother

and be joined to his wife,

and they shall become one flesh.

Genesis 2:24 NKJV

❧ Prologue ❧

September 9, 1846...

"**A**re ya sure, Mama?" Emma wrapped cookies in cloth squares, placing one in each basket. "Seth gets inta everythin'. How'll ya get yer work done?"

Mama smiled. "Yes, Emma Fern, I'll manage jest fine 'til ya come home again. School is important. More important than tendin' lil' boys who get inta mischief." Tucking her finger under Emma's chin, she raised her daughter's face so she could kiss her forehead. "Yer almost seven. Ya've waited long enough."

Emma sighed. It was the same answer she had gotten earlier. She knew better than to ask again. Resigning herself to going to school, she turned back to packing the dinner baskets.

Mark burst through the front door, leaving it wide open and ran straight to the washtub. Scrubbing his arms and hands, he half-dried them on a towel and turned to grab his basket.

"Didya get behind those ears?" Mama asked, even though she already knew the answer.

"Uhhh," Emma's older brother stalled for a clever answer.

His mother reached over to pull his ear out from behind the cover of his hair. "Hmm," she hummed. "Seems ya missed a spot."

Emma chuckled despite herself. Handing her brother a rag, she finished her task.

"I'm gonna be late, Mama. Emma's a real slow walker. Can I jest skip taday?"

Ignoring the pleading look on her oldest child's face, Mama replied quiet but firm, "Mark Wells, when yer at school, ya represent this family. An' I want ya ta make yer Da proud."

With a groan, Mark turned toward the washtub again.

Emma picked up the baskets and turned to wait for him. When he finished scrubbing, he returned to grab his basket from her. Kissing Mama's cheek, he raced out the door. Emma hesitated for a moment before doing the same.

Mama pulled her daughter in for a quick hug. "Try not ta worry. I'll make do 'til yer home." Guiding her out the door, she waved until Emma disappeared along the road.

"Come on, Em!" Mark waited for Emma, where the road curved toward town. When she caught up to him, he took her by the arm to hurry her. "We willna have any time ta play before Teacher rings the bell."

Emma allowed herself to be pulled along. Her mind wandered back to everything Mama and Mark had told her about school. Over and over, she reminded herself of what they said. Reminded herself what was expected of her. *Sit still. Be quiet. Listen carefully. Make Da proud.* It was all so overwhelming. She felt herself sigh again.

"It willna be that bad, Em," her brother scolded. The lines on his forehead disappeared as fast as they formed. "Oh, look... there's James."

Standing in the road ahead was Mark's friend James. James' face brightened into a smile when he saw them. "Was worried ya weren't comin'," he admitted.

"It's Emma's fault. She's scared of school, so she's draggin' her feet," Mark grumbled in irritation.

"I'm not scared," Emma denied. Turning to James, she explained, "I'm worried that Mama will na git anythin' done with that Seth taggin' along. He's jest four! An' it's wash day."

"Yup, scared," Mark repeated as if her words confirmed his theory.

James smiled, amused at their argument. He looked from one sibling to the other.

6

Refusing to be bested by her brother, Emma turned back to James. "Did yer mama have ta check behind yer ears this mornin' too?" she asked, raising her eyebrows. "Because that's the real reason we're late-."

Mark interrupted her with an elbow to the ribs. "Shhh! Em... he doesna have a mama," he hissed in her ear.

Emma saw James look down at his shoe, kicking at a rock. "I'm sorry," she whispered. "I didna know." Her eyes filled with tears at her mistake. Not being able to imagine life without Mama, she felt her heart break for James. Looking down to hide her tears, she saw the cookie sitting on top of the other food in her basket. Without a second thought, she handed it to her brother's friend.

"What's this? I canna take yer food," James tried to refuse, even as his hand reached out for it.

She laughed and insisted, "I helped make that cookie, I reckon I kin help make another."

Smiling, he accepted the treat. He looked down at it like he would like to taste it right there. But instead, he fingered the blue cloth wrapping the treat. "This's pretty."

"It's a scrap from my new Sunday dress," she explained.

He looked up at Emma then. "Thank ya," he said with a quiet smile. The smile made his eyes look brighter.

Emma nodded to let him know she heard him. *I must remember ta bring him another cookie tomorra.*

The school bell started ringing up ahead.

The three children hurried the rest of the way into town. Emma's nervousness returned as she approached the schoolhouse. Taking a deep breath, she slowly climbed the steps. Emma untied her bonnet and hung it on a nail along the back wall with several other hats. A breeze came in through the door, making them sway. How she longed to step back out into that breeze. But Emma never walked away from her tasks, and she was not about to start that day.

Placing her lunch basket next to her brother's, she forced herself to turn toward the classroom and drew in a shaky breath. Determined to make Mama and Da proud, she said a little prayer for help.

Pulling her shoulders back, she stepped further into the schoolroom. A dark-haired little girl waved to her from the front row of benches. Emma was concentrating so hard on looking relaxed that she never noticed her. She was concentrating so carefully that she did not notice anyone, not even Mark and James, as she walked up the aisle between the rows of seats. She did not see that they were walking right behind her.

Ready to help her in any way she might need.

Echoes of Home

❧ One ❧

October 9, 1858...

Emma knew she would have to face the women watching her eventually. Stalling for time, she pretended to search for a place to set her basket of cookies. It wasn't hard to convince everyone. Being one of the last families to arrive, the table before her was already full.

Looking up, she caught Thane's eye. His mouth curved into a lopsided smile. He gazed at her for a moment more before turning back to the conversation he was supposed to be listening to. Closing her eyes, Emma breathed a silent prayer. *Please let Da be right, Lord.*

Her father had convinced the young couple it would help the acceptance of their sudden marriage if they attended the barn raising. Da insisted that having the community see Thane work alongside him would go a long way to gain their respect.

How can the community accept Thane as my husband, when my own brother will na?

Taking a deep breath, she turned her attention back to looking for a place for her cookies. *I can't stand here much longer, or they'll know I'm stalling.* Hardly an inch of the table was showing around the food, so she edged dishes and baskets closer together to make enough room for her own.

Then picking up the crate by her feet, Emma squared her shoulders and walked to where the women were standing together, talking.

"I wouldna doubt if James stayed away taday. Poor dear heart, he has ta be-"

The voices went silent as Emma approached. The silence felt like a warning.

Wherever she went in town, Emma could feel the curious stares. Curious as to what happened during the month she had disappeared. Curious as to what she had endured when she had been stolen away from her family. The silence that greeted her in stores, reminding her that no one had forgotten about her misfortune.

Today was no different. She longed for the time when she had walked down the street unnoticed.

Emma's attention was drawn to the ladies that waited for her with their disapproving frowns. Mrs. Phelps was among them.

"Morning, Emma dear. Such a good day to help the Grahams raise this barn."

Emma felt worried despite the fact that the mercantile owner greeted her with a smile.

"We were na sure ya would be comin' taday. We've never seen the likes of yer Mr. Hawkins at any community events that we could recall." Murmurs stirred around them, agreeing with Mrs. Phelps's words.

Setting her crate down, Emma turned to the group of ladies watching her. "I canna answer fer the past, but Mr. Hawkins is here taday." She caught little Rachel Moore studying her again. She had seen that look on Rachel's face more than once lately. A look of pity- pity but mixed with something more. Emma couldn't figure out what else. *She looks worried*.

A beautiful dark-haired lady pushed through the crowd. "Emma!"

"Oh, Abigail dear," Mrs. Phelps turned her attention to the newcomer. "We didna expect ta see ya here taday."

"I couldn't possibly miss a chance to visit with you all, my dear Mrs. Phelps. And I saw the new window display ya put together. So clever." With a pat on the older lady's arm, Abigail greeted each of the other women around her.

Abigail Spencer had a way of drawing all the attention to herself. It felt good for Emma to settle in her friend's shadow once more. When Abigail turned back to Emma, the crowd around them had shifted their focus away from Emma and her new husband.

"Ya came."

"Of course, I came. I needed ta make sure ya sit and take it easy taday." Emma forced her voice to sound teasing, but in truth, she was more than a little worried about her friend.

Abigail's belly was full and round, but she never let it slow her down. Emma suspected her friend's baby would come soon. The previous day Emma had caught Abigail rubbing her hands over her growing baby when no one was watching. Exhaustion had shown itself in that moment. But when someone turned to her, Abigail plastered a smile back on her face and laughed.

When the exhaustion showed through, it worried Emma. The memory of that same exhaustion on her mama's loving face came to mind. The exhaustion that kept her mama in bed for weeks before she died. Dying only minutes after giving birth to her baby sister. A sister who never drew a breath.

Emma forced a smile to stay on her lips as her worry deepened. Everywhere she looked in the community, she saw families who had lost mothers. A few men packed up their meager belongings when they lost their wives and headed back to east. Some farmers remarried if they had young children. Her own Da had chosen not to remarry. Emma and her brothers were old enough when their mama died that it had not been necessary.

Abigail laughed. "Emma, yer such a mother hen. I'm fine. Though I confess to bein' anxious ta hold my baby boy in my arms, instead of this bushel basket under my dress."

Emma smiled again, genuinely this time.

Laughter surrounded them. Abigail continued to rant cheerfully about wanting to have her figure back and how she longed to see her feet. Emma started to relax. The more Abigail made the other women laugh, the more it distracted their attention from noticing her. Emma figured the less they noticed her, the less they would stare.

Rachel caught Emma's eye again before turning away. Although a quiet girl, Rachel usually had a ready smile. Her distracted behavior made Emma a little worried for her. She shrugged off the uncertain feeling.

Turning back to Abigail, she caught her friend watching her.

Emma was so grateful for Abigail's support of late, but it hadn't always been that way. Her relationship with her friend had become strained over the last couple of years. With Abigail getting married and starting a family, she had wanted the same for her friend. But Abigail's matchmaking efforts had become uncomfortable for Emma. Before her family had announced her engagement to James, Emma had started to avoid her friend altogether.

"Emma, could ya have David bring me my rockin' chair? He brought it in the wagon with us, in case I had need of it." Her friend's voice sounded light, but Emma knew she must already be tired.

She nodded. Turning immediately to search for Abigail's husband, she wasn't surprised to see him working near Thane.

David Spencer had chosen to befriend Emma's husband. At first, it had felt forced, and Emma knew he was trying for her sake alone. But after speaking the first few times, David seemed to relax and really enjoy Thane's company.

Hurrying toward the two men, Emma slowed to a stop to wait for one of them to notice her. Thane spotted her first. When she gestured to David, Thane leaned over and tapped his friend's arm. David saw her then and hurried over.

"Abigail would like her chair brought to her." Emma raised her voice to be heard above the noise.

Worry clouded the young man's eyes. Instead of an answer, he strode off toward the row of wagons lining the road. Emma hurried along behind him. She intended to grab the empty crate and blanket from her father's wagon. Propping Abigail's feet up would do her some good.

"I wish Abby had stayed home taday," Emma said, once they were away from the work area.

David chuckled, rubbing the back of his neck. "I argued all morn' with her. She flat refused ta stay home." He looked like he wanted to say more but stopped with a glance at her.

Emma looked back in the direction of her friend. She knew why Abigail had insisted on coming. "I knew Abigail would show up today... jest ta support me. Even if it means exhaustin' herself," she confessed. She knew that David was too polite to express this himself, but she wanted to be honest with these two people who had stood by her and her new husband. She wanted him to know she appreciated the sacrifices they were making.

Surprised by the openness of her statement, David recovered quickly and nodded in agreement.

When they reached his wagon, David reached into the back to untie the chair. Emma retrieved the crate from her father's wagon. Tucking inside the blanket that she had used on the long ride, she hurried back to where David was waiting. He placed a small pillow in her crate, then lifted the chair over his shoulder.

Emma led him to where Abigail waited, talking to the other ladies. David set the chair down in the shade of a nearby tree. Taking his young wife's hand, he led her over to sit. Emma placed the crate in front of her friend and propped her feet up. Shaking the blanket out, she tucked it around her friend's full lap.

"Well, I declare! Ya'd think I was a queen taday, with all this fussin'," Abigail laughed.

David watched her for a moment, concern on his face.

Emma could tell he wanted to take Abigail home. "I'll make sure Abby rests. If I'm worried fer her, I'll fetch ya."

David nodded once. Placing a kiss on his wife's head, he turned back to the barn being built. Then he was gone.

Tucking the small pillow under Abigail's feet, Emma reprimanded her friend. "Ya shouldna come taday. Ya should be at home relaxin'."

"An' leave ya ta face this on yer own?" Abigail shook her head. "I'll be fine, Emma. Don't ya worry none."

Emma laughed. Her friend looked fierce. As fierce as a very pregnant woman could look. She lowered herself to the ground next to the rocking chair to watch the building in progress.

Small groups of men worked together on various tasks. A group of young men worked on stripping the bark off the logs. Another group attempted to level off the tops for a closer fit. Emma's eyes found where her father and brothers were working. Nearby, she saw Thane and David were discussing something. Emma's brother, Mark, turned and handed some tools to a newcomer in their group. When Mark looked in her direction, she caught his attention. His jaw clenched.

The action reminded Emma of their Da, and she smiled sadly. It seemed that was all Mark did anymore. Flex his jaw. He was still upset over her unexpected marriage. He refused to admit that the abduction was a reason to marry someone- a reason to break his friend's heart.

The change on her brother's face caused the man by his side to turn and face her. Startled at the sight of James, her breath caught.

James' smile didn't hide the sadness in his eyes. After a moment, he turned back to the task Mark had given him.

Closing her eyes, Emma could still remember seeing James' face so full of joy. The way his face had been all that last summer. She had been so blind, thinking his joy had nothing to do with her. How surprised Emma had been when James had confessed his love for her. When he had explained to everyone how he had been in love with her since they were both children.

Those summer days had been happy ones for Emma. She had finally found a friend. She had found Thane. Or rather, he had found her. Thane had started visiting her during her chores, just to talk. Having someone to talk to and laugh with had made Emma blossom. She had

15

laughed more than she could remember in the years since her mother had died. Her joy had been obvious to all those around her.

Nothing could have surprised her more than when her father had explained that he had granted James permission to marry her. When she had tried to protest, her Da had named every time that Emma herself had showed them all that she loved James in return. Every attention that she had given James, leading him to believe she felt the same.

James was her brother's friend. She had never even stopped to think he could be anything different.

Taking a deep breath, Emma opened her eyes and turned them to watch her Da. She could not blame him for his misunderstanding. *No, the fault was mine alone.* When Thane had come visiting, he had always been very proper. But her family had not known about the visits. In fact, they didn't know about Thane at all. So, her father assumed the one thing he could assume. That all her happiness was from James coming around more often. When Emma joked with James and laughed in return? Her father took that to confirm what he believed.

Her happiness had died the day her Da told her she would marry James, but Emma had accepted the arrangement just the same. Her improper behaviors had led James to believe she loved him. She had needed to make her mistakes right.

And she would have married James, too.

But one night, Emma had knelt in the woods and cried out her heartbreak. Just as she had given her life to the Lord to lead as He saw fit, a shadow had separated from the trees and hit her over the head. When she had finally woke, she found that Thane's Pa had taken it upon himself to steal her away. Thane had been angry at his pa's actions. But in the end, it had become necessary for him to marry Emma before taking her home.

Emma's eyes filled with tears as she watched James work in the group with Thane. She watched him set his shoulders and worked side by side with the man who had taken his love from him. Emma could see what he was doing. Despite his heartache, James was trying to help the community accept Thane. Most of all, he was trying to help her brothers accept Thane. After all, if James could show forgiveness and acceptance, how could anyone else reject Thane? James was helping the very man who had caused his world to fall apart.

Wiping the tears away, Emma turned back to Abigail.

The women had turned to greet some latecomers, leaving the two friends by themselves for a moment. Rachel hung back from the group, standing by herself.

"There is talk that lil' Rachel there, may have ta marry. Mrs. Phelps said her brother caught a man embracing her against her wishes." Abigail kept her voice low as she rubbed her round stomach. "I wasn't sure I wanted ta believe the tale. But lookin' at her worried face taday, I fear it may be true."

"Wasn't Mr. Nash courtin' her a while back?" Emma asked, watching Rachel.

"Yes, he was."

Remembering the day Mr. Nash had followed her out of town filled her heart with dread. His intention had been to trap Emma into a dishonorable situation. Being alone with a man was enough reason to force a young lady to get married. She was so thankful that God had intervened that day and sent Thane to her rescue. "Surely, her Da wouldna want her ta marry the likes of him?" Emma asked.

"Lookin' at the worry in her eyes, I fear he may."

Discussing it further was impossible as the other ladies returned. Gathering around the rocking chair again, some settled into the grass near Emma, while others brought chairs and crates closer to sit on. The talk turned to the upcoming quilting meeting.

Emma's mind drifted away from the conversation and returned to Rachel. *Lord, please be with lil' Rachel. Hold her in Yer hands and protect her from harm if it's Yer Will*, she prayed. A smile touched her lips as she looked at little Rachel Moore. She was no longer a little girl. She was a beautiful young lady. A quiet person to be around but always helpful.

No, Rachel was not little anymore. But her mother's name was also Rachel. As a result, the daughter was still called "lil' Rachel."

Shaking her head to clear it, Emma turned back to the conversation around her. When Abigail's cup was empty, Emma rose to fill it again.

The sun rose high over them and caused the men to stop more than once to wipe the sweat from their faces. Emma rose, once again, to take their bucket to the well and fill it. Carrying it over to the worksite, the men in her family dipped some water out to drink. Seth and Mark poured a scoop over the back of their neck. Offering water to some of the other men, she waited until the bucket was empty before getting settled back into the shade near her friend.

When the sun was high in the sky, Mrs. Craig wiped the sweat from her brow and rose from her seat on a crate. Stretching her back, she sighed. "Well, ladies, our restin' is over. Time ta feed those hungry men." Everyone followed the older lady's lead and stood up, smoothing their dresses, and scattering in different directions.

As soon as Emma had her picnic blanket spread on the ground, she heard the dinner bell ringing out over the sound of hammers and saws. She smiled at the abrupt stop to the noise. Grabbing the stack of plates in her crate, Emma barely had time to stand up before Seth was there before her. He held his hand out for a plate and ran off toward the table of food.

"I see Seth still worries the food will disappear before he has a chance to get his fill," David said with a laugh.

"Seth be full?" James joked back. "I'm na sure that'll ever happen."

The rest of the men joined the laughter as they gathered their plates.

After the men filled their plates, the women picked over what was left. When Emma had filled her plate, she joined her family. Sitting on the edge of the quilt next to Thane, she smiled up at her husband.

"Ya doin' alright?" Thane asked.

Emma nodded her head.

"Ya sure? Ya look a little tired."

Smiling at his worry, she bumped against his arm playfully. "I'm fine. Ya tryin' ta get out of all that hard work?"

"Iffen I was, I'd get no mercy from ya." Thane's mouth turned up with a lopsided smile.

Looking over his shoulder, she saw David's worried face. Thinking he was watching his wife, she turned instead to see him concentrating on James. James was sitting on the other side of the quilt, watching her with sad eyes. When she caught him staring, he lowered his gaze to his plate. She saw him push his food around with his fork, but he didn't lift any to his mouth. A sudden movement at his side broke Emma's concentration. She turned and saw Mark's angry eyes directed at her. Turning away, she blinked to keep the tears from coming.

She was beginning to worry that Mark would always find fault with her actions. It had been over a month since she had returned home married to Thane. But Mark was still as angry as he was that first day.

Setting her plate down on the quilt, she stood up and filled a bucket with fresh water. Bringing it back to her family's quilt, she dipped out a cup for each of the men and handed them around. Taking the bucket to the far side of the quilt where David and James sat, she held it out for them to dip from. When everyone had their fill, she returned the bucket to the edge of the well.

When she returned, the silence felt awkward. Emma lowered herself to the quilt but couldn't think of anything to say.

Abigail smiled at her. "I remember when we were buildin' the house fer the Barnes couple last spring. It started out sunny like today, and we thought it would stay that way. Then within minutes of puttin' the roof on, the wind picked up and started ta storm. Blew them shingles all the way ta Vermontville." She continued her story to keep the attention away from her friend.

Breathing a sigh of relief, Emma picked up her food again.

Finally, Da handed his plate to Emma and stretched. "I guess we'd best get back ta it, boys." Putting his hat back on his head, he rose to his feet. Emma followed suit, standing to gather the dishes. Without thinking, she held out her hand for James' dishes. She had been washing his dishes for as long as she could remember. But when he hesitated to give them to her, she wondered if it was still proper. She looked up into James' face. The pain she saw there made her breath catch. She had done it again.

Abruptly, Mark grabbed the dishes from James' grasp and thrust them into Emma's outstretched hand. "Come on," he mumbled, his voice gruff.

Looking away from her, James coughed to clear his throat. "Thank ya, Emma."

Thane appeared before her. His face swam through her watery eyes. Her new husband knew how much she hated to see James suffer. He leaned forward like he was going to kiss her forehead but changed his mind. Emma knew it was because they had agreed not to show affection. No one knew that they had been friends before she was attacked and stolen away. Her family hadn't even known Thane existed. She knew he couldn't kiss her here. But her heart ached for the comfort. Squeezing her shoulder, he slipped his hat on and followed the other men back to work.

Emma felt a tear slide down her cheek as she watched her husband walk away. It was frustrating for her to pretend she didn't know her husband enough to love him. To act like she was merely resigned to her marriage. But for Emma to admit that she loved Thane would mean she had to admit that she knew Thane before his father had stolen her away. She would have to admit she had spent time with Thane. Time that her family knew nothing about.

Taking a shaky breath, she turned back to finish cleaning up. But when she turned around, she found everyone's eyes on her. Even Rachel Moore stared at Emma as she blinked back her tears. It was suddenly too much for her, and she looked down to hide her emotions.

In an instant, Abigail was by her side, hugging her for comfort. Wrapping her arms around Emma's shoulders, Abigail leaned over her big belly to press her lips to her friend's cheek. Suddenly, Emma felt a jolt at her waist. She pulled back in surprise.

Abigail pressed her hand to her stomach and chuckled. "I do believe my boy says ya should kick some sense inta those men of yers.".

Emma returned her friend's laugh, wiping the tears from her cheeks. Looking up again, she caught Abigail wiping tears of her own.

"Well, I'll be... the sun is makin' my eyes tear up somethin' awful," Abigail called out, loud enough for everyone to hear. "We'd best find ourselves some shade after we wash these dishes."

Laughing again, Emma leaned forward and stole the plates from her friend's hands, scolding her. "You, my friend, will find that shade now. No dish washin' fer ya today."

Abigail grumbled good-naturedly about her bossy friend as she settled back into her rocking chair. The other ladies laughed with her, breaking the tension. Only Rachel still looked upset. As Emma walked past her, she couldn't stop herself from reaching out to squeeze her hand in comfort. "Come. We'll scrub these plates, so we can relax in the shade with Abigail." She didn't really need any help, but she wanted to give the young lady an excuse to move away from the group.

Rachel nodded and followed in silence. Standing in front of the washtub, Emma scrubbed her own plates and then started on Rachel's stack. Rachel rinsed each dish without saying a word, drying them carefully. Emma recognized the way Rachel was stalling. She understood her hesitation all too well. She wasn't looking forward to rejoining the other ladies either. So when Mrs. Craig came to stand next to her, she reached for the older lady's stack of dishes and slid them into the water.

"Why, Emma... ya do na have ta wash my plates," Mrs. Craig protested.

Emma smiled. "Well now, I'll bet that not one of yer boys washes them fer ya at home. So, jest sit yerself back and let us pamper ya a little."

Mrs. Craig smiled in delight. "Bless ya both. Ya wouldn't believe the mountain of dishes those boys of mine can produce. I'll enjoy this lil' break." She pulled a crate up beside the girls and began to tell them how trying it could be raising eight boys. "I remember a day when Mr. Craig came in from the fields ta find his three oldest boys strapped inta chairs. He turned his eyes ta me in question, then went ta wash his hands. Scrubbed his hands like he saw nothin' wrong with boys tied ta chairs with their own belts." Mrs. Craig chuckled at the memory. "He sat down ta his plate and bowed his head fer grace. Prayed loud enough fer those stubborn boys ta hear too. Askin' the almighty ta give those stubborn boys wisdom- that they would know to come clean ta their Ma before they starved ta death by their own belts." Sadie paused for a loud sigh. "Now truth be told? I was close ta tears already. Wrestlin' those big boys into those chairs had done me in. But I refused to let them see it. If they had? I already had me those five boys. I would have been overrun in no time. Soon as Mr. Craig said his "Amen"? Those boys of mine started a sniffin'. My second born was the first to apologize ta me. When I accepted and released him from his belted prison, the other two joined in pretty fast. I could have sworn I saw my husband fightin' a smile, but he never said a word about it."

Emma smiled. "What was their crime?"

"Pardon?" Mrs. Craig asked, distracted by her memory.

"What did they do that ya had needed ta tie them there?" she repeated as she kept washing the dishes.

Mrs. Craig laughed. "My oldest had laughed when I got after him. Then proudly stated that his belt would never hurt him when it was used by a woman. As soon as he dug in, the other two dug in their heels as well. So, I had ta show them I was boss in my house. They never questioned it again."

Emma chuckled. The story reminded her of a young Seth. It had irked him to take orders from his older sister. But with Mama gone, Emma had no choice but to make him listen.

"Let me ask Mrs. Peterson if she'd like fer us ta wash her dishes too," Rachel said, interrupting Emma's thoughts.

Emma watched Rachel approach Mrs. Peterson. Mrs. Peterson was new to their community. She had brought three young children with her and added them to the four that her new husband had of his own. They had married earlier that year, after each spending a winter in mourning. This marriage had helped both husband and wife. But with seven young children, Mrs. Peterson was often exhausted.

"That was before my husband died," Mrs. Craig went on. "So at least I had someone ta laugh with when that day was done. Laughter is important when yer raisin' boys."

The other lady's voice brought Emma's thoughts back to her task. "That it is, Mrs. Craig."

Rachel returned with a crate full of dishes. She gave Emma an apologetic smile as she set it by her feet.

"I best get myself a towel and start helpin'," Mrs. Craig stated as she set out for her own crate across the yard.

Emma smiled to herself. *It's a sad day when I prefer scrubbin' dishes ta visitin'*. But she had never been one to waste time. She picked up a stack of plates and set them in the washtub to soak. "We'll need fresh water after this batch of scrubbin' I'm thinkin'."

Rachel nodded in agreement. Putting down her towel, she set off toward the well to pull a fresh bucket of water up.

Mrs. Craig set right to work rinsing the dishes and drying them. When Rachel returned, she set the bucket down and jumped back into the work, handing rinsed dishes to the older lady to dry.

As they worked, they listened to the sweet lady tell stories. "And that Benjamin wouldna stay away from the horse corral. One summer day, that stallion came running out chargin' that boy. Instead of being kicked, he latched onto the horse's leg and wouldna let go. The horse

23

thrashed about and bucked somethin' fierce. But Benjamin held on until we pulled him off."

"Did he finally learn ta stay away?" Emma asked with a chuckle.

Mrs. Craig sighed. "Ya would think that. But what do ya know? He was out there again the very next day. Good thing he's my youngest. Wouldna got anythin' done with another one younger than him."

Emma thought she caught a ghost of a smile cross Rachel's face. *Good*, she thought to herself, *she needs laughter*.

Turning toward Mrs. Craig, Emma gave her a genuine smile. "God sure trusted ya with a big task givin' you those eight boys, Mrs. Craig," she exclaimed.

"Oh, please call me Sadie," she insisted.

They finished drying their dishes and returned them to the people that they belonged to.

Emma felt guilty that she left Abigail alone for so long. But when she finally headed in her direction, she saw that her friend had fallen asleep in the shade. Careful, so as not to wake her, Emma placed Abigail's dishes back into her basket, covering them with her towel so the dust wouldn't collect on them.

Settling into the shade next to her friend, Emma turned to watch the men at work. Surprised at how far they had gotten while she had been distracted by the dishwashing, she searched for Thane among the many heads. She finally spotted him with David. They were carrying something heavy toward the door opening. While she watched, Thane tipped his head back with laughter. It was a short laugh, but it was enough for Emma. *Maybe Da was right. We needed this*, she thought to herself.

In the weeks since Thane returned Emma home, they had kept to themselves. Except when Abigail insisted they stop by. Or when Seth stopped by the farm looking for cookies.

She watched with interest until the men started gathering their tools and putting them into their wooden boxes. Seth stopped working altogether, and Emma saw him leaning against the well, talking to another young man. Emma leaned forward as she watched the two. Seth didn't have his usual teasing smile in place. His frown concerned her.

"Emma?" Abigail drew her attention back to the shade of the tree.

"Yer awake?" Emma said with a smile.

"Ya should've woke me," she answered with a yawn.

Emma shook her head. "Ya needed ta rest."

Abigail sat up and looked in the direction of the well where Seth had been only minutes before. "What has ya so worried?"

Looking for her younger brother, he seemed to have disappeared. "I was jest noticin' Seth. He seems quiet today."

Thane and David approached the shade of the tree, deep in conversation over something. When they saw the girls, they stopped talking and bent to kiss their respective wives.

"Is this ours?" Thane asked, nodding toward the pile next to the rocking chair.

Emma nodded. "This crate and the one keepin' Abigail's feet up."

The menfolk gathered up their belongings. They made a trip to the Spencer's wagon with the rocking chair and baskets, before returning to escort the ladies. Da had the team hitched to the wagon by the time they arrived. Thane lifted her into the back and climbed in with her. Seth climbed up next to their father, quieter than usual.

Da clicked to the team to start them moving. Emma rocked with the motion, holding onto the sideboard. Thane tucked the blanket around her.

"I'm fine, Thane. No need ta worry," she insisted.

"Ya look exhausted, Emma," Thane answered. "It's a long ride home. Why don't ya lay back and rest?"

Her father turned on his bench to look at her. "Maybe taday was a mistake. I hope ya didna overdo it." The worried look returned to his face. The same worried look he had worn every time her head hurt.

"My head is healed, Da," Emma reassured her father. When Thane's father had stolen her away into the night, he had left her with a large lump on her head. She had slept for days. Whenever she had overdone it in the weeks that followed, she would pass out and sleep for hours. "The bump doesna even hurt these days."

Not looking convinced, her father turned back to the road.

Everyone was silent until they approached town. James pulled his horse closer to the wagon, and Emma pulled his dishes out of her crate.

"Thank ya. How are ya doin'?" he asked.

"I am well, thank ya." Emma's eyes wanted to fill up, but she blinked the tears away. The day had been an awkward day for James. Yet, here he was asking her how she had fared. *May God bless you,* Emma prayed.

As the wagon approached the turn off to their farm, Seth turned in his seat toward his sister. "I was talkin' ta the young Moore boy. He told me how he walked behind the barn last week ta see Mr. Nash tryin' ta kiss his sister. He fears his pa will make Rachel marry Nash."

Emma's heart dropped. She had hoped the rumor was a mistake. Now she was losing that hope. "We need ta pray that it doesn't come ta that!" she exclaimed.

"We need ta do far more than that," Mark thundered, turning his horse toward home.

Emma watched her brother ride his horse away. Worry filled her. She knew he was still angry at her, but he also seemed angry at the whole world.

❧ *Two* ☙

mma washed the last of their supper dishes and wiped down the table. Looking toward the window, she wondered where her husband was. Usually, he was in from his evening chores before she finished hers.

Exhausted from the long day, Emma yawned. *Maybe I did overdo it*, she thought. *Perhaps I should leave the rest for tomorrow?* As quickly as the idea crossed her mind, she dismissed it. She never left chores for the next day. The new day would have enough chores waiting for her already. With another yawn, she reached for the broom to sweep the dirt back outside. The dirt they had tracked in carrying in crates and baskets from the barn raising.

Opening the door, she stepped outside to finish sweeping the dirt off the porch. She was turning back to the cabin when a movement caught her eye. There leaning against the open door of the barn was Thane, reading a piece of paper. Putting the broom back inside, she wiped her hands on her apron before stepping out into the evening air.

Thane looked up as he heard her footsteps approach. "I got a letter from Mrs. Preston... from my grandmother," he said when she was near enough to hear. "David saw it at the post office and brought it out to me." Thane handed the letter to Emma so she could read it.

Emma took the paper. Tilting it so the light from the setting sun made the words visible, she could see the fancy handwriting. A breeze blew toward her, moving the paper and wafting the soft smell of flowers. "Is that-?" She brought it closer to her face to sniff the paper.

"Yes," Thane confirmed with a smile. One side lifting higher, making the lopsided smile that Emma loved. "She scented the paper."

"Why?' Emma sniffed it again and then shrugged. Tilting the paper toward the sunset, she read the short letter.

October 4, 1858
My dear Thane,

I hope this letter finds you well.

I am overjoyed to have found you at last. I received the letter Sheriff Granger sent. He explained that you and your young bride have moved into the cabin. This is wonderful news.

I am getting my affairs in order here in Detroit. My hopes are to be finished packing and on my way to Vermontville before long. I wish to make it before the snow flies.

I would very much like to stay with you until another place can be found. We have much to learn about each other.

With Love,
Mary Preston

"Short and to the point," Emma said when she finished. Folding the paper, she handed it back to Thane. "I guess we'll need ta be fixin' that room up fer her," she pointed out. They had spent the last month fixing up the outside of the cabin, getting it ready for winter. But they had not worked inside very much. And they had done no work in the small bedroom. "I have enough material ta sew a mattress cover. Da will let me have some straw ta fill it with fer now. By the time she gets here, I'll have enough feathers ta make a fresh pillow fer her. But it'll be a while before I have enough for a mattress."

Thane nodded, staring off into the hills.

28

Emma had seen her husband looking to the hills often. But in the last few days, it seemed more frequent. She wondered if he missed the quiet life in his cabin. A place where no one judged him harshly because of his father's crimes. But he always shook off his thoughts and returned to his task at hand.

"Emma... now that the shingles are finished, I need to find my pa. I need some answers." He turned to Emma then. His eyes begged her to understand. "Everything will change when my grandmother comes. She'll bring her own truths with her- truths about my mama. Truths about my pa. And I don't even know what was real. My growin' up years weren't like yours. All I had was my Pa after Clara left. An' I couldn't always count on him ta be there. I would tell myself the stories he told me, over and over. They comforted me when I was alone. Now? Now, Emma, I don't know if any of those stories were even true."

"I don't know if I can ask for respect among these people when I don't know if I deserve that respect. How can I, when I'm not sure my family deserves that respect? How can I ask you to be part of my family when I don't know that you should want it?"

The breath caught in Emma's chest. She wanted to be unselfish and give him her blessing to find what he needed. But she was fighting panic. Unable to speak, she tried to smile. She could feel that her smile was shaky, so instead, she nodded her agreement.

He smiled sadly and pulled her into his arms. Her hands curled into fists around his shirt as she breathed in his strength.

"I know ya don't want me ta go. I don't want to be away from ya fer even one day. But I'm hopin' that iffen I go now, I should be back before my grandmother arrives. I'm wantin' ta be back well before winter sets in ta stay." His voice was soft as he spoke against her hair.

Emma nodded against his chest.

"I'll leave after my chores in the mornin'," Thane whispered, emotion making him sound gruff. His arms tightened around her, pulling her against him.

"Tomorrow?" The shock of it made the word come out in a squeak.

Thane remained silent for a moment before answering. "No use puttin' it off. Might as well just get it done."

Emma knew he was right. She also knew she would need a lot of prayers to get through the next day.

❧ Three ❧

October 10, 1858...

*L*ong before the sun rose the next morning, Emma heard the door close behind Thane as he went to start his chores. Rising out of bed, she slipped her dress on and went to make coffee. With a yawn, she watched the fire spark to life. *I'll cook him a big breakfast*, she decided. *It'll keep him fer a few days*.

Slicing a few pieces of bacon, she put them into the pan once it was hot enough. While she was cutting a potato to fry, Thane came into the kitchen with water for the washtub.

Kissing her on the cheek, he watched her work for a moment. "Nothing too big, Em. I want ta get goin' when I finish with my chores."

"I can do chores later," Emma insisted.

A lopsided smile lit up his face, "Ya'll be doin' my chores everyday soon enough. I imagine ya won't be so cheerful about it then." His smile faded a little as he stared into her eyes. "I'm so sorry ta be leavin' ya here alone- ta take care of this farm all by yerself. And ta face the talk in town. But I need answers. Can ya understand that?" he asked, running his thumb down her cheek.

With a nod, Emma turned back to her pan. She blinked a few times to hide her tears. "I'll jest add eggs ta this. It'll be ready when ya are."

Thane hesitated a moment then went back out to finish his chores.

He returned a short time later and washed up before joining her at the table. Emma picked at her food, not really hungry. They ate their breakfast in silence. Neither one knew what to say.

When he rose to leave, Emma felt tears burning her eyes. Turning away, she finished packing food into a bag that Thane could

31

easily carry on his saddle. When she couldn't think of anything else to put in the bag, she followed him outside.

Thane was saddling his horse just outside the barn door. A lantern shone through the door to light his movements. He disappeared into the barn and came back with a few tools that he slipped into his saddlebag. Adjusting the straps, he then set his bedroll behind the saddle. Holding it carefully with his hand, he used his other to pull the straps tight. He looked up as Emma approached. Immediately, he drew her into his arms. "I'm gonna miss ya, Emma."

Emma's chest felt like it was going to explode. She tried to answer him, but she couldn't force words past the lump in her throat. She knew he would only be gone for a few weeks, but just then, it seemed like forever. Squeezing her arms around his waist, she realized she was still holding on to the bag of food. Not wanting to crush his food, she reluctantly pulled away from him. "Yer food," she managed to say.

Thane lifted his hand to take the offered bag. When it was attached to the saddle, he turned around and pulled her back into his arms. Emma leaned her cheek against him. *Please fill my heart with peace Lord*, she prayed. Concentrating on the sound of his heartbeat, she felt a little calmer. A sound that had become very familiar to her over the last few weeks. When Thane pulled back, Emma had her emotions under control.

"I should only be away fer a few weeks," Thane reminded her. "I'm pert' sure I know where Pa headed. I should be back before my grandmother gets here." He cradled her face between his hands and caressed her cheeks. Leaning down, he kissed her softly. "I'm sorry ta be leavin' ya, Emma."

Emma reached up and hugged him to her again. "No more apologies. This's somethin' ya need ta do. No use worryin' about my feelings."

He held her for a moment longer, squeezing her tight, before stepping back. "I love ya, Emma Fern Hawkins," he whispered gruffly.

"I love ya, Mister Hawkins." She gave a watery smile.

Reluctantly, Thane mounted his horse. With one last glance toward her, he guided the horse away from the house and trotted away.

Emma watched until Thane disappeared into the early morning darkness. Closing her eyes, she could hear his horse getting further and further away from her. When she could no longer hear any sounds from the horse or rider, Emma opened her eyes. With one last glance down the empty drive, she walked back toward the house. The door clicked closed behind her, and the sound echoed through their small cabin. A sound as lonely as she felt. Pulling back her shoulders, she shook her lonely thoughts away. Thane would expect her to keep moving. She wouldn't let him down.

~*~

The farm seemed quiet as she nibbled on the piece of bread in her hand. All the emotions that morning had left Emma not very hungry. She had tried to force herself to finish her breakfast from earlier, but her stomach had rebelled against it. She knew she needed to eat something because Da would be there shortly to take her to church, and services had been very long lately. So, she grabbed a slice of bread, nibbling at it.

When Da's wagon finally pulled up the drive, Emma sighed in relief. Setting the bread on the plate, she rose and tied on her bonnet. Wrapping a shawl around her shoulders, she stepped out onto the porch. As soon as the wagon came to a stop, Emma climbed up next to her father and settled on the bench.

"Where's Thane this morn'?" Seth asked before she could explain.

Taking a shaky breath, Emma turned in her seat. "Thane went in search of his Pa. He's needin' some answers that only his Pa can give him. He should only be gone fer a few weeks."

"Kind of sudden, isn't it?" Mark asked, trying to sound amused. But there was a bitter edge to his words.

Emma felt Da look toward her older brother. "A man's business is his own," he reminded him. "He doesn't owe ya an explanation- only ta his wife."

Settling into her seat, she smoothed out her skirt. Da clicked to the team, and the wagon set in motion. Watching her father drive for a few minutes, Emma felt like he didn't approve of Thane leaving his young wife either. "He's been thinkin' on findin' his Pa fer a while now, but there was too much ta do," Emma explained. "Then yesterday, David brought him a letter from his grandmother. She'll be here before the snow flies to stay with us. I think he needs those answers more than I need him here for the next couple of weeks. Thane didna want ta go, Da."

Surprise shone in her father's eyes. He turned in her direction for a moment before looking back to the road before them. With a silent nod of his head, Da let her know he understood.

The rest of the drive was quiet. As they approached the church, Seth jumped down to help his sister.

It felt strange to enter the church without Thane now. With him gone, Emma sat in her old spot between Da and Mark. Sitting that close to her brother, she could feel the tension in him.

Emma's thoughts kept wandering from where Thane was at that moment to worrying about her brother. When they rose to sing the final hymn, she was ashamed that she had not heard what the reverend's message had been.

Every week at the end of services, Reverend Keyes made community announcements. Emma focused carefully as he listed the week's events so she wouldn't let her thoughts drift again.

"We saw the successful raisin' of the Graham's barn yesterday. Nothin' gives me greater joy than seein' this congregation pitch together to help each other." A cloud settled over the reverend's face before he continued. "Robert Moore would like to announce that his daughter, Miss Rachel Moore, will be marryin' Allen Nash in two weeks' time."

Gasps echoed around Emma.

Mr. Nash stood and smiled, gripping the front of his jacket.

At the sight of Mr. Nash's proud face, Mark exploded. Jumping to his feet, he ground out his words. "Mr. Moore, ya should be protectin' yer daughter from the likes of that wolf. Not handin' her over ta him-wrapped in a pretty white dress!"

"Now see here-," Mr. Nash objected.

"What am I ta do?" Mr. Moore rose to his feet. "No one'll have her now that he's disgraced her."

Rachel gasped, clamping a hand over her mouth mortified.

Mark faced her. "Miss Moore, do ya want ta marry that man?"

Tears welled up in Rachel's eyes as she lowered her hand. "What choice do I have?" Her voice quivered.

Emma felt tears fill her own eyes at the hopeless tone in Rachel's words.

"If ya had the choice, would ya marry him?" Mark tried again.

Silence settled around them as the congregation waited for her to answer.

Finally, Rachel shook her head.

Emma saw her brother's jaw flex as he squared his shoulders, resolved in his decision. "Mr. Moore, I ask that ya release yer daughter from her obligation to marry Nash. I'd like yer permission ta marry her myself."

Emma gasped. Trying to stand so she could stop her brother, Da's hand on her shoulder kept her seated. Looking toward her father, she hoped he would interrupt Mark, but his face was set.

Turning back, she saw Rachel's face was filled with astonishment.

Gasps and murmurs echoed throughout the church building before settling back into silence.

Mr. Moore's eyes narrowed. "Are ya sure ya want this? There willna be any backin' out."

With a firm nod, Mark answered. "We must stop these wolves from takin' all our sisters and our daughters. We need to protect them and their happiness."

Emma felt tears flow from her eyes and down her cheeks. The bitterness Mark felt from her marrying Thane ran deeper than she had imagined.

Mr. Moore eyed Mark cautiously.

"Now see here, Mr. Moore- we've come ta an agreement-," Nash protested.

Holding up his hand to Nash, Mr. Moore faced his daughter. "Do ya accept Mark Wells's proposal?"

When Rachel gave an astonished and uncertain nod, Nash stormed from the church.

Mr. Moore turned back to Mark. "Two weeks still stands! Two weeks from this day, ya'll stand before God in this church and promise ta care fer my lil' Rachel," he announced.

Mark nodded, determination shining from his face.

The reverend smiled in relief. "Mr. Robert Moore announces that his daughter, Rachel, will marry Mark Wells in two weeks from today, after Sunday services."

Comments and laughter sounded around Emma.

"Did ya see Nash's face?"

"That marriage willna be a happy one."

Emma looked at Rachel to see if the other girl could hear the whispers. Rachel stared ahead, giving no sign that she heard anything except her own thoughts.

"Let us give our thanks to the Lord in prayer," Reverend Keyes announced.

The congregation quieted and rose to close in prayer. But Emma didn't hear a word of it. The only thought that kept going through her head was that her brother had just agreed to marry a girl out of anger at her marriage. When everyone left their seats and filed from the church,

Emma tried to move closer to her older brother. Once they were outside, Emma reached for his arm. "Mark-?"

Mark pulled his arm away. With a glare in her direction, he stormed away.

Surprised by his behavior, Emma paused for a moment. Then squaring her shoulders, she stepped forward to go after him.

"Emma."

A soft call from behind her stopped her. Looking over her shoulder, she saw James coming toward her.

"I'll go," James insisted. Giving Emma a sad smile, he walked past her to follow the disappearing Mark.

Tears filled Emma's eyes again. It seemed James would continue to suffer from her mistakes.

~*~*~*~*~*~*~*~*~*~*~*~*~*~*~*~*~*~*~*~

Emma flipped the chicken with care, so it wouldn't splatter her arm again. Being lost in thought while frying the chicken had already earned her one blister. She checked the table once more to make sure everything was set out. She decided there would be just enough time to finish cooking if she rang the dinner bell now.

Cooking in her Da's cabin felt so comfortable after being away so long. She ran her fingers along the rail. It felt good to be home for the day. She reached up and pulled the striker from the nail to ring the bell nice and loud. She didn't know where her family had disappeared, so she wanted them to be sure to hear the sound.

As she hooked the striker back over the nail, she smiled. Her brothers had given James such a teasing after his father had let it slip that he had made the dinner bell for her. Making sure it was perfect. The smile froze in place. She hadn't known that James had cared for her back then. If she had known, maybe she could have kept him from getting his heart broken.

The sounds of voices coming closer broke Emma from her thoughts, and she went back into the kitchen. Pulling the pan of chicken from the heat, she carefully lifted each piece onto the platter. Then setting the platter on the table, she moved to stand by her chair.

The men filed in without a word. Emma breathed a sigh of thanksgiving when she noticed that James was not joining them. It wasn't James' fault. She just wanted to talk to her brother if they found a minute. When the men were seated, Emma looked around the kitchen one more time and sat as well.

"Lord, we thank Ya fer this food that our Emma has made fer us. Bless it to our bodies. We thank Ya fer her company as well. In Your name, we pray. Amen." When Da finished speaking, Emma raised her head and noticed Da didn't raise his. There was a sadness there that she hadn't seen for a while.

Turning away, she lifted the platter of chicken and offered it to Mark. He hesitated a moment before taking a piece. Emma could see that he wanted to refuse but the smell coming from the fried chicken was too good to refuse. Passing the potatoes to Seth, she waited for them to make their way back to her.

No one spoke for several long minutes. Emma slowly chewed her bites.

Finally, Da cleared his throat, breaking the silence. "Well, son, have ya thought through yer rash decision?"

Mark's eyes flashed with anger. "I willna be changin' my mind."

Da held up his hand. "Whoa there! Meanin'- have ya thought where ya'll live and such?"

Emma glanced at her father in surprise. He was accepting all this so easy. Couldn't he see that Mark was angry and making bad decisions?

"Oh," Mark replied. The anger whooshed out of him. Picking up his fork again, he pushed around his vegetables. "I was hopin' we could stay on here 'till spring? Haven't got much past that."

Nodding, Da went back to his own food.

Seth rubbed the back of his neck. "Robby Moore was tellin' me that Rachel had asked Nash not ta come courtin' anymore. Then he showed up outta the blue like that. Gettin' her alone. If nothin' happened... and Rachel wasn't wantin' him? Why would Mr. Moore make her marry Nash?"

"Well, it is usually ta protect the girl's reputation. But it seems Nash planned it that way," Da explained.

"Yes, sir. Planned it that way when he saw how well it worked for Thane with Emma," Mark muttered.

Emma dropped her fork. "Thane is nothing like Nash. Ya know Thane had nothin' ta do with his Pa attackin' me. Then we discussed what we should do together. We knew James wouldn't want--."

Mark jumped to his feet, knocking his chair over. "Quit defendin' Thane. He has torn this family apart. He tore James' whole world apart, and ya sit there paintin' him a saint."

"I'm not sayin' Thane's a saint, but he is nothin' like Mr. Nash," Emma clarified.

Placing his fists on the table, he leaned closer to his sister. "It is yer husband's fault that Miss Moore almost had to marry that man. Don't ya realize that yer marriage has given every single man within a day's ride the idea to force young girls inta marriage? And yer smiles' tellin' them all it'll work out in the end. Tells them that those scared girls will love them in the end fer it." Twirling on his heel, Mark stormed out the back door and disappeared into the woods.

Emma gathered her dishes and took them to her washtub. Her eyes filled with tears, spilling over and down her cheeks.

Da continued to sit at the table long after Seth left the awkward silence. When she started washing dishes, he pushed his chair back and came to stand by her. "I get the feelin' there is more to your relationship with Thane than ya are sayin'. Been wonderin' about it fer awhile now." When she hesitated, Da continued. "The Bible tells us that *the truth will set you free*, Emma girl. Maybe ya should set yerself free. Maybe it would set us all free." Placing a kiss on the top of her hair, he pulled his hat over his brow and walked out the back door. She watched him disappear down the path to the creek.

Emma let the tears drip into the wash water without trying to stop them. *Lord... I'm not knowin' what ya want me ta do. I'm not sure it'll help fer my family ta know how I met Thane. I'm not sure I can*, she prayed. Taking in a shaky breath, she lifted her eyes to the window before her. *But iffen it's yer Plan fer the truth ta be told, give me Your strength ta tell it.* Wiping the tears from her cheeks, she went back to scrubbing the dishes before her.

When the last dish was dried and returned to its proper place, Emma untied the apron around her waist and hung it on the nail by the back door as she passed through it. Her feet moved to follow the path to her mama's hill. As the path straightened, Emma had a clear view of her father. Her feet slowed to a stop. Praying for strength, she forced herself to walk forward.

At first glance, it appeared Da was gazing at her mother's gravestone. But as she approached, Emma could tell his attention was further into the hills surrounding them.

Settling herself on the grass beside her father, Emma looked around the familiar hillside. Her gaze settled on the path beside the creek. The path that she took when she gave her life over to God's guidance. Focusing on that path, Emma took in a slow, steady breath for courage. "Yer right. There is more ta my relationship with Thane. I- I meet Thane before his Pa took me," she saw her father's head turn toward her out of the corner of her eye. "Last summer, when it was startin' ta git really warm? Ya'll remember 'twas the week I had to sew myself the new dresses."

Da nodded, knowing the week she spoke of.

Emma cleared her throat, keeping her eyes facing away from her father. "I noticed Thane that week. At first, I noticed him catchin' a door before it hit against me. Then I started noticin' him distractin' strangers from givin' me too much attention. Unwanted attention. He seemed ta be everywhere. The more I saw him? The more it seemed I'd seen him before. But I couldna place him."

Dropping her gaze down, she found a leaf among the grass by her knees. Picking it up, she ran it between her fingers as she continued. "I met Mr. Nash that week as well. Although, I didna know his name back then. He cornered me in the mercantile, and I... I was so worried he'd make a scene. But Thane was there-," Emma glanced up at her father then. "Thane was there and he stepped between us. He convinced Mr. Nash ta leave the store without bringin' any notice ta us. I was so grateful ta him." Dropping her gaze to her hands, she continued quietly. "But Nash and another gentleman followed me out of town." Emma felt her father stiffen beside her. "He planned on followin' me all the way ta the farm. Said he was gonna ask ya permission ta court me."

The fear she felt that day came flooding back through her memories. "I was so scared, Da. But when I turned ta look fer help? There was Thane again," Emma smiled through the tears welling in her eyes. "Walkin' toward me like he was a gift from God himself. He told Nash that I wasn't available and walked me all the way home. Wanted to make sure I was safe before he left."

Emma coughed to clear the emotions that were clogging her throat. "I shoulda asked him ta come ta the fields then... ta introduce him. Ta tell ya what an honor he did me. But I didna think of it then. I was jest so happy ta be back home safe. An' I didna figure I'd see him again. It all felt so strange. He stopped by later ta apologize fer speakin' so familiar with me- with him na bein' introduced ta me. Then he took ta stoppin' by every week ta check on me. Sometimes walkin' me ta town and sometimes jest sittin' nearby while I worked. He was always proper. Always treatin' me with respect. He never came inside. I never thought that him visitin' me might be wrong," she stated softly.

"I donna know. Maybe I would've known if I had really thought about it. But it felt so wonderful ta talk ta someone. Someone who listened ta me talk. Everyone else was always far too busy. It didna seem any different than havin' James here visitin'," Emma felt her throat burn

41

with emotions. Blinking to keep the tears away, she gazed down the path. "I know now that I was far too familiar with James as well. That by jokin' and laughin' with him, I led him ta believe my heart was belongin' ta him. I shoulda been more careful. I shoulda held myself more proper. I shouldna let him get so close. But he feels as familiar to me as Mark or Seth. I canna remember a time without James. But I didna know how it'd be touchin' his heart. I never meant ta hurt him," Emma struggled to keep her voice from cracking.

Taking another deep, shaky breath, she went on, "I woulda done the right thing by him. I was gonna marry him. I tried, Da." Emma raised her hand to cover her mouth, wanting to hide her quivering lip. "I didna mean to disappoint him, Da. I never meant ta disappoint you, either. But I made such a mess of everythin'."

They sat in silence for quite some time. Emma was exhausted from her emotional day. With Thane leaving, then arguing with Mark, and now telling the truth to Da. Her energy was gone. When Da didn't say a word, she turned his way. He leaned forward, propped against his knees. His head was bent down. Emma could almost see the disappointment rolling off his back. Slowly standing up, she straightened her skirt and brushed off the loose grass from the back. "I'd best be headin' home how," Emma stated, her voice soft.

Da didn't acknowledge that she had spoken.

Tears filled her eyes as she started up the path. She walked toward the home she grew up in. But her feet took her past the building and headed toward her new home. The one that didn't feel like home at all.

Four

Stopping to rub her back for a moment, Emma scooped more straw onto the pitchfork and threw it into the stall. She would need to clean out these stalls before long. But for now, she figured the new straw would help keep the eggs clean. Straightening up again, she looked around the barn. She really didn't know what else needed to be done out there. The menfolk in her family had always been responsible for the care of the animals. Other than her chickens, this was all very unfamiliar to her. Mentally ticking off the list Thane had given her, she put the pitchfork back in its place.

With a soft sigh, Emma realized she would have to go in soon. With nothing else to keep her moving, she couldn't avoid the quiet house any longer. In the empty house, she wouldn't be able to ignore the fact that Thane was really gone. How she wished he was there. She wanted to talk to him about her day. She longed to ask him if she should have told Da about their friendship last summer. Her throat felt thick again, burning with the tears she hadn't shed. "Oh, Thane. I fear I made everythin' worse," she whispered.

A shuffling sound behind her made her spin around. Her hope died before her feet came to a stop. It wasn't her husband standing in the doorway. It was her father.

Da stepped into the barn. "I owe ya an apology, Emma girl," he cleared his throat. Lowering his eyes to his hands, he twisted the hat he held there. "-maybe a number of apologies. I never noticed how lonely ya were. If ya were wrong because ya didna know how ta be proper with these young men- iffen ya didna know ta distance yerself from them?

43

Then I was wrong because I never taught ya. Yer mama did such a good job with ya before she got sick- I guess I jest figured ya had everything ya needed. I shoulda got ya a new mama, Emma girl. Instead of leavin' ya ta all that hard work by yerself. With no one fer ya ta talk to." Clearing his throat again, he looked up. "I'm sorry, Emma girl. Ya deserved better than a grievin' Da."

Tears filled Emma's eyes. "I didna need a new mama, Da. Honest! This is na yer fault. It is mine. I shoulda guessed how James felt about me. Iffen I'd been payin' attention at all, I woulda seen it. I could have been more careful and spared him this heartache. When you told me that you agreed to a marriage between me and James, I was so angry. Ya never even asked me if I loved him. But when I quieted down? When my anger had passed? I knew. I knew that by not payin' attention, I hadna thought about what you'd see. When I thought about it from yer side? I could see all the wrong I'd done," Emma paused to clear the emotion from her voice. "And Thane said he knew ta stay away from ya all... na because he thought it was wrong fer me ta be alone with a young man... but because he was a young man from the hills. He told me that he knew no father wants the likes of him for their daughter. We never planned on fallin' in love, Da. I didna even know until ya showed me. Ta us? Ta us, it was jest so good ta have a friend."

Da stepped forward then and wrapped his arms around Emma's shoulders, pulling her tight to his chest. She welcomed the comfort she found there. Breathing deep, she let his familiar scent of hard work, lye, and horses settle over her. It felt like coming home.

"Emma girl, the fact that ya needed a friend... and that God had ta send him to ya in the unlikeliest way... shows me that I was neglectin' ya. I didna even know how often ya went down ta visit yer Mama by the creek, until Thane let it slip in his talkin'. After yer Mama died, I buried myself in workin'. Workin' until I was so tired, I forgot ta miss her. I made sure ya all were fed and clothed. But I never saw that ya were doin' the same thing. Ya were workin' so hard, back at the house, to make sure we were fed and clothed. Ya should have stayed in school longer. Ya shoulda been visitin' Abigail. I never saw yer loneliness because I was too tired."

Placing a kiss on her hair, he pulled back. Settling his strong hands on her shoulders, he gave her a sad smile. "God saw the mess I made of this family. He used the sadness... he used the loneliness... and he used some sorry excuses for men in town... to introduce Thane to yer life. No more pointin' fingers. It doesn't matter why Thane is here. He is here. And he is part of this family. And it helps my old heart ta know ya love this man ya married. No matter why ya needed ta marry him."

Emma's eyes filled with tears again. Da leaned forward to kiss her forehead this time. "I love ya, Da."

"I love ya too, Emma girl." Giving her a quick hug, he stepped away from her. "I must be gettin' back. It'll be dark by the time I get home." Walking to the barn door, he stopped and turned back toward her. "An', Emma? No more secrets, all right? No matter how wrong I am... or how much ya want ta spare my feelings." Raising his eyebrows, he waited to be sure she understood his words.

Tears spilled down Emma's cheeks as she nodded in agreement.

Smiling, Da slipped his hat back onto his head. "Come an' visit when ya have time. Holler iffen ya need somethin'."

"I will. Bye, Da," she answered, wiping the tears from her cheeks. She stood, watching him walk away. She had been so sure he was disappointed in her from hearing the truth. Yet he had only been disappointed in himself. "Would things have been easier iffen I'd been brave enough ta tell Da back then? Thane's Pa wouldna have taken ta the idea of stealin' me away. Maybe Mark wouldna be so angry with me?" she asked into the quietness of the still barn. Shaking her head, she cleared her thoughts. "There's no use worryin' on it now. I wasn't brave enough. No number of wishes can change that."

Going back to the chores on hand, she couldn't wait for Thane to come home again. She already had so much to share with him, and he hadn't even been gone a full day.

❧ Five ❧

rooster crowed, pulling Emma from her sleep. She pulled the blankets over her head and pretended to ignore the sound. But after a few minutes of lying there, she realized that she was not going to fall back asleep. With a sigh, she pushed back the blankets. Slipping a dress over her shoulders, she headed to the outhouse.

When she returned, she filled the coffee pot with water. But the smell of the coffee grounds made her stomach churn. *Must be too early for coffee,* she thought. Pushing the coffee pot to the back of the stove, Emma headed out to the barn to start on chores.

Opening the barn doors wide, she let her eyes adjust to the darkness. Moving forward, she scooped some corn out for the chickens and sprinkled it on the ground. She opened the small gate to let the pig run out into the pen.

Mentally going down the list until the last of Thane's chores were done, she started on her own. She searched the first stall to gather the chickens' eggs and carefully placed them at the bottom of a basket.

When she finally stepped from the barn, a movement at the front of the cabin caught her eye. Her feet came to a stop when she saw her brother coming back out the door.

"Good mornin', Mark," she called out cautiously.

"Mornin', Em," he replied, stepping toward her. "I was wonderin' if ya had time ta talk?"

She searched her brother's face for a moment before nodding. "I havena had coffee yet. Would ya care ta go inside and have a cup?"

With a nod, Mark followed her into the kitchen. He noticed her almost empty kindling box and set to filling it. By the time the coffee was boiling, her wood rack by the back door was stacked high, and her buckets were filled with water.

Emma smiled. If Mark was still angry with her, he wouldn't be thinking of her needs. It sparked hope in her chest.

"What's on yer mind, big brother?" she asked as she set the cups on the table. Returning to the stove, she wrapped a towel around the coffee pot handle. As she approached the table to pour, she studied Mark's face from the corner of her eye.

"I talked ta Da last night," he paused, clearing his throat. "Well, I didna do much talkin'. I should say Da talked ta me last night. He told me how wrong we all were. He told me the story of how ya met Thane." Mark looked up at her then, meeting her eyes for the first time. "Told me how we're beholdin' ta him fer savin' yer honor." Standing up, he paced to the window. When he turned back toward her, his eyes were filled with sadness. "Em... I'm so sorry. All I could see was how happy James was. An' I saw yer laughter... the new life ya had in ya. I jest kept thinkin' of my plans fer ya. What I wanted fer the both of ya. It's tearin' me up inside because I *knew* somethin' else was goin' on. I could see ya worryin' about somethin'. I shoulda jest asked ya!" Looking out the window, he raked his hand through his hair. "An' not got so angry with ya."

Emma put the coffeepot back on the stove as her own eyes filled with tears. Wiping her eyes with her apron, she stepped closer to her brother. "I appreciate ya tellin' me. But the fault's all mine. If I hadna been so lonesome... I woulda realized sooner it wasna proper fer Thane ta be alone with me... no matter how honorable he was. How could ya suspect me of that?" she paused. "No. The fault lies with me." Taking another shaky breath, she wrapped her arms around her waist. "An' poor James. I never meant ta break his heart. When I realized he thought I was happy because of him? That all my laughin' and happiness led him ta believe I was returnin' his feelings fer me? What was I supposed ta do? I was so confused."

Mark walked back to her and pulled her into a big bear hug. "I knew ya were. I jest didna know why."

Leaning into his strength, she took another deep breath. It felt so strange to talk about the secrets she had held close for so long. Da was right. She did feel free. "I told God that I'd put it all in His hands... asked Him to give me peace according ta His Will. And God chose this path."

Remembering how she felt when she woke up high in the hills made her throat thick with emotions. "I woke up in that strange cabin. Not knowin' why Thane was there. It took me a while ta come back ta my promise ta accept God's path fer me. It was jest so hard. I knew everyone'd be worried about me. Knowin' it'd break James' heart. And not bein' able ta give Thane a choice. Would he have chosen ta marry me if he'd a choice? And now... with everyone talkin'. Everyone keeps remindin' me that I broke James' heart. And in my heart? I know... I know I coulda stopped all of this iffen I'd jest been proper."

Mark's arms tightening around her shoulders, pulling her in closer. "'Tisn't yer fault at all. We shoulda taken better care of ya... shoulda noticed ya were lonesome. An' we coulda listened better when ya were so upset." He laughed then. The laughter surrounded her as it vibrated down his arms and through his chest. "I shoulda told James ta come callin' sooner."

She returned his laugh easily.

Mark stepped back as the worried expression returned to his face.

Emma studied him for a moment before breaking the silence. "Mark... I don't know how ta help James so that I willna hurt him anymore. I hate ta see him look so hurt when he sees me," she paused for a moment. Her statement sounded selfish to her own ears. Rubbing her fingers across her forehead, she tried to correct it. "I hate that James hurts every time he sees me. Should I avoid town? Should I stop being nice ta him? I don't know what ta do?" her voice quivered at her last question.

"I do na know either, Em," her brother admitted. Rubbing his hands on the back of his neck, his eyes look off into the distance. "That is the hardest part of all this."

Emma nodded. She agreed that James was the hardest part, but she didn't trust her voice to continue talking about him. With a shaky breath, she searched for a change in subject.

Mark continued to stare off into the distance, deep in thought.

"Are ya still gonna marry Rachel?" The question slipped out before Emma even realized she was going to ask it.

Mark nodded his head once. "Yeah. I canna back out now."

"Do ya regret it?"

Shaking his head firmly, he turned toward her. "No. After Da told me about Nash... how Thane saved ya from bein' trapped inta marryin' that man. Now more than ever, I'm glad I stood up fer Rachel. I wouldna leave any girl in his care. Her brother said Nash kept her behind the barn ta force her inta marryin' him. No girl deserves that."

Wiping her tears, Emma felt a weight being lifted from her shoulders. Mark knew what he was doing, so she was not responsible for ruining his life. "What are yer plans?"

"Seth's gonna move inta yer old room, seein' as our room's a little bigger. We'll be cuttin' trees all winter an' have a house raisin' come spring. Da said he'd let us pick which field we'd like." Lookin' down, he cleared his throat before continuing. "Maybe ya could help us clean some before Rachel comes? We canna clean like ya can. No matter how we try."

Emma laughed outright at his request. Leaning in, she hugged her brother again. "I'd love ta help. Now let's drink this coffee before it's cold."

Sitting at the table, they talked while they drank. Emma reminded herself to thank Da. It felt so good ta feel free from all the secrets.

When the coffeepot was empty, Mark stood up to leave. "I should be gettin' back."

"Thank ya fer comin', Mark."

"I shoulda come sooner." He stepped through the door and stopped. Looking back over his shoulder, he looked thoughtful. "Ya should tell James."

"NO!" she exclaimed, horrified at the thought.

"Em. He thinks ya had so many doubts that ya felt relieved ta marry a complete stranger," he stated softly. His eyes pleaded with her to listen.

"What?"

"Knowin' the truth is so much easier than all the wonderin'. I feel free without all that anger. Da said the same." his voice grew hoarse as he continued. "Doesna James deserve the same, Em?"

Shaking her head back and forth, Emma refused to consider it.

"Jest think about it."

"I donna see how it'd be helpful-," she insisted.

"Jest think on it."

❧ Six ❧

Emma woke the next morning with a peaceful spirit. Her plans for the day creeping over her slowly, like the light shining in through the window.

Throwing back the quilts, she got dressed, eager to get started. The whole day before her would be filled if her father was agreeable to her request. If it all worked out the way she hoped, she would be able to fall in bed later that night, too exhausted to miss Thane. Too exhausted to lay awake in the dark, feeling lonely.

And it would be one more day closer to Thane's return. She smiled as she imagined him riding his horse up the lane to the cabin. The excitement made her hands move faster until she realized she had buttoned her dress wrong, leaving a gap across her waist. Laughing, she chided herself to slow down. Unbuttoning, she started over.

Skipping coffee, Emma went right outside to visit the outhouse and get on with her chores. Letting the animals out, she filled the water trough from the well. Gathering the morning's eggs, she arranged them in her basket.

She scanned the farmyard and realized there was nothing else for her to do. Grabbing a bonnet from inside the cabin door, she set off for the path to Da's farm.

She stepped from the trees just as her brothers were coming from the house. When Seth saw her, he gave a loud whoop. Running toward her, he caught her in a tight bear hug. Mark rescued her basket of eggs from falling off her arm.

51

"Does this mean ya'll make us breakfast?" Seth asked, his face full of hope as he set her down on her feet.

Mark chuckled. "Yer rotten, Seth. All ya think about is food."

"What else is there?" Seth asked innocently, staring at his older brother.

Emma laughed, not realizing how much she had missed their playful arguing. Reclaiming her egg basket from Mark's hand, she set off toward the house. "I'd best get ta cookin' if it's ta be done when ya come in from yer chores."

"I'll fill the water buckets fer ya," Mark stated, as they followed behind her.

Emma had a fire lit, and the stove heating up by the time Mark came in with the water.

"Are ya doin' alright over at yer farm? All by yerself?" Mark asked, surprising her.

Nodding, she smiled. "It's jest so quiet there. And no one ta cook fer. It gets lonely."

Mark nodded and headed for the door again.

Breakfast was still in the pan when her family came in. They went straight for the washtub to scrub.

"I'm sorry. I thought ya'd be a while yet. I'm not quite ready fer ya," Emma explained. She flipped the potato slices to see if they were further along than she thought. But her suspicions were correct. They needed a while yet to finish cooking.

Da looked up with a smile. "We all agreed we could do the other chores after breakfast. Weren't sure how long we had ya today."

Nodding in understanding, she set the plates around the small table. Pouring the hot coffee into cups, she handed them out as they sat down.

"We thought we'd keep ya company as ya cooked, anyway. It's a treat fer us ta have ya here," Da stated.

Emma felt her eyes fill with tears. Confused as to why she felt like crying, she blinked them away. "I find my chores take no time at all these days. An' cookin' fer myself doesn't keep me busy. I thought I'd come over taday ta see you all." Taking the bacon and dividing it among the four plates, she decided to tell her Da the plans for the day. "I was also thinkin' on goin' ta visit Rachel Moore today," Emma explained, ignoring Mark as his head jerked in her direction. "I want ta see if I can help her with the weddin' in any way. An' I thought I'd offer her the material that's tucked away in Mama's chest." The material that Emma had never used for her own dress. The dress she was supposed to make for her wedding to James. Shaking her head to clear her thoughts, she continued. "Would it be alright ta borrow the wagon, Da? Iffen it's not needed, that is."

Da nodded without hesitating.

When he didn't say anything in reply, Emma went back to the woodstove to tend to the potatoes. Moving around the table, she divided the eggs and potatoes among the plates. When the pan was empty, she scooped some water into it and moved it to the back of the stove.

Sliding into her chair, she folded her hands in her lap to listen to her father's prayer.

"Heavenly Father, we thank ya fer the blessing Ya gave us this morning. We ask Ya ta bless our Emma girl as she is settin' out ta spread her comfort ta others. Bless this food ta our needs. In Yer name, we pray. Amen."

"My comfort?" Emma was confused.

"Yer cookin'. Yer visitin'," Da explained.

Emma opened her mouth to object then closed it again. She was just trying to stay busy but was not sure they would believe her.

"This tastes so much better than Seth's oatmeal," Mark stated with a sigh.

"My oatmeal's the best thing I cook," Seth objected.

Emma smiled. "Let me guess? It's too sweet, isn't it?"

Mark nodded. "He shovels in so much brown sugar that it's disgustin'."

Seth's face pulled back in horror. "It's perfect!"

Da chuckled. "I've missed the arguin'. It's been way too quiet here."

Smiling, Emma winked at her Da. "Glad I could bring the arguin' back fer ya."

They laughed and talked well after their plates were empty. When Emma finally rose from her chair to gather plates, Mark stood as well. "I'll go get the horses hitched to the wagon fer ya."

"Thank ya." After her brothers left, Emma turned and saw her Da still sitting at the table.

"There's a little coffee left. Ya have room fer it?"

Holding out his cup in answer, she poured the rest of the pot in.

"I sure have missed yer coffee, Emma girl. How are ya holdin' out? I know it's been a hard week fer ya. I don't want ya bein' strong fer me," he clarified. "I'm wantin' ya ta tell me if yer needin' help... or prayers."

"I'm good, Da. I'm jest lonely. Tryin' ta stay busy until Thane comes home," she reassured him. Pausing, she cleared her throat. "I wanted ta thank ya."

"Fer what?"

"Fer pushin' me ta be honest. It feels good ta not be hidin' the truth from my family," she explained.

Nodding, he drank the last of his coffee and stood to his feet. "Take yer time with Miss Moore's visit today. We have no need fer the wagon." Kissing her on the top of the head, he slipped his cup into her wash water and headed for the door.

She watched her father close the door behind him and then turned back to setting the kitchen to right. When everything was put away, she tucked the material bundle into her empty egg basket. Tying her bonnet on, she stepped outside.

Mark was seated in the wagon. "I think I should go along with ya today. It's time I talked to Mr. Moore about the weddin'."

Emma nodded.

Reaching out, Mark pulled Emma up to sit next to him. Once she was settled, she set her basket under the seat. Mark clicked to the horses, and they set off in motion.

The farm disappeared behind them as they weaved along the road. The silence between them was comfortable as they rode along.

"Is Thane good to you?" Mark asked suddenly, breaking the silence.

Emma looked over in surprise. Nodding, she wondered what prompted the question.

"I know ya thought I was angry with ya- and I was. But mostly I've been worried," he explained. "If Mr. Hawkins was able ta hit ya over the head and drag ya off with no regret? It kept makin' me think that his son would be capable of the same."

Tears blurred her vision. She should have known he would worry. "Mostly, Mr. Hawkins is jest a quiet drinker. His draggin' me off surprised Thane more than anyone." Turning to stare off down the road, Emma thought about the days in the cabin. Thane had been so tormented by what his Pa had done to her. "Thane's always been a gentleman ta me. Always askin' me what I am thinkin'. Wantin' ta hear funny stories of ya and Seth."

Nodding his head once, Mark seemed satisfied. He didn't seem happy for her, but Emma thought it was an improvement. For her brother to just say Thane's name and not growl it was an improvement.

The journey to the Moore Farm took them north through town. It had been a while since Emma had been north of town. When they finally arrived at the farm, she didn't realize how stiff she had become. Laughing, she arched her back to stretch it.

Mr. Moore stepped out of the barn. He did not appear happy to see them with his fists balled next to his side. His sons behind him did not look like they welcomed the intrusion. Mrs. Moore came out of the beautiful farmhouse with Rachel behind her. Rachel clutched her mother's hand, worried.

Mark tensed up, clutching the reins. Everyone stood still as the farmyard fell into silence.

Emma cleared her throat finally. With a silent prayer for guidance, she hoped she was doing God's Will. "Hope ya don't mind me droppin' by uninvited. I thought iffen Miss Moore is ta be my new sister, I wanted ta come an' offer my help," she called out, smiling to hide her nervousness.

Surprised, Mrs. Moore relaxed. With another moment of thought, her face softened, and she returned Emma's smile. "Sure... sure Miss Wells... ahh... Mrs...."

Emma smiled again, embarrassed this time. "Mrs. Hawkins, but please... call me Emma."

Mark finally found his words. "I was wonderin' if I might have a word with ya, sir?" he called out, facing Mr. Moore.

Mr. Moore nodded. His fist hung loose by his side. Emma could tell he was more relaxed, but the way he held his shoulders suggested he was still cautious.

Mark helped his sister down from the wagon and handed her the basket.

Giving him an encouraging smile, Emma turned toward the house.

Following Mrs. Moore inside, Emma caught Rachel's questioning glance. With a smile, she sat near Rachel at the kitchen table. Pulling the material out of the basket, she held it out to her. "I wanted ta offer ya this material for yer dress. I was never able ta use it. I was hopin' ya could."

Rachel reached out slowly to take the material. Running her fingers over the pretty fabric, she smiled. "I am honored fer ya offerin'. Thank ya. But..." Rachel glanced at her mother.

"But we already started her dress," her mother finished.

Emma smiled. Relieved that they hadn't been offended. She was content that it wasn't needed. Reaching out, she wrapped the material up again. "I jest wanted ta offer it... if it could be of use." Tucking it in the basket, she turned back to the group of ladies facing her.

Suddenly one of the younger sisters fled the room.

Emma breathed a prayer for guidance. She didn't know what else to say. Everyone seemed so nervous.

Just as suddenly, the young lady burst back in the room.

"Jane-," Mrs. Moore reprimanded.

"Sorry, Mama," the young lady said, bringing her feet to a walk. Carefully, she laid the bundle on Emma's lap.

Emma picked it up, realizing then that it was the dress they were making. Smiling up at Jane, she realized she had answered her prayer for help. There is nothing like admiring someone's beautiful sewing to break the awkward silence. Made from a softer white calico with a fine print, the dress had fine stitches and delicate pleats. Emma exclaimed over its beauty and her fine taste.

When Rachel's cheeks blushed, she returned the dress to the young Jane. The conversation died out again.

Turning toward the bright window, Emma smiled. "It is such a beautiful day today." Turning toward Rachel, she raised her eyebrow. "Would ya care ta take a walk with me?"

Rachel agreed readily. Grabbing a bonnet from her room, she followed Emma out the door.

"I'm sorry we didn't greet ya better," Rachel stated softly. "My family had me convinced that Mark... uh... Mr. Wells... might try ta back out of his agreement." Giving her a weak smile, she continued. "I shouldna have doubted him."

Nodding again, Emma had guessed that was their fear. "I wanted ta tell ya how sorry I am that ya need ta marry in this way at all. An' I'm sorry ya have ta doubt that someone would honor their agreement with ya." Tears filled her eyes again. Frustrated at her sudden tears, she blinked them away.

"I'd much rather it was Mark," she stated, with a short laugh. "At least with Mark, I respect him already. I fear I'd never have respected Mr. Nash."

Emma agreed to that. "Well, I didna come ta tell ya everythin' will be all right... but I will say that my little family is loving and caring. We'll try ta help ya in every way."

Rachel suddenly threw her arms around Emma. Surprised, it took a moment for Emma to react and wrapped her arms around the other girl. *Please protect this young lady's heart, Lord*, she prayed.

Mark approached them slowly. "We should probably be headed home, Emma. I need to get back." Hesitantly, he turned to Rachel. "I was wonderin' iffen I could return tomorrow after supper? I'd like ta walk out with ya. We can discuss our plans then?"

Rachel nodded shyly. Emma squeezed her hand in encouragement, and they followed Mark to the waiting wagon.

As Mark drove away from the farm, Emma could see Rachel still standing in the yard. She couldn't help but wonder what she was thinking about as she watched the horses draw the wagon away.

⮠ Seven ⮐

October 14, 1858...

Emma glanced over the shopping list in her hand, making sure she hadn't missed anything. It was a short list. Normally, she would put off shopping until a later time, but she wanted to pay a visit to Abigail. The exhaustion she saw at the barn raising had her worried about her friend.

Gathering the extra eggs in a basket, she tied a bonnet under her chin, pulled the door closed behind her, and headed toward the road to town.

The morning was a mild one. The coolness was burning off with the warm sun. There wasn't much of a breeze, but all in all, Emma decided it would be a beautiful autumn day.

When she rounded the last curve before the road, she spotted a pokeberry growing along the tree line. As she approached, Emma laughed. The plant had grown well over her head, and it was the first time she had noticed it. The dark purple berries were beautiful as they reflected the morning sunlight. Her laugh settled into a smile as she remembered the worn curtains that hung in the bedroom she shared with Thane. She had taken them down when they were first cleaning the abandoned cabin. After scrubbing them soundly, they were once again soft. But the sun had faded uneven lines in the middle. "These pokeberries will be jest the thing ta make them like new," she said into the silence around her.

Setting her basket on the ground, she arranged her eggs off to one side and moved the cloth to contain them. She picked a few of the large leaves to layer in the basket and then began to pick the huge

59

berries. The juice stained her fingers a little, making her confident that they would be perfect for dying. Wiping her fingers in the long grass to clean them, she picked her basket up again and set off toward town.

She was excited to have the house fixed up before Thane returned in a couple of weeks. For the first time in weeks, Emma found a song on her lips. She sang her favorite hymns as she walked along until she saw the curve that led into Vermontville. Her simple joy fled as anxiety filled her. Her feet came to a stop. She had not been to town by herself since she was abducted. Between Thane and her father still being worried about her head injury, she always had an escort these days.

Taking a deep breath, she sent up a silent prayer for strength and protection. Then she forced her feet forward along the road. The town seemed busy enough. People walked to and from shops, talking above the sounds coming from the shops and the animals tied along the street. Emma smiled. Just enough people to keep her from being noticed as she walked past. Abigail's house sat on a side street, on the far side of town. Keeping her head down, she walked past the mercantile.

"Emma?"

Emma's heart froze. Turning toward the voice, she attempted to keep a smile on her face.

Standing on the top step of the mercantile was Mrs. Craig. She looked down at Emma with a delighted smile. "You appear ta be in a hurry. Is everything alright?" she asked, letting concern crease her brow.

"Hello, Mrs. Craig," Emma called back, relieved to see a friendly face. "All is well with me. I was simply on my way to visit a friend."

"Oh, do call me Sadie please," she insisted, coming down the stairs to stand next to the younger lady. A smile crept back onto her face as realization dawned on her. "I take it you were tryin' not to be noticed by the mercantile... or its owner?" When Emma blushed, Sadie laughed. "Let me walk a ways with ya, so we can move from here then."

"Thank ya," Emma whispered in gratitude. Sadie took her arm and steered her back in the direction she was headed.

They walked in silence until they were past the last shop. Sadie was the first to break the silence. "Yer a bit young ta have an ache ta yer joints, aren't ya?"

"Pardon?" Emma asked, surprised.

Sadie pointed into Emma's basket. "Yer pokeberries? They aren't fer you, are they?"

Emma glanced down into her basket. She had forgotten about the berries with her anxiety over town.

"Be sure to boil them at least twice. I wouldn't want ya ta end up with stomach pains from not preparin' it long enough," the older lady explained her concern.

Shaking her head, Emma looked up then. "No. No. They are na fer medicine. I picked them ta dye some faded curtains in my husband's cabin."

"Ahhh," Sadie sighed in relief. "Good. Pokeberries are powerful medicine iffen yer not careful. Worried me some." Glancing over at the young lady at her side, she smiled again. "Yer husband's cabin? Wouldn't that make it yers as well?"

Emma felt her cheeks burn. "Yes, ma'am, it would," she replied. Looking over at her companion, she wondered if she could be honest without causing offense. "It's jest that it feels strange. New- I suppose? But it does na really feel like my home yet?"

"Not strange at all." They walked a house length in silence. "I admit ta feelin' the same way when I was a young bride. I imagine with ya gettin' married sudden like... it'll take some time ta get used ta."

Emma's feet slowed as they reached the walk to Abigail's house. Turning toward the widow, she studied her face. She had never talked more than a few sentences with the older lady before the barn raising, but she found herself wishing for more time with her.

"So ya are ta visit young Abigail today?" Sadie reasoned, looking at the beautiful house they stopped in front of.

David and Abigail had one of the few houses in Vermontville that wasn't log built. It really stood out. David had built it himself while he was still courting Abigail. He worked in hours of building around his carpentry business. There was a rumor that he would build well into the night. When he put in the last nail, David decided it was time to ask Abigail to marry him.

"Well, I will not keep ya from her." Returning her gaze to Emma's face, she squeezed her fingers. "If ya find yerself with extra time while yer husband's gone, ya come see me. We'll have a long visit and a good cup of tea."

"I'd love ta," she agreed. Turning reluctantly to Abigail's door, she looked back over her shoulder to Sadie. "Have a blessed day, Mrs. Craig- Sadie."

Sadie smiled gratefully. "May God bless ya too, child."

Sending up a prayer thanking God for answering her earlier prayer, Emma knocked on the door.

When Abigail opened the door, she pushed her hair from her face. Sweat was beaded up on her forehead and ran down her cheeks. Breathing hard, she straightened her shoulders and smoothed her tight gown. "Emma darling!" she exclaimed when she saw who was at her door. "You are here!" Reaching out to grasp her friend's hand, she pulled Emma inside and shut the door.

Emma studied the chaos around her. Rugs were hanging over chairs. A pile of dust lay in the corner with the broom. Plates were piled on the table. The washtub overflowed with dishes as well. "Abigail? What are ya doin'?"

Waving her hand in dismissal, Abigail laughed. "Jest a little cleanin'. I can't sit still taday. Ya can see how dirty this place is. I need ta get it all cleaned up before my boy is born. After that, I suspect I'll jest want ta sit and hold him all day long." Laughing again, she moved toward the stove. "Let me put some water on for tea. A short rest will do me, and my feet, some good."

Emma shook her head. "Ya sit yerself down there. Let me make the tea, and then I'll finish cleanin' up. Yer tryin' ta do too much, Abby."

A scowl crossed Abigail's face for a moment before she started laughing. "When did you get so bossy? I should scold you for using that awful pet name." She moved to a chair without any further prompting. As soon as she was settled, Abigail started explaining everything to Emma that she needed to get done. "And ya should see how wrinkled the baby's clothes are!" she exclaimed, horrified. "I need ta iron them again. But I cannot iron on a messy table. So, I was scrubbin' that and saw a leaf behind the plates. Can ya imagine? A leaf in my cupboard?" Abigail gave a shutter.

Emma tried not to laugh.

"So, I pulled all the plates out and realized that David does not wash the dishes well. They ALL have ta be rewashed. That pesky leaf fell on the floor, though, and I canna find it. I started sweepin' and realized those rugs have ta go!" Blowing out a frustrated breath, Abigail slumped back in her chair.

Emma laughed then, amused at the urgency. She tried to stop when Abigail's face scrunched up in a pout. "I'll help ya put all of this ta right. But first... let's drink some tea."

When their tea was finished, Emma wiped out the cupboards. She washed the dishes and put them back in their places. Once the table was washed, Emma set the iron to heat up for her friend. While Abby ironed, Emma looked for the leaf. When she finally found it, she put it outside. Sweeping the floor was the last thing on her friend's list. She was very careful to get the corners and cracks swept well to keep Abby from being tempted to redo it after she left.

"Ya know yer baby could turn out to be a girl," Emma suggested with a laugh.

Abigail scoffed at the idea. "A mother knows these things. This is a boy I am carryin'."

By the time Emma was ready to leave Abigail's house, she was tired herself. And hot. She rinsed her face and neck in Abby's washtub.

Before Abigail let her leave, she made Emma promise to come again soon.

Promising, she gave her friend a hug and tied on her bonnet.

Emma stopped at the mercantile before she headed home. She hurried around the store locating all the items on her list. She placed them carefully in her basket, so they wouldn't ruin the pokeberries. When she stepped near the front counter, she saw a few bolts of material piled there. Emma ran her fingers over the delicate print on the bottom. The dainty flowers would be cute for a little girl, she thought. She smiled to herself, thinking what a surprise it would be if Abigail's baby ended up being a girl.

Emma felt Mrs. Phelps studying her as she placed her purchases on the counter. Looking up, her smile froze when she saw the scowl on the store owner's face.

"Shame on ya fer bein' so happy here. And in front of James too," she scolded in a low voice. "How can ya be so full of smiles in the face of his heartache?"

Turning, Emma saw that James was indeed in the store. She was mortified to see that he was looking straight at her. Tears filled her eyes. Apologizing, she fumbled to find the handle of her basket and headed toward the door. She just wanted to leave the store quickly. Just short of the door, James stopped her with a hand to her elbow.

"I'd like ta explain somethin' ta you, Mrs. Phelps," James said, speaking loud enough for the whole store to hear.

Emma cringed.

"When Emma went missing, I was beside myself with worry. I prayed and prayed, beggin' God ta help us find her. An'-," his voice quivered, remembering. "And I promised Him I'd do anythin' He asked of me, iffen He would jest return her safe." James cleared his throat before continuing. "What I didna expect was ta have ta give her up. And at first, it was mighty hard ta see her married ta someone else. My Emma bein' someone else's Emma. I'm learnin' ta accept it. But it isn't hard fer me ta see her happy. No. Her happiness is all I've ever wanted fer her."

64

"How can ya be thankin' God when He didna answer yer prayers?" the storekeeper asked, astonished that James was so calm.

"He did answer my prayers, Mrs. Phelps. He brought Emma home to us."

"God did send her home ta us. But surely ya didna pray fer Emma-," she tried again.

Holding up his hand to stop her, he explained. "God answered my prayers. Jest this time- the answer was 'no'," James' voice cracked on the last word. Clearing his throat, he looked down at Emma to see tears streaming down her cheeks. "Are ya done shoppin', Emma?"

Emma nodded. She did not want to stay to purchase the items she had laid on the counter. James pulled the door open for her and stepped back to allow her through. Once on the street, he continued to walk next to her. She noticed that he was keeping a proper distance from her. Guilt filled her as she realized it was the distance she should have insisted on all the years of their friendship.

As they approached his blacksmith shop, her feet came to a stop. Not knowing what to say, she awkwardly picked at the handle of her basket.

"I'm sorry about Mrs. Phelps. I know she means well, but I know how rough that is fer ya."

Tears threatened to fill her eyes again. Blinking them away, she shrugged. "I'm gettin' used ta it."

James rubbed his hand over the back of his neck. "Mark stopped by yesterday. He told me he'd forgiven Thane his part in yer marriage'."

The change in subject surprised Emma. Mark's actions surprised her even more.

"An' then he asked my forgiveness fer his anger. Said he knew how hard it was on me- and that he knew now that he'd made it worse."

Emma just stared at James. She could not think of a good way to reply to him.

James continued, "He also explained that ya had told yer Da a story. A story that helped them all accept this more. He also said that it wasn't his story ta tell. That it had ta come from ya," he paused. "That's what I came ta the mercantile ta ask. Will ya? Will ya tell me?"

Emma looked away. Taking a deep breath to steady her voice, "I do na see how it'll be helpful fer ya, James."

"I think it may help me accept all this better."

Emma's eyes filled with tears.

James rubbed the back of his neck again. "Jest think on it? Pray on it?"

Emma nodded slowly even though she was uncertain that agreeing was a good idea.

"I willna keep ya. I'll see ya Sunday at service?"

Again, she nodded and turned to the road back out of town. Not trusting her voice to say good-bye, she gave a simple wave.

"Hey, Em?" James called out again.

She stopped walking but didn't turn back toward him. She felt him step closer.

"When ya were in the mercantile... ya smiled so brightly. It's the first smile I've seen in weeks."

Emma could hear him twisting the hat in his hands.

"What made ya smile?"

Facing him then, Emma laughed through her tears. "I was thinking... what a shock Abigail will have if her boy turns out ta be a girl after all."

James returned her smile, almost sad. "It's so good ta see that smile again." Settling his hat back on his head, he nodded to her and strode off toward his shop.

She looked away from him quickly before her tears spilled over. "Oh, James," she whispered. She had broken his heart. Emma knew that. Yet here he was, happy that she found something to smile about. Wrapping her free arm around her waist, she took a shaky breath and started for home.

❧ Eight ❧

October 18, 1858...

Emma sat in the shade of the porch. Pushing with her feet, the rocker moved back and forth as she looked around the farmyard for something to do.

She had moved the chair to the porch the day before. Tired of being in the house by herself, she had wanted to be outside. *At least outside, I'll be able to see the animals running about.* She could not handle the quiet cabin anymore. She assured herself that she would feel better outside in the sunshine and the breeze.

But there was no breeze. Nothing moved at all. Even the chickens were quiet in the barn, not stirring out of their stall.

The laundry caught her attention. Water dripped slowly from the clothes to the ground. The drops were the only movement anywhere in the yard, each causing a small splash in the pool forming below.

Looking back up to the line, she saw her two dresses hanging limp on the line next to her nightgown. They looked so lonely on the line by themselves. But Emma knew it wasn't the dresses that were lonely. It was her.

Thane had been gone for over a week. She had seen her family as often as could find an excuse for. But still, she had never felt so alone.

Her eyes scanned the road for any sign of her husband, and just like the numerous other times that week she had looked for him, the road was empty.

She was alone.

Emma stopped moving her feet. As she sat there, in the quiet world around her, an idea formed in her mind. *I did promise Abby I*

67

would come again soon. Standing up, she strode inside to get her bonnet. She splashed water on her face and neck before tying the hat on.

Closing the door behind her, Emma started toward Abigail's. She would see how her friend was faring. Anything was better than just sitting there. With the baby coming soon, she imagined her friend was getting anxious.

If I'm lucky, she'll have work for me to do. The thought made each step lighter.

The trip to town went quick with the excitement of having something to do. Before she knew it, she was knocking on Abigail's door.

"Hold on," Abigail called from inside.

Hearing the exhaustion in her friend's voice, Emma opened the door and stepped inside. "It's Emma."

Abigail had half risen from the chair she was sitting in. Hearing Emma's voice, she sank back into her seat. Once she was settled, she turned to her friend with a smile.

Emma could see the exhaustion in Abigail's face. Closing the door, she went to kneel on the floor. "I came for a visit, but ya look tired. Iffen ya want I can come back later."

"No. I'd love the company. I jest need ta rest for a moment, and I'll make us some tea," she said with a smile. "Then, I'll finish my dishes."

Looking around the kitchen, Emma could see some dishes in the washtub, and a pan was still soaking from the morning meal. It was unlike Abigail to leave dishes for washing later. She studied her friend again. The dark circles under her eyes and disheveled hair made Emma a little more worried. "Did ya sleep last night?"

Shaking her head, Abigail leaned forward to rub her back. "I couldn't get comfortable. When I couldn't get to sleep again, I got up. But walking around isn't comfortable either."

"Do ya want me to fetch David?"

"No," Abby shook her head.

"How long have ya been up?"

"I'm not certain. It was long before David woke."

Emma sighed. "Ya need to rest. Let's get ya ta bed."

"But my dishes-," Abigail protested.

"-your dishes will wait. I'll get you settled an' come back to them."

Abigail looked like she wanted to protest more but relented. "Very well."

Standing, Emma helped her friend to her feet. They walked at a slow pace to the bedroom door, and Emma helped Abigail climb into bed. She unlaced Abigail's boots and slipped them off. "Mama used to put a pillow under the baby," she suggested as she reached for David's pillow.

"I'll try anything," Abigail said.

They arranged the pillow under her large stomach. Once it felt comfortable, Emma covered Abigail up. She set her boots against the wall and headed for the kitchen. At the door, she turned back to look. Abigail was already breathing evenly. *Please let her be alright, Lord.*

Heading to the kitchen, she turned her focus to the work she found there. *Once this is cleaned up, I'll find David,* she promised herself.

~*~

Emma woke to pounding. Disoriented, she felt her head behind her ear, but it didn't hurt to touch.

The pounding stopped.

Confused, she couldn't decide if she was still dreaming. It reminded her of waking in the cabin, high in the hills, when her head injury had been its worst.

The pounding started again. More awake now, she realized it was coming from the front door. Emma pulled back the blanket and quickly wrapped it around herself.

Hurrying to the door, she slid back the lock and unlatched the door.

James stood there.

"James? What are ya doin' here?" Emma asked, trying to think why he would be at her door in the middle of the night.

"David asked me ta fetch ya. The baby's comin' and Abigail won't let him go for the midwife until you are there with her."

"Fetch me?" Emma echoed, confused. The image of Abigail, from that morning, flashed through her mind. How exhausted she had been.

James nodded.

Slowly, Emma mirrored his action. "Let me get myself ready." Closing the door on James, she returned to her room.

Emma had been worried about Abigail all day. She had found David at the mill, then returned to watch her friend sleep until David had been able to come home. *Please keep Abigail safe, Lord*, she pleaded.

With shaky hands, she dressed and pulled her hair up. She wished Thane were there. She longed for one of his hugs. Sending up a prayer for strength to get through this day, she hastened to the front door.

When her hand gripped the latch, her heart stopped. James did not own a wagon. He only owned a horse, and there was no way she could ride on a horse with him. Taking a deep breath, she opened the door, ready to explain she would walk.

But there, next to James in the moonlight, stood the Spencer's wagon. Relief flooded through her.

Hurrying forward, she accepted his help onto the wagon seat.

"I know I shoulda gotten Mark ta fetch ya. But David seemed so panicked- I didna know what ta do," he confessed.

"It's all right, James. I was jest surprised was all."

Driving at a fast clip, James sped to town. When he pulled up in front of the Spencer's house, he leapt down and reached up for her.

Once her feet touched the ground, she turned to hurry inside.

James' hand on her elbow stopped her. She looked over her shoulder in question.

"Em? I'd like ta try ta be friends still. I miss talkin' ta ya," he admitted.

"Do ya think that's a good idea?"

"I practiced jest bein' a friend ta ya fer so long. It comes easy ta me," James said with a shrug.

Emma nodded. "Until ya marry," she added.

James' head jerked up. She couldn't see what emotion was there in the dark- what emotion clouded his features. Taking a deep breath, he relaxed his face to reply, "Yeah. Until I marry."

The door flew open, and David ran from the house. "Thanks fer comin', Emma. I'll hurry!" Giving a squeeze to Emma's arm, he climbed into the wagon and drove away.

Emma watched him go with a trembling heart.

"Ya gonna be alright?" James asked.

"I sure could use some prayers," she said with a quiver to her voice. "We all could use some prayers." Giving James a smile, she turned toward the open door.

~*~

With one last pat of the towel, Emma decided the baby was dry enough. Carefully, she swaddled him in a soft blanket. Abigail held out her arms as they approached the bed. Her friend's face was radiant behind the exhaustion.

"There's my little man."

Emma laughed. Some of the tension in her released with the action. "I admit it. Ya were right."

"Of course, I was right. Mama knew ya'd be a boy," Abigail cooed softly to her baby. Tugging the knitted hat down a little so it covered his ears, she planted a kiss on the top of his head.

As the midwife finished tucking the clean blankets around Abigail, she smiled. "I guess I'll be fetchin' Da now, won't I?" Lifting the heavy basket of soiled linens they had gathered, the lady opened the door.

David rushed to meet the older lady, worry etched into his forehead.

"Well now. Put yer worries away. Yer Abby has someone who wants ta meet ya."

He scurried around the midwife and into the room. At the foot of the bed, David froze. All the worry that had shown only moments before was wiped away.

Suddenly, Emma felt too warm. She hurried outside and knelt in the grass. The cool evening air easing back the feeling of sickness. Taking deep breaths, she slowly relaxed. She assumed it was nerves from the long day. And she admitted that seeing David had made her think of Thane again. Emma let tears of thankfulness flow down her cheeks as her thoughts turned back to Abigail. Bowing her head, she decided to finish the prayer that she had been adding to all that day. *Lord, I thank ya for helpin' Abigail deliver her boy safely into this world. Thank ya fer guidin' my hands ta know what needed ta be done. In yer name, Amen.*

She turned to find Mark and James watching her. They looked worried. Like something bad had happened. She forced herself to smile as she stood to her feet. "I do na think Abigail is quite ready ta show off her baby yet."

Both men relaxed as she approached. Mark's lips twitched into a half-hearted smile. "Was she right? Did she have a boy?"

Emma laughed. "She sure did. No one'll be able ta convince her she isn't right again."

James echoed her laugh. "An' you? Are ya fine? I saw ya earlier. Looked like ya were gonna be ill."

Emma looked down at her hands. "Jest too many emotions, I expect. I prayed pert near all morn. Prayed fer God's hand ta protect Abby and the baby. When it was all over? I jest felt so relieved."

"Has it happened before?"

She shook her head. "I better get back in ta help."

They both nodded in understanding.

James called out as she walked away. "Tell Abigail I can't wait ta see if her boy lives up ta all her braggin'."

After dinner had been eaten, Emma's father and her brothers rode up. Da pulled Emma into a tight hug as soon as he could reach her. She gripped his shirt, feeling the tears pull at her eyes. "I was worried fer ya all day. James came ta tell us ya were here. Told us ya could use some prayer." He pulled back to see her face. "I knew this would be hard fer ya. Rememberin' yer Mama. Ya good?"

Emma nodded and wiped at the tears in her eyes.

Mark stepped forward then and gave her a quick hug. "Seems like we're always makin' ya cry these days," he teased with a smile and held out a basket covered with a towel. "Brought ya a clean dress."

Emma looked up, surprised at how thoughtful her brother had been. He had always been helpful but thinking of her needs wasn't usual for him. Maybe getting ready to be married was starting to change him.

Mark rubbed the back of his neck, uncomfortable under her gaze. "James said ya'd be in need of it... and a nightgown. He didna figure ya'd be in a hurry ta leave yer friend. We knew it'd be improper fer him ta bring it."

Da laughed outright. "I wondered where ya got the idea."

Mark laughed good-naturedly. "Let me know if ya need anythin' else brought ta ya."

❧ Nine ❧

October 20, 1858...

Emma had been stirring the laundry for forever, it seemed. She was no longer standing in the shade. The sun was now blazing directly over her instead of behind the tree. Standing over the boiling water, she was sweating. The bedding and clothes used during the birth needed to boil long enough to remove the stains and soiled coloring. The last time she checked, she could tell she was nearly done.

Mopping the sweat from her brow, Emma went back to stirring. She would be done none too soon. Her stomach was feeling queasy again. Working with lye had been making her sick lately. She had avoided using it at home that week. But here with these soiled fabrics, she had no choice but to rely on it. Leaning on her stir stick, she thought about Thane's habit of sitting with her on laundry day. She knew that as his duties picked up next spring, that would probably change. But she had grown to look forward to the time spent visiting with her husband as he read sections of the Bible and discussing it together. Her throat tightened as she realized how much she missed him. Wiping tears away, she started stirring again.

Mark and James approached from the side of the barn, talking quietly. Shaking away her sad thoughts, she watched them approach. A smile crept onto her face. It did her heart good to see their relationship repaired.

As they stood there talking together, Emma turned back to the job before her. She didn't want to get caught staring at them. Breathing in the lye, her queasiness returned. The feeling was overpowering this time, and she turned away from the fire completely. Leaning against the tree behind her, she took in deep breaths. Mark was by her side before she realized it, taking the stick from her. Keeping his eyes on her, he stirred the laundry

James fetched a fresh bucket of water from the well for her to drink from. Soaking a clean cloth that he grabbed off the nearby line, he handed that to her as well.

Emma tried to laugh it off, but her eyes filled with tears.

"Is this still from yer bump?" Mark asked, worried.

The bump that had left her unconscious for days that fall had given her plenty of dizzy spells over the weeks that followed. Emma couldn't help thinking this felt different but didn't know what else it could be. "I'm sure it must be. It seems I'll never be rid of it."

Mark and James looked at each other before turning back to watch her lean against the tree.

"Emma, jest sit yerself down there and rest," Mark instructed. He held up his hand when she tried to protest. "It may be time ta see the doctor again."

Emma sunk down to sit on the ground. "The doc told us last time it could take months. Besides, I've no time fer that. I've more water to tote. I need clean water to rinse those in," she stated, pointing to the laundry being boiled.

James jumped up from where he knelt close by. He grabbed the buckets as he walked past them. Mark continued to stir the washtub until the second washtub was filled with water.

Tears clouded her vision as she watched their hard work. *Why do I have ta cry all the time*? Frustrated, she leaned her head back against the tree.

Mark cleared his throat. "Now what, Em?"

Rising to her feet, she went to take the stir stick from her brother, but the smell of the hot lye made her stomach churn again. Turning away, she held her breath.

"Jest tell us what ta do," James insisted.

When the waves of nausea passed, Emma turned toward the men again. She kept back from the heat this time. "I have ta lift each piece out with the stick. When it's cooled enough, I wring it out then put it in the rinse water," she explained, pressing her hand to her forehead. "It's jest the smell of the lye turning my stomach. Iffen ya help me lift the laundry from the lye, I can do the rest."

But neither her brother nor James would let her near the washtubs. They lifted the heavy sheets from the boiling tub, following her instructions carefully. Squeezing the water out of each item, rinsing them and squeezing again, then they shook them out to hang. When they realized the last few things were Abigail's undergarments, they turned the job back to her.

While Emma rinsed the last few garments, they emptied the boiling water into the weeds, far back by the woods.

"Looks like yer done fer now," Mark pointed out.

James pulled his hat off to run his hand through his hair. "Do ya need anythin' else done before I go?"

"I'll be fine. Thank ya both. Once I grab a bucket of water to fill the washtub inside, I'll be done fer awhile." Emma pressed the back of her hand to her forehead. "You go on now." When she looked up again, she saw James walking away from her with the bucket in hand. Emma sighed but set about cleaning up her mess.

Mark kicked dirt over her coals and waved to his sister.

Emma paused in the doorway to the house. She could hear James talking in the kitchen, and the midwife answering in reply.

"Jest the same, Mrs. Clem," James said, his voice filled with concern.

"Oh please, it's jest Maggie," Mrs. Clem insisted.

"Maggie, iffen ya can keep an eye on Emma. Not let her work too hard until she's feelin' better, I'd be obliged."

"I didna know she was feelin' poorly," the midwife's voice came from further away.

Emma opened the door slowly, feeling she shouldn't stand there listening any longer and stepped into the room.

James went back to pouring the water into the washtub when she entered. "Is there anythin' else yer needin,' Em?" he asked as he walked past her to leave.

Maggie Clem watched James move around the room and sighed. "So nice ta see a man bein' considerate of a young mother's condition. Don't see it often enough."

Emma froze.

Feeling awkward, James tried to smile. "The heat's jest gettin' ta Emma taday, that's all. She's tryin' so hard ta be a help ta Abigail."

The midwife chuckled. "Looks like it'll be yer turn soon enough."

"Turn fer what?" Emma asked, fear settling cold in her heart.

"What ya been married? 6 weeks? Plenty of time ta have new life growin'," she chuckled again.

"What?" James uttered. The look on his face said he wasn't really sure he wanted to hear her answer.

"Yer young wife's gonna have a baby," Maggie announced, not noticing the tension in the room.

Emma's mind overloaded with emotions. Grief for James' unhappiness. Stress over the birth of Abigail's baby. Worry over Thane being gone. Loneliness from being at the new farm alone. *And now... a baby?* At the realization that the midwife thought it was James' baby, it suddenly became too much. Emma's stomach rolled over, and she fled out the door she had just entered. She ran past the barn and collapsed into the tall weeds.

Emma had not missed James' sigh as she fled.

~*~*~*~*~*~*~*~*~*~*~*~*~*~*~*~*~*~*~*~

Sometime later, Emma's stomach had settled, and her tears subsided. She heard someone approaching cautiously. Looking up over her shoulder, she saw James squat down near her. When he saw her look up, he handed her a wet towel.

Taking it from him, she pressed it against her face.

"I explained ta her that we aren't married. She apologizes ta ya. She'd heard, back in August, we were ta be married. But then has been gone from Vermontville for some time. A whole number of births in a row. She hadna heard of yer abduction- or yer need ta marry another," James explained. "I told her that Mark and I had stopped by because we're concerned about ya, and she promises ta keep an eye on ya." Pausing, he cleared his throat. "I'm sorry. I may have opened ya up to talk, Em."

"Please stop apologizin' ta me. I brought all this upon myself. I thought I could protect ya from it. But here ya are-," her voice cracked. "Here ya are gettin' drawn back in again."

"How could ya have brought this on yerself, Em? Ya've done nothin' wrong."

"I've done everythin' wrong," Emma sighed. Maybe Da and Mark were right. Maybe explaining how she met Thane, would help James understand. At least, James would see how improper she'd been. Maybe then he would want to stay away.

Taking a deep breath, Emma stared off over the field she was facing. "The night I was taken was not the first time I met Thane. I met him earlier during the summer," she started. She heard James' breath catch, but when he made no comment, she continued. "Someone in town tried ta-." She couldn't bring herself to put the actions of Thane's father into words. Clearing her throat with a simple cough, she looked down at her fingers instead. Fidgeting with the cloth she held in her hand, she searched for a different way to explain.

"Thane stepped in before there was a chance ta ruin my reputation. He distracted the man away from me. But then when I went ta town again? I met Mr. Nash. He cornered me in the mercantile... and wouldn't let go of me. I started ta panic. Then suddenly, Thane was there by my side again. He made Nash let go of me. Talked him inta leavin' the store before he made a scene. But Nash wasn't nearly as easily distracted. He followed me- followed me down the road." Emma heard James' sharp intake of breath. Her eyes filled with tears.

"When Nash caught up to me, I was alone. So scared. And then Thane appeared again. Almost as if I had willed him into appearing. He had guessed what they were after before I could. Once Thane made them realize I wasn't available? That marriage wasn't an option? Then Nash and his companion finally left me alone."

"So that's what Nash was talkin' about that day," James commented.

Emma nodded. "Thane walked me home, ta make sure I was safe. I never thought ta see him after that, so I didn't think ta introduce him ta Da. But he did come back, apologizin' fer bein' so familiar with me that day. I was so used ta you and my brothers bein' around... and he was always so proper- I didn't stop ta think that it was wrong fer him ta be there. All we ever did was talk. About the Bible, our lives... I told him stories about my family. I started lookin' forward ta those talks. Missed them when he didn't come around." Looking up then, she met James' gaze. "And then Nash came to the farm. I realized then that I should tell Da. But it was so hard. I knew he'd be so disappointed in me. And then- I never got the chance."

"We all assumed it was me. Ya were so happy... and lively. Ya smiled so often and were making treats for all of us. It is like you woke up after a long nap. And so distracted. I wanted, so badly, ta believe that it was me that made ya so. Ya seemed so happy whenever I came around. Ya started teasin' me again... and sharin' jokes,". His voice barely above a whisper, but Emma could hear the sadness in it.

"I didna know," Emma said, letting tears slide down her cheeks. "I had no one ta tell me what love was. What love looked like. I didna know I'd done wrong until Da told me I'd made ya believe I loved ya. I realized I'd done wrong then. But by then it was too late ta fix anythin'. I knew I'd hurt ya if I told the truth about Thane. So, Thane... he agreed ta leave. And I knew I should marry ya." She paused, trying to find the right words. Her throat burned, remembering how frustrated she had been those weeks.

"Only it got harder and harder. I prayed- and tried ta stay busy. But without Thane being there, no one even stopped ta talk with me. Everythin' was so new, and no one asked me what I was feeling." Her chest filled with a longing for Thane. "When I couldna hide from my feelings anymore, I followed the trail ta that abandoned farm. The farm that ya planned to make yers. And I prayed. I told God that I'd follow His will- if He'd jest show me which way ta go. An' I asked fer His peace. His peace filled me up. Right there- kneelin' in front of that house. And then? Then I was taken." Emma's voice fell to a whisper by the end. "I never wanted ta hurt ya, James. I chose ya so I could spare ya the pain."

"But God chose Thane," James stated, emotions making his voice raw.

She nodded once, hanging her head. She knew he would be disappointed in her.

They sat in silence for a time until James cleared his throat.

"Did I-? Did ya ever have feelings fer me? Did ya even want ta marry me?"

Emma turned to look at him finally. His eyes were pleading with her. Asking for some reassurance. The tears pooling in her eyes overflowed. "Any girl woulda counted herself lucky ta be yer wife." Emotion clouded her voice, "I jest never had a chance ta get used ta it. I'd no idea really. I thought ya only came around fer Mark. You're Mark's friend. Then it all changed so fast." Emma stopped there. She couldn't go on.

"Then, we all assumed. Pushed it on ya," James finished for her. "I'm glad God stepped in. Glad He stopped us. I wanted ta marry ya, Emma. I woulda done anythin' fer ya. But I never woulda wanted ta marry ya that way. Forcin' ya-. Ya woulda hated me in time."

"I could never have hated ya, James." Emma denied. "Yer such a good man."

James stood, brushing off his pants. Turning to walk away, he paused. "I always thought I was yer friend too."

"The only time I ever saw ya was at church or when ya were lookin' fer Mark," she pointed out, confused.

James laughed then, but the laughter didn't reach his eyes. "I was always lookin' fer you. Makin' excuses ta stop by the cabin. Always comin' ta check on ya. Ya jest assumed I was lookin' fer Mark. I used any excuse I could ta spend time with ya, Emma. Even spendin' hours with ya on schoolwork. I guess I always thought ya knew. Thought ya 'd guess why I was comin' `round."

Emma didn't know what to say to that. She should have seen it. He was always there. Always around to talk to. How could she tell him she had never noticed?

"Thank ya fer telling me, Emma," his voice sounded weary. With one last look at her face, James strode away.

Too exhausted to cry anymore, Emma just stared out over the field. She was too tired to even wish Thane was there anymore.

Ten

A baby? Emma placed her hand over her flat stomach once again. Her heart raced every time she thought of a baby growing there. The memory of Abigail's pain flashed before her. And Mama. Remembering the sorrow she saw on her Da's face when her mother didn't pull through, made her feel a little queasy. Uncertainty filled her.

Emma watched Abigail feed her son, the look of love shining from her face. A little of the worry left her. *I wish Thane was here. Ta tell him my worries. Ta talk this through with.* The roll of her emotions from joy, to worry, to missing Thane made her stomach feel queasy again. Breathing slowly, she got through the worst of it.

"I never had much sickness," Abigail said from across the room. She studied Emma's face. With an impish smile, she said, "Bet yer gonna have a girl. Then when she grows up so pretty like her Mama, my boy won't be able ta resist askin' her ta marry him."

Emma chuckled, "Hope she's a good deal prettier than me then."

Abigail's smile faded. "Emma. I know ya think you're plain. But ya have a beauty. A beauty from within. It shines through yer face- through yer calmness. Yer always so sure of what ta do. Ya make people feel better, jest by bein' in the room," she insisted, stroking her son's head. "I always felt like a better person when ya were around me. I made better choices." Glancing up to her friend again, she smiled, "Is it any wonder half the men in town fell fer ya?"

"Don't," Emma pleaded.

"Don't?" Abigail raised an eyebrow in question. "So, ya truly canna see the effect you have on the people around you?"

"Abby..."

"No, Emma. Ya turn heads wherever ya go-," Abigail insisted.

"-No! Abby, no," Emma interrupted her friend, embarrassed at the attention.

"Verra well," Abigail paused for a moment, studying her friend. She looked like she wanted to argue but eventually just shrugged. "Did ya know David told me he wanted ta dislike Thane, fer James' sake. Even while we wanted ta give ya our support. But watchin' Thane take care of ya, changed his mind. Stayin' by yer side to protect ya," she paused with a smile. "Him worryin' at how he'll support ya. Hard ta not like someone that honorable."

Emma smiled at that, relieved at the change in subject. She had noticed David's stiff attempts at friendship in the beginning. He had relaxed and became more natural over the weeks that had followed.

Just then, the midwife came bustling in, clicking to herself as she tidied the room around her.

Emma moved too fast as she stepped out of the way, and it made her head swim again. Holding her breath, she waited until it passed.

Maggie stopped her cleaning and smiled broadly. "That there baby'll be a girl child. Mark my words."

"A girl?" Emma choked. First, Abigail was sure it was a girl and now the midwife was predicting the same.

"Only girl babies steal their Mama's beauty. Makin' them swell all up and sick all the time," she clicked. "Yes, `am! Yer havin' a girl, all right." With that, she bustled back out of the room.

Emma met Abigail's eyes. They both burst out laughing at the same time. The merriment felt good, but Emma felt a little queasy afterward. Sitting down, she leaned her head back against the chair.

~*~*~*~*~*~*~*~*~*~*~*~*~*~*~*~*~*~*~

Giving Abigail one last hug, Emma tucked the blanket firmly around her. Leaning over the baby carefully, she gave him one last kiss and headed out the door. "I'll be back as soon as I git the farm cleaned up," she laughed. "Or Rachel will run fer the hills when she sees it."

Emma decided to head directly to her Da's farm. She wanted to see how much work was needed before she headed back to the cabin. When she stepped into the kitchen, it felt so familiar to her. Like an old friend that greeted her. She almost sighed until she saw James sitting in the corner.

He sat with his back to her, facing the corner with the cookstove and cupboard. Apparently, he had not heard her light steps because he didn't turn toward her. He stared at something in his hands. A small piece of cloth he twisted in his fingers.

Emma hurried to flee the kitchen, embarrassed that she had intruded.

"Em?" James called after her.

She stopped in the door opening, still facing outside. "I didna mean ta intrude on ya."

"Ya didna intrude. It's yer kitchen," he pointed out. "I jest came-" he stopped himself. He seemed to think better of his answer. "Everythin' all right at the Spencer's? With Abigail?"

Emma nodded. "They're all well. I was comin' ta straighten up before Mark brings Rachel here. I can come back later."

James put his hand on her arm to keep her from leaving.

She jumped at his touch, not realizing he had approached.

Clearing his throat, he asked softly, "Emma? If I had asked ta court ya sooner, would ya still have married Thane? Would it have made a difference?"

"I'm not sure what good thinkin' like that would do."

"I jest need ta know. Did I even have a chance?" his voice cracked with the emotions he held in check.

"James, I had no time ta be more'n a friend ta anyone when I was younger. I was so sad and confused. It was all too much with Mama

84

gone," she cleared her throat to lessen the ache she felt growing. "Ya deserve someone who'll make ya happy. Someone who chooses ya above all else. I could never choose between you and Thane. I had ta let God decide."

Dropping his hand from her arm, his voice sounded gruff. "I wish I could go back and do it again. Not wait ta tell ya my feelings. I did everything wrong."

"Ya didna do anythin' wrong, James," Emma faced him then. "It's jest that Thane... well? He saw past my plainness. Really saw me."

James stood so still that Emma wasn't sure what to think. "I don't see plainness when I see ya, Emma. I never have. But Thane-, he saw somethin' we didn't. We were so busy takin' care of ya and keepin' ya safe. We never saw that ya were lonely. We didna see that ya needed someone ta sit and talk ta. Thane saw that. I see how happy he makes ya. And that's what I want. I want ya ta be happy." Tucking a stray curl behind her ear, he held his hand there for a second- barely touching her. Abruptly, he pulled it away and walked out the door.

Sinking down into a chair, Emma let the tears stream down her cheeks. As she thought of how he had come to her old kitchen to feel closer to her, she cried harder. An ache filled her chest to know that he was hurting. And knowing that it was her fault made it almost impossible to breathe. *Please, Lord*, she prayed. *Please*. She did not what she was praying for. She only knew that it was all too much. Lowering her face into her hands, her shoulders shook.

When her tears had finally subsided, she stood to wash the evidence away. Approaching the washtub, she found it empty. A movement off to her side caught her attention, James stood in the doorway, holding buckets of water. He had returned to fill her tubs, but her tears had stopped him.

The misery on his face made Emma want to hug him tight. To tell him how sorry she was for everythin'. But she knew that it wouldn't be proper. *And havna I ruined enough because I've never done the right thing?* Wrapping her arms tightly around her ribs, she instead stepped away from the washtub.

James quickly filled the washtub and left the kitchen.

His thoughtfulness through the pain he had to be feeling brought tears back to Emma's eyes. Sending up a prayer for healing and peace, she took a deep breath. Wiping at the tears, she focused her attention on the much-neglected kitchen before her.

✎ Eleven ✎

October 23, 1858...

Saturday dawned, warm and breezy. *I wonder how long these beautiful days will last*, Emma thought as she headed to the barn to take care of the animals. The extra chores were easy for her now that she had done them for a couple weeks. She found that she actually enjoyed being outside in the early morning.

With a smile, she remembered her decision to bake bread at Da's cabin later. Without an oven, baking bread was not easy to do. It was even harder not to burn it. Her father had agreed that she should use the oven she was used to.

And the cabin she was used to.

No matter how she tried, Emma could not feel comfortable in her new kitchen. It felt like it all belonged to someone else. It was such a relief when she could relax and cook in her mama's kitchen, surrounded by everything familiar to her.

As she headed back to the house, she made up her mind to have breakfast with her family. It had been over a week since she had eaten with them.

Deep in thought, she stepped over a package on her doorstep. With her hand on the latch, Emma froze. Looking back, she stared at the package laying there in surprise. The bundle was wrapped in brown paper and tied with string.

Checking from side to side, she didn't see anyone. *Was this here when I stepped out this mornin'? How did I miss it?*

Reaching down, she pulled a paper from where it was tucked into the string. The front merely said her name. Opening it, she found a note inside.

Emma,
I fashioned this for you months ago, for you to take with you to our new home. I want you to have it still.
May God Bless your marriage and your new home.

Happy Birthday!
Your friend,
James Abernathy

"My birthday." She had forgotten about her birthday.

Curious, Emma carried the package to the kitchen table inside. Untying the string, she peeled back the layers of paper. Her breath caught when she saw the new dinner bell laying there. James had made her one to replace the bell she left at Da's. The one she couldn't bear to move from its place on the front porch. This new bell had a twisted design around its shape. As she tapped the striker against the triangle's side, it made the most beautiful sound. Tears filled her eyes. This gift had been made with love. And then given in selflessness. "He is such a good man, Lord. Please fill him with peace and blessings," she whispered.

Heading to the barn, she searched for a hammer and a nail to hang the bell from. She found them quickly and returned to the front steps. Not quite tall enough, she was looking for something to stand on when she saw Seth coming up the lane.

"Whatcha got?" he called.

Emma held the bell out for Seth to see. "My birthday present."

"It's the 23rd already?" Seth asked with a smile.

"Apparently," she confirmed. Handing her little brother the nail and the hammer, she pointed above her. "I canna reach that spot there. Could ya hold this while I get a chair?" She stepped inside and heard Seth pound the nail in.

She turned back to see his impish smile. Trying hard not to respond to his irresistible teasing, she replied sternly, "It'd be easy fer me too... if I was built like a giant."

Seth helped gather up the supplies she would need for the day's baking. Carrying the bulk of it himself, they set off toward Da's. Laughing and joking along the way, Emma saw the roof of the cabin before she was even tired.

Once she stepped through the trees into the yard, Mark and her father came out of the barn to greet her.

"Happy Birthday, Emma girl!" Da gave her a tight hug.

Emma laughed. "Seth made it sound like ya all forgot what day it was."

Seth rubbed his hand back and forth through her hair, loosening a hairpin in the process. "Canna have ya gettin' a big head now, can I?"

Pretending to be annoyed, Emma tried to keep herself from smiling. She pushed her brother's hands away from her head and then tried to smooth the ruffled hair as best she could. "I thought I'd spend the day here, gettin' some bakin' done. Iffen ya do na mind."

"Don't mind at all," Da stated with a laugh as he watched his children tease each other.

Mark echoed their father's laugh. "Maybe ya could make a better cake than the one we baked ya."

"Ya baked me a cake?" She felt her eyes fill with tears.

Da took the basket from her arm, "Maybe ya should save yer tears until AFTER ya taste it."

All day, her family stayed inside with her as much as their chores would allow. They sat at the table, visiting with her as she cooked. Taste testing what looked irresistible.

After the noon meal, they ate the cake that the boys had baked her. "It's a little dry, but it tastes good," Emma praised.

"Good?" Mark questioned. "I'm thinkin' Seth's shoe would taste better."

Da laughed loud. "I wouldna be tastin' Seth's shoe. He doesna watch where he is walkin'."

Emma smiled at the laughter around the table as they poked fun at the cake they had baked her. The first thing they had ever baked. Her heart was overflowing with love that they had even tried to make her something special. "My heart is full, no matter what it tastes like. Thank ya fer this treat."

They all turned to her and smiled.

"Ya could really thank us by makin' some cookies ta leave behind," Seth replied with a twinkle in his eye.

"Yer rotten, Seth," Mark teased. "She already made ya cookies."

"Those? But I already ate most of 'em. I meant some that'll be fer tomorra-," Seth explained.

Da's laugh interrupted what else his youngest child was about to say.

Emma's cheeks hurt from smiling so much. She met Mark's eyes and loved seeing the joy there. She wondered how much their lives would change by adding Rachel to their family the next day. A little of her happiness dwindled at the thought. She knew it wouldn't be a bad thing with Rachel there. Just different. Not the way they were used to things.

Much like her brothers had to get used to not having her around. At least with Mark's marriage, they had a couple of weeks to get used to the idea. Shaking the somber thoughts away, Emma decided to make it the best day she could.

"Alright. I'll make ya more cookies, Seth," she said with an impish smile of her own. "But I was thinkin' I'm gonna need ya ta do somethin' fer me."

Seth nodded. "I'll do anythin' fer cookies."

"I'm gonna need a couple chickens iffen I'm gonna make fried chick-," Emma was interrupted by her little brother's whoop.

"Oh boy," Seth jumped up and ran for the coop without closing the door behind him.

Mark stood as well. "I'll make sure he doesna get that old cranky hen. She'll be bitter- even in the pot."

Closing the door behind him, Mark left Emma alone in the kitchen with Da. They were silent for a few minutes as she set about making another batch of cookies. "Do ya want some more coffee, Da?"

"No," he answered. "I think I'm good fer now." He gathered up the plates and put them in the washtub.

"Jest leave them. I can get them in a minute," Emma protested.

Da chuckled. "I've washed many a dish in my life. A couple more won't hurt me." He watched his daughter work for a moment. "Ya comin' today has put Mark at ease. His nervousness this week has been buildin'. Ya've taken his mind off that today. But I think ya knew that. I think that was what ya planned. Even forgettin' that it was yer birthday." He washed another cup and set it on the towel to dry. "But ya've also made my old heart happy. Havin' today with all of ya together and happy. It's jest like the old days. Days that I didna know ta be thankful fer until they were gone. Thank ya fer that." He looked toward her then.

The tears she saw there were too much for Emma. She put her arms around his waist and leaned her head against him. "I've missed this ta be honest, Da." Her own tears soaking his shirt front.

Clearing his throat, Da chuckled again. "Emma girl, it seems I've dumped wash water down yer back."

Sure enough, Emma felt the wetness as the water cooled against her skin. With a laugh, she pulled back. "Oh well. It will give me somethin' ta wash on wash day. With it jest bein' me, washday is mighty borin'."

Da smiled. "Yer Mama would be so proud of ya."

91

Emma's breath caught. She had spent so many years worried she had let Mama down. To have Da say those words was the best birthday gift she could receive. "Thanks, Da."

"Now," Da said, tying an apron around his waist. "Tell me what ya want me ta do." When he saw her look at the apron in amusement, he smiled. "Unlike you, we have a lot of laundry on washday, and no one skilled enough ta get stains out."

With a laugh, Emma turned the bowl in her hand over to her father. "Stir this until it's fluffy."

"Fluffy," he echoed and tried to stir the egg and sugar mixture. His big hands held the small fork awkwardly, but he soon fell into a rhythm.

With a smile at this man who had always been in her life, she set about making cookies with him. Determined to enjoy every minute of it.

When the sun began to tuck behind the trees, Emma gathered her things to go home. It was hard to leave. Except for the new life growing inside her, it felt as if she had never left. At the edge of the path, she stopped and turned back. Da stood on the porch, watching her go. For a moment, Emma was torn. Part of her wanted to stay, especially after the wonderful time they had together that day.

But the memory of Thane's lopsided smile passed through her mind. A smile that she missed. And that smile was a part of her future.

Da raised his hand in a wave. Emma returned the gesture and turned back to the path before her.

❧ Twelve ❧

October 24, 1858...

izziness washed over Emma as the wagon jostled along over the bumpy road, and she gripped the bench.

"Are ya feelin' alright?" Da asked as he pulled back on the reins.

Emma tried to assure her father she was fine, but the wheel hit a rut in the road, and a wave of nausea swept over her. Placing a hand over her mouth, she slowly shook her head from side to side.

Da reined the horses to a stop. "Would ya rather walk?"

Shaking her head again, Emma took a moment to answer. "I willna make Mark late fer his own wedding."

"We have time," Mark insisted. "We needna hurry... not in her condition."

Her brother's words made her smile despite her discomfort. His desire to give her extra time had more to do with his nervousness. She had seen his hands shaking on more than one occasion that morning. "My condition?" Emma repeated, lifting her eyebrow. "I'm havin' a baby... not dyin'."

A smile crept on his face. "Well, with ya moanin' all the time? It seems like the same thing."

Happy to see her brother's attempt at teasing, Emma tried hard to keep herself from smiling in response. She turned back to her father. "I'm better now."

With a click, the horses began moving forward again but at a slower pace. Even with the slower speed, they still arrived at the church with plenty of time before services began.

When Mark caught sight of Rachel standing with her mother and sisters, he froze.

Nudging her brother in the side, Emma nodded toward Rachel. "She is probably nervous. Go tell her how beautiful she is today."

"Women know how beautiful they are." Mark pointed out. As if Rachel knew they were discussing her, she turned toward them. With a determined set of his jaw, he nodded in her direction and then hurried into the church.

Emma covered her mouth to hide the smile that sprung to her lips. Taking her father's arm with her other hand, they followed Mark inside and found their seat.

Reverend Keyes stepped up to the podium and greeted his congregation. "It is a beautiful day that the Lord has made us today! A beautiful day to join together in Worship. I'd like ta remind you all that the wedding ceremony that will join Mark Wells and Miss Rachel Moore together forever, will immediately follow today's service."

Mark's color went slightly green at the word "forever." Squaring his shoulders, he gave a single nod. Emma wondered if he was confirming the words to himself or to the reverend.

As voices rose in song, Emma turned away from her brother to allow him a moment to gather his strength. *Help him to be strong, Lord,* she prayed. Reaching out, Emma took her brother's hand and gave it a squeeze. Mark squeezed back.

Rachel sat motionless on her bench. Unlike Mark, she did not fidget or move at all.

When the sermon was over, Reverend Keyes called the couple forward. As soon as Rachel stood, Emma could see that her calmness did not mean she wasn't nervous. Her face was white and terrified.

Not for the first time, Emma found herself thankful that Mr. Nash hadn't been to church since Mark had asked for Rachel's hand. *Of course, I don't mean that, Lord,* she corrected. *I know even men with black hearts need church. I... I jest think it would make it worse fer Rachel is all.*

As Mark moved forward, he saw Rachel's nervousness too. It brought him out of his own worries for a moment, trying to make her feel better. "Do na worry yerself, Miss Moore," he stated. "Ya'll be jest fine, I promise ya." Rachel tried to respond to Mark's reassuring smile but was not quite successful.

One of Rachel's sisters stood up as a bridesmaid. She smoothed the bride's simple dress and tucked in a few stray wisps of hair. With a small bouquet of flowers in hand, Rachel squared her shoulders and faced the reverend.

Emma couldn't help but wonder if she had made Mr. Nash's bad attentions known earlier if it could have saved these two from getting married. Well, the townsfolk know now, she thought. And Rachel could have a worse man. Much worse.

Remembering her own wedding among strangers, Emma wondered if she would have liked this better, having a friend to stand up with her. Shaking her head, she realized all the well-wishers and whispered comments would have stolen the joy she had felt that day.

As James stood up next to her brother, he turned and met Emma's eye. Her breath caught. There was such a sadness about his expression that it made her chest hurt. She wondered if he was thinking about the wedding they were supposed to have had. The wedding that never happened. When her eyes filled with tears for him, he startled. Trying to smile, he didn't quite succeed and turned back to the ceremony instead.

Emma took a shaky breath and turned her attention back to her brother. She couldn't deal with James' sadness here in public, or she would end up crying.

Rachel repeated her part of the vows, her voice quiet and hesitant. Emma could not imagine promising to love and honor someone she did not know. Watching their stiff and polite exchanges, she couldn't contain her smile. No wonder the preacher's wife had known there was more to her and Thane's relationship than just honor. She could never have stood so coolly next to Thane. She remembered how his voice had caught during the vows. *Yes. I imagine we were a sight different than this one.*

Mark repeated his section of the vows with a strong voice and his fists clenched. When he finished, he slipped Mama's ring on Rachel's finger, squeezing her fingers in reassurance. A faint smile appeared on her lips then. Relief showed in her eyes.

"Ya may now kiss yer bride," Reverend Keyes announced, breaking through Emma's thoughts.

The young couple both blushed as Mark leaned forward for a soft, quick kiss. As soon as their lips touched, they both jerked away from each other.

Reverend Keyes placed Rachel's hand on top of Mark's. Turning them toward the congregation, he proudly announced, "May I present to you all, Mr. and Mrs. Mark Wells."

Rachel's family rose and were the first to surround the newlyweds. Emma followed her father to stand behind them. Mrs. Moore caught Emma with a surprise hug. "Bless yer family fer steppin' forward fer my Rachel. Bless ya all."

No one congratulated them on their marriage. But as each congregation member stepped forward, they were wished well, and everyone gave their blessing. As the line of people grew shorter, Emma stepped outside into the sun. The makeshift tables they used at community events had already appeared. She went to the wagon to retrieve her soft biscuits and the basket of bread. Unwrapping the cloth from around them, she placed both on the long table. Then she went in search of a place to lay out their picnic blanket.

James stayed near Mark all afternoon. Emma began to wonder why. Mark and Rachel had a constant line of people talking to them, leaving very little chance for the two friends to talk together. When James handed Mark a cup full of water, Emma saw her brother's hand shake slightly as he took it. She smiled to herself. Her strong, confident hero of a brother was nervous.

"Was wonderin' if ya'd care fer some company this evenin', Emma girl?" Da's question broke the silence around her.

"Sure," Emma replied with a nod. "I can come by home-- the farm-- tonight."

Da smiled. "Actually, thought Seth and I would come by yer place. We haven't been that way much."

Realization dawned on Emma. Her father was trying to give Mark and Rachel some privacy. "Sounds fine. What time can I expect ya?"

"I figured we'd have Mark drop us off at yer farm before they headed on home," he answered. "Seth and I could walk on home in the morning."

Nodding to Da, Emma's eyes went back to the awkward newlywed couple. Standing stiffly next to each other, not touching or talking to each other unless they had to. Yes, she agreed with her father. These two needed some time alone.

✒ Thirteen ✒

November 12, 1858...

Emma put her hand to her forehead. Holding it there, she hoped her dizziness would pass quickly. She heard footsteps, and her eyes flew open. Her hope died when she saw her brother approaching.

Feeling her eyes fill up, she blinked the tears away. Every day she hoped that Thane would come home. Then every day when the sun set, she tried to hide her disappointment.

"Sorry, it's jest me. I see yer disappointed," Mark said with a small smile.

Wiping the tears away, she laughed at herself. "I thought ya might be Thane fer a moment." Standing up, Emma wiped her knees off. "I switch from sick ta cryin' with the blink of an eye these days. I canna help it."

"Seems a miserable life," he agreed, trying not to laugh. "What are ya doin' here?" He pointed to the holes she had dug.

"It's where my garden will be. I canna till it, but I've loosened the large stones and started movin' them," she nodded to the pile of stones next to the barn.

Mark was silent for a moment. "I'll send Seth over this afternoon to till it up for you. It'll be faster than diggin' it up by hand. And it'll be better fer ya."

"I thank ya," Emma replied. She had been so used to her brother's predicting her needs that she had never realized how hard it was to do certain tasks. Like tilling a small garden.

Pulling an envelope out of his pocket, he held it out to Emma. "I brought ya yer mail. Didna know when ya'd be goin' ta town again."

"Oh, thank ya." Reaching out for the envelope, she saw it was addressed to Thane. She wondered if she should open it, but quickly decided she would wait. Thane should be home any day now. "I'll put it on the mantle fer Thane ta open when he gets home."

"Shouldn't ya open it? It might be from his grandma. Ya wouldna want ta be caught unaware," her brother pointed out.

"I'm stuffin' a mattress with straw. And collectin' feathers every day for a new pillow fer her. I canna do much more than that, I'm thinkin'. Besides, I'd feel a mite strange openin' a letter not addressed ta me," she admitted.

"True." Mark took his hat off and ran his fingers through his hair, looking around the yard. "If Thane doesna come home soon, we'll need ta do some work around here."

She knew he was right. Emma hated to ask her family to help her. But if Thane wasn't home to help, she wouldn't have another choice. She could not do everything on her own when she couldn't even keep down her breakfast.

"Well, hopefully, my husband'll be home soon." Emma noticed the expression on her brother's face. "How are you and Rachel doin'?"

Mark rubbed the back of his neck, looking away from his sister.

"Ya don't seem ta talk much."

"I do na know what ta say ta her. She is so quiet."

"It'll take some time ta get used ta each other."

He tapped his hat against his thigh a couple of times. Without looking up, he went on, "I'm afraid ta push a relationship on her. I don't want ta be like... Nash. I jest want her ta be happy."

Emma guessed from his hesitation that he was about ta say her husband. "Thane never pushed anythin' on me, Mark. He was always courteous and careful. We mostly jest talked in the beginning. He asked questions. Jest showed me he cared."

Mark cleared his throat. "I was actually thinkin' about James. But I know he didna mean ta be pushy."

"Oh." Silence settled between them. Emma had never thought of James as pushing his affections on her. Maybe it had appeared that way to Mark, though. "I never felt like James was pushy. Misunderstandin' my feelings maybe- but not pushy. James always knew what I'd allow and I wouldna stand for."

Pausing for a breath, Emma wondered if she should go on. "Mark... Do na let my mistakes color yer choices. Otherwise, it'll make my sins so much worse than they are."

"What are ya meanin'?"

"I mean that ya seem hesitant with Rachel. Don't let it be because I blundered my way through figuring out love. Ya offered this girl a life with you. Ya need ta go forward and make that life now."

Nodding in agreement, Mark sat in silence. "What do I do?"

Emma smiled at her brother. "That is easy. Go home and find yer wife. Sit down next ta her and ask her ta tell you a story from her growin' up years. Or take her fer a picnic lunch. Ask her what she likes ta do in her quiet time. Then keep askin' her questions from there. Her favorite flower, her favorite cookie. Even her favorite time of day." Mark listened so careful that it made her smile get bigger. "Once yer knowin' more about each other, it'll be easier ta talk ta each other."

With another nod, he shoved his hat on over his hair. "Well, I best be headin' on back then. I'll send Seth ta ya after his noon meal."

ᦓ Fourteen ᦓ

November 17, 1858...

Emma let the gentle breeze blow through her hair. It was uncommonly warm for this time of year. November usually meant strong winds and cool temperatures. But that morning didn't feel like autumn with the gentle breeze and the warm sun.

With a spring in her step, Emma continued to her father's farm. As she approached the house, she could hear Seth talking to someone. Stepping through the doorway, Seth came into view. He was leaning close to Rachel as she washed the dishes.

Mark's new wife looked exhausted. She wiped her brow then went back to scrubbing the pot in the washtub.

"When Emma makes these cookies, I think she uses more ginger? Or more molasses? I'm not sayin' yers aren't good, but maybe if ya ask her what yer doin' wrong-?"

"Seth Wells!" Emma scolded from her place in the doorway. "Are ya tellin' poor Rachel how ta make ya cookies? When she cooks fer ya all day long? Ya should be happy ya get cookies at all! Now get out of here." She was appalled at her little brother's manners. Turning to Rachel, she apologized. "Pardon my little brother. Apparently, growing up without a mother's care has addled his brain."

Seth had the good sense to look sheepish as he made for a swift exit to the barn.

Rachel gave Emma a shy smile as she shrugged her shoulders. "Seth doesn't bother me any. He jest misses ya. And misses yer cookin'. No shame in that, I'm guessin'."

"Hmm," Emma murmured. "Jest promise me ya won't take his harassin' ya."

Rachel nodded as she continued to scrub the pan.

A smile played across her lips. "Did ya make oatmeal this mornin'?" Emma asked.

Another nod was her only answer.

"Let me guess," Emma stated, pretending she was thinking hard. "Seth told you that ya didna put enough brown sugar in it. And probably explained the benefits of extra spices?"

The young lady looked up in surprise. A smile slowly spread across her lips, "How could ya know that?"

Emma laughed easily. "I have been cookin' fer my little brother for many years. He's been using the same arguments these last few months as he did when he was 10. And he wonders why I never change my mind." With another laugh, she started drying the dishes on the cup board. "So, no, my new sister. Seth doesn't miss my cookin'. He jest craves *more* sugar and spices than we can afford ta give him."

Rachel laughed despite herself. A low but cheerful laugh. It delighted Emma.

"Let's do somethin' fun today, Rachel. It's such a fine day outside," she suggested.

Unsure, Rachel looked out the window. "I should really use this nice weather ta get caught up on laundry. Bedsheets and quilts will be easier in this fair weather."

"You've been workin' non-stop since ya married my brother. What say you, we get Mark ta hitch the wagon and we take ya ta see yer Mama?"

Hope filled her face. "Do ya think he would?"

"Of course, he will," Emma assured her. "The Wells men canna say "No" to their women."

"They're na allowed?" Rachel asked, confused.

"Oh, they're allowed ta." A laugh escaped Emma. "They are jest na capable of sayin' it."

Almost as if speaking of Mark would make him appear, he opened the door and walked into the kitchen.

Emma raised her eyebrows to Rachel and turned toward her brother. "Mark, it's been weeks since Rachel has visited with her mama outside of church. We'd like ta drive the team up there, iffen ya've no need fer the wagon today. It'd be a shame ta be inside on this beautiful day."

"I'll hitch it right away," Mark said with a nod in agreement. Whatever he came inside for was forgotten as he turned and headed back out the door.

As soon as the door closed behind him, Emma burst out laughing.

Rachel's smile broadened as she put the last dish onto its stack. "Ya seem very happy today. Have ya heard from Thane?" she asked.

Shaking her head, Emma's smile slipped a little. Thinking of Thane reminded her how much she missed him. "No," she stated simply. "But today was the first time I woke up and didn't get sick." She had still needed to sit on the edge of the bed frame for a few minutes before standing. But it had felt nice to not bolt for the outhouse the second she sat up.

By the time the ladies ventured outside, the wagon was hitched and waiting for them.

"Anythin' else ya be needin'?" Mark asked.

Emma smiled at the proper way her brother addressed his wife. "I canna think of anythin', kind sir." Smiling at Rachel, she asked. "Can ya?"

Rachel shook her head.

Mark helped his little sister and then his wife into the wagon. His hands lingered on Rachel's waist for a moment before releasing her, heading back to the barn.

Wasting no time, Emma clicked to the team, and the farm disappeared behind them in no time.

"It feels so good to be goin' home." Rachel smiled, excitement shining from her eyes.

Turning toward Rachel, Emma studied her face. Focusing back on the road in front of them, she agreed. "I couldna wait ta find an excuse ta go home when I first married Thane. I missed the familiar smells. I missed the chaos Seth brought with him. But it didna take long before I felt like I was jest visitin' my Da's house too." She let the scenery roll past as she thought of those first few weeks. "And yet Thane's farm does na feel like my home yet either. Almost like I do na have a place I belong ta."

Rachel cleared her throat, "It's the same fer me. Not that I don't feel welcome. Jest that it doesn't feel like it's mine yet."

Emma smiled, "Exactly."

She slowed the team and drove carefully through the town. A child ran out in front of them, but a man grabbed him and pulled him back to safety. After that, Emma slowed down even further. She released a sigh of relief as they left the town buildings behind.

As the Moore farm came closer, Rachel was having a hard time keeping still in her seat. She was so excited. *The wind feels the same way*, Emma mused. It had picked up energy and seemed to be pushing them to arrive at their destination faster. When they pulled into the yard, the family met them on the porch. Rachel jumped down and ran to her mother and sisters. They were all laughing and hugging.

"How long can ya stay?" Mrs. Moore asked.

"Until the noon meal."

"Poor Rachel has been harassed by my little brother for far too long. I brought her for a nice relaxin' visit," Emma joked when they looked to her. She felt awkward standing among these women who knew each other so well. But it warmed her heart to see Rachel so happy.

Coffee was put on to boil, and a sweet bread was produced from the room behind the kitchen. Laughing and talking, the sisters set plates of treats on the table.

With seven kids in the Moore family, their house was larger than the one Emma grew up in. She could see the original log home in the center, where the kitchen and sitting area surrounded the fireplace.

Building on, the newer rooms jutted out like fingers. Behind the kitchen, there was a lean-to that enclosed the root cellar doors. From the far side of the sitting area, another addition was built to make one large sleeping room for the boys. Emma didn't know what the other small lean-to held since she hadn't asked.

"So young Seth has been harassing ya?" Mrs. Moore asked Rachel, concern showing on her face.

Rachel turned to Emma before answering her mother. "He's been tryin' ta convince me that Emma used ta cook larger meals fer him."

"An' use more spices. An' I imagine askin' fer cookies when ya are the busiest?" Emma added with a laugh. Her eyes sparkled at the remembered mischief that her little brother was known for.

"But Emma is helpin' me set him straight," she explained. "Should make it easier- until he comes up with new stories."

"When I was younger, I used ta think he was a little devil," Emma chuckled. "If there was trouble within a stone's throw, Seth could find it. When he was eight, he was convinced that porcupines would be good meat iffen ya could git under the quills. So, one day he lassoed one, leading it right inta the farmyard. Perty near every farm animal ended up with a quill in it before Mark could shoot it." Smiling at the memory, she took a sip of her coffee. "He still tells people ta this day that the reason Mark can shoot so straight is from the number of critters he brought home. I don't know that he isna right."

The ladies all laughed.

"Tell us a story of Mark," the youngest sister spoke up.

"Mark?" Emma put her cup down carefully. "Mark never went anywhere without James. They were always the heroes. At least in their own memories." Laughing to herself, she continued. "One spring, their friend George took to messin' with my braids. I was so frustrated that finally, I asked Mama ta cut my hair short. The next day, George didna return ta school after dinner break. It was hours later that we found him. Well... Abigail found him. Mark and James had tied him inside the outhouse. Poor Abigail thought it was a bear trapped. After hours of

105

yelling, George was so hoarse he jest took ta growlin', hopin' someone would hear him."

"Did George leave yer braids alone?" Rachel asked.

"Yes, ma'am. He wouldna even look at me fer the rest of the school term."

Rachel blushed. "Could ya tell me more? Yer brother's so much older than me. I do na remember him from school." Her request was hesitant like she was intruding on his privacy.

Emma studied her brother's wife. She could not imagine living in marriage with someone that you knew nothing about.

"I could talk about my brothers all day," she answered with a smile. "One year, for Mama's birthday, Mark wanted ta surprise her with fresh honey. He was little, and he thought all bees made honey. So he searched and found a busy hive. Figurin' bees slept like little boys do, he snuck out after everyone was asleep with a cannin' jar. He shimmied up that tree, pulled the hive from where it hung, and tried to pour the honey out into the jar. But try as he might- no honey came out."

"Oh, no." Rachel's eyes were huge as she listened.

"Oh, yes." Emma laughed. "When he realized it wasn't gonna work, Mark tried to carefully put the hive back. But that hive would not stick back to the branch. So... he propped it in the corner of a branch and started climbing down. Halfway down the tree, the wind picked up and blew the hive off its ledge, crashin' ta the ground below. Terrified from the sound of all those angry bees, Mark shimmied back up the tree. Da found him in the morning, huggin' the verra top of that tree, still holdin' that cannin' jar."

Mrs. Moore shook her head with a small smile. "Likely gave yer poor mama a panic to find him gone."

"Yes, ma'am."

"Do ya have another?"

Rachel's expression made Emma's heart happy. "There was the time-,"

106

"Hold on now," Mrs. Moore stood up. "Let me get the mendin' basket. Might as well get somethin' done while we are enjoyin' ourselves."

Young Jane ran from the room. "I'll fetch it."

When Jane returned, each lady grabbed a needle and thread, repairing rips and seams while Emma shared story after story. They all listened, interrupting only with laughter.

~*~

Just before dinner time, the door opened, and Mr. Moore stepped inside. A great gust of wind came in with him and blew a paper off the cupboard. One of Rachel's sisters raced to retrieve it.

"Sorry ta interrupt yer hen housin'. But the wind has set ta blowin', and the sky is gettin' dark perty fast. I believe a storm is blowin' in. The boys are hitchin' up yer wagon, Mrs. Hawkins. Ya need ta head back. With a steady pace, ya might make it home before it hits."

Rachel nodded to her father. "Yes, Pa."

Emma stood up and started gathering the dishes around them. Mrs. Moore shooed her away. "Never mind ya the dishes. We can git these ourselves. Ya need ta be headin' out. Mr. Moore doesn't worry unless there's a need." Handing the girls their bonnets, Rachel's mom held the door open for them.

"Oh, the wind has picked up some," Rachel pointed out, seeing the trees sway back and forth. Kissing her mama's cheek, they hurried to the waiting wagon.

"I'm wishin' I wore a shawl now," Emma stated. They gave a quick wave to Rachel's family on the porch before clicking to the team. The horses seemed as eager to get home as the ladies. They pulled at the reins, anxious to be home.

Emma had jest past over the river when she saw Rachel give a shiver. "I guess this isn't such a fine autumn day. Sorry, Rachel."

Rachel smiled, "How could ya have known? Mark didn't suspect either, or he wouldna sent us off."

"True. It was a fine visit. Well worth a chilly ride home."

"I agree," Rachel smile grew bigger.

The snow started falling in large flakes. It looked so peaceful when the wind wasn't gusting. Emma thought how beautiful the drive would have been if they weren't both so cold. The wind picked up again. Soon, the snow was falling so thick that she had to strain to see the road.

When the back wheel hit a rut along the edge of the road, Emma steered the horses back on to the road and reined them to a halt. Taking a deep breath, she handed the reins to Rachel. "Take these. I'm gonna walk next to the mare. I should be able to keep us from goin' off the road again. We won't be able to go very fast."

"Emma let me walk. Ya'll get too tired with the baby, " Rachel reasoned.

Shaking her head, Emma climbed down. "I reckon the horses know me better. And they already seem a little spooked."

Looping her fingers around the bridle strap, Emma clicked to the horses. They started off again. Wanting to go faster than she could walk, Emma frequently had to pull them back to slow their pace. It wasn't long before Emma could no longer feel the pain in her cold fingers. Taking one hand at a time, she placed her fingers in the crook of her elbow to warm them.

Suddenly the ground below Emma's feet sloped away from her. "Whoa," she cried as she slid forward. Her weight, balanced against the horse, was the only thing that kept her standing.

"What is it?" Rachel called.

Emma leaned her forehead against the warmth of the horse. When her heart stopped hammering, she turned toward the wagon. "We missed the curve toward town. We have to back out of the ditch," she explained.

"We're only halfway ta town?" Rachel asked. Disappointment added an edge to her voice.

"Yes. Only a little further," Emma forced more cheerfulness into her words than she felt. "We'll stop at Abigail's when we get ta town and warm ourselves."

Taking a deep breath, Emma returned her attention to the horses. "Back," she commanded them. But they didn't want to go back. They sidestepped in their harnesses nervously. Stepping in front of the mare, she nudged her chest. "Back!" she called again, trying to sound more like Da. The horses took one step back and sidestepped again. "Come on," Emma begged.

"Do ya hear that?" Rachel asked against the wind.

Emma stopped struggling with the horses. Turning her head, she didn't hear anything. "What did ya hear-." Out of the corner of her eye, she saw a shadow emerge from the wall of white.

"Emma?"

She would have cried if she had any energy left in her. Relief made her knees weak.

Mark jumped down from his horse and ran toward her. Pulling off his jacket, he tried to put it around her.

"Rachel," she called against the wind, pointing toward the bench of the wagon. "Go ta Rachel. She is freezing." Her words were jumbled with her shivering. She watched her brother run toward his new wife. Her throat tightened as she watched them together. Mark gathered Rachel against his chest, rubbing her arms and back to get her warm.

Watching them, Emma longed for Thane to be there, running toward her with a warm coat. Pulling her to him for warmth and comfort. How she wished to collapse into his arms. A sob threatened to escape her lips. *Now is not the time for hysterics.* Taking a deep breath, she leaned against the mare again. *Please, Lord, give me strength.*

The weight of something across her shoulders startled Emma. Grabbing out to catch herself as she slipped back down the snow-covered slope, she felt hands steady her and pull her back to solid ground.

Turning with relief, she felt hope fill her heart. "Thane?" she whispered. Her heart fell as she looked up into James' worried face. She couldn't help the sob that escaped then. "Oh, James," she choked out, her throat raw with disappointment. He pulled her into his arms for an awkward hug. Trying to push away from his hold, James only pulled tighter. "Don't, Em," James scolded. "Yer freezing. I need ta get ya warm. Yer lips are turnin' blue."

Wrapping the weight around her shoulders tighter, Emma's hands were trapped in front of her, inside of the material. She knew that he was right. She knew that she needed his warmth. *But why does it always have ta be James?* She knew it had to hurt him, always being this close to her. "I wish Thane were here," she whimpered, the emotions in her throat making her voice thick. If Thane was there, James wouldn't have to help her all the time. He could heal and move on.

James' hands stopped rubbing her shoulders for a second. "So do I, Emma," he whispered against her hair. "So do I. He could hold ya closer than I can... properly." He started rubbing the fabric against her arms and back again, in an effort to warm her up. She relaxed into him, greedy for the heat he brought. "I feel so helpless," he admitted.

"I'm so sorry, James." Her jaw clattered together as her shivering increased. "I always seem ta need ya. I wish I could jest leave ya be."

"Don't ever wish that," James growled in her ear. Putting his arm under her knees, he lifted her with ease. Emma tried to protest, but James shushed her. "I'm gonna put ya in the wagon to rest. We need ta get ya both home."

Laying her in the wagon bed, he wrapped a blanket around her legs and feet. Then another quilt was tucked around her back and shoulders.

"Ya'll need yer coat," Emma protested as she tried to sit up.

He stopped her with a finger on her lips. "I'll be fine. Ya need it more'n me."

As he turned to leave, she reached out and grabbed his wrist to stop him. "James... we missed the turn off ta town. We're headed in the ditch." James tucked her hand back inside the blanket. "I couldna get them ta back up."

"We'll get 'em headin' right," he assured her as he tucked the quilt around her again.

Rachel appeared next to her in the wagon bed. Rolling close, they huddled together to keep warm. The wagon seat above them sheltered them from most of the wind. But still, Emma felt colder by the minute. *How can I be feelin' colder now?* she wondered incredulously. She reasoned that she probably hadn't been aware of the cold as she worked with the horses, trying to get Rachel home.

The wagon jarred into motion. She heard the men calling to each other and commanding the horses. The wagon started moving forward finally. The bumpy, rutted road jarred the girls' chattering teeth. Even though their adventure had taken a toll on their energy, there was no way for the girls to rest. Emma wrapped the blanket around her hand and held tight to the rail above her head.

Rachel burrowed closer to Emma to get warmer. Emma reached out to pull the younger girl against her, holding them both in place. Slowly their shivering subsided. The cold was still there, but it wasn't as overwhelming. By the time Emma heard the noises of town going past them, she had stopped shivering completely.

"Hey, Em," Mark called over the wind. "Do ya want ta stop at Abby's to warm yerselves?"

Emma uncovered her face to see Mark leaning over the edge of the wagon. He was much closer than the sound of his voice made him seem. "How 'bout it, Rachel? Ya want ta stop?"

Rachel shook her head, "I jest want ta go home."

Emma smiled as she thought of their carefree conversation earlier that morning. Looking up at her brother, she spoke loud enough to be heard, "We're alright now. We jest wanna go home."

The sky was so dark and white at the same time. If Emma didn't know better, she would think it was almost nighttime, instead of late afternoon. Not wanting to disturb the quilts around Rachel, Emma lifted her head to look behind the wagon. She knew from the sounds that she should be able to see the buildings, but all she saw was white. She could see the grooves that the wagon wheels were leaving behind. Several inches of freshly fallen snow were on the ground. As if on cue, the wagon slid sideways. The wheels did not traction well in the snow. Da rarely switched to the sleigh rails after Mama had died. He just used the horses to get around.

"Whoa," Mark calmed the horses, as he steered them back onto the road.

Laying her head back down, she pulled the quilt back over her face. It wasn't long after that Emma felt the wagon sliding around the curve toward Da's farm. Toward home. She had not wanted to admit how much she missed her home to Rachel. But in truth, her childhood home was the only place that felt comforting to her.

As Mark pulled the horses to a stop, Emma pulled the quilt back from her face again. Struggling to sit up with the tangled quilts, she noticed that Mark had pulled the wagon right into the barn. Suddenly Emma felt herself being lifted over the side. Knowing whose strong arms held her, she protested, "James, I can walk."

"An' I can carry ya.".

Da waited for them with an open door. Emma saw the blazing fire as soon as James stepped inside. Nothing had ever looked so beautiful to her. Piles of blankets sat on the table in clumsily folded piles. James set Emma down in her rocking chair, so close to the fire that she thought her quilt would catch fire. Da stepped up in front of her and tucked another quilt around her.

"James," she called out, watching him head for the door. "Yer coat?" She started to shrug out of the blankets, so she could remove the garment from her shoulders.

James looked back at her and nodded, "I'll be back fer it." He held the door for Mark as he carried Rachel in.

"Here, let her have this one," Emma told her brother, trying to stand up. The blankets clung to her legs making movement difficult.

Mark lowered Rachel into a kitchen chair across from her.

"I'll not be takin' yer chair from ya," Rachel murmured.

Letting the heat seep into her hands, she leaned back against the chair back.

Da ladled soup into cups and handed one to each of the girls. "Drink this." The soup was mostly broth, but Emma didn't mind. It was warming her insides.

"Thank ya, Da," she said, curling her hand around it.

Untying her bonnet, he smoothed her hair back and kissed her forehead. "I'm so glad yer home, Emma girl."

Home? thought Emma. *Will anything else ever feel like home?*

"From now on, I'm takin' a coat with me ta my Ma's house. Even in July," Rachel stated seriously, taking another sip of her soup.

Emma smiled at the girl across from her. *She had not complained once today.*

Da chuckled at her words. "Now THAT would be a sight ta see."

~*~*~*~*~*~*~*~*~*~*~*~*~*~*~*~*~*~*~*~

After the horses had been dried off and draped with blankets, the menfolk came in and warmed themselves by the fire. Kneeling between the girls' chairs, they held their hands out to the warmth. Da draped quilts over each of their shoulders. Neither one protested. Once both men were sipping soup, the house was silent except for the sound of the wind whipping around the cabin.

Emma shivered at the sound. If Mark and James hadn't come along when they did, she would still be out in that wind. Looking over at Rachel, she saw her eyes drifting shut. Tears sprang to her own eyes. This brave new sister of hers, struggling to stay awake.

"I reckon it was a bad idea I had this mornin'. I'm so sorry, Rachel."

Rachel opened her eyes and turned toward Emma. "Ya couldna known about the storm. I've never known it ta snow so hard this early in the season," she pointed out. "An' it was so warm this morning."

"It rolled in fast, Em," Mark agreed. "We didn't even suspect it until the snow was already fallin'. Or we'd have set out fer ya earlier."

"Luckily yer Da thought ta send blankets with us," James said, staring into the fire. "We forgot ya didna have coats."

Emma looked up then. "Ya musta been freezin' yerselves with no coats."

"I do na care how cold we were, Emma. We wouldna ever taken those coats back."

She knew her brother was speaking the truth.

Pride stirred for her older brother. Riding out into the storm and sacrificing his comfort for that of his young wife and his sister. She felt tears prick at the back of her eyes once more. Emma leaned her head against the rocking chair and let her eyes close. She felt someone take the cup from her fingers as sleep crept in. Her thoughts drifted away as she listened to the fire crackle.

"Do ya think the cold will hurt her baby?" asked a voice, soft and far away.

"That we have no way of knowin'," Da answered. "Only time and prayer will tell."

My baby. Did I harm my baby? Her last thoughts were on the small life within her as sleep finally claimed her.

❧ Fifteen ❧

November 18, 1858...

The crackling of the fire was the first sound she heard as she woke. Slowly, she opened her eyes and gazed into the hearth. The warmth of the coals and glowing logs was comforting against her skin.

Da reached past her to add more logs. "Do ya want fer anythin', Emma girl?"

Emma nodded. "I'm verra thirsty." Her hand was almost immediately wrapped around her cup. The coolness soothed her sore throat.

"Where is Seth?" she asked. She noticed that he wasn't laying on the floor by the other men.

"He's at yer house," came her father's voice behind her. "Carin' fer yer chores."

"He went out in this alone?" Emma asked, worry creepin' in.

"He stayed on earlier when we went lookin' fer ya both."

That helped her relax, knowing her animals were cared for. And knowing that Seth was safe as well. Her gaze fell on James asleep on the floor. His back was pressed against the wall, facing the fire. He looked so relaxed in sleep, but a sense of sadness still lingered.

"I couldna have kept him from comin' ta ya," Da stated, reading her thoughts.

Her throat burned with frustration. "Why does this stuff keep happenin'? I never wanted ta hurt James, yet it happens over an' over again. I canna steer from trouble fer long. And James is always right there, always ready ta help me. Ready ta give me his coat while he is

115

freezin'. And he gets nothin' in return. Nothin' but pain, Da." Her voice cracked at the last word.

Da looked back at James, watching him sleep. "Such a good lad. He's had a tough road, that's fer sure and certain," he agreed. "He fears causin' talk around ya. Yet... he canna resist rushin' ta yer side when ya need him."

"What could God's purpose be ta have him suffer this way? I know the Bible says that *'All things are beautiful in their time.'* But --," she looked at Da through tears. "But I do na want him ta suffer anymore."

Da cleared his throat. "Then pray yer husband comes home soon and starts takin' care of ya better." Turning back to the fire, his jaw flexed.

"Da-," Emma protested.

Throwing a stick into the fire, he blew out a frustrated breath. "I know. I know, Emma girl. That wasna fair," he admitted, running his fingers through his hair in the same fashion the boys did when they were flustered. "Thane no more asked fer any of this then you did. I know he needed answers."

The silence stretched out as she waited for her father to continue.

"I understand it... but then I look into that boy's eyes every day. Watch as James fights so hard ta fight his own feelings so that ya can have a good life with someone else. An' it feels like somethin' breaks apart inside."

Emma tried to swallow the lump in her throat, but it wouldn't go down. The burning emotions overflowed and tears ran down her cheeks. "I know, Da," she finally whispered, forcing the words through her emotions. "I canna bear it, sometimes. He feels as much a part of my growin' up years as Mark was. I try ta stay away from him, ta keep people from talkin' about us. But it feels like I am losin' a piece of home when I do."

Da nodded in understanding. "But yer gonna have ta, Emma girl. Yer gonna have ta be the one ta stay clear of him. Because he canna do it. I do na think he has it in him."

Swallowing again, Emma lowered her eyes. "What if that hurts him more? I do na know which way is right."

Silence fell between them. Only the crackling of the fire could be heard over the light snoring behind them.

"We'll have ta explain it ta him," Da said finally. Picking up a stray stick from the floor, he threw it into the fire. "We'll jest explain it's fer the best."

Blinking back the tears, Emma knew he was right. "I'll tell him in the mornin'."

✎ Sixteen ✎

mma wrapped her coat tightly around herself and straightened a button. *Quit stalling.* With a deep breath, she stepped into the blacksmith shop. Blinking a couple of times, her eyes gradually grew accustomed to the darkness.

James was standing at his workbench, his back to the door. He had not seen her enter.

"James," Emma called out.

He turned at the sound of her voice and took a few steps toward her. But he stopped halfway, looking torn. "Mornin', Emma." His eyes looked sad and tired.

"Ya left before I woke yesterday. I didna have a chance ta give ya back yer coat." Pulling the folded coat out of her basket, she held it out to him.

James edged closer and reached out for it.

"And I want ta thank ya."

His head came up then, his eyes meeting hers for the first time since she entered. "Thank me?" he repeated, confused.

"Fer lettin' me use yer coat," Emma clarified. She cleared her throat before she could she continue, "and fer comin' after us in the storm. I didna know what we were gonna do. And then God sent Mark and you. When ya boys stepped through that storm, I almost cried." Looking down at her basket, she took another breath. "And then I was so worried about what people would say if they saw us together again, I forgot ta thank ya proper. I'm sorry I was rude ta ya. I appreciate everything ya did fer me. I jest-." Closing her eyes, she tried to swallow back the emotions that filled her chest.

"Emma, don't," James pleaded.

Emma looked up, tears falling down her cheeks. "Don't? Don't what?"

"Don't do this. I heard ya talkin'. When ya were talkin' ta yer da by the fire," he admitted. "I know ya both think this is hard on me bein' friends. But it'd be harder iffen I had ta go through every day of my life with ya crossin' the street ta avoid me. I couldna bear it." His voice was raw with emotion, pleading for her to understand.

"But, James-."

"No, Emma! Please? I'll be more proper, I promise ya. Jest a nod and a smile iffen yer not with yer family," he explained. "Jest, please? Please don't block me out?"

The pleading in his voice, paired with the pleading in his eyes, made Emma's chest hurt more. She knew she was passed being able to speak. Nodding her agreement, she averted her eyes. *Maybe I should have let Da talk to him? No. This isn't his problem to solve.*

Clearing her throat, Emma held out the basket on her arm. "I brought ya a loaf of bread and some jam. An' the extra eggs from the week. Sorry, it's not more, but the storm spooked the hens. Only a few eggs today."

"It's plenty. We are grateful for the treats," James assured her. "Let me jest put these inside, so I can return yer basket ta ya." He disappeared through the back door of the shop.

Wrapping her coat around herself again, she tightened her arms across her chest.

"Good day, Mrs. Hawkins," called a voice behind her.

Turning toward the voice, she saw Alistair Scott entering the shop behind her.

"Good day ta ya, Mr. Scott," Emma returned. Dread filled her heart at the sight of him. Never one to hold his opinion to himself, she began to wish she had jest told James to keep the basket.

"Howdy, Alistair," James called out as he returned through the door to the house.

"Good day ta ya, James."

The two shook hands. With a nod in Emma's direction, Alistair raised his eyebrows. "With all the talk around town about you two, I'm surprised ta see ya together. It's not proper fer ya ta meet this way." Alistair leaned closer to James, not noticing his stony glare, and studied his face as he continued, "As a fact, I've heard more'n once that Mrs. Hawkin's baby may na be belongin' ta Mr. Hawkins at'all."

James' fists clenched down by his sides, and Emma saw his jaw flex. Her breath caught. *Please, Lord, do na let him strike this man. It canna help this.*

Relaxing his hands, he stepped toward Emma. "Mrs. Hawkins merely stopped by for me to buy eggs from her hens. Jest as she has done since she was 10. It is perfectly proper fer her ta bring them ta my shop." Handing her the basket with one hand, he pressed a coin into her other.

Emma stared at the coin and blinked. She had never taken his money before, but she didn't know how she would be able to give it back to him today.

"As fer her baby, I expect she'll come out lookin' like her daddy. Until that day, I'm sure there'll be doubts in some corner of this village." James stepped closer to Alistair then. "If I happen ta hear someone insult Mrs. Hawkin's honor- hear them doubtin' her baby's growin' properly where she is? I willna be so calm. And I canna be responsible fer my action."

Turning back to Emma, James nodded his head in her direction. "Good day ta ya, Mrs. Hawkins. Thank ya fer bringin' by the eggs. Please give yer family my regards." He turned back to his other customer then. "Now, Alistair," his calm voice distracted the other man from watching her exit. "What brings ya in today?"

"Ya know talk is- that her husband won't be comin' back ta her? I know ya've heard it too," Alistair's voice followed her out the door.

Emma's breath caught. *Is that what people think?* She didn't care how long Thane had been gone. She had no doubt that he would come home to her- if he could.

Worry sprang up at the possible situations that Thane could encounter. Weather and wilderness were unpredictable here in Michigan.

Please keep Thane safe, Lord. Emma took a deep breath to clear the worried thoughts away.

Wishing she could just go straight home after that scene, she had to take several cleansing breaths to force herself to turn toward the mercantile. She dreaded what she would find there.

When she opened the door and stepped into the mercantile, it was surprisingly empty. Mrs. Phelps glanced up and smiled. "Hello, Emma dear," she called out. "How are ya today?"

Emma was taken by surprise when the storekeeper seemed to be waiting for her reply. "I am well," she answered quietly.

"Good. Good." Going to stand behind her high counter, Mrs. Phelps held a hand out in Emma's direction. "What brings ya in today?"

Handing over the list in her hand, she replied. "Mostly, I jest need molasses so that I can make Seth those cookies he loves. He came over and took care of my stock yesterday during the storm."

"That storm came out of nowhere. Everyone was caught unaware. We heard you and young Mrs. Wells got caught on the road home from her Ma's place? It seems ya made it home safe."

"Yes, we were Blessed! Da sent the boys out after us, ta bring us home." Emma was careful not to say which boys. She figured the Lord knew it wouldn't be helpful in this situation.

Nodding, the storekeeper leaned over the counter. "Will ya be buyin' material for the baby today?"

Emma swallowed her frustration. This was the second person who mentioned her baby. She had avoided saying anything, wanting Thane to be the next to know. *No use fretting about it now. I canna undo what's been done.*

121

"Not today, Mrs. Phelps. But soon," she replied once she found her words. With a forced laugh, she continued, "I'd hate fer the baby ta have all her sewing done before her own Da gets home to hear of her existence."

Mrs. Phelps studied Emma's face. Then with a single lift to her shoulders, she seemed to make a decision. Turning to gather the items on the list in her hand, the storekeeper started to catch Emma up on happenings in town.

"And Abigail's little man is certainly growing fast enough. With yer little one comin' this summer, our little town is growing in number again. I expect Mark and his new bride will be announcing news soon as well?" Mrs. Phelps asked with her eyebrows raised, hoping to gain new information.

Emma blinked. "If they have news, they have not shared it with me."

Disappointment flickered across the older woman's face. But not for long. She soon found something else to talk about. Emma smiled and waited patiently for her order to be completed so she could go home and breathe easier.

✎ Seventeen ✎

A scream escaped Emma. After not seeing anyone all day, the last thing she expected was to see a child standing in the middle of her barn.

Emma had heard about people with dark skin when she had attended school. The teacher had taught that they had been enslaved because of their skin color. However, she had never actually seen anyone with brown skin with her own eyes. Once the panic had settled from her startled body, her eyes took in the dark skin, the bare cracked feet, the torn dress, and ended at the beautiful little face. However, when Emma looked into the child's eyes, she saw terror still residing there.

"Oh! Pardon me fer bein' so rude," Emma rushed to console the little girl. "I scared ya with my screamin', and then here I stand jest starin' at ya." Rubbing a hand across her forehead, she tried to think of a way to calm the girl. "I didna mean ta scream, I was jest startled ta see ya in my barn. Thought I was alone today, so I didna expect ta see anyone out here."

With a glance around the barn showing no one, she prepared herself to see someone else stepping out into the open. *I wonder where her family is. Surely, she couldn't be traveling by herself.* When nothing else moved, she turned her attention back to the child in front of her.

The terror in the child's eyes was being replaced with curiosity. But the shaking of her shoulders did not lessen. "Oh," Emma exclaimed. "Yer freezing." It dawned on her the reason for the child being in the barn. Though the barn was still chilly, she could no longer see her breath in front of her face. Taking the shawl from around her shoulders, she wrapped it around the child.

Eyes huge, the little girl stared up into Emma's face.

Emma's own eyes twinkled as she remembered the trunk of Annie's things. "Oh, yes," she laughed. "I have some clothes that will fit ya! They'll be a mite warmer than the ones yer wearin' now. Should I fetch them fer ya?" she asked, tugging at the torn edge of the girl's summer dress.

After a moment to think, the girl nodded.

Emma turned and all but ran to the house. Throwing open the trunk, she moved the quilts on the top to look through the dresses available.

Over the previous couple of weeks, everything had quieted down. Emma had found herself with plenty of extra time on her hands. She had explored this trunk with all its treasures. At first, it had felt strange. Going through someone else's belongings. But in the end, she felt like Annabel was a little less forgotten.

Finding two dresses that would probably fit with some hemming, she put them with the socks and woolen bloomers. The shoes would most likely be too large. But they would keep her feet warm. Draping the clothes over her arm, she piled a quilt on top. Then carefully holding the shoes and her sewing basket, Emma hurried back to the barn.

A short distance before she stepped into the barn, Emma felt a movement off to her right. Turning, she expected to see the child's parents, but all she saw was darkness. "Hello?" Emma called. "Yer welcome ta come inta the barn where it's warm." The young girl stepped into the open doorway.

The reflection from two eyes emerged from the dark shadows. But they weren't human eyes. A terror gripped Emma's heart as she saw the powerful cat slink out of the shadows toward her. The terror kept her feet frozen in place. Frozen until the piercing scream came from the barn. Looking toward the sound, she saw the young child standing out in the open.

"Get back," Emma yelled, running toward the child. "Close the door!" Each girl grabbed a door and pushed it to block out the giant cat lunging at them. With inches to go, the doors stopped. Snarling sounded from the other side of the boards. Claws swiped at the small opening, trying to push their way in. Without thought, Emma pushed the girl back and threw her back against the opening. Catching the wildcat by surprise, the doors slammed closed. The unexpected motion caused Emma to stumble backwards. Quickly bracing her feet for leverage, she leaned heavily into the door. "Please, Lord, protect us," escaped her lips as she prepared to protect the child in front of her.

The sound of a board hitting the door above her head opened her eyes. She looked up just in time to see the long board slide down into the groove of the door. Not a moment before the weight of the cat hit the outside of the doors again. Emma pushed with all her might to support the door. When the snarling sound quit, the movement of the cat lingered outside the door for what felt like forever. When the heavy steps moved further from the barn, Emma squeaked out an order to the girl next to her. "Go check the latch on the other door. Make sure it's firmly in place. Hurry!" The girl flew to the backside of the barn. When the latch was solidly in place, she ran back to Emma's side.

Emma sat in the dirt of the doorway. The shock wore off, leaving her shaky. Looking up at the terrified girl, she tried to smile. "Thank ya fer yer help," she whispered. Looking the girl's arms over, she checked for scratches. "Are ya hurt?"

The young girl shook her head.

Laughing then, Emma pulled the girl into her arms as her eyes filled up with tears. She knew the young child didn't need the hug as much as she needed it herself, but the girl did not struggle. "The Lord was lookin' out fer us ladies tonight." Emma closed her eyes and breathed a simple prayer of thankfulness.

After her heart calmed to a normal beat, Emma opened her eyes to the mess before her. "Oh, no." In her haste, she had thrown her armload of clothes onto the ground in a heap. The shoes had landed in something particularly messy. Her eyes filled with frustration when she saw the overturned sewing basket. Wiping the tears away, she laughed at her foolishness. "No use cryin' over spilled buttons when we're both safe." Releasing the child from her arms, she sighed.

Not keen on the idea of moving from her spot guarding the door, she pointed to the clothes in the dirt. "If you bring me a dress... and find me a needle from the dirt... I can fix you up something warm ta wear."

The young girl dutifully rummaged through the dust until she found a needle and thread. Sliding the first dress over the child's head, Emma quickly put in a higher hem. When the dress hem was finished, Emma explained the undergarments to her young friend. She explained how they would keep her warm, and the girl scurried off to an empty stall to put them on. She came back to have Emma help her lace the shoes. Sighing in exhaustion, Emma wrapped the closest quilt around the girl's shoulders and pulled her close to her side to keep her warm.

On the verge of sleep, Emma heard the child's stomach growl. "I shoulda thought ta grab ya a biscuit," she realized. "We'll have some eggs and biscuits come first light.". She felt the child nod, and then Emma fell asleep.

✑ Eighteen ✑

December 10, 1858...

MMA?"

Emma heard the voice in the distance, wondering who would be calling her.

"EMMA?"

"EMMA?"

More voices broke through her sleepy fog. *Why is everyone calling me?* Slowly, she stretched her stiff back.

Suddenly, something slammed into Emma's back. Crying out, her eyes flew open. Surprised, she looked around the barn from her place in front of the door. The place she was too afraid to move from last night. The place she slept. Her eyes scanned the barn for the little girl, finding no sign of her.

The door hit her in the back again.

"Ouch," she called out before she could stop the words.

"EMMA?" came a chorus of voices. She heard feet run toward her.

"Jest a moment, I have ta get up," Emma called out so she wouldn't be hit with the door again before she had her feet underneath her. The quilt was wrapped around her tightly, making it a little difficult to stand. The door shook behind her. Blowing out a breath at their impatience, she finally stepped out of the quilt bundle and reached for the board holding the door in place. No sooner was the board loose, then the door was being pushed toward her.

Blinking at the light pouring in, Emma could see her brothers in front of her and James standing further behind. Wiping the sleep from her eyes, she yawned. "What are ya doin' here so early?"

127

No one answered her for long moments. Then Seth broke the silence by bursting into laughter. Confused, she looked at her younger brother. Soon, Mark and James joined him, chuckling in relief.

Looking to her older brother, she raised her eyebrows in question.

"We searched everywhere for ya... fearing the worst... and ya come crawlin' out of the barn? Do ya sleep in the barn often?" he asked with a cocked eyebrow.

Emma felt the edge of her mouth curl up against her will. Sighing, she rubbed her hands over her face. *Should I tell them about the little girl in the barn? Would they have to report it?* "Oh!" she exclaimed, remembering the real reason she slept in the barn. Turning around in a circle, she frantically searched for signs of the wildcat.

"Emma? Ya alright?"

"There was a wildcat!" she whispered against her fear. *Did they come out during the day?* She started edging toward the barn door. "I came out ta check on the animals. They were makin' all sorts of noise. And-," she decided to leave the girl out of the conversation for now. "And there was suddenly this cat. It was bigger than Dawg." Her eyes searched the trees behind her brothers as she backed away.

Mark grabbed Emma's elbow. "There was a mountain lion here?"

Turning toward her brother's alarm, she shrugged. "It was sand-colored... I think? It was so dark outside. I couldn't really see it."

"*WHY* would you come outside, Em?" Mark growled in frustration.

Emma blinked in surprise. Pulling her elbow away from her brother's grip, she replied, "Because my animals were alarmed. There is NO ONE else here, Mark."

James stepped closer, holding back Mark from reaching for his sister again. "Emma? Why don't ya go inside? We'll look around some."

Emma nodded in relief and turned back toward the barn.

The laughter behind her stopped her. "He meant the house, Em," Seth was amused. "Maybe ya ARE used ta sleepin' in the barn."

Emma felt her cheeks flush in embarrassment. "Oh, of course." Turning around, she fled in the direction of the cabin.

Taking the time to wash her face and comb out her matted hair, Emma had just finished making herself presentable when she remembered the little girl. *Is she in the barn still? Did the boys startle her away, calling so loudly?* Remembering the quilt tucked unexpectedly around her body, she began to suspect the little girl had been gone before the boys had shown up.

Opening the door, she saw James standing guard. When he heard her step out, he turned to face her.

"James," she spoke in a low voice, worried about Mark overhearing. She hadn't spoken a word to James since that day in his workshop. Guilt weighed on her that she was only breaking the weeks of silence so he would do her a favor. "There was a girl in the barn last night. She had dark skin-," she paused with his sharp intake of breath. Looking down at her hands, she continued. "The girl was gone when I woke this mornin'. Could ya-," her eyes darted toward where Mark was running through the woods.

"Ya want me ta look in the barn fer her?" he asked, guessing the rest of her request.

Nodding her head in gratitude, she felt relieved.

"Iffen ya go back inside, I'll check fer her," he assured her. Before she could turn back, James continued. "Why didna ya want Mark ta know?"

Her cheeks burned. "Mark gets so- At times, he- He's already frustrated with me," she answered with a shrug.

Nodding in understanding, James turned toward the barn. "Go back inside, Em."

A short while later, her brothers filed into her small kitchen. James stepped in behind them. With a short shake of his head, he let her know he did not find the little girl.

"There are cat tracks all over yer farm, Em. It was definitely a mountain lion," Mark reported. "From now on, you must carry a rifle everywhere."

Emma coughed in surprise. "A rifle? I don't have a rifle," she pointed out.

All three of the men turned to her in surprise.

"What?" she asked, uncertain of what she said wrong.

"Thane left ya without a rifle?" James demanded.

With her short nod, all three groaned in frustration.

"I wouldna know how ta use one, any way."

"Of all the -."

"James," Mark warned, cutting off whatever James had planned on saying.

James took his hat off in one swift motion, raking his other hand through his hair. Then slamming the hat back on top of his head, he turned and strode off into the woods.

Mark watched his friend walk away before turning back to Emma. "We need ta keep searchin' fer the heifer. She wandered off last night. Da thinks she may be close ta her time." Pausing for a moment, he looked around her secluded farm. "Don't go wanderin' off yerself. We're not sure how far the mountain lion traveled."

"The heifer? Which one wandered off?"

"The dark brown one," Mark answered.

Catching her by surprise, Mark leaned in and gave his sister a quick hug. Stumbling back when he released her, Emma laughed. "What was that for?"

"We thought ya were gone- when we found yer house empty this mornin'. Empty before daybreak with no sign of where ya'd gone," His voice was gruff with emotion.

Emma nodded, her chest tightening. Her family had been through so much this past summer when she had disappeared. Taken. From this very spot. The shadow of that worry hovered under the surface of her older brother's face. Leaning over, she wrapped her arms around Mark's waist. "I'm sorry I worried ya again."

Mark wrapped his arms around her shoulders and gave her a fierce brotherly hug until she grunted her surrender. Loosening his grip, he looked down at her. "Jest take care of yerself, alright? Maybe carry a big stick until we get ya a rifle?" He lifted his eyebrows in question while trying to keep a straight face.

"Yeah," she returned. "A big stick won't scare the hens off from layin' eggs at all."

Mark laughed. Lifting his hand to ruffle her hair, she ducked quickly and backed up a step. Laughing louder, he waved and turned to follow the other boys into the woods. There was a barely noticeable trail wearing down between the two farms. Worn down by the numerous trips she had made in the last couple of months.

Emma watched her brother disappear among the trees, then turned back toward the barn to look around. In the stall where the chickens sat upon their nesting boxes, lay the shawl folded over her sewing basket. Picking up the shawl, she saw that the contents of the basket had all been found through the dirt and organized in the basket again. Tears gathered in her eyes at the thoughtfulness of this young child.

Taking the basket to the house, she set it inside her front door. She wrapped the shawl around herself and started walking around the buildings. Calling to the girl, she peered into the shadows of the early morning sun. Rounding the back corner of the barn, where it meets the lean-to, she ran right into a cow. Surprised, she scrambled back and then froze.

Between the trees and the lean-to, the cow stood in the shadow of the barn almost completely hidden.

After a couple of breaths, her heart rate slowed to normal, and she laughed at herself. Her surprise encounter with the wildcat the night before had made her jumpy this morning. Her laugh startled the heifer, causing her to step away from her. As the cow moved, Emma saw the calf at her feet. "Oh, yer baby," she exclaimed.

All around Emma was evidence that the calf was freshly born. Its hide was still matted with fluid, as steam poured off it's back in the cool morning air. He arched his back in protest against leaving his mother's warmth and protection. He looked at Emma in indifference through his half-closed eyes and shivered.

"I'm so glad ya waited until morn to join us." The thought that this calf could have been a meal for the prowling mountain lion made Emma's heart ache. She dropped to her knees in front of the calf, taking her shawl off her own shoulders and placed it around him. Rubbing back and forth, she talked to the small animal, trying to soothe the little calf. "Ya should've come in spring. It's much warmer in spring. Ya wouldn't be wishin' ta go back to yer Mama's warmth, then." She continued to talk in a low voice as she rubbed around its ears, back, and finally the legs. Hoping to rub warmth into the cold calf.

"Now I've seen everything."

Emma started at the voice behind her.

"Bathing a wild beast?" Seth's voice teased, pretending to be shocked by his sister's behavior. "No wonder that mountain lion stopped by. He jest wanted a bath."

Emma stopped herself from giving her young brother a scowl. She knew that animals could take care of their own babies. And she assumed that Seth would never let her hear the end of this. Choosing to ignore Seth's comments, she insisted, "This young lad is freezing, it's the least I could do fer him."

Seth laughed with glee. "Oh look, Em," he knelt down, pretending to have a closer look. "Ya coddled that boy cow so much ya turned him inta a girl cow."

Her hands froze. Emma didn't need to look to know her brother was probably correct. Willing herself not to smile, she turned toward Seth. "She is such a sad lookin' creature, refusing ta rejoice in her own birth... I jest assumed she was a boy."

Seth's eyes sparkled as he laughed again at his sister's teasing. "When yer done there, Da sent me ta fetch ya home with me."

"Home with ya? I have'na even ate breakfast yet."

"That shouldna worry ya. Ya can cook us breakfast, while Da makes sure yer safe with his own eyes," Seth insisted. As if in agreement, his stomach growled loud enough for her to hear.

Emma laughed at her brother's blatant begging for a cooked meal. "Let me grab a rope ta lead this mama home," she replied. When she returned with the rope, she saw that Seth had already hoisted the calf up around his shoulders. Tying a simple sliding knot around the cow's neck, she guided it along the path to her Da's farm.

❧ Nineteen ❧

December 10, 1858... morning

After the bone-crushing hug her father gave her, Emma helped Rachel prepare a big breakfast for everyone. They were all starving from their early morning search through the woods.

Everyone squeezed in around the table when the meal was ready. Seth barely waited for his father to bless the meal before he retold his version of Emma bathing the boy cow right into a girl cow.

The menfolk sat and continued to talk while the girls cleaned up. Finally, Da looked up and spoke to Emma. "Emma girl, until we get ya comfortable with a rifle, yer gonna sleep here."

"Da-," Emma protested.

"No arguments," he interrupted. "Mountain lions aren't something to be reckoned with."

"Da, be reasonable. I've animals ta care fer. And I need ta be there fer when Thane comes back," she pointed out. "Besides yer rooms are full here."

"Yer gonna take my room," Seth stated.

"I'm not takin' yer bed."

"It used ta be yer bed."

"What about my animals?"

"I'll be sleepin' at yer house ta protect yer animals," Seth pointed out. With an impish smile, he added, "with a rifle."

"Seth'll make sure the animals are fed, and the chores are done," Da reassured her.

"Why do I always have ta do her chores?" Seth teased. "Next ya'll have me scrubbin' laundry. And bathin' newborn calves."

Emma turned to throw her towel at her little brother, but his impish smile stopped her. How she missed his teasing and that crazy smile. Tears flooded her eyes. Quickly, she turned back to the dish tub. Exasperated at her moods, she wiped her tears away in frustration.

"Rotten kid," Mark stated. "Quit makin' her cry all the time." Swinging at his younger brother, Mark missed when Seth dodged out of the way.

"That's impossible. Ever since she found herself in the family way, she's been a mess. Cryin' fer anythin'," Seth whined, blowing his hair out of his eyes.

"You try carryin' a life around inside ya and doin' all her chores. Ya'd be cryin' too," James muttered.

Da burst out laughing suddenly. When everyone turned to look at him, he quieted. "You three boys need ta be gettin' used ta those tears. All three of ya will see them in yer married years."

Seth looked mortified, "All women do that?"

Rachel's face flushed, which made Emma chuckle. "I'm sure other women are more sensible than I am. Rachel will handle this all much better, I'm sure."

"Rachel's gonna have a baby too?" Seth practically shouted in horror.

Rachel's face burned in embarrassment. Mark looked at his wife and flushed red too.

Emma threw a towel at Seth. "Hush ya, little boy. Yer embarrassin' yer new sister."

Seth threw an apologetic glance in Rachel's direction. "I didna mean anythin' by it. Jest don't know if I can handle two women cryin' all the time."

James laughed. "We'll pray it isn't time- for Rachel's sake. If Em cries that much and only has ta see Seth fer hours at a time? Jest think if poor Rachel had ta suffer with him all day long?"

Seth smiled despite the teasing. Opening his mouth to answer it, he was cut short.

"That's enough, boys," Da stated. Their father was amused by their joking but put an end to Rachel's embarrassment. When everyone quieted down, he turned serious. "We need ta get yer things before long, Emma. If ya make a list, we'll send Mark after them."

"Da-," Emma tried to protest.

"Enough, Emma girl. Ya need ta think of yer baby. Yer not stayin' there alone."

"Yer baby?"

Everyone in the room froze when they heard the voice come from the doorway.

Emma turned and saw the door hanging open. There stood Thane, his hand still on the latch. Joy flooded her. She took a step toward him but was blocked in by her brothers. As she looked for a path around the table, her gaze fell on James.

James looked at his hands, clenched on the table. Emma froze. How could she run to Thane without hurting James? Again. Was it even proper to kiss in front of others? She wondered. She had seen her Mama kiss her Da. But never away from home. She couldn't remember seeing anyone else kiss- except Abigail and David. Frustrated, she turned back to set down the dish she had been drying. Tears spilling over her cheeks.

"Yer pregnant?" Thane repeated the question, not getting an answer the first time.

Hearing the words finally, Emma turned back toward her husband. The anger on his face made her breath catch. How many times a day had she wished he would return so she could share the news with him. Share her joy and her worry. Now he was here before her, and he was angry?

She nodded, unaware of the tears on her cheeks.

Seth laughed, trying to lighten the tension in the room. "Ya'll get used ta the tears. The rest of us have."

Thane's eyes turned toward the table then. Taking in everyone there, he stopped at James. Emma could see the hurt in his eyes but didn't understand it. Why would he be hurt by James? Looking up at his wife again, he cleared his throat. "I came ta let ya know I've returned. I need ta unpack." He turned to leave, pulling the door closed behind him.

Emma stood there, staring at the closed door.

The room was so quiet, the ticking from the mantle clock could be heard. No one spoke. No one even moved. Finally, Da pushed his chair back from the table. He walked around the table to pull Emma into his arms.

Breathing in his familiar scent, she gripped his shirt with her fingers. Her Da could always scare away her fears when she was young, but she didn't think it would help this time.

Her father's hands settled on her shoulders as he pulled back. "Go ta him. No matter who's ta fault, ya never let the sun set with anger in the house. Hurt feelings ruin a home." With a sad smile, he wiped the tears from her cheeks.

Rachel stepped closer, taking the towel from her hand. "I'll finish up here. Not enough work for two of us, anyhow."

"Thank ya, Rachel," she whispered. Walking past her brothers, around the table, she kept her gaze on the door. When her hand gripped the latch, she looked back over her shoulder. Around this table sat her family. All of them watching her leave. All of them sitting in the only home she had ever known. The only place she had felt safe and sheltered. She had felt loved in the house Thane provided for her, but never secure. Never safe. Never felt like she belonged like she had here in this home.

Tears filled her eyes as her throat burned. "Thank ya all fer always bein' here fer me." With a shaky smile, she lifted the latch in her hand and stepped into the open air.

Taking a deep breath, Emma walked toward the path through the woods. She needed to find Thane.

The Road Home

ℒ Twenty ℛ

December 10, 1858... late morning

A s the cabin came into view, Emma's steps slowed. Her heart hammered in her chest. *Has he regretted marryin' me?* The thought made it hard to breathe. *Does he hate havin' ta come back here?*

If Emma didn't know Thane had headed this way, she would have doubted anyone was here. Doubted that it was any different from this morning or yesterday when she wandered this lonely farm alone. No sounds came from the cabin or the barn. The only sound was the wind blowing through the trees. Squaring her shoulders back, she took a deep breath to steady her heartbeat and forced herself to head toward the cabin.

Pushing the door open, Emma's eyes fell upon the pile of quilts and the sewing basket by the door. She gasped at the mess. Ashamed of herself for not remembering to fold them before heading to her father's house that morning, she picked up the top one to fold.

Was it only this morning I woke in the barn? It feels like ages have passed.

"Looks like ya left in a hurry," Thane spoke from behind her.

"I -," Emma stopped. *Where should I begin? Tell him I went to look for a little girl hiding in the barn? Should I tell him about the wildcat? The newborn calf? Had all that happened just last night? Was it only one day since I prayed so hard for God to send Thane home soon?* And here he was, standing before her. But in place of the joy she thought she would feel, she felt a new worry start to grow. Her throat thickened and refused to let her speak. Instead, she nodded.

Thane watched in silence as Emma folded the quilts and set them on the table. She kept her gaze down so she wouldn't have to see the anger she heard in his voice. "Are ya hungry?" she asked finally. Not knowing where else to start a conversation, she thought food was a good place to start. At least it would give her hands something to do after she finished putting the quilts back in their trunk.

"No. I'm not hungry," Thane stated. His words were short and harsh, showing his displeasure with her.

Emma's hands froze. "I'm sorry I left the cabin with such a mess."

"I don't care about the mess." Thane voice echoed through the cabin.

She looked up then. Never had she heard Thane raise his voice to her. What she saw on his face, she couldn't describe. It wasn't disappointment. Nor anger. Whatever emotion it was, it was intense. And it confused her.

"Then what do ya care about? I canna fix it if I do na know Her voice cracked, betraying her emotions. She stepped closer to her husband, cautiously.

Thane's face hardened as the emotions left it. "Ya cannot fix everything, Emma. Jest like ya couldn't bear ta live in my house. Jest like the wood box doesn't fill itself as is evident with it bein' empty. How long did ya stay here before ya returned ta yer Da's farm? One day? One week? The dust on the hearth tells me it wasn't long."

Emma's gaze turned to the hearth, as his angry words echoed through the cabin. There was indeed a layer of dust there. It hadn't occurred to her to actually dust the hearth with all the ashes and soot piled there. Realizing that he was waiting for an answer, she pushed words past her aching throat. "The fireplace doesn't work. There's something wrong with the chimney. I was gonna ask Da ta look at it -."

Her words were cut short by the angry groan that came from Thane. He jammed his hat down over his hair as he walked past her, his arm brushing against her shoulder as he went by.

"Thane?" she called out, turning to watch him walk away.

"Why don't ya go back ta yer Da's? Everythin' here is fallin' apart. It's really not worth yer trouble."

The anger and hurt in his voice, with the sight of his retreating back, made Emma's chest hurt. "I tried ta keep it all up, Thane. I really did."

Thane stopped in the doorway. His hands shot up, running through his hair. Emma thought he would turn back toward her then, but he just stood there. His knuckles flexed around his hair, but they didn't release it.

Emma couldn't breathe as her throat swelled with frustration. She wanted to rush to her husband and comfort him. To be comforted by him. But his anger confused her. Did he even want her comfort? Would that make him angrier? She squeezed her eyes closed as they filled up with tears. Wrapping her arms around her waist, Emma tried to get her emotions under control.

The sound of movement from the open doorway brought Emma's eyes open again. Thane had not turned to face her, but his hands were down by his sides. The muscles in his arms flexed as he clenched them in fists.

"Emma?" His voice sounded uncertain. "Do ya regret marryin' me? Are ya wishin' ya'd chose James?"

The hesitation in his words brought more tears to Emma's eyes. "Is that what ya think?" Very little sound making it past the lump in her throat. Clearing her voice, she tried again to answer him. "For me, there has only ever been you, Thane. My heart broke when I thought I couldna have ya. And it's breakin' now because I've made ya doubt yerself. James is a friend ta me. Nothin' more." Emma's voice cracked on the last word, as her emotions choked off her ability to speak.

Thane looked over his shoulder in her direction. Seeing his wife's arms wrapped around herself and the tears on her cheeks, he spun around. Within a moment, he was at her side and weaving his arms around her waist. He pulled her tight against his chest, resting his face against the curve of her neck.

A sob escaped Emma as she moved her arms up around his shoulders. Taking a deep, shaky breath, she quickly got her emotions under control. Gripping his shirt with her fists, she felt him pull her closer. He squeezed her so tight that she couldn't move. But she didn't fight against him. She relaxed and leaned into her husband's strength.

Several minutes passed before Thane raised his head and pressed his lips against Emma's hair. "Oh, how I've missed ya," he murmured, his own voice thick with emotions.

Emma's arms tightened around his neck. When she trusted her voice to speak, she loosened her grip and raised her head. "I've missed ya too. Ya were gone so long."

"I rode back through the night. I found myself so close ta home that I couldn't sleep. So, I broke camp as soon as I'd set it up and started ridin' again. I rode all night and into the morning. Only to arrive and find ya not here. I set off again ta yer Da's, only ta find ya laughin' with James," Thane stated, stiffening beneath her arms. Pulling back slightly, he looked down into his wife's eyes. "When ya looked up and barely smiled before returnin' ta yer work? I thought my heart stopped there-."

Emma put her fingers over his lips to stop his words. Tears flowed down her cheeks to hear his heartache and hurt. "I wanted ta run ta ya when I saw you standin' there. Wanted ta feel yer arms around me. But ya looked at me so strange. And then at James- an' I didna know if it was proper to hug ya with James standin' there- with him not bein' family. I've already made everythin' so complicated with me not bein' proper. I didna wish ta make it worse. Especially fer James," Emma dropped her hands as she shrugged uncomfortably. Her eyes turned to look out the door. "So, I jest stood there. Cryin'. Cryin' jest like I do every day since I found out about the baby." She cleared the emotion from her voice again, struggling to find the words to go on. "And then ya seemed angry. I was so confused."

"I wasn't angry. I was jest so hurt. Thought ya'd be waitin' at the cabin fer the second I rode up. That you'd be so happy to see me. When ya didn't seem ta care?" Thane paused, squeezing her. He didn't seem to be able to explain his emotions in words. Silence filled the air until Thane pulled back to look at her. His hand lifted her chin so her eyes would meet his. "Why would James be knowin' about our baby before me?"

The hurt and question in his eyes, made Emma push away from her husband. As she took a few steps away, she wrapped her arms around her waist again to gather strength. She knew Thane would not like to hear the story she had to tell, but she needed no secrets to tear them apart.

"When Abigail sent fer me- when her time came- I had been feelin' pretty sick in the mornings. I still do in the early light. But in those first days, I thought I had an illness. Other times, I thought it could still be my head botherin' me- from this lump yer pa gave me. I really didna know what it was," squeezing her eyes closed, she continued. "But I didna think anyone else noticed. I paid little attention to it myself. Then James saw me get sick. He got worried. He tried ta send the midwife ta look after me." Emma had to swallow a lump in her throat before she could continue. Even then, her voice still cracked. "Widow Clem had been away from town fer quite some time. She hadna heard about yer Pa takin' me. Or my marriage ta you instead- instead of James."

She paused again. "She announced the baby happily ta James, thinkin' it was his." Emma's eyes filled with tears, and she felt her throat burn with emotion. "Hearin' about the baby like that? Seein' the emotions he was feelin'? It was too much fer me. I ran out ta be sick- again. I left James there ta explain everythin' ta her. Left him ta explain how I had married another man. And that the child I carried? It wasn't his." Wiping tears from her cheeks, she finished in a whisper, "That's how James came ta know of yer baby before ya did."

She felt Thane's chest against her cheek as he pulled her back into his arms. As his arms tightened around her, they broke loose her control over her emotions. The emotions that ever seemed to be tumbled together lately. "I keep makin' a mess of everythin'."

Thane squeezed her tightly and spoke against the hair above her ear, "It isn't yer fault, Em. Ya aren't makin' a mess. I don't know what God has planned fer us. but this path we're on is the path He chose fer us. And ya've shown me, time an' time again, that God is promisin' us that everythin' will be beautiful in its time. We jest have ta give it time."

How could James' heartache ever be beautiful? Emma let the tears run down her face and soak Thane's shirt front. But in her heart, she knew he was right.

Thane pulled back. Using his thumbs, he wiped the tears from her cheeks. "It's mighty hard ta remember that God has His own timin' when I haven't slept in days. Sleep that I chose not to take..." a lopsided smile graced Thane's lips for a moment before he became serious again. "Emma, I'm so sorry I yelled at ya. I didn't know how I was gonna live if you didn't want me as yer husband anymore." Covering her lips with his thumb, he kept her from interrupting. "But I should've gone ta ya and asked you. I should have pushed all yer brothers out of the way ta get ta you. To hold you close the way I've longed ta. I'm truly sorry fer yellin'. An' fer doubtin' you."

Emma moved the thumb from her lips with her hand. "James is a part of my life- he's a part of my brother's life. I'm gonna run inta him from time ta time. But he's jest a friend. I woulda married him because I made everyone think I loved him with my familiarness ta him. I woulda married him because he's a good man. But it has always been you in my heart. Ya canna doubt that every time ya see me near him."

Thane closed his eyes and took a deep breath, releasing it slowly. He nodded his head.

When he opened his eyes, his lips slipped into a slow smile. "So, we're gonna have a baby?"

Teary-eyed, she nodded. She couldn't keep a blush from creeping into her cheeks any more than she could keep the smile from her lips. His reaction at Da's farm had made her fear he wouldn't want children. But the pride shining from his face now showed her she couldn't have been more wrong.

Laughing, Thane picked Emma up and twirled her around.

Emma returned his laugh easily.

When he stopped turning and set her back on her feet, she looked up into his happy face. She found herself blurting out the midwife's theory. "Widow Clem thinks it's a girl. She says girl babies steal their mama's beauty. Makin' them sick and swell up. Not that I have much beauty ta begin with," Emma admitted, with a short laugh.

"Well, I'll have ta scold her fer makin' it so hard on ya- ta be carin' fer her like this." He chuckled. "A little girl?" He repeated, continuing to look into her eyes.

"The midwife's jest guessin'. I think only God'll be knowin' what's growin' in my belly," Emma reasoned with a smile.

"Until she is born," Thane stated with a teasing smile.

"Yes. Until she is born," she answered. Her heart swelled to see her husband so happy.

Thane's fingers slipped into his wife's hair as he pulled her closer. As his lips touched hers, Emma felt a hairpin release from her bun. But she didn't mind. Thane was kissing her. A kiss she had begun to fear would never happen. But it was jest as beautiful as she had imagined it would be- maybe even more beautiful.

Twenty-One

December 11, 1858...

The rooster crowed, announcing that it was morning. Emma tried to pull the blanket closer to her neck, knowing she would need to get up soon to do the chores. When the blanket wouldn't move, she opened her eyes. The room was quiet. Trying to figure out what was out of place, she started to sit up.

"Don't get up yet," Thane mumbled into her hair, pulling her back into his chest. Emma tensed for a moment before she woke up enough to remember that her husband was home again.

"I've dreamed of wakin' up next ta ya fer weeks. Let me enjoy it for a few minutes more."

Relaxing against him, she wrapped his arms tighter around her. "I'll na kick you out of bed."

"Soon yer daughter may make it hard to get this close to ya though. I may find myself without enough room ta lie in the same bed."

Knowing he couldn't see her face, she smiled at his teasing. "In that case... I might as well get up ta do the chores then."

Thane tightened his grip around her with a chuckle. "Is that so-?"

"Hello in the house."

Thane was out of bed and pulling on his pants before Emma realized that she didn't recognize the voice outside. "What is it with people comin' ta visit when it's dark?" she grumbled.

Thane's movements stopped as he looked at her curiously. But the sound of horses outside caused him to turn toward the door.

Emma hurried to slide her dress over her head, an uncomfortable feeling settling in her stomach.

147

"What can I do fer ya?" Thane's voice broke through the dark silence.

Holding her breath, Emma listened for a reply.

"I didn't mean ta wake ya, sir," a voice answered. "I was reckoning no man lived on this farm when I didn't see anyone stirrin' about. Never met a farmer who slept past a rooster."

She could hear laughter in the stranger's words. Frustration boiled up inside her.

How is he to know that your husband hadn't slept in two days? came a quiet voice in her head. Closing her eyes, Emma sighed a prayer for forgiveness.

"Well, I reckon when I rise is my business. If my wife has no objections, then your opinion makes no difference to me." Emma heard the firmness in Thane's reply.

"Ah... a young wife." Men chuckled.

"What can I do fer ya at this early hour, deputy?" Thane repeated.

There was a moment of silence before the stranger continued. "We've tracked a fugitive to the edge of your property."

"What kind of fugitive?"

"A runaway slave. He stole some property from his owner and fled. We've been on his trail fer a couple of weeks."

"So, he's on horseback?" Thane asked, sounding worried.

"No, sir. They're on foot."

Thane paused. "So... there is more than one slave?"

"We believe someone is helping the slave."

Silence met Emma's ears. She took a step toward the window but couldn't see anything in the darkness.

"How can I be of service, ta ya?" Thane asked.

"Have ya seen any slaves wanderin' around anywhere?"

"No, sir, I haven't."

Emma closed her eyes and prayed they wouldn't come in to ask her.

"Do ya mind if we search yer barn?"

Putting her hand over her mouth, she barely covered the gasp. *What if the little girl came back last night?*

"By all means. I need ta be feeding my animals anyhow."

Through the faint morning light, Emma watched her husband lead the deputy and his men into the barn. Light shone through the cracks in the loft as they moved about searching the corners.

Thane went about his morning chores, but Emma noticed that he kept the men within his sight.

When the deputy was satisfied that there was no one hiding in the barn or any of the outbuildings, he returned to the barn door. He shook Thane's hand and saddled up.

Emma stepped out onto the porch as the men rode out of the yard. Thane watched them ride away and headed to where she stood watching.

"Thane?" Emma started. Her voice cracked, and she paused to clear it.

Hearing the uncertainty in his wife's voice. He looked down into her face.

"Uh. The night before last -?" She paused and looked down at her hands. Taking a deep breath, she squeezed her eyes closed. "The night before last, I found a dark-skinned little girl in the barn."

Thane rubbed his chin. He watched his wife in silence before he nodded.

"I didna see a slave. Jest the little girl," she explained. "What do ya think the slave stole?"

"Likely, he stole the little girl."

Surprised, Emma was silent for a moment. "Why? Why would he take a child?"

"I suspect it is his daughter."

"But then it wouldna be stealin'. If it's his daughter."

Thane sighed. "Some slave owners consider the children of slaves to be property."

Emma felt tears well up. "But that's -."

"I know." Thane murmured as he pulled her into his arms. "Not all slave owners are like that. But if I had to guess, I would say that part of the runaway's family was about to be sold off."

She let the tears run down her cheeks as she thought of the little girl from her barn. Finally, she pulled back from Thane's arms. "Will ya need to find the deputy? Ta correct the lie we told?"

One side of Thane's mouth tipped up. "Well, since I haven't seen any slaves, and you certainly hadn't told me of any. I didn't lie. And they never asked you. Did they?"

Emma shook her head.

"Then I feel no obligation to track down the deputy."

"What'll ya do if he comes back?"

Leaning forward, Thane kissed his wife on the forehead. "Let's pray they don't come back."

After breakfast, they decided to go ask Da's opinion.

As Emma and Thane walked into the clearing near her Da's cabin, her family stepped out of the barn. As they stepped closer, her father handed her a crate. "I was jest headed ta pick out some vegetables from the cellar fer ya. Now yer here ta do the pickin' yerself."

"Da-," Emma protested, even as her hand reached out obediently to take the crate. She could tell by the flexing of his jaw that he intended to speak to Thane about yesterday.

"Be a good girl, Em, and listen ta Da," Mark interrupted.

Thane squeezed her hand before he released it. "Go ahead. I'll be fine." Even with his reassuring look, Emma wasn't so sure.

Seth reached out to take the crate from her. "Here, I'll come with ya, ta help carry it." He didn't look like he wanted to stick around to hear what his father had to say.

With one last look around, Emma followed her little brother around to the back of the house. Gathering the potatoes and carrots she would need for the next week, she began climbing the steps out of the cold cellar. Thane's voice stopped her when she reached the top.

"It was a little hard to see James and Emma together," Thane admitted.

Emma felt Seth step up beside her as Mark's voice exploded in the silence, "She was in her father's house! It's the only place she will even speak ta him anymore!"

"Is she that uncomfortable around him?"

Mark's irritation could be felt in his voice. "No, Em is not uncomfortable around him. She is jest so tired of makin' James' life harder than it needs ta be. And James doesn't want any more talk spreadin' about her. So, they only nod politely when they see each other. Unless she is surrounded by her family. Or unless she is in her Da's house."

Da studied Mark's face for a moment. "I think ya have chores that need doin'."

Mark looked like he wanted to argue. But when he caught sight of Emma approaching, he nodded and stormed away.

When Emma reached Thane's side, he turned back to Da. "There's somethin' we came ta tell ya, sir. There was a posse out ta our farm this morn. They were lookin' for a runaway slave. And some people possibly helpin' them travel. I let them search my barn, but we found nothin'. To be truthful, I hadn't seen any sign of travelers. So, I didn't worry about what they'd find."

Emma felt Thane turn to her. "But I have, Da. A couple nights back, there was a young girl. Her skin was dark-."

"In the barn?"

Emma nodded. "I didna know she was a slave. But I did know she was hidin'. She was cold and hungry. So, I..."

Thane hesitated for a moment when Emma stopped talking. "I know that not all slave owners treat their slaves coldly. But if this one chose to run-? I can't think his owner was a good one."

Da stood silent. Emma could see his jawline tense.

"No man has a right ta own another man."

Emma reached out to her father's arm. "So, we did right? Ya do na think we should find the deputy?"

Da stepped forward and kissed the top of her head. She smiled at how it still made her feel like a little girl. "Ya did good, Emma girl."

"One more thing, sir. And then we'd best be headin' home." Thane said, "Seems our chimney is plugged solid. I am looking for something to clean it out with. Do you have a long pole? Otherwise, I can cut a long stick from a tree."

Da went into the barn and returned with a long pole. On the end of the pole was a homemade hook. "Here's what I have used to dislodge mine."

Thane took the pole from him and inspected the end. "Yes. I think it'll work. Thank ya, sir."

~*~*~*~*~*~*~*~*~*~*~*~*~*~*~*~*~*~*~*~

Thane carefully balanced the pole in his hand as he climbed the ladder. Once he had his footing, he looked down to where Emma was building a fire. Determined to get the chimney fixed so that it would be the last meal she would need to cook out of doors, Thane turned his attention back to the chimney.

He looked down inside the opening and saw the shadow of a blockage. Pulling some of the debris away from the chimney top, one of the bricks jiggled loose. Thane pushed it back into place, and a squirrel popped its head from the top.

Thane started laughing. Seeing Emma turn toward him, he called down to her. "It appears a squirrel made its nest in the top part of our chimney. He popped out at me, and I pert near jumped out of my skin." He laughed again at the concern on her face until a movement caught his attention.

James walked into the yard carrying a small rifle and a little wooden box.

Thane swung his leg around to climb down the ladder, jumping down from the third rung to meet him.

"James," Thane called out as he approached the other man. "I'd like ta apologize ta you fer my rudeness yesterday. I've no excuse except that I hadn't slept in days." He offered his hand to James. "But that wasn't yer doin'. I was out of line. I'm sorry."

James shook Thane's hand without hesitation. "Apology accepted."

"Ya out huntin'?"

Looking down at the rifle in his hand, James shook his head. "No. I brought this here rifle for yer wife. It was my first rifle as a youngin'."

Emma saw Thane's back stiffen. "Thank ya jest the same, but she won't be needin' it."

James' face hardened. "She'll be needin' it the next time ya go off fer months leavin' her here unprotected."

"What I do and where I go are no business to anyone but my family," Thane's voice was calm, but Emma could hear the firmness behind the words.

James' knuckles turned white where he gripped the rifle. "It becomes my business when we are all out searchin' fer yer wife because she slept in the barn because there was a mountain lion in your yard. Without a rifle to protect herself, she couldn't return to the house."

Thane froze. "A mountain lion?"

"Yes, Thane. A mountain lion," James' face lost some of its anger as Thane stood there quiet. "How on earth could ya go and leave her here without a rifle, Thane?"

Thane turned to Emma. His shoulders slumped in shame. "I didn't think about it."

The farmyard was quiet for a long while.

James put the rifle forward again. "This is the rifle I learned on. The kick is small. There are enough bullets here to get her started," he hesitated for a moment. "Ya'd be doin' me a favor usin' it. I won't have to keep cleanin' it ta keep it from rustin' up."

153

Thane took the rifle slowly and then extended his other hand to shake James' again. "I thank ya fer this."

James cleared his throat. Nodding toward the roof, he changed the subject. "What are ya fixin' on the roof?"

"A critter made a nest in the chimney. I was jest noticing a few bricks are loose. So, I'm settin' to clear it out. Can't have Emma cookin' out of doors all winter."

"Would ya like a hand?"

"Wouldn't want ta bother ya," Thane began.

"No bother," James said as he rolled up his sleeves and started up the ladder.

Thane watched him a moment before he turned to Emma. "A mountain lion?"

She nodded. She had planned on telling him, but everything had been so chaotic.

Thane moved forward and leaned his forehead against hers. Pulling her closer, he took a deep breath. "Is there anything else that happened while I was gone?"

Emma chuckled. "Abigail really *did* have a boy."

Thane laughed outright. Pulling her into his arms, he lifted her off the ground. Then with a sigh, he put her down and headed for the ladder.

≈ Twenty-Two ≈

December 11, 1858...

Emma watched her husband read the letter. Mark had been right. It was from Thane's grandma. That had been Thane's only comment before he fell silent. Refilling his cup with coffee, she went back to washing the morning dishes.

"Grandmother says she's suffered a fall cold and hasn't recovered. The doctor says her journey will have to be delayed." His eyes skimmed over the page again. "She hopes we have settled in and will see us when she can travel."

"I hope she gets better," Emma added up the years and realized Mary Preston would be close to 60. It made Emma worry more. She really wanted Thane to be able to meet someone from his mother's family. "Did yer Pa tell ya anythin' about yer mama's story when ya saw him? Did he explain anything'?"

"When I found him, he was already pretty deep in the drink and mumblin' about a curse. My questions seemed ta just make him drink more. He was sleepin' it off the next day and then just disappeared." Thane folded the letter and slid it away from his cup. "It'd already taken me weeks to find him that first time. After lookin' fer him another couple days, I realized he'd not be sharin' anythin' with me."

Emma watched her husband as he sat there. He was quiet as he stared at his cup, but she wondered at the thoughts going through his head.

"I'd like to show ya how to shoot the rifle before I leave today."

The change in subject surprised her, but she knew that he wanted her to learn to handle the rifle before he left the yard. "I've all day. So, jest let me know when you are ready." Emma only had a few chores to do since it was Saturday.

"I'd like ta get some work done to get the traplines set up. Do some scoutin' as I go. I could be gone quite a bit if the weather holds. So, I'll get a target set up for you. That way, when you are done here, we can get right to it." Thane took his last swallow of coffee and put his cup in her wash water. With a kiss on her head, he pulled his hat on and headed out into the yard.

Emma finished up the last few dishes and put them in their spot on the shelf. She turned back to grab the washtub just as Thane came inside.

"Let me dump that for you." He lifted the heavy tub without any effort and left Emma to close the door behind him.

Emma grabbed the buckets to fill. It would be hours before she needed them, but the water would warm if she placed the buckets near the fire. As she neared the door, Thane stepped in. He set the washtub in its place and reached for the buckets in her hands.

The door closed and left Emma alone in the cabin. Thane had already filled the kindling bucket and stacked the wood high by the backdoor. The chickens had been fed as well as all the barn chores. She knew she should be thankful for the help. But somehow, after the months of doing the chores all alone, she felt like she was of no use.

Thane stepped back through the door he had just closed, kicking it closed behind him without spilling more than a few drops of water.

Absentmindedly, Emma reached down to wipe up the drops.

"Jest leave them, Emma. I'll wipe them up."

Emma closed her eyes and breathed a prayer for patience.

"Why don't ya slip on a coat? I need to grab James' rifle, and we are ready."

Emma wondered if he would let her pull the trigger on the rifle. *Or change his mind and just do it for me.*

You're not being fair, a small voice reminded her.

She closed her eyes again. She knew she wasn't being fair. Taking another deep breath, she grabbed her coat and slipped it over her arms.

Outside, Emma saw there were a few objects set on the chopping block at the edge of the yard. Her heart started beating faster at the simple sight. She wasn't sure she wanted to learn to shoot.

She didn't have time for doubts. Thane was already explaining the different parts of the rifle to Emma. He showed her each step in loading the shot. Pulling it into his shoulder, he showed her where to position it and explained that she needed to pull it tight or it would hurt. He pointed out that she needed to keep her eye clear of the hammer as it might spark. As he aimed toward the chopping block, he warned her again about the kick. The pinecone shattered and went flying off the log as the sound exploded from the rifle.

Emma had thought that shots were loud from far off. But she had never been so close before. She felt the pressure from the sound even though she wasn't touching the rifle yet.

"Do you think yer ready to try?"

Nodding, even though she wasn't sure at all, she reached a shaky hand for the rifle.

Emma turned the weapon over in her hands. It felt heavier than it looked. Thane brought her attention back to him as he placed his hand over hers to help her reload the shot. Repeating which powder went in which hole. "Remember- this small flask of powder goes in the small divet by the flint. This bigger flask is the gunpowder." She pulled it into the curve of her shoulder. Looking down the barrel to site in the small box on the log, she started to close one eye.

"Keep your eyes open, Emma. You'll aim better."

Opening her eye, she adjusted and took aim again.

"When you are ready, squeeze the trigger."

Emma took a deep breath and then squeezed the trigger. It felt like the rifle was pulling from her grasp.

"Hold it tight." Thane reached out and pulled the stock back into her grasp. "You hit the log. If you hold the rifle in place this next time, I think ya'll hit the box."

Emma nodded. Her ears were ringing a little.

"Are ya all right?" Concern filled his eyes when she rubbed her ear.

Nodding again, she gave him a reassuring smile. "I'm jest na used to the noise. My ears are ringin'."

Thane looked like he was ready to take the rifle back from her. He glanced toward the barn for a moment before he turned his attention back to his wife. "I'm sorry, Em. I wish you didn't have to learn this. But with mountain lions and search parties comin' on the farm-."

Emma interrupted him. "Thane, we both know this is necessary. I probably should have learned long before this." Standing on her toes, she kissed him. "Now. I need to reload before I can try again. You said... powder... patch... ball. And now I ram it into place."

"Keep pushing it down. You should only have three finger-widths showing on the rod when it's all the way in place."

"What happens if I don't get it all the way down?"

Thane slipped his arm around her as he helped her position it against her shoulder. "If it's not in place. It won't shoot. Now... keep your eye further back from the flint. You don't want that in your eyes."

Emma concentrated on the target. Then she took a deep breath and held it as she squeezed the trigger. The box jumped to the side an inch as the bullet grazed the edge.

"Good job, Emma. That was close."

Resisting the urge to hold her ears, Emma started reloading the rifle again. She was determined to hit the box.

With the third shot, the box flew off the log. Emma gave her husband a triumphant smile as he kissed her head. "Well done. You are a natural shot. I think we need to let you rest now."

Rest? Emma thought to herself. She had barely been allowed to lift anything all morning. The rifle might have a kick to it, but it wasn't likely to tire her out.

"I hope you'll never need to fire it. But I'll be gone a bit this winter. Knowing how to shoot will keep you safe. Even if it's just a shot in the air to let your family know you need them."

"Thane? Why will ya need ta be trappin' so much? I thought we would be clearing these fields of brush. To get ready for spring."

"The crops won't come in until harvest. So, the farm won't be givin' us any money back until fall. That's a long way off. We need money now." Thane got quiet for a moment. "We need to fix things here on the farm. We need food. The baby is going to need more things. Everything costs money. Trapping will bring us that money for this season."

Emma understood the reasoning. "Da says we can have all the vegetables we want from the root cellar."

"We can't keep takin' food from him, Emma. Besides. We have a mountain lion roaming around. I need to find him."

Hearing an edge to his voice, Emma didn't say anything more. Heading back inside the house, she finished up her chores.

When Thane came to say good-bye and disappeared into the wooded path, Emma started sewing on a nightgown for the baby. But she couldn't concentrate. Finally, she slipped a coat on and headed down the path to her family's farm.

Her father was working on the wheel in the yard when Emma stepped into the clearing. "Broken again?"

Da looked up. "Hello, Emma girl. Nope, it's not broken. Just greasin' the axle. What's worryin' ya?"

Emma shook her head, "There's nothin'-."

"Emma girl." Interrupting her, he grabbed the rag next to him to wipe his hands. "I ignored that look fer far too long. I willna ignore it again. What's worryin' ya?"

There was a moment of silence while Emma thought. "I'm not really-," she stopped herself. Looking down at her hands, she realized she had been thinking a lot. "Well– I-."

Emma's father walked toward her. "Is it the baby?"

Shaking her head, she cleared her throat. "No. It's Thane. I reckon I thought with havin' the farm, he'd be around more. But he still insists on trappin', and-."

When she didn't continue, Da repeated her last word. "And...?"

She felt her eyes fill up with tears. "And I thought when he returned, he would be around the farm more." Wiping her tears away in frustration, she looked up at her father. "I just don't understand why he wants to trap still."

Da nodded. "I see." He walked past Emma and opened the door to the house.

They entered the kitchen, and Emma watched Da start making coffee. *Is he mad that Thane is leaving the farm again?* She wondered if she should defend Thane. Realizing that her accusation sounded like her husband was being irresponsible, she searched for a way to explain.

"Last summer when you talked with Thane?"

Emma was startled by her father's question. "Yes..."

"Did he tell you he was a trapper?"

She nodded.

"And you fell in love with him anyhow?"

Again, she nodded.

"Did he ever mention wantin' ta be a farmer?"

Confused, she shook her head.

"So-," he paused to stoke the fire under the coffee before turning to her. "So, Emma girl, you married your husband knowing he was a trapper? Expectin' him to be a trapper? And you were alright with that?"

Emma nodded again. Slower this time.

"Good." He set cups on the table. "But now? Ya canna expect him ta change. You married a trapper. Ya said yerself that you love him that way. If he never decides ta farm? You must be acceptin' that."

Silence filled the cabin. Emma listened to the logs crackling in the fire, trying to sort out her thoughts. Da's words made sense, but her heart wanted to argue. Nodding finally, she turned to find her father looking at her. "I find nothin' wrong with trappin' I jest hoped..." she stopped. She realized her words were selfish.

Da smiled at her. "Ya look so much like yer mama. She would get that look." Crossing the room to her, he pulled her to him and kissed the top of her head. "Read 1 Corinthians 13. It was your mama's favorite passage for comfort."

Recognizing the verse, Emma was confused. "*Love is patient, love is kind?* But mama was always so happy," she protested.

"Emma girl, I drug yer mama a thousand miles from Vermont to here. I took her away from her family and everything that was familiar. She went from a cultured community to carvin' a life out of the forest. She needed to remind herself frequently what it meant to love," Da chuckled. "An' when I saw her readin' her Bible? I assumed it was because I was testin' her love." With a wink, Emma's father kissed her head again. "If ya look in her Bible, ya'll see her underlinin' that last verse... *And now these three remain, faith, hope, and love. But the greatest of these is love.*"

Emma studied her father as he moved about the kitchen, insisting on waiting on her.

His words were still going through her head as she walked home later that day. *Could Mama have been frustrated with life too? Did she accept things she didn't want to accept for the good of our family?*

The barn came into view, and Da's words echoed in her ears. *If he never decides ta farm? You must be acceptin' that.*

Emma closed her eyes and breathed a prayer. She didn't even know what she was praying for. Knowing she could not be selfish but not sure she was able to pray for Thane to continue to be gone from home so much.

The chickens squawked from the barn and brought Emma's eyes open. Quieting her breathing, she heard the horse moving around its stall. He snorted. She started toward the barn.

Thane stepped out of the woods. The sudden movement startled her, and her hand flew to her mouth to catch the strangled squeak that escaped it.

His mouth settled into his lopsided smile as he approached her. "What has ya so skittish?"

"I jest didna expect ya at that moment. I was listenin' to the animals. They're actin' a bit strange and-."

"You weren't goin' to look."

"Well... I was-," she started.

"Where is the rifle?" he frowned as he saw her empty hands. "Emma, go inside."

Emma started to protest, but Thane was already easing his things to the ground and reaching for the door latch. She could hear the animals reacting as her husband walked deeper into the barn. The quiet made Emma nervous, and she headed to the house to get the rifle.

She was just pulling the rifle down when Thane stepped through the door.

"Next time, just stay in the house. Leave the animals until I get home," Thane pleaded. Emma could hear the worry in his voice.

"Did ya find anythin'?"

"No, but the animals sensed somethin'. None of those animals are worth you or the baby getting hurt."

"What if it's the little slave girl comin' back?"

"Then you leave her until I return. Don't leave the house to check. Please?" Walking over to the fire, Thane warmed his hands for a moment before stripping off his outdoor clothing.

"I was on my way back from Da's when I heard them. I didna even think ta grab the rifle first," Emma admitted.

Thane looked up at his wife. "Ya walked to your Da's? Without the rifle?"

Emma froze. "Ya want me to take it with me?"

Running his hand through his hair, he took a deep breath. "Yes," he stated, finally. "Ya need ta carry the rifle with ya until we see no signs of that wild cat."

A worry formed as she looked down at the weapon in her hand. "When the cat jumped out last time, it was fast. How will I have enough time ta load and fire?"

Thane looked up at her then. "It should already be set ta fire. Is that rifle not loaded?"

With a shake of her head, Emma held it out to Thane.

After a moment of silence, Thane took the offered weapon. "Alright. From now on, in this cabin, we need ta keep this rifle loaded and hangin' near the door. At all times."

Emma started to protest, but the worry that shone in her husband's eyes stopped her.

"But isn't that dangerous?"

Thane shook his head. "As long as you don't have it cocked- and the flint guard is in place. Then hold its barrels away from anyone. You should always be good. It is more dangerous to go out with an unloaded weapon. Or to not have a weapon at all," his gray eyes begged her to understand what he was telling her. "I need to know you'll be safe. Otherwise, I'll worry whenever I am checkin' the lines."

Emma's heart sank a little at the reminder that he would be away. *Ya fell in love with a trapper.* Squeezing her eyes shut, she nodded in agreement. "I'll keep it loaded and keep it with me."

Thane pressed his forehead to hers. "Thank you."

"Thane-." Emma breathed a prayer to steady her. "I-, I shoulda realized that you'd still be trappin' this winter... and I know that's what you do. But I'm wonderin' if we need quite so many lines?"

"Emma, I have to provide for you and our baby-."

Putting her hand on his chest, she interrupted him. "I know that. But I... I feel like our home isn't made up of things we need to provide or fix. It's in the closeness we have always felt."

Thane nodded. "Sounds about right."

"I miss you. You jest returned and are already plannin' to be gone again." Emma looked down at her hand against Thane's chest. She could feel his heart beating below her fingers. "And I understand yer tryin' to provide for us. I jest wondered iffen perhaps we can do without extra things. The unnecessary extras. So, we can spend more time together."

"Balance," Thane whispered. He put his hands on her cheeks and stroked them with his thumbs. "Yer askin' for balance. I can do that. I won't let you go without necessities, but I do miss spendin' time with ya. It's more important than the extras. At least for this season." He placed a soft kiss on her lips and leaned his head against hers again. "Sometimes? I get so busy working to get everything done that I forget where I am. Forget where God has put me. Then I'll catch sight of ya. And I'm surprised all over again when I remember He gave me you. When I'm realizin' how good my life is and that I get to keep my Emma for as long as I live," he cleared the emotion from his voice. "You are so precious to me."

❧ Twenty-Three ❧

*E*mma hurried to get her chores done so she could start baking. She wanted to have all her family's favorites for Christmas dinner, but Thane was constantly telling her to rest. With only two days until Christmas, Emma worried she wouldn't get them all made.

At breakfast, Thane had announced he was going up to his Pa's cabin again. He needed to check on the roof and get more of his trapping tools. Excited to be alone for the day, she figured it was enough time to get the extra baking done. Emma had sent her husband on his way with more energy than she usually did. As he readied himself to go, he had hesitated a moment before closing the door behind him.

Emma smiled, remembering the concerned look on his face. Grabbing the empty bucket, she headed out to fetch clean water for the dishes that needed washing.

The air was cold on her lungs as she carried the heavy water up the path back to the house. Her foot slid on an icy patch, causing her to set the bucket down at her feet. Emma rested for a moment to make sure her feet were solid under her, then lifted the bucket again.

"Emma, stop!"

Startled, Emma dropped the bucket. The water splashed over her boots and the snow around her. As it soaked through her laces, she could feel her stockings getting wet. She looked up to see Thane stepping into the yard from the trees.

"Thane Hawkins, donna ya be yellin' at me!" she said sternly. Fighting back the tears in her eyes, she put her hands on her hips. The

165

movement caused her feet to slide sideways, and she put her hands out to catch her balance before she fell.

"I told ya to leave the heavy stuff, and I'd get it," Thane hurried to her side and held out a hand to help steady her.

"Well, you were off in the woods. An' I needed water." She stepped off the path. The snow hadn't been trampled down, so it was deeper there, but it gave her more traction so she didn't slip. "I've been gettin' my own water... fer months now. I've had ta do a lot of work while ya were away. I reckon one more trip isn't gonna kill me."

Thane stepped forward and pulled Emma into his arms. He pressed his forehead against hers. "I'm sorry fer yellin'. I saw ya strugglin'... and it jest scared me was all."

Emma let her frustration slip away. She pressed a kiss to his cheek and let her arms wrap around him. "I'm sorry fer losin' my temper."

They stood there in the snow with their arms wrapped around each other. Then with a gentle squeeze, he bent down to pick up the empty bucket. "Let me go fill this. It's the least I can do fer makin' ya spill it."

Realizing how cold her feet were, Emma hurried inside. She stripped off her boots and stockings, setting them near the fire to dry.

Thane came in close behind her. "You've more bakin' ta do?"

Emma looked at the ingredients she had set on the table. "I usually make cookies and bread to go with our Christmas dinner. I thought that I'd use today to get a start on them since I've my other chores caught up."

"Is that why you were so happy ta send me off this morn? Afraid I would set ta eatin' them all? Like Seth?"

Emma chose her words carefully. "I was jest wantin' ta bake without bein' told ta sit down. Without bein' told ta jest leave it."

Thane froze. "I didn't mean ta-."

The emotions stormed through his eyes and across his face. Emma could see the concern and the apology form before he even uttered the words.

"I'm sorry, Emma. I- I can see how that'd be hard fer ya. An' I should have... I jest worry. So many things can happen when yer carryin' a baby around. But I shouldn't have..."

Feeling terrible for saying anything, Emma put her finger over Thane's lips to stop him. "I know yer worried. I shouldna said anythin'."

Thane pulled away from her hand. "I'm sorry my worryin' frustrated ya. But I'm not sorry ya told me. Otherwise- I would've jest kept pesterin' ya ta sit down." He smiled for a moment before seriousness clouded back in. "The truth is... I'm worried. Both our mamas died after bringin' a baby inta this world. I'm so excited fer this lil' one," he paused to form the right words. "but I'm worried too. I don't want ta learn ta live without ya. Like both our fathers had ta."

Emma couldn't speak around the lump that formed in her throat. She nodded and let her husband pull her into his arms.

With a kiss to her head, Thane headed for the door. "I circled back to let ya know I found tracks from somethin' big nearby. It might be yer mountain lion comin' back around. Animals get mighty brave in winter. It's when they are most hungry. Be watchful when you go outside."

~*~*~*~*~*~*~*~*~*~*~*~*~*~*~*~*~*~

Emma dumped the washtub and stopped to rest. With only one batch of bread left to bake, she was happy with the number of treats she had baked. But she was exhausted. It was a good feeling. She had cooked and baked for hours. Only stopping for a small meal. With the mess cleaned up, she had only to wait for Thane to come home before cooking the simple meal she had planned.

As if her thoughts had brought him home, Thane stepped into the yard. Emma saw that something different was in his expression. Excited but unsure. Catching sight of his wife, he started forward with a lopsided smile. As he came closer, Emma saw that his shirttails were untucked and held tightly in his fingers, creating a bowl. Thane pulled back his hand and showed Emma his shirt front full of berries.

"Oh, winter berries. I love ta see these growin' down by the swamp. Especially when it's full winter. The color against the white snow darin' us ta believe that spring is comin' soon. That is– 'til the birds eat the last one." She set the berry back in the pile. "Thane," Emma paused. She did not want to hurt his feelings but wasn't sure how to get around it. "These berries aren't – ya canna eat them."

The corner of Thane's mouth tilted up. Looking down at the berries, he hesitated. In that moment, Emma thought her husband looked like Seth. The moment right before Seth would suggest something he knew she would never agree to.

"I know we can't," Thane lifted his eyes to hers. "When I was small, I remember sittin' around fires with a trapper my Pa called Fred. Fred would tell tales of growin' up across the ocean. His childhood in Germany. Now, most of these tales seemed farfetched, and I think he told them jest ta see me smile. But my favorite stories he would tell were about how they decorated for Christmas."

"Decorated?" Emma hadn't meant to interrupt, but he had surprised her.

"Yes. He said they would chop down trees and bring them inside. String up berries and treats. Then wind them round the trees. He even said they'd put candles on the branches by melted wax," he paused for a moment before continuing. "I'm pretty sure he was pullin' my leg about bringin' the tree inside the house. But he showed me how to string berries together one winter, and we wrapped them around a tree. He looked so happy as he watched the berries twinkle in the firelight."

Tears filled Emma's eyes as she watched her husband recount a good memory. His childhood had been so hard that it filled her with happiness to hear this glad tale. *Of course, happiness means tears with a baby on the way*, Emma thought as she wiped the tears away. "So, yer wantin' ta bring a tree into our house?"

"No." Thane's shoulders seemed to relax when he realized she wasn't opposed to his plans. "I'm pert sure he told that part to see a young boy's eyes pop."

She laughed. "Well, Abby's been beggin' David ta chop down a tree and bring it inta her parlor since last Christmas. Said it's all the fashion back East. I think David has much the same opinion as you."

Thane laughed outright at that.

"What would ya like ta do with the berries then? I'm guessin' ya want me ta string them up for ya?"

"I'll help ya," he answered enthusiastically. "Fred said they would string them up on the eve of Christmas and light the candles." Turning her toward the barn, he nodded toward a small evergreen tree. "I'm not wantin' ta bring it inside. But I thought we could put the berries round that little tree. That way, we can see it from the window."

Emma couldn't pull her gaze from the excitement in Thane's face. It seemed a strange thing to spend time on, but she knew she would agree to anything he asked with that expression. The gray of his eyes seemed to sparkle, and the storms were gone. "Well, the eve of Christmas is tomorrow. So, I guess we could string those berries tonight after supper. I'll go lay them out to dry a little. They'll make less of a mess that way."

She made a bowl from her own apron for Thane to pour the berries into, but he only laughed. "Best only one of us gets stains on our clothes."

Turning toward the house, Emma was surprised when his hand reached out to keep her from walking away. Looking over her shoulder, she saw Thane take a step closer to her and reached his hand up to her face. He closed the distance as he let his thumb trace her cheek. "I'm the luckiest man alive. I love you, Emma." He pressed his lips to hers carefully.

Emma breathed him in. She wanted the memory of that moment to be burned forever in her mind. Reluctantly, she pulled back. "I love you, Thane Hawkins. Now let's get those berries in a basket– before yer shirt gets so stained it won't wash out. No matter how hard yer poor wife tries to scrub it."

Thane laughed and pulled her back against his side. "The stains will remind me of this kiss." He lowered his mouth to hers once again.

Emma agreed. The stains and the berries that made them would always remind her of that kiss.

❧ Twenty-Four ❧

December 25, 1858...

Emma woke to the darkness. For a moment, she did not know why she woke.

"Merry Christmas, Emma, my love," Thane whispered against her forehead and then kissed her.

"Merry Christmas, Thane."

She felt his arms tighten around her, and then he was gone. The darkness blocked him from view, but she could hear him moving about the room, getting ready to feed the animals.

Emma's dress had just settled over her shoulders when she felt another kiss being placed on her head. "I'll be back in soon."

She felt him leave, even though she could not see it. "Forgot how dark these winter mornin's can be," she muttered as she felt for the matches to light a candle. Once she had a light to see by, she soon had coffee over to boil and set about cutting up some bacon.

A flutter moved in her stomach. Emma stopped to place her hand over the movement. Next Christmas, they would have a little one crawling around. *This will be our only quiet Christmas.* As if to agree, Emma felt the baby flutter again.

With a smile, she set about finishing breakfast.

Just when the coffee smelled done, Thane returned.

"Perfect timing," she said as she set a cup on the table for him. "Get warmed up while I finish this."

"Mmmm. Smells delicious." He sat down in his chair and reached for his coffee. He had nearly finished his first cup by the time Emma set his breakfast in front of him. Refilling his coffee, they ate in silence.

171

Emma's thoughts kept going over the day's plans in excitement.

After cleaning up the dishes, Emma reached for the Bible on the mantle.

"The story of Jesus's birth is in Luke 2." She opened to the well-worn pages. *"And it came to pass in those days that a decree went out from Caesar Augustus that all the world should be registered. This census first took place while Quirinius was governing Syria.*

So all went to be registered, everyone to his own city. Joseph also went up from Galilee, out of the city of Nazareth, into Judea, to the city of David, which is called Bethlehem, because he was of the house and lineage of David, to be registered with Mary, his betrothed wife, who was with child.

So it was, that while they were there, the days were completed for her to be delivered. And she brought forth her firstborn Son, and wrapped Him in swaddling cloths, and laid Him in a manger because there was no room for them in the inn.

Now there were in the same country shepherds living out in the fields, keeping watch over their flock by night. And behold, an angel of the Lord stood before them, and the glory of the Lord shone around them, and they were greatly afraid. Then the angel said to them, "Do not be afraid, for behold, I bring you good tidings of great joy which will be to all people. For there is born to you this day in the city of David, a Savior, who is Christ the Lord. And this will be the sign to you: You will find a Babe wrapped in swaddling cloths, lying in a manger."

And suddenly there was with the angel a multitude of the heavenly host praising God and saying:

"Glory to God in the highest,
And on earth peace,
goodwill toward men!"

So it was, when the angels had gone away from them into heaven, that the shepherds said to one another, "Let us now go to Bethlehem and see this thing that has come to pass, which the Lord has made known to us." And they came with haste and found Mary and Joseph, and the Babe lying in a manger.

Now when they had seen Him, they made widely known the saying which was told them concerning this Child. And all those who heard it marveled at those things which were told them by the shepherds.

But Mary kept all these things and pondered them in her heart."

Pondered, Emma echoed.

Looking over at her husband, she saw he was deep in thought as well. Love welled up in her as she watched him.

"I got ya a little something."

Thane looked up. "Me?"

Emma rose from her chair and pulled out a pot from under the cupboard. Reaching inside, she retrieved a stuffed sock. Setting the pot back in its place, she moved to put the sock on the table in front of Thane.

Thane stared at it for a moment.

"Look inside."

Reaching in, Thane pulled out a rolled-up sock. He flattened it.

"That is the other one to match. Ya didna have a sock without holes, so I made a pair. It didna make sense ta just make one."

Smiling, he ran his fingers along the sock. "I canna remember a time someone made me socks."

Emma smiled at his expression of wonder. Kissing the top of his head, she urged him to empty the sock.

Pulling out licorice and small candies, he smiled at each one. But his hand stilled as he unfolded the small paper.

Sketching "I love you," and signing her name had been an afterthought for Emma. She had added it to the sock even though it was of no value.

Thane slipped his arm around Emma's waist and pulled her into his lap. "I love you." His whisper against her neck brought tears to her eyes.

Abruptly, Thane set Emma back on her feet. He slipped his coat back on and left through the door. He reappeared before she had time to wonder at his behavior. His lips curled up on one side as he stepped toward her.

Emma watched his gray eyes brim with happiness and love as he approached. Seeing so much happiness there made Emma's throat hurt. She couldn't look away.

Thane paused for a moment. He seemed hesitant to break their connection. When he finally looked down, Emma followed his gaze and rested her eyes on a puppy. A brown puppy with mixed tones of brown all melting together. The head and the paws looked enormous compared to the puppy's tiny body.

"Awww."

The sound made the puppy turn its head to the side as it studied Emma.

"It looks like he's smiling at me."

"Well, *he* is a girl. But that smile is why I picked her out instead of her brother. I wanted someone to bring happiness to your life." Thane placed the puppy into Emma's arms. "Well, her smile and the fact that she'll be teachable. She doesn't mind being rolled on ta her back. So, she'll not be challengin' ya."

As if to prove him right, the puppy rolled onto her back, almost asking Emma with her eyes to rub her belly. Laughing, Emma obliged her.

"What will ya name her?" Thane asked with a lopsided tilt to his smile. "Dawg two? Dawg the second?"

Emma could tell he was imitating the way she called her dog at Da's farm. She tried not to smile as he continued to list names for her to choose from.

"...Baby Dawg? Queen Dawg? Oh- or Emma's Dawg?"

Trying to come up with a funny comeback, Emma looked up into Thane's eyes. She saw love shining there. The love that drove him to pick out such a precious animal for her. The retort died on her lips, and she smiled. "Jade."

"Jade?" he repeated in surprise.

Nodding, she looked down at the puppy again. The puppy was studying Emma. Her eyes half-closed as her tongue hung to one side. *She does look like she is smiling.* Emma scratched under her chin and watched the puppy's eyes close in contentment.

"Jade," she confirmed. "I have always wanted to see what Jade looked like- what it feels like. See with my own eyes why a jewel could be so precious to anyone." She paused. "But in this moment, I realize some things are more precious than a rock. And nothing is more precious than this bundle of love right here."

Jade jumped out of Emma's arms and put her paws up onto the front of her dress. Barking once, she licked Emma's cheek.

Thane laughed. "I'm thinkin' she approves. Jade, it is."

When Jade barked again, Thane picked up the puppy. "Alright, Jade. That'll be enough of that. We won't be encouragin' ya to bark fer no reason." Thane turned his gaze back to Emma. "I worry about leavin' you alone so much. I'm hopin' that Jade will grow into a fine companion fer ya."

Emma smiled to herself. Her Da had told her much the same thing when he brought Dawg home to her. After her Mama had passed away, she spent much of her days alone at the farm. The boys still went to school and Da in the fields most of the day. She knew her father had worried about her. When he had brought Dawg home for the family, he told her having a dog around would make the days to not be as lonely.

The sound of a wagon pulling up to the front of the cabin brought her out of her thoughts.

"Hello in the house," Seth's voice sounded cheerful.

Thane walked to the window. "Looks like yer Da sent Seth with the wagon. Either that or yer brother couldn't wait another minute for the treats you baked him." His mouth curled into the lopsided smile that she loved. "I'm bettin' it's the treats."

Emma laughed out loud.

Thane's face went serious. He walked to her and leaned his head against hers. "I love to see ya so happy. That is my hope. To always make you laugh."

Wrapping her arms around her husband's waist, she leaned against his chest. His heart beat loud in her ear. "I love you, Thane Hawkins."

"I love you, Emma Hawkins." He squeezed her closer. "I still don't know why God blessed me with you. But I'm so grateful."

Jade jumped up onto the door as footsteps approached it. "Em? Do ya need help carryin' any baskets to the wagon?"

Thane pulled back from Emma and looked down at her with a smile.

"I know those cookies can get real heavy... and with ya already carryin' a baby..." Seth called through the door.

They shared a laugh as Thane went to let Seth in.

The men made short work of putting all the baskets and crates of goodies in the wagon as Emma straightened up the cabin. When Thane asked if she wanted to take Jade with her, she went to find a basket big enough for a blanket and the puppy. When she returned with one, she found that Thane had fashioned a harness for Jade. Lifting her by the harness, she settled her in the basket.

Thane helped her up into the wagon seat and turned to climb in the back.

"Ya all set?" Seth asked around the cookie in his mouth.

"All set," Thane called from behind them.

Seth clicked to the team, and the wagon easily pulled through the light dusting of snow.

"What did ya name this little gal?" Her brother reached into the basket to ruffle the puppy's ears.

"Jade." Emma squeaked as she managed to catch the little animal as it leapt toward the horses. "Her name is Jade." She repeated as she tucked Jade back into the basket. Emma kept her fingers looped through the rope harness. She understood the wisdom that her husband had shown when he took the time to make it.

Looking up once the puppy was secure, Emma saw the mischievous look in Seth's eyes.

"What are ya up ta, little brother?"

"Me?" Seth didn't even try to look innocent as he winked at his sister with a laugh.

Shaking her head at his nonsense, Emma looked over her shoulder and saw that Thane was watching them in amusement. She smiled at him. Her heart was so full that her eyes started to fill with tears. Brushing them away before Seth could comment, Emma turned back to face the road.

Da's cabin came into view as they rounded the next bend. Da stepped out onto the porch with a wave. Emma waved back as new tears filled her eyes.

Before the wagon came to a stop, Thane was beside Emma. She was surprised that he had moved so quickly. Grasping her waist, he lifted her down. The way his gray eyes searched her face told Emma he had seen her tears.

Standing up on her toes, she kissed her husband's cheek to reassure him that she was alright. "What a glorious day."

His mouth tilted into a smile in relief. "Indeed, it is." Leaning down, he pressed his lips to her forehead.

"Do na worry, Thane. Ya'll get used ta the tears," Seth mumbled as he moved past them.

With a smile at her husband, she turned to Da and the open door. "Merry Christmas, Da." She gave him a hug with her free arm.

"Merry Christmas, Emma girl." He kissed her head and then ushered her into the warm kitchen.

Stepping inside, Emma saw Mark sliding the roaster pan into the woodstove oven. A fat duck lay in the pan on a bed of vegetables. It was the first year that Emma could remember not preparing the Christmas bird, and it felt strange for a moment. *Rachel is a good cook. Enjoy the break.*

Emma's attention returned to Mark. His head tilted close to Rachel's as they inspected the fire under the duck. A smile lifted the corner of her mouth. There was a sweetness to the way Rachel laid her hand on Mark's arm.

Mark looked up to find Emma watching them. His cheeks turned pink, but he did not move away from Rachel.

"Merry Christmas, Mark. Merry Christmas, Rachel." Emma set the basket with Jade on the floor so Rachel wouldn't catch her staring. Straightening again, she moved to hug the rest of her family.

"Merry Christmas, Emma. The duck's in ta roast." Rachel gestured to the woodstove. "I rubbed it with lard like ya told me ta-."

"I'm sure it'll be delicious," Emma assured her new sister. "I've brought some sweet treats if ya have some coffee fer us."

Rachel set about boiling some.

The rest of the menfolk brought the crates of baked goods with them. Seth helped himself to a variety of cookies and settled into his chair at the table.

Putting a few of each cookie on a plate, Emma placed them on the table for the others to enjoy. When Seth reached for another one, Emma playfully swatted his hand away. "Eat the ones in yer hand first."

Seth laughed. "Hey, Em. What's with the berries in the tree at yer farm?"

Everyone turned to Emma in curiosity.

"Actually," Thane interrupted, "that's from me. It's somethin' I'd always wanted ta do." He told them about the trapper from across the ocean while they waited for the coffee to heat.

Emma smiled as she sank into the chair next to her husband.

~*~*~*~*~*~*~*~*~*~*~*~*~*~*~*~*~*~*~*~

Cleaning up after dinner, Seth started teasing Emma. "You know, Thane, you left my sister alone for far too long."

The room went quiet. Thane looked to Emma, guilt showing in his eyes.

"Boy-?" Da's tone warned Seth to be careful, but his youngest didn't pay him any attention.

"She's a little daft now. Bathin' baby calves. Carryin' the farm animals in baskets."

"Ya, little rascal. That puppy isn't a farm animal."

Seth laughed as he dodged away from his sister. The swipe of her towel missed his backside. He laughed from the safety of the next room.

"But ya did bathe a calf?"

Everyone turned toward Rachel.

"I'd like to hear this one as well," Thane agreed.

Emma opened her mouth to deny it, but Seth interrupted. "I saw it with my own eyes. Emma kneelin' in front of the wet calf, towel dryin' the little beast. And talkin' ta it like a lil' baby."

"That calf had just been born. I merely shared my shawl with it."

Thane's laughter rang out into the room. "What didn't happen while I was away?"

Emma's cheeks burned. "I may've come ta be a little daft in my old age, but what about you, Seth Wells? Sometimes I think ya were born daft. Stealin' honey from hives in the heat of the day. Forgetting to latch the barn door and lettin' the pigs escape."

"For sure and for certain, I am a daft boy. But we weren't talkin' about me. We were talkin' about where the world is going when womenfolk start carryin' around the livestock in baskets on their arms."

"That puppy is hardly livestock."

"I think someone is feeling safe now that he has hidden the rest of the cookies away in the larder in hope that ya'll leave them here," Da's voice was full of laughter.

"What about Mark?"

Emma turned from her father's joyful face to her new sister. "Mark? What about him?" Glancing at Mark's face, she saw confusion there too.

Rachel's cheeks turned pink, and she paused for a second before explaining. "Do you have any more stories about Mark? From when he was little?"

Emma smiled. "Yes. Of course, I do."

"Emma. No." Mark pleaded.

"There was the time Mark and James tied George in the outhouse."

"He kept dippin' Emma's braids in ink. I was defendin' her honor," Mark answered, stepping close to Emma.

Rachel smiled. "Ya told me about that one the day of the snowstorm."

Emma evaded her brother, walking to the other side of the table. "There was the time that Mark and Seth thought they could get out of choppin' wood by rubbin' berries all over their arms ta look like they got cut. While Mama was tryin' ta decide how to punish them for the deceit? They started to itchin' something fierce. Mama made them-"

"Emma!" Mark interrupted, panic in his voice.

Trying not to laugh in response, Emma winked at Rachel. "Let's just say they didn't have to chop wood for a few days. So, they got their way."

"And we didna even get punished for that one," Seth announced, proudly.

"Oh... we were punished. Just not by Mama," Mark grumbled.

Rachel's smile grew at her husband's grumpy tone. "What else?"

Mark's eyes pleaded with his sister. "Emma? Please?"

Emma was tempted to do as her brother asked and not tell the story she knew he was thinking about. But laughter was what made families grow. And she wanted to see Mark and Rachel happy.

"Well there was this time, Da sent the boys out to find a heifer who was about to drop her calf." Ignoring the groan from her brother,

180

she sat next to Rachel. "Da wanted to make sure they brought them both back home so we could get the milk and make sure nothin' got that calf. They found the cow next to the swimmin' hole. The calf happily nursin' from his mama. But the boys decided to pretend like they needed to wait for the heifer to finish...while they went swimming."

Rachel gasped in amused shock.

"Emma..." Mark pleaded.

Da chuckled near the fire.

"After a few hours, Da went in search of them and found them swimming still. So, he gathered up the boys' clothes and put the calf around his neck. They were makin' such a racket. He led that cow away without the boys knowin'."

Mark's hand shot out and covered Emma's mouth. "Emma... how about we talk about something else?"

Emma pushed her brother's hand away, amused that he was embarrassed.

Mark pulled his wife to her feet and covered her ears with his hands. "Rachel. You don't want to hear this."

"Oh, but I do," she replied as she pulled his hands away.

Cradling her face, he pleaded. "Surely, there is no need to hear of the mischief of my youth."

Rachel gripped her husband's arms. "Sure, there is. I'd like ta be knowin' the boy you were. And besides, I'll need ta be tellin' these tales to our children someday."

At her last words, Mark's face softened. His fingers relaxed against the side of her head, framing her face. The two stood silent, looking into each other's eyes. Mark trailed his thumb down her cheek.

Emma watched the tenderness on her brother's face, and her eyes teared up. Feeling like she was invading on their moment, she looked away only to see that everyone else was also watching the tender moment as well.

Seth caught her eye and gave her a cheeky wink before he cleared his throat to continue. "I didna have a worry. I marched home to tell Mama somethin' stole my clothes."

"In his drippin' wet long underwear," Da added from his place across the room.

"But not Mark. Nope. He waited by the swimmin' hole. Hopin' Mama would take pity on him and bring him some clothes," Emma chuckled at the memory.

Mark protested. "I was lookin' for the cow and her calf. I thought they were still out there."

Everyone studied Mark's red face in silence while he struggled to maintain his innocent look.

"He was definitely waitin' for clothes."

Everyone laughed in response to Seth's words.

When the laughter died down, Seth smiled at Emma. "It's nice ta hear ya tellin' stories about someone other than me fer once."

"It's nice ta hear our Emma tellin' stories again. No matter who they are about," Da added.

"Yeah," Mark agreed. He looked down at his sister with his arms still around his wife. "Tis nice ta hear your stories again."

"My stories?"

Mark nodded and then looked over at Thane. "My sister used to tell the funniest stories around the dinner table. When they were borderin' on the *unladylike*? Mama would send Emma off ta do a chore," a smile crept onto his face, "so that Mama could laugh without Emma knowin'."

"Mama never laughed at me."

"Oh, Emma girl," Da sighed. "Yer Mama used to complain about havin' to bite her cheek ta keep from laughin' at your stories."

"Why?"

"Yer Mama wanted ta raise ya to be a lady. Even here in this rough country. So, she'd discourage any stories that were na ladylike," he paused to raise his eyebrow. "Like tellin' tales of her brothers in their long underclothes."

Emma's cheeks burned. Her Mama would have interrupted her story if she had been there. "Oh..." Turning to Mark, she opened her mouth to apologize.

"I dinna mind, Emma. 'Twas worth it to hear you tellin' stories again." He smiled. "Even if they were about me."

Not knowing what to say, Emma just looked around at her family.

"Besides," Rachel interjected. "I've already seen his long underwear." When everyone turned to look at her, she stumbled to continue, "-in the washtub every week."

Everyone laughed as Rachel blushed.

Emma rose and walked over to Thane's chair. Resting her hands on his shoulders, she closed her eyes and listened to everyone talking. She wanted to remember that moment for a long time.

~*~

They arrived home in the dark. Seth had offered to drive them, and they had accepted gladly. The cabin was dark and cold when they arrived. Emma sunk down into the rocker by the fireplace and let Jade out of her basket.

Thane had a fire blazing in no time and sat down at Emma's feet. "Joseph must've been worried sick."

Curious, she turned from the flames. "Who?"

"Joseph. From the Bible this morning." His eyes met hers, and she could see the emotions in his gray eyes. "You are exhausted from a short trip ta yer Da's house. Can ya imagine how worried Joseph would have been to take her on a long journey? *Heavy with child*, it said. He had no choice, but he had to have been so worried for both Mary and the baby."

Emma watched as Thane turned his attention back to the fire. He added a few more sticks and settled his back against her legs.

183

Hearing the story of Jesus's birth every year, Emma felt very familiar with the words. She even remembered thinking the stable sounded like an adventure. But today's trip to see her family had been long enough for her. The thought of a longer journey made her think of Mary's journey a little differently. She would not find it an adventure to have her baby come into the world in a stable. Far from her family. She would find it terrifying.

Reaching for the Bible, she opened it to Luke 2 and scanned the story again.

"Would ya read it aloud?"

Nodding, Emma started at the beginning. She read the familiar words, and for the first time, understood how Mary must have felt.

Twenty-Five

January 7, 1859...

L ooking out the window, Emma realized she would be hanging the laundry inside again. The clear skies at breakfast had disappeared behind thick clouds. Strong breezes would dry the clothes in no time, but not without the sun.

Her attention turned to the road and searched for any sign of Thane. Watching the road had been a constant that morning. The same way she watched it any time her husband was gone for more than a day.

The wind shook the window, almost as if to remind her of the clothes waiting for her. Moving back to the washtub, Emma swished around until she found one of Thane's socks and began scrubbing it against the washboard. Rinsing it, she added it to the growing pile to hang.

Jade barked at Emma and lunged for the basket. Grabbing the sock off the top, the puppy ran under the table and started chewing on it.

"NO, Jade!" Emma bent down after the naughty dog, but her growing belly made it difficult to reach her. Settling onto her knees so she wouldn't topple forward, she tried to take the sock from Jade's mouth. The sock made a ripping sound as Jade pulled back.

Emma groaned. That sock made the fourth thing Jade had ripped in the last few days.

Jade dropped the sock and barked at Emma again. Happy to have Emma's attention, Jade bent her shoulders low to the floor and wagged her tail.

"No, Jade. I'm not playing." Emma tried to stand up, but Jade darted between Emma's legs and her raised skirt, sending her back to her knees. Landing with a grunt, she rested for a moment to let the pain pass.

A sound behind Emma brought her attention away from her pain. She saw Jade struggle to get over the edge of the washtub for one second before she flipped inside. As soon as the cold water touched the puppy's skin, Jade scrambled up the washboard. Puppy and washboard toppled out of the washtub, spraying water all over the kitchen. There was nothing Emma could do but watch helplessly as Jade landed on the edge of the laundry basket and flipped the clean, wet clothes onto the floor.

Emma covered her face with her hands and prayed for patience. She let her tears fall between her fingers.

Thane had been gone for a few days, checking his trapline, and Emma hadn't been sleeping well since he left. She was worried about him being gone, and Jade was keeping her awake at night. She had needed to start tying Jade in the kitchen. Emma wasn't sure what was worse, Jade whining to come sleep with her or having a growing puppy crowding her bed.

Jade jumped into Emma's lap and started licking her tears. Emma pulled her hands back to pet Jade's ears and secured the dog's harness. "I know ya jest want to play, but yer makin' more work for me than I can handle."

Emma led Jade out to the barn and put her into an empty stall. It was the stall where they kept the extra tools and things, but Emma didn't think the puppy could hurt anything. Closing the gate before she could escape, Jade started whining.

Ignoring the sound, Emma made the cold trek back into the house to repair the damage that was there. Scooping up fresh buckets of snow, she left them on the hearth to melt. She used the towels she just cleaned to mop up the floor and dropped them back into the remaining wash water to wash again.

Stretching her back, she knelt to put the clean clothes back into the basket. She decided the best way to sort through them was to shake each item out and decide whether to hang them up or rewash them. She stretched the coiled rope across the kitchen, near the fireplace, and looped it over the nail Thane had put in the opposite wall.

She could hear Jade whining from the barn but ignored the sound as she got to work. It didn't take long before everything was cleaned up. Emma poured the last water from the tub into a bucket and took it to dump in the trees.

Returning to the kitchen, she sank into the rocker by the fire and just rested her head back.

Jade's whine brought the puppy back to her mind and fresh tears to her eyes.

"What is it, Emma?"

Emma turned her head to see her husband standing in the door. "Oh, Thane!" She bolted up to meet him in a hug just as he closed the door.

"Are ya all right?" he asked after a moment.

She nodded against his shoulder.

Pulling back a little, Thane searched her face. "What happened?"

Emma felt fresh tears start as she explained the puppy's adventures in the last few days. She was ashamed as she told how frustrated she had gotten before she put Jade into the stall.

Thane didn't say a word as he listened to her talk. When she finished, he simply nodded. "I wondered when I heard the whining from the barn."

Wiping her tears away, she looked toward the door. "I know she wasn't being bad. She jest wanted to play. But Thane- if I canna even be patient with a puppy, what kinda mama will I be?"

Thane pulled Emma back into his arms and leaned his head against his wife's. "A pesky puppy ripping holes in yer laundry is a mite different than motherin' a baby, I'm thinkin'. But I imagine we'll be havin' days that try our patience jest the same." Silence settled around them for a moment before he continued. "I'm certain we won't be perfect parents, Emma. But I have a feeling that ya'll still be amazin'."

Emma smiled. She wasn't convinced, but she felt a little better.

Jade barked again from the barn, and Emma groaned. "I guess we should go let her out, now that the mess is cleaned up."

"Not *we*... but you. If you had to shut her away, she needs it ta be you that comes back to get her. That way, she learns to respect you. And, in turn, will trust you."

Thane's logic made sense. With an exhausted sigh, she headed to the barn.

She could hear Thane close the barn door behind them as she reached for the stall gate. Jade gave her a huge smile when Emma called her out. The puppy ran forward until she caught sight of Thane. She changed direction and jumped onto the stool to get to Thane, so excited to see him after his days away. But the stool was broken and tipped over as soon as the puppy's weight landed on it. Jade fell over the short stall wall and into the chickens that roosted there. The chickens scattered everywhere.

Thane pulled Emma out of the center of the ruckus and into the safety of his arms.

Jade chased the chickens as they flew around until she got distracted by a feather in her mouth.

When everything was quiet, Emma looked around at the cracked eggs and the feathers floating in the air. Looking up at Thane with a raised eyebrow, they both started laughing. Pulling Emma closer, Thane kissed her forehead, then tilted her chin up and placed a kiss on her lips. "You've been workin' too hard. I have ta run into town ta see James. Go get cleaned up, and we'll see if Abby has time for tea with ya."

"I do na have time. I have laundry dryin' and ..."

"That laundry will dry whether you're watchin' as it hangs or if yer visitin' yer friend," he reasoned.

188

"That's fer certain. But I'm too tired to walk that far," she admitted.

"Well, I guess ya won't be walkin' then, will ya. The horse is already saddled." Thane kissed her again and called Jade back over to the stall. Filling a bucket with water, he set it inside for her.

"Oh-, water. I didna think..." Emma started.

"She was fine fer the short time. But I have a feelin' she will be stayin' out here more." He cleared some of the extra things out of the stall, but he paused as his hand felt a nail on the wall. As he twisted it to the side, a board swung loose on a hinge hidden under the window.

Thane studied it for a moment more and turned to look at Emma. Neither one said anything, but Emma couldn't help but think it was a strange place for a hinged board.

Hooking the nail again, he made sure it wouldn't come loose. "Don't want Jade gettin' out that way, to be sure."

"Thane?" Emma started to ask, but he interrupted.

"I will explore the stall later, but for now, I need to get to town while it's still light out. Exploring the barn can be done by lantern light."

Nodding in agreement, Emma turned toward the house. "A visit with Abby does sound good." At the door, she paused. "What are ya needin' from James?"

"Another one of my traps was pried open. This one will need James' help to repair. He fixed it last year when the bear bent it. I'm hopin' maybe he'll be able to help me decide what's doin' this damage."

Emma watched the frustration cross over his face. Nodding in understanding, she turned to go into the house.

~*~*~*~*~*~*~*~*~*~*~*~*~*~*~*~*~*~*~*~

The ride into town was a short and peaceful one. Rocking with the motion of the horse almost put Emma to sleep. Leaning back against Thane, she let her eyes drift shut.

"Here we are, Emma."

Emma opened her eyes as Abby opened her door. With a squeal, she hurried to open the gate as Thane lifted Emma down.

Thane kissed her forehead and swung back onto the horse. He tipped his hat to Abby before riding away.

"Come on in. It's so cold out here today." Abby pulled Emma over to the fireplace and took her jacket from her. "I'm so happy you're here... and surprised. My Emma, taking a break in the middle of the week to have fun? Are ya feeling alright?"

Her friend stopped to look Emma over.

Emma laughed. "Yes, I am well. Thane just thinks I work too hard, especially with Jade being all pent up in the cabin."

"Jade? Is that the puppy Thane got you?"

Nodding, Emma sat on the chair Abby held out for her.

"Jade is the happiest girl. She looks like she is smiling at you all the time. Her eyes shine like the brightest jewels." She sighed before she continued. "But she also knocks the water buckets over and grabs bread off the table before it can even cool. Grabs laundry out the basket and chews Thane's socks. I have a whole pile of things to mend because of her. Then today, she catapulted the washboard out of the tub and knocked the laundry about. I was so frustrated that I locked her in the barn. Then? When Thane returned home, we went to let her out. She got so excited she tried to jump on him and accidentally landed in the chicken stall. There isn't a single egg that wasn't broken." Shaking her head, she took the teacup Abby handed her. "But ya canna stay mad at her. She smiles up at ya with those beautiful eyes. Urgh."

After a moment of silence, Emma looked up at Abby. Her friend just sat there, watching her.

"I'm sorry. It has jest been so long since I heard ya tell a story. I forgot how much I enjoy them."

Emma remembered Mark's comments at Christmas. "Mark told me the same thing at Christmas. I didna realize anyone liked hearing me talk."

"Oh Emma. Ya could always take the most dreadful tale and turn it into the funniest thing the way ya told it. I didn't realize how much I loved them until you stopped telling them."

"I stopped?"

"Yeah. When your mama got sick. Your stories stopped. Until today. This Jade sounds like a source of many good stories. I can't wait until you can tell them to my little man."

Emma laughed. "Are ya ever goin' ta call that little man by his name?"

Abby and her husband had finally decided on a name for their son, but she had called him by the pet name for so long that Emma doubted she would ever be able to stop.

"Of course, I will. When little *Thomas* wakes up, he will be so happy to see you." Abby took a sip of her tea to hide her smile. "What about you? Have you picked names yet for your little girl?"

"No, we have na. An' only God will be knowin' if this young life is a boy or a girl."

Abby smiled.

Emma knew what Abby was thinking before she even opened her mouth to talk.

"I was right about my little man. I knew." Abby smiled with confidence. "You'll be havin' a daughter."

Laughing, Emma looked down her stomach. "Ya hear that? She says yer a girl." Feeling her friend study her face, Emma looked up again.

"How are you doing, Em?"

"Oh, I feel well enough now," Emma took a deep breath. "I jest worry that I'll na know what I'm doin' as a mama."

Abby laughed. "None of us really know. But you had a lot of practice with Seth. Ya'll be a sight better than I was."

"I do na remember Seth as a baby, though. As a pesky kid toddlin' around, yes. But diapers and feedings? It'll all be new."

"Well, it is a lot of work. After a while, it begins to feel like ya always knew." Abby reached forward to squeeze Emma's hand. "What else is worryin' ya?"

Emma stared into her cup for a moment. "I do na know why, but there is this part of me that canna forget that both my mom and Thane's mom died bringin' a baby inta the world."

"Oh, Em." Abby put her cup down and knelt by her friend's chair. "Yer Mama was sick for a long time before she had your sister. And ya know nothin' about Thane's Mama. You aren't sick. You're strong. You are always telling me that God has us in His hands. You have to have faith that He will take care of you."

Tears filled Emma's eyes. "Yer right. I canna borrow worries that may never happen." She squeezed her friend's hand, so thankful that Thane had suggested a visit. She remembered months back when she had avoided Abby. It seemed so long ago. "Now. Tell me what your Thomas is doin' now. Is he ready ta go work at the mill with his papa yet?"

Abby laughed. "Of course not. But he is holdin' his head up. And you should see my little man turn his head toward people. Almost as if he is listening to what they are sayin'. He is so smart." Rising and settling back in her chair, Abby told Emma every detail of little Thomas's day.

A hearty cry from the other room let them know that the baby had woke from his nap. Abby rose to get him.

As she stepped from the room, a knock sounded on the front door.

"Could ya get that, Emma?" Abby called.

Emma could see Thane's face through the window as she neared. She smiled as she let him in.

"I'm sorry to cut yer visit short, Emma. But the temperature is starting to drop. I don't want ya to be caught in a storm." He retrieved her coat from the hook by the door and held it out to slip around her.

"It was a wonderful visit. Even if it was short."

Abby entered the room with Thomas. "Oh. Must you be goin' already?"

Emma crossed the room to hug her friend. "Thane says it's getting colder. But I'll come again soon." She kissed Thomas's head. "You take care of yer mama, little man. Let her sleep tonight."

Thane held the door open for Emma. The sky was dark, and the air felt heavy. "Are ya warm enough?"

Emma nodded. "Was James able to help ya fix yer trap?"

"No. But he does think it was pried with a small tool."

"Tools? So, a man is doin' it?"

Thane lifted Emma carefully onto the horse's back.

"But why?"

Stepping into the stirrup, he swung his leg up behind her. "Stealin' furs is pretty common up in the North. I've jest not had a problem around here."

The ride home passed quickly. Emma couldn't talk to Thane because the wind was blowing too hard to hear. He pulled her close and tucked his coat around her shoulders.

Jade was barking as they approached the barn. Emma went to open her stall as soon as Thane lifted her down. She froze when she noticed the puppy barking at the floor.

"Thane?"

She felt Thane lean over the wall between the stalls, just as Jade stopped barking to dig at the floor.

"Whatcha got there, girl?" Coming around to them, Thane knelt on the ground and pulled the straw back. He put his finger in the crack Jade was the most interested in, and the boards swung up.

The barn went silent. Thane studied the hole in front of him for a moment before looking over his shoulder at his wife. "Do you have that pile of quilts out here still?"

"No," her voice barely above a whisper. Clearing her throat, she tried again. "I took them back inside."

"Can you go fetch them? We have guests, and they look cold."

"Runaways?" The memory of the little dark-skinned girl shivering in her barn flashed through Emma's mind, and she sprung into action. "I'll be back."

Once inside, she gathered the blankets and balanced the rest of her loaf of bread on top. When she stepped back outside, the wind took her breathe away. Trying to pull her coat closed, she hurried to the barn.

"Will they be warm enough out here?" Emma asked, concerned that she should gather more.

That concern was mirrored in Thane's eyes. "It is better than they would have outside." Handing the blankets and bread down into the hole, the shadow of hands reached up to take them. "Would ya care for some boiled eggs?"

Silence met his question. Emma began to doubt they would answer when she heard a deep voice. "We'd be obliged to ya, sir."

Thane nodded. "We'll bring some out to ya soon."

Replacing the boards, Thane spread the straw back over the door. He stood and went back to care for the horse. "Do we have enough eggs for now and for the morning?"

"How many are there?"

"Four."

Nodding, Emma went to check the nesting box and found a few more eggs. She headed to the house to boil all the eggs that she had. *Life must be pretty difficult for a man to take his family out in this weather to escape.* Rubbing her hands together, she warmed them over the flames. As soon as the fire was blazing, she swung the pot of water over the heat.

Taking the clothes off the lines, she dropped each item in the basket and then set them aside to iron after their meal.

Thane came in a short time later, bringing Jade with him. The puppy jumped onto Emma's leg and yipped at her before running off.

"Was the little girl with them? She wasn't dressed for this weather Thane."

He shook his head. "They aren't staying in the area, Emma. Just stopping here on the way North. Canada is most likely. Your girl is likely long gone to safety."

Nodding, she folded Thane's socks together. "It is such a cold night."

Thane turned Emma toward him and pulled her against his chest. "The heat from the animals will keep them warmer than being outside. And the barn will shelter them from the wind and weather." Running his fingers over her hair, he reassured her. "We can't bring them in, Em. If the deputies came here, the family would be in danger. The barn is the safest bet."

Squeezing her eyes shut, she knew that her husband was right. She breathed a prayer that they would be warm enough.

"The eggs will help warm them. They can keep the extra ones in their pocket, and it will be a little warmer for a while."

"I didna think about that. I cooked all 12 of them. Figured they needed them more than we did."

Placing a kiss on her forehead, he looked down at her. "You are right, of course." A smile crept onto his face. "I guess I can share those last few cookies. They need them more than I do."

"Thane, do you think they're the ones messin' with yer traps. Ta get the meat out?"

He looked thoughtful for a minute and then shook his head. "No. This has been happenin' for a while. These folks are just passin' through. I'll be lookin' for someone stayin' in this area." With another hug, he headed out. "I'm gonna walk the yard and make sure there are no tracks leadin' to the barn. The snow is startin' and will cover everythin' soon enough, but I don't want to take any chances. I'll be back for the eggs."

Emma watched her husband disappear from the window. *How can helping people feel so wrong?* Closing her eyes, she breathed a prayer for peace. She didn't stop until she could smell that the eggs were done.

Twenty-Six

"Do ya see that red sky?" Seth nodded to the window as he poured water into her washtub.

Thane had been gone for two days, resetting the traps on his line. Seth had been coming over to do the barn chores even though Emma insisted she could manage. But at that moment, she was thankful that Seth had ignored her. The wind had picked up that morning, and the house felt really cold. She had already broken the ice on the wash water since breakfast.

Emma moved to the window to see the vibrant color shining in. "Wow! That is a beautiful sight."

"It's gonna snow," Seth predicted as he brought in another bucket of water.

"Yes. Just like it snowed yesterday," Emma stated. "Along with the day before that. And the day before that."

It had been snowing so much that Thane had tied a rope from the house going to the barn. Just in case they needed it to guide them along the path.

Laughing, Seth set the extra buckets of water next to the fire so that they would get warm. "Da says that sailors prepare to battle nature when the skies are red in the mornin'. I'm thinkin' it'll be a sight more snow than yesterday."

Emma glanced out of the window. "You think so? The blanket of snow from yesterday will be making Thane's progress slow. More snow will keep him stuck."

"Yer husband is a smart man. He'll see that sky this mornin' and find a place to stay iffen he canna get home." Seth grabbed a cookie from the basket on the counter. "I'll make sure the animals have plenty of fresh beddin' jest in case the temperatures drop. Then I'll be headin' back." He slipped a couple of cookies in his shirt pocket with a mischievous smile.

Pretending to be annoyed, she shooed her little brother out the door. He headed to the barn with a bounce to his step.

Emma smiled at the sight. Seth might have always been extra work for her growing up, but she always felt his joy for life was contagious.

The snowflakes caught her eye, and she looked up at the red sky. Breathing a prayer of safety for Thane, Emma turned back to her laundry and pulled the door closed behind her.

The laundry didn't take long to wash. With Thane gone most of the week and it being so cold, they hadn't dirtied much laundry. Emma hung the last shirt on the line over the hearth, thankful that she did not need to wash blankets in the winter.

Emma pulled her shawl around her shoulders as a cold breeze went through the cabin. She had not realized how cold it had gotten while she worked.

Lifting the washtub, she headed to the door to empty it. When she opened the door, a solid wall of white greeted her. The snow was so solid she could not see the barn. Setting the tub on the floor, she quickly closed and latched the door. Wrapping her shawl tighter, she peered out of the window. The wind shook the window in its frame.

I wonder where Thane is? He'll be lost fer sure if he tries to travel in this. When the wind shook the window again, Emma shivered. *If he stays out there, will he be warm enough?*

She looked around the cabin for something to keep busy with. "I'll make a warm stew in case he comes home."

Speaking to Jade had become more common as the days without Thane grew. Jade tilted her head to one side as if she was considering her choices then barked once in agreement.

Emma laughed. Jade made her times alone more bearable.

Cutting a roast, she set it to browning while she cleaned up the potatoes. Even with her hands busy, she was distracted, worrying about Thane and where he was.

Movement caught her attention. Jade stood on her rocking chair and stretched to reach Thane's church shirt. "No, Jade!" At the sound of her name, Jade leapt for the garment and pulled it down with her as she fell. Emma called for her again, but it seemed to make the puppy more excited. She ran into the bedroom and leapt onto the bed. Her feet caught in the quilt and caused her to tumble onto the other side and fall to the floor. Jumping up, Jade ran under the bed pulling the shirt with her.

Emma could hear the happy dog's tail wagging against the ropes under the mattress. With a sigh, she knelt by the bed. "Come here, Jade. Drop it."

She couldn't quite reach Jade or the shirt. And no amount of calling was encouraging the dog to come out. Finally, she crawled under the bed and succeeded in getting a handful of the shirt. A burning smell reminded Emma that her dinner was over the fire. She shimmied from under the bed then hurried to the pot to save her stew from burning. She set the rescued shirt on the cupboard and pulled the pot back to sit on the ledge. So intent on getting the meat off the bottom of the pot while the heat settled down, she didn't see that the shirt landed right in the dishwater.

Looking around the room at the mess she had, Emma sank into the rocker and blew out a long breath. Jade pushed her nose under Emma's hand and smiled. Knowing she couldn't stay mad at the puppy, she scratched Jade behind the ears. "Well, little lady, this mess won't clean itself.

Wringing out the shirt, Emma set it aside. She poured water into the pot to cover the meat and swung the pot back over the fire. Then she finished chopping up the vegetables.

When all the vegetables were in the pot, she turned to Thane's shirt. She decided, with a thorough rinsing, it would be good as new. She set the washtub on the table and poured water from the bucket over the shirt. Wringing it out, she concentrated on carefully rinsing in a few spots. Then a final rinse before hanging it back in its place. She moved her rocking chair closer to the fire so that Jade wouldn't be able to repeat her game. She knew better than to let it become a habit.

As she wiped up the water on the floor, Emma realized how much colder the room was away from the fire. Getting her hands dry, she pulled her shawl back around her.

Jade walked toward the door and barked once. Her usual easy-going nature disappeared behind the tension in her shoulders.

"What is it, Jade?"

Jade looked up at Emma. Even her eyes weren't as bright as they usually were. She barked once and turned her attention back to the door.

Emma peered through the window toward the barn. She couldn't see anything beyond the swirling cloud of snow. The glass rattled against the wooden frame. Even though it was only midday, the sky was dark.

Her breath froze against the glass where she had leaned close. She used the edge of her shawl to scrape it off.

Jade's growl brought Emma's attention back inside. The dog laid on the floor in front of the door. Her ears were pulled back, and the hair on the back of her neck stood straight on end.

Emma turned back in the direction Jade was growling. The barn was hidden from view still. The wind gusted strong, shaking the cabin again.

She sighed. She did not want to go out in the cold. It was cold enough where she stood by the door. But she worried about the animals if Thane did not come home.

Thane had said he would be gone a couple of days this time. Staying up in the old cabin and working the line from up in the hills. That morning had been day three.

Jade barked again as if to hurry her along.

"Alright. Alright. No need ta bark at me. I reckon the mountain lions will be too smart ta come out in this weather. An' Thane did put up the rope fer such a time as this. It will be guidin' me sure enough. Right?"

Jade barked again as if to agree.

With one last look out the window, Emma sighed and then turned to get layered up. She pulled an extra pair of Thane's pants under her dress and tied them up over her growing belly. Buttoning up an extra shirt, she tucked the shawl close so it would stay in place. There was only one time in her childhood that she remembered it being so cold. Her mother had given her Seth's clothes to keep her warmer than the dresses would.

She smiled as she remembered her mom telling her that warmth was a greater gift than beauty. And how pride wouldn't keep her as warm as her brother's old work pants would.

Jade barked at the door again.

"I'm goin', dog." Emma sighed again. Reaching for her coat, she pulled it on. She only hesitated a moment before she reached for Thane's extra jacket and pulled that on as well. The cold pushed into the room through the door and made Emma shiver. Pulling her coat together, she realized the buttons would no longer close. Worried about her stomach sticking out into the cold, she looked around for a moment before seeing the small blanket on the back of the rocking chair. Pulling it over her stomach, she tucked it into the ties of her apron.

"Jade. Come here, girl." Emma tied the puppy to her coat. Jade made it difficult as she continued to scratch at the door.

As soon as Emma lifted the latch on the door, the door swung in and pushed against her. The wind took her breath away. Suddenly more thankful for the rope connecting the door to the barn, Emma stepped into the wind only to be pushed back inside. She stepped back in surprise and looked up into the face of her husband.

Thane stepped into the room and shut the door behind him. Pushing against the blowing wind, he bolted the latch down. The snow had blown in and left small piles next to the snow Thane's boots had tracked in. Only when he made sure the latch was secure did he turn toward Emma.

Emma smiled. "You're back!"

Thane smiled as he set his things down and pulled her into a hug. "Yes, I'm back. When I saw the sky this mornin', I packed up and set out fer home. Anythin' on that line can wait. I didna want to leave ya alone in this storm."

Emma pulled him closer and breathed him in. "I'm so glad. I was worried." She didn't realize how worried she had been for him until that moment as her whole body relaxed.

Jade barked again, jumped up against them, and then pawed at the door.

"Yeah. I hear ya, girl." Emma pulled away from her husband with a sigh.

Thane's smile turned into a frown as he looked at her outdoor clothes for the first time. "Where are ya goin'?"

"Jade keeps barkin' at the barn. I was headin' ta check on the animals. Figured I'd feed them while I was all bundled up."

Jade barked at the door as if to show Thane.

"Emma. Ya shouldn't be goin' out in this storm ta deal with the animals."

Emma looked out the window for a moment. "But Seth didna come tonight. I think it was too stormy. So, I was just headin'-."

"Seth didn't come because he knew it wasn't safe. The animals will be fine until morn."

Watching Thane's face, she saw the concern planted there. "But Jade was barkin' at the barn. What if the big cat came back?"

"The mountain lion? Then I really don't want ya out there." Thane grabbed the rifle off the wall and headed back out the door. "Hang your coat up. I'll be back in a few."

Annoyed at his tone, Emma hesitated. But she knew it was childish to leave on the extra layers just because she didn't like to be told what to do. *He is likely just worried*. She took a deep breath and blew it out as if she could blow her frustration away with it. She was surprised when she could see her breath in front of her.

Emma hung up her coats and pulled the blanket off her apron. Standing at the window, she tried to peer through the snow again. She couldn't make out anything. If she didn't know the barn was there, she wouldn't have guessed it. It was like being in a stormy cloud.

The wind shook the cabin again.

Emma shivered. Despite still having the shawl, she realized how cold she was. *I hope the baby is warm enough*. Wrapping the blanket back around her stomach, she felt a little warmer. She decided to keep on some of the extra layers.

With one last look out the window, she went back to her chair by the fire. Pulling the stew away from the heat, she stirred it and swung it back to stay warm. She leaned back in the chair, rocking as she waited for Thane.

The wind blew the fire as the door opened. Sparks flew everywhere, and Emma moved her legs away. Making sure none landed on her dress, she turned to Thane.

Thane stomped the snow off his boots before moving further into the room. Pulling the scarf off his mouth, he warmed his hands over the fire. "The air is so cold it hurts to breathe."

"Do you think the animals will be warm enough?"

Thane smiled at his wife. "They will be fine. I won't be bringin' the chickens in here. Or the cow. I'll need to bring in extra buckets of snow to melt for them, though. Eatin' snow would make them colder."

Emma nodded. Standing to move the pots off the hearth, she stopped when Thane grabbed her wrist. He stepped closer and pulled her to him.

"Emma. I never want ya to go outside if the dog is barkin'. Especially if you are here alone."

She opened her mouth to object, but he placed a finger over her lips.

"What I need ya ta do, is shoot the rifle into the air. It'll let yer family know ya need help. They'll come to you. It'll scare off any animals that don't belong here too."

"So, I canna go outside?"

Her husband shook his head.

"An' ya jest want me ta fire off the rifle?"

He nodded one time.

Struggling to keep a straight face, she sighed. "I understand. I guess you'll be patchin' a lot of holes in those shingles. Last time I checked, rifles don't take kindly ta bein' fired in the house."

It took a moment for Thane to realize what she said. With a low growl, he wrapped his arms around her waist and lifted her off the floor. "Someone needs to be tossed in the snowbank."

Emma laughed, knowing that she was safe as the wind howled. "I was jest repeatin' what ya told me to do."

"You know what I was meanin'." Her husband laughed in return.

"Yeah, I gathered."

Setting her on the floor again, Thane grew serious. "Promise me ya won't go lookin' for trouble when I'm not here."

Emma nodded. "I promise."

Thane kissed her head and then lifted her chin to kiss her properly. "That stew smells heavenly."

"It's ready ta eat."

"Let me bring in some snow ta melt fer the beasts, and then I'd love a bowl- or two."

Emma had their bowls dished up by the time Thane returned with the buckets. As they ate, her husband told her about his adventures in the hills.

The stew warmed them, but the room was getting colder. The snow Thane tracked in still sat in piles by the door, unmelted.

"I'd best sweep those piles outside if we want it ta warm up in here." His words formed clouds as he spoke.

"I'm na sure that'll be helpin' any." Emma washed the dishes quickly, not wanting her hands to be wet any longer than they needed to be. The temperature dropped further as Emma took the clothes off the line.

"It's so cold, my hands hurt." Emma cupped her hands together and breathed into them. "And my nose."

"Here." Thane took her hands in his and rubbed some heat back into them. "Let's get the rest of these down so ya can warm yerself by the fire." Once the last of the laundry was in the basket, Thane wound up the rope. "Are ya wantin' to iron these now?"'

"No. It's been a long day. They'll keep until tomorrow." She yawned.

Thane watched his wife for a minute. He cast a worried glance toward their bedroom. "I'm thinkin' it'll be too cold fer ya to sleep away from the fire tonight. But I don't want ya to sleep on the floor. What if we bring the mattress out here? And make up a bed by the fire?"

"I can sleep on the floor. Ya do na have ta wrestle that heavy mattress out here," Emma insisted.

Thane shook his head. "The ground will be too cold fer you and the baby ta sleep on."

"Alright. If you bring it out here, I'll make up a bed fer us."

With a kiss to her head, he turned toward their room to do just that.

Emma set the basket off to the side of the room. Then moved the table back to give the bed more space. Thane maneuvered the mattress onto the floor without getting too close to the fire. Then he went back to their room to scoop up the sheets and quilts.

"I'll go give this water to the animals. Then we won't be letting anymore heat out tonight." He grabbed two of the buckets and headed out the door.

Getting right to work, Emma shook out the sheets and quickly made the bed. Then adding wood to the fire, she had the room warmer by the time Thane returned carrying more buckets of snow.

Emma turned to wash the bowls they had set aside earlier, but her wash water was frozen solid again. She set about refreshing it, but Thane stopped her.

"Those dishes will be there tomorrow, no worse for sittin' fer a night. Come get under the quilts. We need to get ya warm."

Emma started to protest that it was still daylight, but Thane wouldn't listen. He set her in a chair and unlaced her boots for her. "I can take off my own boots."

"As I have seen you do every day."

With a smile, Emma leaned forward and kissed her husband's forehead. "I have missed you."

Catching her eye, Thane smiled. He reached up and tucked a curl behind her ear. "An' I've missed you." He leaned up and placed a kiss on her lips. A shiver passed through Emma's lips, and Thane pulled back. "Come on. Let's get ya warm."

Emma crawled into the sheets as Thane refilled the wood box. Then he crawled in with her. She leaned her head on his arm and pulled the quilts tight around her shoulders.

"How was your day today? Quiet?" Thane asked.

She laughed in response. "No, it wasna quiet. Seth was here before the sun was up, askin' for cookies. Jade snatched yer good shirt right off the line and drug it all over the house."

Hearing her name, Jade woke up from her place on the hearth and jumped onto the bed. Thane chuckled in Emma's ear as the dog trampled both of them to get comfortable. "It's a good thing she isn't full grown yet."

When Jade finally settled, they relaxed again.

"Now. Start again. And tell me everythin' that happened while I was away." Thane smoothed the hair back from her face, twirling a curl around his finger.

Emma smiled at the gesture. She started at the beginning and told him about every antic that Jade had done that day. She took extra care to make it funny so that she could feel Thane laugh.

Twenty-Seven

February 8, 1859...

Emma looked up when she heard a noise at the edge of the woods. She set the heavy bucket of water down and smiled as Thane stepped from the forest. Her happiness was replaced by confusion as a young boy followed her husband out of the shadows. Her eyes searched out Thane's as he stepped toward her.

Thane leaned down to kiss Emma on the forehead. Without acknowledging the boy behind him, he lifted the bucket of water by her feet and carried it into the house. She followed behind him and set out to prepare a simple lunch.

"You'd best be washin' up in the corner before you sit down to Emma's table, son," Thane spoke softly but with a firmness that Emma had never heard from him. Keeping her attention on the meal in front of her, she couldn't help but see the boy move to obey from the corner of her eye.

When the boy returned to the table, he sat with his head bowed and his hands in his lap. As Emma set the food on the table, she saw the thread barren material of his jacket and the hole in his left shoe. His attention perked up at the plate set before him. His hopeful glance went from the plate to Thane's face and then back to the plate of salted pork and bread before him.

Emma felt her husband stiffen beside her.

"Eat up, son," he spoke gruffly. "You have a lot of work to do to repay me your debt." Thane's words were firm, but Emma recognized the kindness in them. Once again, she searched her husband's face for a clue. His stormy eyes met hers, and he gave her a small smile. An array of emotions passed over his face.

Emma looked once again to the boy, only to realize that he had been watching her. "Ya'd best eat up. A growin' boy like ya will need it." She turned back to the cupboard to grab her own plate before she sat in her chair.

The boy looked at the food with torn interest. Emma could tell he was hungry, but still, he hesitated.

"What's on yer mind, son?" Thane asked, breaking the silence.

Looking up from his plate, the boy met Thane's gaze. He couldn't have been more than ten, Emma guessed. But she hesitated at the maturity in his eyes.

Clearing his throat, the boy turned his attention to Emma. "The food looks mighty good, missus. But I jest don't feel right, eatin' my fill when my family's so hungry back ta home." He nodded nodded to confirm his conviction.

Emma searched the young man's face. She could see traces of pride and strength around the underfed surface. When his eyes flicked back down to the food placed in front of him, Emma looked away so he wouldn't see the tears that filled her eyes.

Thane took a deep breath as he leaned back in his chair. "Well, son, the way I see it, ya'll need ta eat that food iffen ya plan on supportin' yer family. A weak man can't do a hard day's work. And ya'll be needin' ta work hard ta pay us back fer stealin' from our traps."

Emma saw the boy's head dip in the corner of her vision. She turned to Thane to protest, but his eyes asked her to trust him. Closing her mouth, she turned back to watch the boy nod.

Moments of silence passed as no one at the table moved.

Finally, Thane leaned forward to take his first bite of food. "Emma? Would ya happen ta have an extra loaf of bread this week?"

Emma did not often make extra bread because it was wasteful. But something in Thane's voice made Emma feel like it was important to agree.

Thane took another bite of food, chewing as he thought through his next words. "Emma, would ya be willin' to trade a loaf of yer bread to this boy, iffen he has time to muck the chicken stalls? After he does his work fer me?"

The boy's head jerked up.

"Would save me a mighty backache," Emma answered. She was curious as to why Thane was giving the impression that she cleaned the stalls. Instead of questioning him, she continued, "I'd be glad fer the trade."

"Do you agree ta the trade?"

Nodding quickly, the boy's eyes sparkled.

"Then ya best eat up, so you've time ta finish yer work, son," Thane stated, starting in on his own food again.

"Avery," the boy corrected, stuffing a big bite of bread in his mouth.

Emma and Thane paused to look at him.

"M'name's Avery," the boy explained.

Thane nodded in understanding and continued eating. Emma looked toward her husband and caught his wink. A smile sprang to her lips. She wasn't sure what was going on, but she knew that he had it under control.

When Avery had cleaned his plate, Emma reached for it to refill the food. Reading her thoughts, Thane put his hand on her arm. With a shake of his head that Emma barely saw, Thane turned to the boy.

"Emma. Avery admitted that he has been stealin' animals from our traps fer quite some time. He claims it's ta feed his sisters," Thane paused for a moment and locked eyes with the boy. The boy did not look away. "Avery and I decided that he would come back here and work off the damage he has done to my traps."

"But, Thane," Emma started to protest but stopped when he held up his hand.

"Avery, why don't ya head out to the barn. I'll join you in a minute."

Standing immediately, Avery headed to the door. "Thank ya fer the meal, missus," he called over his shoulder.

When the latch clicked shut, Emma turned to Thane. "Thane, they are starvin'," she started before he interrupted.

"Emma, I need ya ta trust me on this."

Hurt flashed in Thane's eyes. Hurt that she would doubt him. Closing her eyes, Emma bowed her head. "I'm sorry. I do trust ya. I always trust ya."

Thane reached over and pulled one of her hands up over the table. He pressed a kiss to her palm then wove her fingers between his. "There were many times as a kid that I went without food. Many times, I thought stealin' would be the answer. But then, somehow, I always found food before I needed ta steal."

Emma felt her throat tighten at the thought of Thane being hungry as a child.

"I think God sent this boy ta steal from our traps fer a reason, Emma."

"Then why not jest help him feed his family?" she asked, needing to understand.

Thane nodded slowly. "That would seem ta be the most neighborly thing to do." Pausing for a breath, he squeezed her hand. "Avery is goin' ta be providin' fer his sisters fer quite some time. But he won't be an adorable young man forever. Underfed boys draw pity and charity. But underfed men? Underfed men look scary- and'll get rifles drawn on him. Or worse."

Emma knew this was true. She felt her chest tighten. "What will ya do?"

Thane smiled at her. "We'll let him keep his pride. Let him work off his debt." Standing up, he pulled her to her feet. "Then I'll teach him ta provide fer his family himself. How ta hunt and find work."

"But he's so young," she protested. "He should be in school."

"He isn't as young as he looks," he said softly. "They've been strugglin' fer some time. Even before his mom died. School can wait."

Pulling her close for a hug around her growing belly, he kissed her head. "Can ya put together a basket to send home with him? More than just the bread? But not too much-," he interrupted her before she could protest. "-not too much. If they eat too much food, after they have gone without for so long, they will get sick, Emma. Trust me."

Taking a deep breath, she pulled away with a smile. Through the tears in her eyes, she put her hands on his cheeks. "I trust ya. It jest hurts me ta think of kids strugglin' so."

Thane gave her another smile and then headed for the door.

"How many sisters, Thane?"

He paused with his hand on the door. "Avery said five. There were six, but they buried the baby before they buried their mama."

She swallowed past the lump in her throat. "Are they all younger than him?"

"No. He has one older," Thane turned back to her. "We will help him, Emma. I promise you. But I want ta help him the right way. So, make him up a basket of food... and I'll follow him home ta see what else he might need." Sadness showed in the smile he gave her as he once again headed out the door.

Closing her eyes, she breathed a prayer for peace. Then she set about making up a basket of food to send. She paused only briefly at the cookies and instead went to fetch a jar of jam.

~*~*~*~*~*~*~*~*~*~*~*~*~*~*~*~*~*~*~*~

The sun was dipping down behind the trees before Thane brought Avery inside. "These winter days are mighty short. Avery has promised to come back tomorrow to finish what he started. He looks like a man of his word, so I told him he could take the bread he would have earned home to feed his family."

Avery looked anxious to Emma.

She smiled to set him at ease. "I made up a basket of goodies for yer sisters. I'm happy ta have new neighbors."

Thane reached into the basket and pulled the towel-wrapped loaf of bread and handed it to Avery. "You can carry the bread you earned. I'll carry the basket and bring it back home to Emma once it's empty."

Avery started to protest, but Thane kissed Emma on the forehead and left through the door, leaving the startled boy to hurry in order to catch up.

Emma followed them to the door and watched the two walk into the woods. *Please, Lord, help this young boy and his family.*

She turned to start a stew that could simmer until Thane returned.

Twenty-Eight

February 21, 1859...

Thane pushed his plate back. "I need ta see yer Da this morning. Is there anythin' ya'd like me ta take over with me?"

Emma waited to see if he would explain why he needed to go see her father, but his silence told her he didn't plan on it. Breathing in slowly, she nodded. "I should send some of these cookies for the boys." Placing a towel at the bottom of the basket, she set cookies in the bottom and covered them for the journey through the woods. She wanted to walk with him, but her feet had been hurting more and more by the time night fell these days. "Tell Mark ta eat his first. Iffen he wants any at all."

"I think Mark knows that lesson by now." With a smile and kiss pressed to her hair, Thane carefully stepped across the porch and headed in the direction of her family's farm.

Jade chased after him, but as soon as her feet touched the icy boards, her front paws slipped, and her face hit the porch. Trying to right herself so she could catch Thane, she pushed up with her front legs, only to knock her back feet out from underneath her. She struggled to get up on her feet and seemed to run in place for a few seconds, until her feet slide in different directions. She landed flat on her stomach, facing the door that she had just come from. Jade looked up at Emma with a look that seemed to beg her not to tell anyone.

"Aww. Poor girl." Emma tried not to smile but it was hard. "Come on, back inside with ya."

Jade pulled herself up to her feet. Placing her feet carefully, she managed to walk across the icy porch and back into the house.

With a glance to see that Thane had disappeared into the woods, she turned back to her chores for the day.

Emma started heating water over the fire. She wanted to get the laundry washed and hanging to dry before lunch so she could get some sewing for the baby done. As she rubbed her sore back, she was startled by a soft knock. She dried her hands on a towel and moved toward the door.

Avery had been coming to work on the farm for over a week. Thane had found him in the barn working before the sun was even up, but he never came to the house without Thane.

Opening the door, Emma saw Avery standing there with a small toddler in his arms. The child was wrapped tightly in a blanket, but the blanket did not look like it held the cold out. Behind him stood a couple of girls, the oldest huddling a cold baby against her chest.

"Come on in, Avery," Emma hurried them in to stand by the fire. "These must be your sisters?"

"Yes, missus Hawkins," Avery answered. He sounded out of breath. "Mister Hawkins asked me ta bring my sister today ta be helpin' ya with the laundry. But my sister couldn't come without the little uns."

"Of course, she couldna," Emma replied automatically, wondering why Thane hadn't mentioned asking the girls to come.

"Right on time," Thane called to Avery, as he opened the door. Hands full with a crate, he kicked the door closed behind him. "Emma, yer Da sent some laundry ta be mended. That Seth is awful hard on clothes."

Emma's smile waned a little. So much for getting some sewing done. She reached out for the crate, but Thane's raised hand caused her to pause.

"Linsy here told me she is mighty quick with a needle. Yer Da said if she passes yer test, Emma, he'll pay her to do some mendin'."

"Linsy?" Emma repeated as she turned to the sisters surrounding Avery. The oldest girl gave a clumsy curtsy.

"I'm Linsy, missus Hawkins. My mama taught me ta mend. She knew I'd need ta know how." The girl never raised her eyes to meet Emma's.

Emma met Thane's eye over the crate of clothes. Rachel had been doing the mending, so the size of the pile surprised her. "Even Seth doesn't tear that many clothes."

One side of Thane's mouth tipped up. He started to pull a few items off the pile. Underneath, Emma saw her old coat peeking out and a pair of worn boots.

"Linsy, Mr. Wells offered to pay ya in cash for your work. Or in trade for a few items he no longer needs." As he laid three coats of varying sizes over the back of the chair and set the boots on the table, the girl raised her eyes to stare at them.

Emma recognized one of the coats as one that Rachel wore to do chores outside. She felt tears fill her eyes and turned away.

"And in this crate are some vegetables. If you and Kay are willin' ta help my Emma with the laundry today, I'll carry this home fer ya tonight. I figure it would go mighty fine with the meat that Avery's been trappin' fer ya." The room was quiet as the kids looked to each other. Thane walked to Emma. "I was hopin' ta surprise ya with free time ta be sewin' fer our little one."

Emma smiled up at her thoughtful husband. "That would be wonderful."

"Well, Avery, all that's left for us is ta haul in more water fer the ladies, and we can get ta our repairs." Avery handed the toddler in his arms to Linsy and followed Thane out the door, leaving the girls to an awkward silence.

Emma cleared her throat. "Well, Linsy, I'll set ya up ta do yer mendin' job while the water is heatin'. Do ya think ya'll want the coats or the cash fer yer work?"

"We'll take the coats, ma'am. If that's all right, missus Hawkins." Linsy replied in a small voice.

"Oh, please call me, Emma."

215

Thane and Avery brought in buckets of water for the washtub and went out to refill them to use for rinse water. Then they bid the girls good'bye until dinner.

At first, the girls didn't utter a sound and the silence was strange. Finally, Emma started singing hymns to fill the air. The little ones listened and watched. Soon, Emma heard the small voice of Kay join hers and she smiled to encourage her.

She looked around the cabin for something for the kids to be entertained with but didn't come up with much.

Emma checked over Linsy's mending and found her stitches to be small and even. "Very nice," she complimented her.

Linsy nodded once. Emma thought she saw the trace of a smile before it disappeared.

When the water was hot, Linsy put the mending down and helped Kay scrub the clothes.

Seeing that they had it under control, Emma sat down to finish the sleeping gown she had started for the baby. When it was finished, she held it up to show the girls. "I'm tempted to be puttin' lace on the trim," she said with a wink. "But only the Lord in heaven knows if Mr. Hawkins will be havin' a son or a daughter."

Linsy looked up. "A son will be a bigger help to him than a daughter."

Emma paused at the words. *Had someone made her think girls were not as needed as boys?* "My Da used ta say he'd be lost without his girls." Pausing, she thought carefully. "But sons and daughters are each a blessin' to their parents in their own time."

Without agreeing, Linsy went back to scrubbing the last few items in the tub.

As she cut out the next garment for the baby, she watched the girls work. "So Linsy is the oldest. But then comes Avery? Or Kay next?" Emma knew the answer but really wanted to get the girls talking.

Kay answered for them, surprising Emma. "Then comes Avery. Then me. Then Sarah," she pointed toward the little girls playing near

216

the fireplace, "-then Nettie... and then Betty, of course. Betty's the one with red hair like mama."

Emma smiled. "Those are all beautiful names."

The girls smiled at the compliment and then fell back into silence. All three older girls worked together to get the wash rinsed and wrung out before the noon meal.

All work and no smiles. Emma gave up on trying to get them to talk. She went out to get a portion of the venison to slice thin and set to frying. Once the meat was browned, she added water and some vegetables. Stoking the fire under the tall legs of the pot, she left it to cook. She figured it would be done about the same time the girls finished clearing away the washtubs.

~*~

Emma watched Kay move the baby to her other hip, just before stepping into the woods. Little Betty's legs dangled low enough to hit the bottom of Kay's dress. *She is too big for Kay to be carryin'*, Emma thought with a frown. But she also knew it was too far for the baby to walk. Avery and Linsy couldn't help because their arms were far too full.

Linsy waited for Sarah to lead Nellie behind the others and disappeared into the trees as well. "We shoulda asked Da fer the wagon."

"Wagon won't make it ta where their cabin lies."

Thane had offered to walk along with them and carry the heavy crate, but Avery and Linsy refused. They insisted they would be able to manage easily with their new coats.

The memory of them arriving in the thin blankets sent a shiver down Emma's back. "Thane?" Turning away from the kids, she looked up to search his face. "Why didna ya tell me they were comin'?"

"I wasn't sure they would come."

She paused for a moment. Hurt. "Ya coulda still mentioned that ya offered it ta them."

Silence hung in the air. Emma watched the emotions roll through her husband's eyes. Da's words echoed in her ear. *Patience.*

"Patience?"

"Oh." Emma didn't realize she had said the word out loud. "Da reminded me that *Love is Patient*. I'm tryin' ta be patient. An' tryin' ta wait fer ya ta be sharin' yer thoughts with me. Ya go off inta the woods and go off ta Da's house. Sometimes I donna know what yer thinkin' from one minute ta the next." She smiled up at him. "I'm na askin' ya ta ask my permission ta do these things. I jest want ta know what yer thinkin' on- where yer mind takes ya. I want ta share in yer worries- and yer joys. Yer thoughts. Not jest the good times. But the good, the bad, sad, and frustratin' too. I love ya, Thane Hawkins. An' I want ta be sharin' this life with ya."

Thane pulled Emma into his arms and pressed his forehead to hers. They stood there in silence for a moment. "I went ta ask yer Da how I could find work fer these young'ns ta support themselves. We talked fer a little. He came up with the mendin'." Emma waited for him to continue as the silence lay between them. "I'll work on tellin' ya my thoughts. But I am guessin' that ya've been worryin' on this fer some time." He pulled back from Emma and lifted her chin.

She could see the emotions in his eyes. "I have. But Da told me that I need ta remember that love is patient and that it will na fail. So, I've been prayin' on it."

Thane nodded. "Seems we've both been goin' ta Da?"

"Seems so."

Studying her face, he remained quiet for a moment. "It feels like I'm always doin' things wrong. Livin' this close ta people, I don't know everyone's rules and the way things are here. I didn't want ya ta worry about me. So, I've been talkin' ta yer Da about the duties of a man." He raised his hand to tuck a curl behind her ear. "Perhaps we should agree to have our talks with Da and pray about our worries. But then tell each other what we are worryin' on. I'm thinkin' it's like the animals trapped

218

in my snares. Even if those animals knew ta stop strugglin' and remain calm, they'd still need help from someone else ta be set free."

Emma put her hand over Thane's and pressed it to her cheek. "I'll tell ya about my thoughts. And I'll ask ya about yers."

Thane kissed Emma's forehead. "And I'll talk so much ya'll be beggin' me ta be more broody."

Emma laughed then. Rising up onto her toes, she kissed her husband. "Love is patient. Go ahead and test me."

Twenty-Nine

March 14, 1859...

Sparks flew everywhere as the log popped and split in the fireplace. Emma stepped back and shook her skirt to see if any of the sparks were stuck in the folds. "I do na need more holes in this skirt."

"Hold on. Ya missed one." Avery rushed forward to kneel beside her. He held out her skirt edge to flick a coal back into the fire. Licking his fingers, he pressed them onto the burnt hole in her skirt. "Ow!" He stuck his finger back in his mouth and sucked on it.

"That water is pretty cold. Best soak that burn." Emma pointed to the bucket on the table. Taking her washrag, she pressed it to the hole to make sure the fire would not make it bigger.

Avery put his hand in the bucket and grimaced. "That is cold."

Chuckling, she shook her head at the boy. "The fire's too hot. The water's too cold."

Smiling, he watched as Emma made him a plate of breakfast. "Missus Hawkins...?"

"Please, call me Emma."

"Missus Emma...?"

When he paused, Emma turned to him. He looked down at his food and didn't seem ready to finish his sentence. Yet, he made no move to pick up his fork either. "Yes?"

"A few days back..."

When he didn't say anything else, she prompted him to continue. "Go on."

Squaring his shoulders back, Avery met Emma's eyes. "A few days back, I was cleanin' the stalls. And- Jade kept pawin' at the boards and I thought she broke the wall. I tried ta fix it but– I found another door. When I opened it… I found a family down there under the barn."

"I see," Emma wasn't sure what to say. Her attention drifted to the barn but was brought back to Avery as his voice wavered.

"Those lawmen said they was lookin' for *'thievin' slaves*, and I know I shoulda told ya when I found 'em down there. But…"

"But…?"

"They didn't look thievin'. They looked like they was starvin'." Avery met her eyes, begging her to understand. "They was likely the same slaves. They all had dark skin. But they never said it was a family. I saw that family huddled together in the dark. Shiverin'. When I saw those deputies again- I- I couldna turn them in," Avery bent his head. "Should I have turned them in? After I knew where they were?"

"Hmm… Do ya feel Thane should have turned you in to the authorities for stealin'?"

He thought for a moment before he shook his head. "No. But there is more."

Emma waited for him to speak.

"They looked so hungry. I gave them my breakfast bread… and- and a couple of eggs from the chickens." The young boy looked up then and bravely pulled up his shoulders. "I know they weren't mine to give but I remember feeling that hungry. And I didna know if ya'd want them there. But I shoulda asked ya. I'm sorry."

Kneeling in front of Avery, she squeezed his arm with affection. "I'm proud of ya for tellin' me, Avery. And from now on? You can feel free to be generous to any starvin' people ya find in that barn. Sound good?"

Avery nodded with a smile.

Thane stepped through the door and stopped. Looking from his wife to the young boy, he raised his eyebrow in question.

"Avery here was just confessin' that he gave his morning bread... and a few of our eggs... ta some extra guests we had in our barn." Standing to her feet, she continued. "And he explained that he didna tell the deputies where they were stayin' when they questioned him." The fact that the deputies were still around worried Emma.

Thane roughed up Avery's hair. "Good man."

The praise brought a smile to the boy's face.

"Now, eat up before your food is cold." She dished up food for Thane and set it before him. "Was it a man and wife with small children?"

Avery answered around his food. "Twas two little boys with their mama. They was all pretty young."

"I'm guessin' that this farm was bein' used for the underground slave path ta Canada while it was abandoned," Thane seemed deep in thought. "When did ya find the family, Avery?"

"Last week. Day after my sisters was here."

"They *were* here." Emma corrected.

Avery's fork froze in the air. "That's what I said."

Emma shook her head in amusement as he resumed his eating. He reminded her of Seth at times. Especially when nothing could pull his attention from the food in front of him. But Seth has never known hunger like this boy. The smile on her lips faltered. Even after all the food they had given him, the boy still had shadows under his eyes. She pulled the bacon off her plate and slipped it onto Avery's plate as she sat.

Thane caught her eye. His own gray eyes were full of concern.

She wanted to ask him what was worrying him, but her husband flicked his attention to the young boy sitting with them.

"Well, Avery. You and I have some work ta do today if we are ta be ready ta work those furs tomorrow." He stood up and put his plate in the wash water.

Avery shoved the last of the food on his plate into his mouth and pushed his chair back. Pulling his hat down over his head, he nodded to Emma. "Thanks for breakfast, Missus Emma."

"Avery." Thane's tone stopped the boy in his tracks. He gestured with his eyes toward the plate left on the table.

Avery looked at the plate in confusion. Finally, he looked back at Thane and shrugged.

"The best way to tell Mrs. Emma thank you is fer you ta put your plate in the washtub." He indicated the tub with a flick of his hand.

"Why? That's... girl's work."

The corner of Thane's mouth curled up into the lopsided smile that Emma loved. "That may be. But the way I see it? Mrs. Emma can keep makin' us piles of delicious food ta eat- which is a lot of work fer her. Or," Thane held his hand out toward Avery. "she could start makin' us porridge. And who knows if she'll find it in her heart ta put brown sugar in it?"

Avery blinked as he looked from Thane to Emma. Looking down at the plate on the table, he squared back his shoulders and passed the plate to Thane's waiting hand without another hesitation, then almost bolted from the room.

"You'll have him terrified ta forget ta help me now," Emma said in amusement as soon as the door latched.

Thane took his wife's hand and pulled her to stand. "You work too hard fer us boys fer us to not do our part." He leaned his forehead against hers for a moment. "Besides... you give that boy all your bacon."

When she started to protest, Thane chuckled. Placing a kiss on her lips, he turned to leave.

"Thane?" She waited until he looked back. "How did I get so lucky ta love ya fer all my days?"

"I am the lucky one." He kissed her again and then disappeared through the door.

~*~*~*~*~*~*~*~*~*~*~*~*~*~*~*~*~*~*~

The sun shone down on Emma's face. She closed her eyes as she turned her face up to catch the warmth. The tightness in her boots brought her attention back to her job at hand. Shifting her weight, she tried to ease her discomfort.

The promise of spring seemed to be all around her, but Emma knew it wouldn't last long. She was using the lapse in snow and wind to get some jobs caught up. With the rugs beaten and the quilts aired out, she stepped into the barn.

Sighing, Emma knew that her chores would have to be done soon. Her feet were really starting to ache. More than she could push through. Searching the nesting boxes, she put the eggs in her basket and headed toward the house.

The last few steps to the house were excruciating, and Emma sunk into the chair right inside the door. Working quickly, she unlaced her boots and slipped them off. Sliding off her stockings, her feet were swollen and unsightly. She tried to rub them, but her growing belly made it uncomfortable.

With another sigh, she hobbled to the washtub to scrub her hands. Drinking a full glass of water, she decided to lay in her bed and prop her feet up. *Just for a few minutes.*

~*~*~*~*~*~*~*~*~*~*~*~*~*~*~*~*~*~*~*~

Emma woke to the sound of men talking and horses outside her window. Rising, she was pleased that her feet didn't hurt as bad as earlier. *I must have worked too hard.*

Hobbling to the front rooms, she did not have time to put her stockings and shoes back on before the door opened. An elderly but elegant lady breezed inside. She paused for a moment at the sight of Emma standing there and frowned at her bare feet before she continued.

"You must be my grandson's wife. I am Mary Preston." She turned away without waiting for an answer, opening the door further. "Bring the trunks in. Yes, set them against the far wall. My grandson will move them into my room when he arrives."

Emma shook her head to get the sleepiness out. "We have the room ready for you now if ya'd like your trunks put in there." She moved back and opened the door to the second bedroom.

Mary studied Emma for a moment before stepping forward. With a quick glance in the smaller room, she moved across the walkway and stepped into the larger room.

"I think this room will hold my things better. And it will allow space for a second bed once the baby is here." Turning around once more, she nodded. "We will leave the trunks in the main room to give you a chance to move your things to the other room."

Emma was stunned. "This is the room that Thane and I share."

"Yes. I can see that," the older lady replied. "But if I am to care for the baby, I will need this room because of the extra space it provides."

"I plan on keeping our baby in our room for the time being," Emma stopped herself frustrated. "Thane will be home soon. Would you care for a cup of coffee?"

Mary studied Emma. "I will brew some tea. It is plain to see that it was difficult for you to even dress today. I would not want to trouble you."

Closing her eyes, Emma prayed for patience.

"My wife was up and workin' long before the sun rose this mornin'. So havin' someone pamper her with tea would be a welcome break."

Emma opened her eyes to find Thane standing in the doorway, holding his hat.

Mary turned with a gasp. "Thane?" Her eyes filled with tears. "You look so much like my Annabel."

Thane moved forward to shake her hand, but his grandmother pulled him in for a hug. She hung on tight before planting a shaky kiss on his cheek.

Emma reproached herself for being frustrated with this woman. She obviously was looking forward to this moment.

He looked down into his grandmother's face with his lopsided smile for a moment longer before he stepped back. Putting his arm around Emma, he smiled down at her. "You've met my Emma?"

Mary nodded. "I have."

Not knowing what to say, Emma just smiled up at Thane.

"Why do I find ya both in our bedroom?" He asked, confused.

Emma looked toward Mary.

Instantly, the older woman was in motion. "We were discussing which room would be easier for me to care for the child in. Obviously, it makes more sense for him to be in with me for nighttime feedings and such. This room has more floor space for the extra bed and trunks. Maybe even a set of drawers."

"The baby?" Thane watched his grandmother move about the room. "I think the baby'll need ta be close ta her Mama fer quite some time."

Thane's grandmother sighed. "If only it were that simple."

The room fell into an awkward silence for a few minutes.

Finally, Emma cleared her throat. "I can care fer one baby easy enough with the help of Thane."

Mary took a step toward Emma. With a firm shake of her head, she explained. "No. You won't. For you will never survive the curse. And when a baby loses her mother, she will need someone other than her father to care for her."

Emma's breath caught in her throat.

Thane stepped forward, pushing Emma behind him. She leaned her head against his back.

"Ya can't come in here and tell my wife she's gonna die. We don't know what God's plan is. You can't know what God's plan is."

Thane's grandmother looked up into his face. With a sigh, she looked down. "I should have started at the beginning. Let me make us some proper tea. I will need to find the trunk it is packed in." Moving back into the main room, they noticed several trunks had arrived. "Then I will tell you all about the curse that has been taking mothers from their young ones since Annabel Douglas defied her father all those years ago. Defied him with fire flashin' in her gray eyes jest like they used to in my Annie's." Turning her own gray eyes to her grandson. "I imagine jest the way they do in yours."

With the tea located, Mary closed the trunk and turned toward the hearth. "I will say I did not miss this wretched thing." She took her gloves off, one finger at a time, while staring down at the cold fireplace with disdain. With a sigh, she set to brewing the tea.

The whole situation struck Emma suddenly. The invasion without so much as a knock, the large amount of luggage for one person, the request for the larger room, the announcement that Emma would die, and the desire for a proper tea. A soft chuckle escaped her lips.

Thane looked down at his wife with concern. Pulling her close, he studied her face.

Emma smiled to reassure him. "Your grandmother has finally arrived."

The corner of his mouth tilted up. "That she has."

"Do you have more kindling than this?" Mary asked, inspecting the basket of wood.

Thane leaned his forehead against Emma's. Taking a deep breath, he moved to start the fire.

Emma watched the two of them. The grandmother trying to interact with her grandson. The adoration was apparent in every look. But Thane moved stiffly, freezing under her touch on his arm. After a lifetime with no family, Emma could tell he was uncomfortable.

Turning from them, she pulled the cups down. She put a few cookies on a plate and set it on the table.

A cold breeze blew over her feet, and Emma realized she had not put her boots back on. Picking them up from where she had left them, she took them to her room.

When she returned, Mary was chatting about the weather over winter and the illness that detained her. Thane looked up as Emma entered the room and shot her a grateful look. She patted his shoulder as she passed him.

Mary poured hot water into the teapot and hung the kettle back on the arm over the fire. Placing the teapot on the table to seep, she sat next to Thane.

"A long time ago, our Douglass Clan lived in Scotland. Along the family line, there was a girl, daughter to the Laird and Lady. She was named Annabel. All the stories say she was fair of face. Dark curls and blessed with clear skin. No sicknesses had marred her beauty. And she had our same gray eyes."

"Now Annabel, they say, was promised to a young apprentice. The apprentice was nothing to look at. But he had done a great service to the clan leader. The stories changed over time. Who he was apprenticed to and how he helped the Laird change in each story, but what we know for certain is that he was an honorable young man, and the stories say he was mad in love with young Annabel."

"Misfortune has it that an English Captain was also madly in love with Annabel. He was ordered by the English king to squash a rebellion in the area and ran into her often. The Captain was friendly with the Clansmen and was invited often to eat at their table- not knowing that he had a growing affection for the girl."

"As for young Annabel? A powerful and rich man was showing her attention. A contrast to her shy, pox-faced betrothed. It was not long before she was torn. The Captain asked for her hand and was informed of the promised marriage. He left the highlands broken-hearted."

Thane looked toward Emma for a moment before turning back to listen to Mary.

"The stories say he returned with an edict from the King, ordering the Laird to allow the marriage to take place. Even promising lands in return for his continued help."

"The Laird refused. The marriage was a debt of honor that needed to take place. And everyone in the clan knew of the young apprentice's love for his betrothed. The Laird arranged for the marriage to take place that same day, instead of waiting for the apprenticeship to be complete."

"Annabel disappeared before the ceremony."

"Weeks later, she returned in a carriage. Married and coming to ask for forgiveness."

"Her family would not give it. What they did give her was a curse. A curse that the Bible promised them. That her sins and the sins of her husband would be visited upon three generations of her children and their children."

"Annabel left broken-hearted. Months later, she died in childbirth. They say her shame had made her weak. The curse had already taken effect."

"Annabel's captain was heartbroken. He returned the baby girl to the Laird and his Lady and begged them to raise her. The baby girl who was the spitting image of her mama was too much for the captain to see."

"So, the Lady raised the baby to understand that it would be her responsibility to break the curse for their family."

Mary paused to pour the tea.

Emma looked toward her husband. He was deep in thought as he reached for the cup his grandmother passed him.

"When Annabel's daughter reached of age, she was promised to her mother's apprentice. He was no longer a young man but still owed a debt. They married and had a daughter of their own. A girl with dark curls and gray eyes. Theirs was not a love match, but they did well in life, and the clan prospered. It's said that the land flourished, and the flocks doubled as the girl grew.

"Annabel's daughter raised the girl to understand her duty. But no matter how much they explained the curse, the girl- Annabel's granddaughter- was rebellious against the marriage the Laird had arranged for her. When her betrothed arrived with his clan to celebrate their marriage, the girl disappeared with the stable boy."

"They say that the lands shriveled up and nary a drop of rain came down until a year had passed. It's said that the day that stable boy returned with a baby, a girl with dark curls and gray eyes? That very day, the skies opened and watered the highlands again."

"Annabel's daughter raised her new grandbaby to understand the great suffering her mother had caused. She grew and married whom her grandfather chose for her. And again, the clan prospered."

"But try as we may? The Douglass women could not get three generations of daughters to marry honorably. My mother and I almost made it. We both did our duty. And I named my baby Annabel, to finally come back to where fate started us. To finally cleanse our family of this curse once and for all. My Annabel was a joy to us, but she was stubborn. She insisted she would be honorable but refused to marry without love. When her father promised her hand to a prominent businessman, a man that would have made her very comfortable, Annabel refused to honor it. She apologized to the man but insisted she would not marry where there was no love."

"I tried to reason with her and told her love would come later. Still, she refused his attentions. As a result, her father lost his position, and the bank called in our mortgage. And still, Annabel refused to marry the man." Mary paused to sip from her teacup.

Emma felt Thane's eyes on her and turned to meet his gaze. She could see the emotions churning in those gray eyes. Offering him a smile, she reached out to hold his hand. He squeezed it in return before turning back to Mary.

"We were forced to sell all that we owned and move west. Hoping to start fresh out here where no one knew of Annabel's ruined reputation. We arrived here in this town, built this cabin, and tried our hand at farming. However, we could not get anything to grow.

"One day, a young man came across my husband in the fields. He suggested they bury fish along each row. Said that he had seen the Indians do it when they planted their fields. The young man had a mangled hand, yet he helped William, your grandfather, catch enough fish to fertilize the whole field.

"A very nice young man, your father. Annabel did not pay any attention to him at first. But one day in town changed all that. Suddenly, the two of them were asking William for permission for Nathaniel to court Annabel.

"William refused. He explained that while he was a nice young man, he wouldn't be able to support a wife and family with only one hand.

"Annabel was furious with her father. She was convinced he was punishing her for refusing to honor his wishes in Vermont. They quarreled. Annabel was so sure that he would change his mind. When the months went by, and he did not? They slipped off to elope without so much as a word.

"We were frantic as we searched for her."

Thane squeezed Emma's hand then. Emma glanced toward him, remembering a time when the town was searching for her.

Mary continued, "Eventually, everyone stopped searching. Everyone except her father. One morning, Mrs. Wells came to keep me company while William searched."

"Mama," Emma whispered.

Looking up in surprise, Mary nodded. "I can see Lilianna in you. I had no idea." She looked thoughtful for a moment before continuing. "Your mama sat with me, and we prayed for Annabel to return. And then Annabel walked right through the door. While I was still hugging my daughter to me, William returned. He was so relieved at first. But those two always clashed.

"Annabel asked us to forgive her. But her father couldn't forgive her for leaving without so much as a note. She insisted she had left one on the chest in her room. But I never found a letter. In the months since she'd been gone, I had cleaned her room so many times. Hoping for a clue. There never was a letter. Annabel left in tears, and I never saw her again," Mary paused, sorrow filling her expression.

"Months later, Nathanial returned with a baby. And the news that Annabel was gone. He asked us to keep the child, a boy, until he was older. William refused. Said if the child was truly Annabel's, that the curse would die with him. In grief, I denied that the child was hers. There had never been a boy born to the Douglass Clan since the first Annabel had brought on the curse. So, I reasoned that this baby could not be from our blood. And I let them walk away."

"How I wished them back. How I wished you back. Your face haunted my dreams."

"William would not stay here after that day, but he insisted on keeping the house. So, we boarded it up and headed into the city. We found good work there and had a good life. But it felt empty. When William died, I set my mind to find my grandson. When a young man wrote to me asking to buy my farm, I decided it was time to make a trip out here to find you myself."

Mary leaned over to pat Thane's arm. "Then to know they found you and me being to sick to travel. I was so impatient to get better." The smile slipped from her face. "When they told me of your young bride, I knew I needed to hurry. I heard of the way you stole her away in the night. I expect you knew no better being raised in the woods by your father. But you-," she looked to Emma, shaking her head, "you would have been better off marrying your betrothed. That would have been an honorable marriage."

Emma felt Thane stiffen and pull his arm from his grandmother's grasp.

"Thane didna steal me away. But he was there ta protect me. He is honorable-." Cut off with a wave of the older woman's hand, Emma felt her impatience grow.

"You have to see the curse at work here, Thane. You and I need to make ready to raise this child to set things right with God."

Emma felt her husband's arm tense again.

"I'll not have ya scarin' my wife with tales of death from a curse. Whatever past you and yours had, it has no effect on my family."

232

"But my family is your family." Mary reached for Thane's hand only to fall short as he pulled it away.

Thane stood. "If you insist on carryin' on with this curse talk, I'll ask you to leave."

Mary's face hardened.

But Thane held his hand up to prevent her from continuing. "And iffen you're gonna say that the gift of this farm comes at the cost of scarin' my wife into dyin' while bringin' our daughter into the world, then you can keep yer farm. We'll be packed in an hour and on our way."

No one spoke as Mary digested what Thane had said.

Finally, the lady sipped her tea and smiled. "Of course. This all comes as a shock to you. We will leave it all in the Lord's hands."

Emma refused to give in to the need to shiver. The chill in Mary's attempt at a smile did little to lighten the ominous mood. Looking down at the forgotten tea in her cup, she realized she didn't think she could stomach it. Breathing a prayer for strength, she rose to start cooking the evening meal.

Thane rose as well. "I'll move your trunks into the extra room. First, let me move my mother's trunk out of your way."

"Actually," Mary stopped him. "Just move the small one. The room is too small for all of them. Just leave Annabel's trunk in there. I'd like to see her things again."

Pausing to think it through, he turned to Emma. "Will the trunks be in yer way where they sit?"

The trunks were piled against the far wall. Emma shook her head. The room was small, but they wouldn't be in the way where they sat. "They'll na bother me there."

Mary smiled then. "You speak just like your mother. How is she?"

Realizing how long Mary had been gone, Emma hesitated for a moment. "Mama died awhile back. A sickness made her weak. It took her and my baby sister from us."

The sadness that filled the elder lady's gray eyes took Emma by surprise. They looked so much like Thane's eyes at that moment. As frustrated as she was with the chaos Mary had brought with her, Emma remembered that this woman was Thane's family. A link that he had been looking for. And she seemed to have a fondness for her mama. *A greater fondness for my mama than fer her own Annabel.* Shaking the negative thought aside, Emma breathed a prayer of forgiveness and set about making a nice meal for Mary.

∾Thirty∾

April 28, 1859...

Emma caressed her feet for a moment longer before sliding them into her boots. With a sigh, she stood to tidy the kitchen from breakfast.

Her feet had been hurting so much lately that Emma had chosen to cook breakfast without boots on. But with Mary staying with them, she knew the older lady would be up soon. And she would be ready with her disapproving looks at the bare feet. *Besides, with the menfolk coming to help, I'll need to be running to the fields.*

The day before, Emma had spent hours baking bread and cookies for the men to eat. Baking cookies in spider pans was not as easy as using the oven at Da's. The long legs of the pan kept the cookies from burning. But even with the biggest of the pans, Emma could only make six at a time. It made for a long day over the fire, bending and lifting. By evening, her back and her feet were aching.

When Thane and Mary had arrived home for the evening meal, Emma could barely stand. Her husband had insisted she sit in the rocker and prop her feet on a crate. She could feel Mary's disapproving gaze as Thane waited on her.

Shaking her head to clear her thoughts, Emma turned her attention back to washing the last few dishes.

As she dried the last plate and set it in its place, she heard Thane's grandmother stir in the other room. Knowing she would want tea, Emma swung the kettle of fresh water toward the fire. Setting cups on the table, she got everything out that Mary would need.

Mary opened her door and headed straight for the outhouse. Looking over her shoulder as she stepped outside, she saw what Emma was doing. "Oh. Emma dear, I'll just have coffee this morning. No need to make a fuss." Pulling the door closed behind her, the older lady disappeared in the direction of the outhouse.

Emma watched her leave, then closed her eyes. Breathing a prayer of patience, she began putting the tea and sugar in their homes again.

Swinging the iron arm away from the flame, Emma put in the coffee beans and returned it to the heat. By the time Mary returned, the water was already boiling. She sat at the table and pulled her shawl around her shoulder. "Brrr, the days can be so beautiful this time of year. But the mornings can still be a bit frigid."

Emma started to plate up the breakfast she had kept warm for Mary, but Mary waved her away. "Oh, you mustn't make a fuss for me. I won't have you serving me when you are so tired all the time. I'll just cook something in a little while.

Her hand froze a little way from the table. She set the plate on the cupboard. "That's ok. Avery'll be here soon. He can never get enough to eat."

The door creaked open, and Avery stuck his head through. The impish smile that spread across his face hinted to Emma that he had heard her statement.

"Mornin', Missus Emma."

"Good mornin', Avery."

"Would ya have any breakfast left? I'm real hungry this taday."

Emma fought to contain her smile. The wink he gave her reminded her of Seth. *Likely from spending the last few days with him in the fields.* "Jest so happens I have some left." Heaping the last helping onto the plate that she had offered Mary, she placed it in front of Avery.

With the first fork full of eggs, Avery made a satisfied sound. He continued to fuss and compliment the food with every bite until Mary gave an annoyed sigh and excused herself.

As soon as Mary's door latch slid into place, Avery quickly finished the rest of his food in silence. When he rose to give Emma his plate, he cocked his head to one side. "I don't know why anyone would turn down a meal from ya. I haven't eaten such a tasty meal since my own mama passed. Thank ya fer always makin' sure I'm fed."

Avery settled his hat on his head in a way that reminded Emma of her Da and gave her a nod before disappearing in search of the menfolk.

Emma watched the boy trot across the farmyard for a moment before closing the door.

Mary came out of her room with her coat and hat on. "Well, I must go into town today. I need to check the post.". She left without any other comment.

Watching the door close behind Thane's grandmother, Emma breathed a prayer. *Lord, fill me with patience fer this lady. I'm na understandin' her at all.* She took a deep breath and felt peace flow through her. Turning away from the door, she set to work.

The rest of the morning was filled with preparing a big meal for when the menfolk would come in. She figured a nice soup would warm them and be ready whenever they finished. She sliced some bread and lay a cloth over it to keep it soft and fresh.

Peeking through the window, the yard looked quiet. So, Emma stepped out. She took in a deep breath of fresh air and decided to pull her rocker onto the porch to rest for a bit.

No sooner had she sat, Avery ran into sight.

Emma groaned. She had hoped she had a moment to rest her feet before the men wanted their meal.

Avery didn't notice her disappointment as he stopped in front of her. "Emma, guess what?"

Noticing the absence of the usual "Missus" in front of her name, she was curious. But she didn't answer fast enough before Avery continued.

"Well, ya never will guess. So, I'll jest tell ya. James came again taday ta help dig rocks. An' he's always praisin' how hard of a worker I be."

"Am-," Emma corrected.

The boy didn't notice the interruption. "Jest a few minutes ago, when Thane asked me ta fetch the water before you made the trip out with it?"

Guilt crept in as Emma realized she forgot all about the water bucket.

"Well, James stopped me, an' he offered me a job blacksmithin'!"

"Blacksmithin'?" Emma echoed. The hot forge seemed a dangerous place for a young boy.

"Yeah!" He confirmed with excitement, not noticing her worry. "I'll be his apprentice!"

Emma didn't know what to say.

Avery seemed to feel her disapproval then. Stepping closer, he knelt in front of her.

"Don't ya see, Missus Emma? I'll be able ta provide fer my own family. We won't be hungry anymore."

Pride shone from Avery's eyes.

Emma remembered the defeat and shame that this boy had felt when he first arrived, stumbling through the trees behind Thane. Hungry and afraid. The confidence she saw as he knelt before her made her heart ache.

Realizing that he was waiting for her approval, she cleared the emotion from her voice. "Well, of course, James would want ya ta work with him. Such a hard worker is hard to come by."

A smile erupted onto Avery's face.

Emma put her hand under the boy's chin. "Promise me that ya'll be careful in the shop."

Reaching up to squeeze her hand, he nodded. "I will. Thane always tells me ta mind where my fingers are."

Thane had told her that his father's mangled hand had always reminded him to be careful. It seemed he was passing that caution on to this boy in front of her.

Emma smiled. "So, you've come ta fetch a water bucket then?" Rising from her chair, she went inside to the kitchen.

Avery followed her. "Seth said ta remind ya that you promised him cookies."

A laugh escaped her. Handing Avery the empty bucket, she reached for the basket of sweets that she had prepared. "I'll carry the sweets while you draw some water from the well, my little blacksmith."

Her words won her a full smile from the boy. He ran to the well while she closed the door behind her. Wrapping the shawl closer, she headed to the fields. Avery caught up before she had gone very far.

"I'll be missin' yer breakfasts every mornin'. My sisters don't rise before I leave."

Emma smiled over at him. "If ya stop by tomorrow before ya go ta James' I'll send some sweets and bread ta go with what he feeds ya."

"Thank ya, Emma. I mean, Missus Emma."

Smiling again, she assured him. "*Emma* is jest fine. No need for the *Missus*."

With a nod, he hurried ahead to pour his water into the drinking bucket on the wagon. The men had all drank a dipper full of cool water before she made it the rest of the way.

"Finally!" Seth cheered as he reached for the basket.

"Finally?" Emma pulled it away from his hands and raised her eyebrow.

Changing his expression to one of a pouting boy, Seth begged her. "Please, Em? Thane said ya baked my favorite molasses ones. I have na had them in so long."

"Rachel jest baked those for ya last week," Mark reminded him.

"Yeah, but that was Rachel. Nothin' beats Emma's cookies," Seth winked at his sister.

Emma laughed and handed the basket to Seth. Just as he pulled it to him, Mark tapped the back of Seth's head.

"Rotten kid," Mark muttered. "I'll tell Rachel ta na bother with spoilin' the likes of you."

Seth laughed and dug through the basket. Pulling out a handful of the molasses cookies, he thrust the basket toward their father.

Da simply shook his head as he watched his son's antics. Then taking a cookie off the top, he handed the rest to James. When James returned the basket to Emma, she put a hand on his arm to stop him.

"Thank you," she said, her voice soft so Avery wouldn't overhear. When he squinted in confusion, she continued. "Thank you fer what ya did fer Avery."

His eyes widened. With a nod, he touched his hat and returned to work.

Thane stepped forward with a question in his eyes.

Smiling, she offered him a cookie as she explained. "Avery came ta the house, fair ta burstin' with pride at the thought of his new job. I jest wanted ta thank James."

Thane nodded in understanding.

"And you- I'm glad I trusted you. You said that holdin' him responsible for his actions would be the best thing for him. Ya've changed that scared boy into a man. I couldna be more proud of you, Mr. Hawkins."

He smiled at the affectionate way she used his formal name. "Well, I couldn't do it without all of these delicious cookies, Mrs. Hawkins." Pressing a kiss to her hair, he smiled down at her. "I better take another one before Seth comes back fer another handful."

She laughed and held out the basket. He took one off the top and headed back to the field.

When Mark stepped in front of her, she jumped in surprise. "Oh! I didna see ya there."

He smiled. "I'm na surprised. I didna want to interrupt your sweet moment. But I couldna pass on a sweet treat this mornin'."

240

Laughing at his teasing, she held out the basket once more.

He smiled at his sister and grabbed a few. "I'll take a couple ta Avery. His head is too far into the clouds to remember mere hunger." With a nod, he headed back to where the men were digging.

Watching her brother hand a cookie to Avery, she smiled then headed back to the house to check on her soup. With the men having their snack, they would likely be another hour or so before they would want a meal. That gave her time to prop her feet up.

The rest of the afternoon went by fast. The men came in for their meal and left a pile of dishes for her to wash. But even that task was easy as she thought about the laughter and teasing around her table. Most of it had been aimed at poor Avery, who had not stopped smiling all day.

When she heard the wagon roll into the yard, she set her sewing aside and went to wave to everyone. Not seeing Da in his wagon, she assumed he was in the barn. When no one came out for quite some time, Emma headed in that direction.

Stepping through the doors, Emma overheard Thane talking. "I'm jest not sure what ta make of this curse. She really seems ta believe in it."

Emma brought her feet to a stop at the words. Wondering what her father would think of the nonsense, she waited for his reaction.

Da nodded as he continued to work the leather in front of him. Quiet settled around them. "Our Scottish people love a good story, fer sure and fer certain. And a story wouldna be complete without superstition or a curse- often fueled by strong drink." Wiping the sweat from his brow, he leaned against the stall post. "I'm no' an expert, fer that ya'd have ta ask the reverend what that verse means by *three generations*- but the God that Jesus teaches us about, wouldna be punishin' kids for their parents bein' a little headstrong. Otherwise, there'd be a whole lot of bairns runnin' around without someone ta look after them. I do na think God woulda sent His son to save us- jest ta turn around and punish these young mamas. Doesna make any sense ta me.

Truth is… it's hard work bringin' bairns inta this world. Women have been dyin' from birthin' fer a long time- with or without a family curse."

Emma squeezed her eyes shut. *Dyin' from birthin'*. Thinking on the rest of her Da's words, she stepped closer to Thane's side.

Her husband saw her then and put his arm around her, drawing her closer. "At first I thought this farm was a blessin', but then it started ta feel like a curse of my own. It came with someone else's expectations. Things that I didn't know how ta do. I didn't know where ta begin. And then there were the people. So many people all the time. People tellin' me what ta do. People askin' me questions. And me not sure who ta listen to. Not sure who deserved an answer and who jest wanted ta gossip about us. Even the good people- watchin' me and hopin' that I do right by Emma. It was too much for me in the beginning." Thane paused and looked out the barn door, toward the hills. "It all felt like too much. And the peace of the trees was callin' me. So, I went ta search for my Pa. Search for some answers I needed about the past but also questions I had about my future." Thane looked back to Emma then. "I know that ya only know the worst of my Pa. An' what ya saw was horrible. But he could be pert' wise when he wasn't deep in the drink. And we'd always been close. He's all I knew."

"Of course, ya'd go ta him, son." Da agreed.

"But when I found him, he was already deep in the drink, and my questions didn't help. Questions about Clara, and this grandmother. He muttered about a curse- which I thought was nonsense. But now I realize he made perfect sense." Thane gave a short laugh. "It makes perfect sense now. But in that moment, I thought I was goin' nowhere with gettin' answers. So instead, I jest sat with him. Explainin' my worries, while he drank. I was hopin' that he'd give me some advice on what I should be doin'. But in the end? He just muttered, *Emma is home*. Which I already knew. That's when I realized I might be wastin' my time. I decided to try again the next day. But when I returned ta talk ta him, he was gone. I looked for him again, but I was missin' Emma."

"Son," Da stopped working then, stepping closer to Thane, "Yer Pa gave ya the best advice of all. Ya jest didna know how ta listen yet. *Emma is home.* Emma was at yer home, fer sure, but she also *is* yer home. The home for you. Wherever that girl of mine is? That is where your heart is. That is where ya belong. I saw that the first time I met ya. Yer Pa might be misguided about a few things, but he gave ya the best advice to all yer worries."

Thane's eyes widened. Emma saw how they glistened as tears gathered.

Swallowing hard, she felt tears gather in her own eyes. "Da's right. Yer Pa is right. Wherever you are? That's where I want ta be. And Thane? If ya'd rather be in the hills, trappin'? Not bein' a farmer at all? I'll go with ya. I married ya knowin' that ya were a trapper. None of that has ta change, jest because someone gave ya a farm and people expect ya ta use it."

As Thane turned his face down to look at his wife, the tears escaped down his cheeks. "Ya have no idea how beautiful those words are ta me. I'll not back down from this challenge. I want ta try my hand at farmin' this land. But knowin' that ya'll accept my decision if it doesn't work makes it easier somehow. Yes, Pa was right. I should've seen it. Ya are my home. That is the answer ta everythin'."

Da stepped forward with tears of his own. Putting a hand on each of their shoulders, he kissed Emma's head and then kissed Thane's too. "I couldna be any prouder of you two. Your road together might na be easy. But if ya walk together? Ya'll get there."

~Thirty-One ~

May 20, 1859...

"Once we get those last stumps out that field will be cleared." Thane pointed in the direction he meant.

Emma could see the stumps in the far corner of the field. She couldn't believe that they had cleared almost to the creek.

When her eyes settled on the berry bushes there, she smiled. Thane had been careful to avoid the berries so that they would have them for jam. While she was looking forward to making jam again, mostly those bushes reminded Emma of the first weeks of getting to know Thane. Losing those bushes would have been like losing memories.

The baby kicked, bringing her attention back to the present.

"Yer Da suggested that I jest farm these fields this year. So, if I can get these stumps out today-."

Thane was interrupted as Jade ran between them, pushing them apart. A few feet in front of Jade was a squirrel scrambling for its life. The dog was close on its tail when the squirrel changed directions, climbing a post of the corral and easily leaping into the tree next to it. Running up the trunk, it raced across the branches and jumped into the next tree. Jade was oblivious to the squirrel's continued journey. She dutifully stood at the base of the first corral post, barking her accomplishment for the whole barnyard to hear. Her tail wagging so hard it almost caused her to lose her balance.

They laughed at the puppy's antics. Thane touched Emma's arm and pointed to a tree. "Look." The squirrel sat on a branch watching Jade. "It doesn't understand what happened either."

Emma shook her head in amusement. "I think we can check hunting off her list."

"Yes. It's a good thing I know how to trap varmints. If I was counting on this ole girl, we'd be empty-handed." He reached out and pet Jade behind the ears.

Jade's eyes shone, smiling from ear to ear.

Suddenly, Jade turned and darted between them again.

Emma turned to see Avery walking up the road.

Thane met him and shook his hand in greeting, the same way he shook David's when he saw him. Emma hid her smile at the way the boy pulled his shoulders back. The confidence she saw in the young man was a nice change from the scared boy that first sat at her table.

"Good mornin', Avery," Thane greeted him.

"Mornin', Thane. Mornin', Missus Emma." He touched his hat in a salute to her.

"What can we do fer ya?"

"I wanted ta see if ya need help clearin' that last field. Otherwise, I'll be headin' back home and see what help Linsy needs."

Thane nodded. "Ya sure that James does na need ya today?"

Avery paused for a moment, looking from Thane to Emma. "Did ya not hear?"

"Hear what?" Thane asked.

When Avery didn't offer up any information, Emma prompted him. "What should we have heard?"

"Well... yesterday we had a horse with a temper somethin' awful. He was teachin' me how ta clean the feet, but I got too close ta its hindquarters. And well? He pushed me out of the way in time- but it caught him in the head."

"James got kicked?" Emma barely got the words past the lump in her throat.

Avery shook his head. "No. No. It was Mr. Abernathy. He was teachin' me."

A gasp caught in her throat. She remembered Mr. Abernathy sitting at their family table last summer. A nicer man was hard to find. "Will he be alright?"

The young man shrugged his shoulders. "The midwife lady says she won't know until he wakes up- if he wakes up."

"Midwife?" Emma was confused about why the midwife was there.

"Doc is out of town. Someone had an accident, but they don't know what direction he went in. So, they fetched Widow Clem, and she came ta stitch him up." When neither Emma nor Thane responded, Avery continued. "David was sitting with James this morning. He told me James wouldna be working taday."

When Thane turned to her, Emma wiped the tears off her cheeks. "Thank ya fer lettin' us know, Avery. I'm sure your sister has chores for you ta help with."

"She sure does. Wants me ta work in the garden fer her." He stepped in the direction of the woods, then stopped and looked over his shoulder. "Oh yeah, the lady at the mercantile said to say that yer stove was delivered." When he saw Thane's scowl, he froze. "Oh yeah. She also said it was a surprise."

"A stove?" Emma echoed. She looked from Avery to her husband.

Thane ran his hand through his hair and balled his fist in frustration. With a sigh, he looked up at Avery. "Thank you, sir. That'll be enough help fer today. Go help yer sister with her garden."

Avery gave an apologetic smile to Thane then ran into the woods.

"A stove?"

"Yes. A stove. Abby was goin' ta have ya over fer tea when it came in so I could set it up. Well- yer Da and me. I don't want ya cookin' around the fireplace with a young baby. I thought this would be helpful. We wanted it ta be a surprise."

Emma smiled when she thought about a cookstove. *No more bending over.* The smile had barely formed before she remembered Mr.

246

Abernathy's injury. *Seems silly to be happy about a stove when James' pa is barely alive.*

Thane wiped the tear that ran down her cheek and pulled her close. "You don't have ta feel guilty for a moment of happiness. James' pa wouldn't expect that."

Surprised, Emma lifted her head. "How did ya-?"

The corner of Thane's lip lifted. "Emma Hawkins. Every emotion ya feel, flashes across your face."

Another tear drifted down her cheek. "I love you." The simple phrase didn't come close to the feeling she felt when she looked at her husband. But Emma couldn't find any other words to describe how happy she felt at that moment. How understood she felt when she was with him.

"I know," Thane said simply. "I can see that flash across your face as well. Like the brightest sunshine. And knowin' that sunshine's jest fer me? There are no words ta describe that feeling."

Thane kissed his wife's upturned mouth. With a sigh, he smiled. "Next ya'll be askin' me ta take ya ta James' house. So ya can see if you can be of help."

"Hmm. Did ya see that on my face as well?"

"No," he kissed her again, "but I know yer heart almost as well as I know my own. I knew that ya'd be wantin' ta go as soon as Avery explained what happened."

"But yer stumps?" Emma reminded him.

"I reckon those stumps have been there twenty years or more. One day more won't make a difference."

Thane headed to the barn to saddle the horse. Emma watched him for a moment before heading into the house for a shawl and a bonnet.

When they arrived at James' shop, everything looked dark and quiet. Feeling strange, Emma turned toward the house next door. She couldn't remember ever going to James' house. He had lived there with his pa ever since she could remember. She always knew where they lived. But whenever she had followed Mark to find James, it had always been to the blacksmith shop.

Stepping up to the door, Emma felt uneasy. When she hesitated, Thane put his arm around her side and pulled her close as he knocked.

"It feels weird ta look fer them here," Emma explained. "They are always in the shop."

Knowing what she meant, Thane nodded.

David opened the door. "Hello, Thane. Emma."

"We came as soon as we heard.".

Backing up, David let them enter the room.

The kitchen was small but clean. The sitting area was filled with another table. Tools and unfamiliar things were spread across its surface.

"James has been trying to finish some work while his pa sleeps. He doesn't want to be far away, but he hasn't been getting much done." David explained when he saw her studying the extra table.

Voices from the other room brought their attention to the door in front of them. Emma looked around and realized it was the only door in the house.

Thane took her hand and led her to the door.

Emma saw the midwife and Sadie talking. James just sat in the chair next to his pa's bed, leaning his face into his hands. Mr. Abernathy lay in the bed with a bandage wrapped around his head. His coloring was pale.

"Check the bandage from time ta time. Make sure it hasna set to bleedin' again. Send fer me if it does." The midwife was gatherin' her things into her basket. "I donna understand the good Lord's timin', but I canna be in two places at the same time."

Sadie nodded. "Well, Maggie, I can sit here and watch this one sleep jest the same as you. An' I can send fer ya if he wakes." She paused as she noticed Emma enter. "Oh, child. It is so good ta see ya." She pulled her into a hug and then looked down at her hands. "Yer hands seem a might puffy. Are they like this every day?"

Maggie came close and took Emma's hand in hers. "Hmm."

"Somedays they are. Other days they are thin." Emma was uncomfortable with the attention on her. She looked toward the bed, hoping she hadn't offended James by drawing attention away from his father.

James had stood to his feet and looked concerned.

"I'm sure it's fine." Emma was embarrassed, pulling her hand away.

Maggie studied her. "Likely it is. But you can never be too careful." Seeing Thane standing close to her, she squinted at him. "So! You must be the husband who's finally come home. Hmm. Get yer lady some fresh meat when ya can. Too much salt meat won't be good fer her." She gave him another stern nod and left the room.

David spoke from the door. "I'll check in with you when I return, James." He shook hands with the menfolk then turned to leave.

Once the outside door was closed, James turned to Emma. "Are ya feelin' alright?"

Emma nodded. "Yeah, I'm well. Just a little swollen. How is yer Pa?"

James looked back to the bed. "He hasna changed. Jest lies there. So quiet."

"Is there anythin' we can do?" Thane asked.

Running his hand through his hair, James took a deep breath. "Well, Sadie here said she would sit with Pa so that I can finish a job I had promised. And I have a horse half-shoed in the barn."

"Can I give you a hand? Is it the same horse that injured him?"

James studied Thane's face. "'Tis the same horse." Looking back to his father once more, he nodded. "I'd be honored for your help, Thane. It'll make my work go more quickly."

"I'll stay here with Sadie. We can visit while we keep an eye on Mr. Abernathy." Giving them a smile, Emma sank into the chair James had been using.

The menfolk gathered a few things from the front room and exited to the attached shop.

"Haven't seen ya much this winter. How've you been?" Sadie had been missing from services a lot this winter. The times that the weather allowed Emma to go, she hadn't seen her. "It was a mighty winter this year. We were snowed in for many a day. But I was worried about you. Were ya ill?"

Sadie nodded. "I was ill fer a time. Then my horse was lamed. She seems ta be healed up now. Maybe it's the warmer weather?"

"Seems reasonable. Jade is happier now that it's warmer to be sure."

"Jade?"

"My puppy. Though she's close ta full-grown size now. She's still a babe at heart." A smile formed on her lips as she remembered her silly antics from that morning. "If somethin' is movin' around the farm, Jade is chasin' it. Or knockin' things over. Or draggin' Thane's socks off the line." With a laugh, Emma told Sadie how Jade had destroyed the house in the middle of a snowstorm along with the other happenings around the farm.

Emma thought about telling Sadie of the visitors in her barn, but a knock at the front door interrupted them.

Sadie waved Emma to sit back down as she went to see who it was.

"Good day to ya, Sadie. I brought James a pie and ta check on Mr. Abernathy."

Emma heard Mrs. Phelps's voice, followed by footsteps traveling across the front room. The thought of the mercantile owner approaching made Emma's heart sink. When Mrs. Phelps entered the door, Thane's grandmother was just behind her.

"Mr. Abernathy is much the same as he was," Sadie offered as she found a towel to cover the pie. "Widow Clem was called away and just asked me to sit a spell."

"Oh? The midwife is still here?"

Sadie nodded. "Until the doctor returns, she's Mr. Abernathy's best hope."

Turning, Mrs. Phelps's face lit up when she saw Emma.

Emma dreaded what would come next. She had stopped going to town by herself because visiting the mercantile had become so miserable. The older woman's comments had always been uncomfortable for Emma, but since she Thane had returned, Mrs. Phelps had criticized everything she did. So, she had started asking Thane or Da to take her to town. She knew they assumed it was the growing size of her belly but she didn't correct them.

"Good afternoon, Mrs. Phelps," Emma forced herself to say. Her voice came out softer than she had intended. Clearing her throat, she spoke up louder. "Good afternoon, Mary."

"Come now. Mary here has been tellin' me she is Thane's grandmother, come back. Surely, you should call her as much."

Mary dismissed the notion with a flick of her hand. "They'll become used to me, by and by."

Sadie entered the room. "I'd heard tell that Thane's grandmother had returned. Nice to meet ya in the flesh."

Barely acknowledging Sadie's greeting, Mary stepped closer to Emma's chair. "I'm surprised to see you in a sick man's room. You need to take better care, Emma dear." She patted Emma's shoulder. "We should get you home."

Clicking her tongue, Mrs. Phelps agreed. "Too true. Mary here already lost too many years with her grandson because her daughter was careless. You must be careful while yer with child."

Emma's heart dropped. She had hoped that Mary would not be telling others her idea of the curse. "I'm in no danger. Mr. Abernathy was injured. He isna contagious."

Sadie looked from Emma to the other woman. "Tis true. She is in no danger here."

"Sounds like our Emma is in danger anywhere." The mercantile owner clicked her tongue. "The dishonor that brought Mrs. Preston's family out to our community, when it was still new, was passed down ta yer young Mr. Hawkins when he was born inta their family." Turning to Sadie, she leaned close to explain. "Poor Mary's daughter was drawn in by Nathaniel Hawkins, that drunk. The curse that plagued her family sent her to an early grave. Isn't that the way of it, Mary?"

Emma met Sadie's eyes and hoped she wouldn't believe what the shopkeeper was saying. She had never cared for the gossip-mongering. Now that the stories were about her family, she cared for them even less.

"I'm afraid it is. My poor Annabel- if only she had chosen honor, she might be alive today. And my family would be rid of this curse. But I'm here ta help Thane now."

"A curse?" Sadie was curious.

"Mmm-hmm. Started by an ancestor in the old country. A young lady dishonored her clan and died, bringing her daughter into the world. Ever since that fateful day, the daughters that dishonor their family die, bringing their daughters into this world."

"Sounds like a good story to scare daughters inta listenin'," Sadie mumbled as she moved to check Mr. Abernathy's bandage.

"Well, it didn't work with my Annabel. She stubbornly chose her own path," Mary stated, "and she left her son here alone in the world. She would have been the third generation and would have been the end of it."

Sadie looked up. "Third generation?"

"The Bible promises us that the sins of the father will be visited upon three generations," Mary explained.

"Annie didna break any honor by marryin' Nathaniel. My Da said she wasna promised to another. He also said that Jesus wouldna be punishin' children fer the sins of their fathers."

Mary smiled at Emma. A smile that adults used on children. "Annabel was promised to another in Vermont. She refused to honor that promise. And I'll keep my trust in the Bible. No offense to your father."

"No offense taken. My Da said he was goin' ta talk ta the Reverend about it when he came ta town. That way, he had the right knowledge ta give ta us."

Mary look startled for a moment.

"Well, ya better pray the Reverend has an answer fer ya." Mrs. Phelps stated. "Otherwise, the ill-gotten way yer marriage came about will get you the same fate as poor Annabel."

"This is hardly helpful," Sadie protested.

Pulling her shoulders back, Emma stood in front of Mrs. Phelps. "I've always been a good daughter. Always prayed fer God ta guide me with what He wanted from me. So, if yer comparin' me ta Annabel? Then I reckon that means Annabel tried ta do the honorable thing too."

The shopkeeper was surprised.

Emma had never spoken harshly to anyone before. She wasn't sure why she chose that moment to speak out. The whole room was stunned into silence. Emma saw Sadie smile at her from the corner of her eye, but she also saw Mary was about to answer her. Her heart sank as she wondered if she was about to regret her words.

"Good afternoon, ladies." Seth stepped into the room.

Wondering how long he had been there, Emma moved toward him. "Hello, Seth."

"Em. Your husband asked me to see ya home as it's gettin' late." He indicated the front door.

Emma knew that it was a coward's way out to leave a conversation in the middle, but she was suddenly very weary. "Let me gather my things." She pulled her shawl around her shoulders and tied on her bonnet.

Sadie walked with her to the door, giving her a hug and a smile before she returned to the injured man's bedside.

Seth helped her into the wagon and clicked to the horses.

Once the town buildings were behind them, Emma turned to ask her brother what he had heard. The smile on Seth's face silenced her, though.

"Wait until I tell everyone ya took on that old biddy." The impish look made Emma ashamed of her words.

"I shouldna said those things ta her, Seth."

"She needed ta be set in her place, Em. And that grandmother? I always thought that grandmothers were supposed ta be kind old ladies. She's horrible. Tellin' ya yer gonna die?"

"Seth-," Emma started.

"No, Em. I willna be quiet on this. I'm proud of what ya said. There's nothin' that ya should be regrettin'."

Closing her eyes, she breathed a prayer. Prayer for what, she wasn't sure. Emma knew in her heart that she was still scared of dying while bringing the child in her belly into the world. She was putting her faith in God's plan. But she was still worried. Mary's talk of curses was making that worry come alive again.

But God is bigger than Mary. He has a plan for you. Who are you going to put your faith in? A small voice reminded her.

Breathing out, Emma prayed for God to take her doubts. *And forgive me for my worries.*

"Might as well say a prayer fer me too," Seth whispered into her ear. "I might have laughed a little... at the look on that woman's face."

Emma could hear the smile in Seth's words. With a raise of her eyebrow, Emma prayed aloud. "And Lord, please forgive my lil' baby brother. He wasna raised ta delight in another's pain, but he sometimes forgets it."

"Amen!" Seth chimed in.

"Amen." She echoed. Studying her brother's face, she saw how much he had changed over the winter. He no longer looked like a little boy. Even with the mischievous look on his face, he looked older.

He caught her staring at him and winked. "Did ya forget how handsome I was?"

Emma laughed. "Jest when I thought ya had grown up."

Laughing with her, Seth clicked to the horses to guide them onto the road to Emma's farm.

"Actually, Seth, could ya let me down here? I think I'd like to walk the last bit?"

"Whoa." Pulling back on the reins, it was his turn to study Emma's face. "Are ya sure?"

Emma nodded. "I need to stretch my legs. I've been sitting all afternoon."

Seth jumped down and helped her to the ground.

Her feet protested as she started walking, but she felt like it would get better as she walked more. Waving to her brother, she turned toward home.

Each step grew more and more painful. She was so thankful as she rounded the last bend. The house looked good as it came into view. She could not wait to go in and take her boots off. Swinging the door open, Emma went right to her rocking chair.

The swelling in her feet made unlacing her boots difficult, and she struggled to pull them off. Finally, she leaned back. She knew she should start cooking but she needed to prop her feet up for a minute. Closing her eyes, she sighed in relief as her feet relaxed against the crate.

It didn't seem very long before the door creaked open, and Thane stepped inside. His eyes took in the sight of her bare feet.

"Jest give me a moment, and I'll cook ya some supper. My feet are near ta burstin'." She smiled at her husband. "Did ya get James' work finished?"

Thane stood with his hand on the latch for a moment more before he closed the door. "Yes. Everythin' that was pressin'." Sitting on a chair near the door, he removed his muddy boots.

"Ya don't have to take yer boots off. I'll sweep it out when it dries."

"I'll not be makin' more work fer ya. Besides... you'll not be wantin' this soot to be stickin' to yer bare feet."

Emma smiled at her husband. He looked exhausted and yet was so thoughtful.

Setting his boots outside on the porch, Thane moved to kneel by Emma's feet. He moved the crate to one side so her feet could rest in his lap.

She pulled her feet away in protest. "I should be rubbin' yer feet. You're the one workin' long hours in the sun and fields."

Thane smiled and captured her foot again. Kneading the knots in slow circles. "I reckon you work jest as long and as hard as I do. With none of the company or help- except with sitting a spell with Mr. Abernathy. Not to mention growin' that wee one inside ya."

She relaxed her foot. Watching her husband's thumbs move in circles over her aching muscles, her mind slipped back to the times they would sit on Mama's hill and just enjoy the quiet.

Thane's thumb pressed on a tender spot, and Emma winced.

"Sorry." He paused for a second and then concentrated on kneading the spot softer. "I saw yer Da use a bit of liniment on his horse's leg when they-."

"I'm na one of my Da's horses, Thane Hawkins!" Playfully nudging his chest with her foot, she gave him a stern look before giving way to a smile.

Thane's mouth curled into the lopsided smile that Emma loved. Her breath caught the way it always did.

"Nay. You're not. But I'm wonderin' if it helps their swollen joints- it might jest bring some relief ta yer swollen feet." He continued to rub her feet in silence for a few moments. With a twinkle in his eye, he tilted his head to meet her gaze. "Come ta think of it. The only other animal that ever kicked me in the chest was a horse."

Emma laughed. Pulling her feet away, she sat up.

"Don't be upset-."

"I'm na upset with ya." Emma leaned forward, around her round belly, and pulled her husband's face to hers. Placing a gentle kiss on his lips, she looked into his eyes. "I love ya, Thane. More than I ever imagined."

The baby chose that moment to kick against Emma's ribs. She arched away from Thane to give the baby more room. "Hmmm. I guess yer baby said we were crowding him."

Concern passed through Thane's eyes for a moment until Emma smiled again. Rising to his feet, he leaned down to give her another kiss. "Well, I think she'll have ta get used ta me kissin' her mama. I don't think I'll ever tire of it."

The soft reminder that he thought the baby was a girl made Emma smile.

Seeing that smile, he gave her another kiss. Then he put the crate back under her feet. "You just sit yerself there. I'll cook tonight." Emma started to protest, but Thane just smiled at her. "Ut- Don't argue, Emma. You need ta rest."

Settling back into the chair, Emma watched Thane set about making the evening meal. Once the vegetables were in the pot and set over the fire, he knelt by her again. "Seth said my grandmother has been," he paused for a moment as he searched for the right word, "spinning some tales with the ladies from town."

Emma nodded. She hadn't wanted to speak badly of her, so she had not decided if she was going to bring it up with her husband.

He nodded to acknowledge her answer. His shoulders seemed to sag a little. "Were ya gonna tell me?"

When she hesitated, he nodded again. "Seth said ya tried to defend my mama."

"It just doesna seem fair fer her ta be tellin' tales on someone who canna defend herself," she hesitated a moment, "but it doesna seem fair fer me ta complain ta ya about yer family either."

Thane laced his fingers through Emma's and pressed them to his lips. "I can't imagine ya ever complainin' about anyone in a way that would offend me. But I can't imagine you tellin' me that someone treated ya poorly either." He pressed another kiss to her hand. "But I worry. I need ya ta be able ta tell me if my grandmother becomes too much."

Emma shrugged. "I jest pray for her when I donna know what ta do with her."

A slow smile spread across Thane's face. "Well. God probably knows a sight more than I would on how ta handle the lady." With a squeeze, he released her hand and went to check on the progress of his cooking.

Thirty-Two

May 28, 1859...

Snowflakes settled on the rug that Emma was beating. Her paddle paused in midair. Looking up at the sky, she saw that darker clouds had blown in. With the clouds, the temperature had dropped.

Emma's eyes swung to the far field. Thane was still working on the last stump. She could see him putting a log in front of the stump before adjusting the chain on the saddle. Squinting to see what he was doing, she thought she saw him give her a wave. Emma smiled.

Raising her paddle, she finished beating the dirt from the rug and carried it inside. The heat from the fire felt good. Emma didn't realize how cold she had gotten. She washed the dust from her hands and moved to the fire to warm herself.

The stew bubbled in the pot. Emma stirred it once and then sat in her rocker to finish the seam on the baby's gown. Her thoughts drifted to Thane's morning.

The stumps should have been pulled days before, but things kept going wrong. First, James' pa got injured. Then the chain had broken. It was an old chain, and Thane had needed to take it to James to repair it. She knew how Thane worried about bothering James with his repairs. Finally, that morning her husband had made good progress. Until Jade had planted herself too close to the horse. When the horse had stepped back at Thane's bidding, it had stepped on Jade's tail. The dog's yelp startled the poor horse and it jerked the chain from Thane's grasp. The horse didn't go far, but the chain had knocked Thane's hat off, grazing his forehead.

Coming in for his noon meal, Thane had a jumpy horse, a bruised dog, and a bleeding cut. Only to find that his wife had lost track of time while she cleaned.

Emma had felt terrible as she cleaned his wound. He assured her that he understood. But she felt disappointed in herself watching him grab some salt pork and a slice of bread for a quick meal.

Jade still sulked under their bed.

To make it up to Thane, Emma had put a stew together. Stew was his favorite meal on a cold day. She had cut up extra vegetables and meat to compensate for the missed meal.

Hoofbeats approaching brought a smile to her face. *That stubborn stump must have finally relented.* Rising from her chair, she filled the bowls and set them on the table.

Emma lifted her head as she realized the stirring outside was from multiple horses. Knowing Thane was alone that day, she moved to the door in curiosity. Opening it, a group of strange men stood in her yard. Jade appeared at her side, growling.

"Stay, Jade." Emma moved through the door and closed it behind her. Away from the house, she could see dogs being led around her barn on ropes. Hearing the dogs growl sent a shiver down her back.

One of the deputies rode his horse up to the porch's edge. "Hold 'em," he called to the men holding the dogs back. He lifted his hat in greeting. "Evenin', ma'am."

Emma heard growling closer. She looked down to see Jade standing between her and other dogs. Frowning, Emma realized Jade had not stayed in the cabin. It wasn't the first time she had darted out the door without Emma knowing. "Leave it, Jade." She looked back at the man. "What can I do fer ya?"

The dogs started snarling at the barn again. One almost broke free from the handler.

"Well, ya see, we've been trackin' us some runaways today. And our dogs tracked em right up to yer barn."

Emma's eyes drifted to the barn door. "There's no one in my barn. I've been here all day."

The man was quiet as he studied her. "There are laws against hidin' slaves."

"I'm aware of the laws. But I was jest in the barn, and there was no one there." Emma's voice was strong and didn't betray the emotions she was feeling.

The dogs were pulling at their ropes. Their lips were pulled back as they snarled. *Please don't let those dogs hurt anybody.*

"We're gonna need to search yer barn."

Emma walked toward the bell. "Let me call my husband in."

"That won't be necessary-."

"Actually, it is necessary." Emma looked toward the field to see Thane entering the yard. She let out a sigh in relief. He must have left his work when he saw they had company. Her husband didn't stop walking until he stood in front of her.

"What can I do fer you, gentlemen?" Thane asked.

The deputy focused on Thane. "Good evenin'-."

An approaching horse interrupted them. Everyone turned toward the road.

Emma recognized her brother as he pulled to a stop. Looking from his sister to the strangers in their yard. "We need all able-bodied menfolk in town. There has been another kidnapping, and we want to get on the trail as soon as possible. We do na want to make the same mistake we made the last time-." Mark faltered for a moment. He met Emma's eye. "Last time we waited too long. We could not track in the dark and we lost the trail. We willna do it again."

The trail? Emma's thoughts went to that dark night the summer before. "The creek."

"What?" Confused, Thane faced her.

"The creek. He took me along the creek," Emma repeated. The snowflakes were getting bigger as the light disappeared.

"The creek?" Mark thought about that for a moment and then nodded in understanding. Suddenly remembering the deputies, he returned his attention in that direction. "And what might you boys be doin' here? Surroundin' my sister?"

"We tracked some runaways right to this barn. We're about ta search it."

Emma stepped out from behind Thane. "I asked him ta let me call Thane in, and he refused."

"Refused?" Thane repeated.

"Well, that doesna seem very gentleman-like," Mark stated as he pulled his rifle from its holder and lay it across his elbow. "Would you all happen to be the same fellas that Sheriff is lookin' for? The ones that roughed up Widow Craig and almost torched her barn?"

"Sadie?" Emma gasped. Worry filled her for the older woman.

Thane stepped in front of Emma again. "Is that right?"

Smiling, the deputy balanced his elbows on the saddle horn, bored with the conversation. "Torched is a strong word. It was a little... singed."

Chuckles erupted behind the man.

"Besides, we only had to restrain her when she wouldn't cooperate," the deputy's smile widened.

Mark's fingers turned white as he gripped the gun. "Do ya enjoy preyin' on helpless women?" He raised his eyebrow in question. "My sister is anythin' but helpless. An' she isna alone here on this farm."

Thane studied the man before him. "Emma. From now on, you come outta the house with a rifle in hand and fire it off as soon as ya see these boys ridin' in."

Looking at Mark holding a gun on these men, Emma began to realize the danger she had been in. This stranger smiled at his misconduct. She realized there was no honor in him. "I will."

"Now, now. There's no need fer such precautions. We meant no harm. We simply followed the scent of some runaways. An' we'll be searchin' yer barn. With or without yer say so."

Emma felt Thane tense under her hand. Wondering if he was as worried as she was about the hidden cellar they had found, she prayed that room stayed hidden.

"You can search the barn. But yer dogs will stay here. I'll not have them killin' my animals," Thane stated, leaving no room for argument.

The deputy straightened in his saddle. His relaxed demeanor disappearing. "The law says we can search."

"Aye. But the law doesna say anythin' about savage beasts bein' necessary." The farmyard was quiet except for the snarling of the hounds. "My brother here will shoot any animal that enters my barn. Law says I can protect my livestock from wild animals."

Mark cocked his rifle back. He left the flint cover in place but left his finger close by.

The tension increased as the search party waited for orders. Their hands hovering close to their own guns.

Finally, the deputy relaxed in his saddle. Taking his hat off, he ran his hand through his hair with a smile. "Of course, the hounds will stay outside. But we will search every inch of this barn."

Thane watched him in silence. "Expected nothin' less. But you won't break an egg or spill a drop of water. I won't hesitate to send for the sheriff."

The deputy studied Thane for a moment and then called out to his men. "Search the barn! Leave the dogs outside."

A couple of the men tied the snarling dogs to the corral posts. Emma cringed as they bit each other for being too close.

Mark eased his horse closer to his sister, keeping his eye on the dogs. "If they break loose, I'll shoot them, Em. They willna hurt ya."

She didn't want the dogs to get hurt, but she admitted to herself that they did scare her. Jade growled near her feet, as if in agreement with Emma's thoughts. Emma bent and scratched her ears. "Good girl."

When no ruckus came from the barn, Emma calmed down enough to remember her brother's purpose in coming. "Who is missing?"

"Little Lydia Fender."

"Lydia. She isna little at all."

Mark looked down at his sister for a moment and then back at the dogs. "I suppose she isna." He was quiet for a moment. "I havna seen her since I stopped school. But then... I still think of you as little too."

Emma smiled at that. She believed he did. "They've no idea who she went with?"

"Her Pa insists she was taken, but he has no idea who." He hesitated, looking down at her again. "Da thinks it best if Thane is there..."

Frowning, Emma knew what her brother was leaving out. "So that he can prove it isna him? Why would he take a random girl?"

Her brother shrugged. "All we can do is join the search and show his honor. They canna cast shadows on us if we are all there in the light."

The men all immerged from the barn. None of them looked happy. The snow was now deep enough to show their footprints as they returned to their horses, reminding Emma of the trail they hoped to follow.

"Mark- ask them to join the search party. Their dogs could track in the snow. Ya could say they can keep lookin' fer the runaways." In her heart, Emma hoped the runaways were moving in the other direction.

Her brother hesitated as he watched the men.

Emma chose her words carefully. "If she was taken? It's her best option. If she left willin'ly? Hopefully, she makes it to where she was wantin'."

Mark met her gaze then. Guilt passed over his eyes before he nodded in decision. "I'll talk to them. Go get a warmer coat on. We have to leave soon."

"Stew is ready to eat. I can have coffee boiled in minutes."

"There is no time. Sorry, Emma." Thane called out as he approached. "Get some warm clothes on while I go unhook my horse."

Mark interrupted. "Go eat your dinner. I'll gather your horse and water it. You'll need your strength for the long night ahead." He paused a moment. "Last time-," he looked uncomfortable. "Last time, the ladies all met at the parsonage. They kept coffee and food there. For the search parties as they circled back to warm themselves... and get updates. For when we..."

Thane knew that Mark couldn't finish his statement. "When you were searchin' fer Emma. I can't imagine how hard that was."

"There are no words to describe it," Mark confirmed.

With a nod, Thane went into the house.

Emma watched him go inside. She knew the guilt still ate at him. "It was hard on him, too."

"Pardon?"

Turning to her brother, she saw the confusion on his face. "It was hard on Thane too. He begged his pa to take me back. When his pa refused? And then I wouldna wake? He begged God ta tell him what ta do. I'd never seen a man so broken. It's why I knew I could trust him."

Mark stared at the door to the cabin. "I didna know."

"I know."

The baby pushed against Emma's stomach. With no room to move, he had started stretching against the edges. Putting her hand against the baby's foot, she held her breath until the baby relaxed.

Mark's face was filled with concern. "Maybe ya should stay here."

She shook her head. "Yer right. We all need to stand united. So, no one can blame Thane." She followed her husband inside.

Thane was just finishing washing up when she entered. They sat at the table and ate the stew she had dished up. When they finished, she cleared the table and moved the stew off the swinging arm of the hearth. Lifting it to put it on the table, Thane stepped in and finished for her.

"That is too heavy fer ya."

Knowing that she wouldn't win, she didn't argue. Instead, she wrapped a loaf of bread in a towel and put it in a basket.

Thane went in search of Mark and the horses, while Emma washed the bowls they had used. When she finished tidying up, she met the men out front.

Emma and Thane arrived at the parsonage as Mrs. Keyes was coming out of her door. "Oh, hello there, Emma. Mr. Hawkins. I'm just headin' over to the church. It was deemed a better meetin' place for the search party. After last time-" she froze, and her eyes darted to Emma's face.

Emma felt Thane tense behind her. *When they were looking for me.* She gave the reverend's wife a weak smile. "We'll head over ta the church then." She pulled Thane's arm closer around her. *Will tonight be a constant reminder to Thane of what his pa did?*

Thane guided their horse to the church and stopped in front of the steps to lift Emma down. When her feet touched the ground, she felt a cramp radiate from her side around to her back.

Thane tightened his grip on her arms when she gasped. "Are ya alright?"

When the pain eased up, Emma smiled to reassure him. "Yeah, I'll be fine. My back is jest stiff from overdoin' it today." With another smile, she turned to go inside.

"Emma? Should ya just go back home?"

Looking over her shoulder at the uncertain tone in Thane's voice, she saw the worry in her husband's beautiful gray eyes. "I promise I'll sit and take it easy inside. And I will go home if I get uncomfortable."

With a nod, he tied his horse to the rail and followed Emma inside. As soon as they entered, everyone stopped talking.

A man that Emma did not recognize stepped forward. "Why did ya even bother to show up. This is all yer fault." Taking slow steps toward Thane, he growled his dislike into every word. "You steal a girl away in the night and then inherit a farm. Now every low life scum around is goin' ta snatch up the nearest girl and force her ta marry him."

Emma saw her husband's shoulders tense. "Thane didna steal me away in the night. This isna his fault."

Another young man sneered at Emma and agreed. "Aye. It isna his fault. The fault lies with you."

Her breath caught in her throat.

The man stepped closer. "We all see ya. With yer happiness and daydreamin' smiles. Any man fer miles around saw you. And it encouraged every scoundrel ta know that the wife he kidnaps... Well? She'll be a happy wife- once she accepts her fate. So, what's gonna stop them now?"

The whole church went quiet again. Emma tried to speak past the lump in her throat but couldn't think of anything. Wrapping her arms around her round stomach, she felt Thane push her behind his back.

"If anyone has an issue with my wife bein' happy-," Thane started.

James interrupted. "If anyone has a right ta be angry with Emma's happiness, it'd be me."

Thane turned toward James in surprise. The men around them all nodded in satisfaction.

"But I'm not."

Silence returned.

"I wanted ta hate Thane Hawkins." A murmur rose around them, but he held up his hand to silence them. "I wanted to- but I couldn't. Thane is an honorable Christian man. He did the honorable thing when he thought all hope for honor was gone. I canna blame him for that. But I can thank him. He took care of Emma when none of us could. He protected her honor and nursed her back to the livin'. Then he married my Emma. And I wanted ta hate him."

Sadie came to stand beside Emma. Her Da and brothers pushed through the crowd and made their way to stand by Thane, shielding Emma.

"Only she wasn't my Emma. She is jest, Emma. She belongs ta no man. Sure, I wanted those smiles to always be shinin' on me. But one thing I always knew Emma would do was find happiness wherever she is. She is jest like one of her mama's flowers. They bloom where the wind plants them. I'd think that any pa in this town would want their daughters to look up to a young lady that can smile in a storm."

No one said anything. Some looked around while others looked at the floor. But silence settled over everything.

The door opened suddenly. Mr. Nash walked in. All heads turned to him.

A young man advanced on him and yelled out. "Why do ya even bother ta show up?"

Nash met Emma's eyes. "Because I chose not to join the search last time and was accused of kidnappin' Emma here. I'll not make the same mistake again." Kicking the snow off his boots, he looked away.

"How can we be sure ya didn't steal her and stash her in your barn before coming here?"

"I guess you'll have ta have a look in my barn fer yer--."

"Mr. Nash didna steal anyone tonight. He was at my house havin' dinner when the news came in of her disappearance."

Emma looked at Nellie in surprise. Nellie had been a few years ahead of her in school, and she had been shy. Then when both of Nellie's parents had passed away the year after Emma's mama, she had been forced to get a job.

Nellie met Emma's gaze and studied her expression.

Mr. Fender entered the church and headed for the woodstove. "The tracks out behind my house came from the North and lead back to the North. So, it clears anyone in this room."

The young man looked taken aback. "Are ya sure?"

The girl's father nodded. "Zeke, I'd like ta get followin' the trail before it snows anymore. So, can we point the blame later?"

Zeke headed for the door without answering.

Someone put a warm coffee in the worried father's hand, and he drank it. When he looked up, his eyes locked on Emma's face, and he frowned.

Looking away from the man, she moved to the window. She saw that the posse had arrived outside. Their dogs seemed calmer.

Hands wrapped around Emma, and she felt herself being pulled backward. "Are ya feelin' alright?" Thane's voice was quiet in her ear. When she didn't answer, Thane turned her toward him, studying her face.

"I'm alright. It just took me by surprise."

Studying her face for a moment more, he finally kissed her on the forehead and headed back to get his horse. As he reached for the door latch, it swung open toward him, forcing him to step away. Thane's grandma walked straight for him.

"Such terrible news. And they are sayin' it's yer father's fault," Mary announced, her voice loud in the small room.

Thane's shoulders tensed.

"I will say it makes me sad. The poor choices my daughter has made has led to the ruin of this town- and the ruin of your honor."

Emma prepared to defend Thane again.

"No."

A shadow stood in the door. It moved forward until Nathaniel Hawkins' face came into view. A hush fell over the room as he stepped inside.

"I came back ta find my son and make amends fer my poor choices. Ta ask fer forgiveness- where forgiveness is possible. But none of this is Thane's fault. Nor will this ruin his honor. Because my boy has always been an honorable man."

Mary had turned to face Nathaniel as he walked toward her. The room froze as they watched the two.

"No, Mrs. Preston. If there is guilt for this night, then it'll lay at your feet. Yours and yer husband's. Annie wrote ta you. Beggin' ya ta forget about this curse and give us yer blessin'. But ya refused. Because of yer stubborn pride- our Annie died. She asked ya for help, and you refused." Nathaniel took a step toward Mary, dropping his voice lower. "I couldn't find work around here because no one trusted me after the way your husband treated me in this town. So, I was forced ta continue trappin'. I wasn't there when the chimney caught fire. But I was there

269

when the chimney collapsed. It was too cold fer her ta stay there. But she had nowhere ta go." Nathaniel stepped closer again and lowered his voice, deep with emotion. "And when I asked you fer help in carin' fer Thane after our Annie died? Ya refused again."

Mary opened her mouth to protest, but Nathaniel waved away her interruption.

"Annie was so sure ya'd help raise her baby once you saw that he was a boy and that your curse was finally broken." Emma saw tears form in Mr. Hawkin's eyes. "She had faith in you even after ya'd turned her away. But ya let her down, refusin' ta help Thane. Ya refused ta help an innocent babe."

"So, I had no choice... but ta turn ta a stranger ta help me raise this boy. Ta marry another, with no time ta grieve. I was broken and lost. And I didn't see the precious gift she left fer me. A boy who was better than I could ever be. Even when I never spent the time to raise him good- he still turned out honorable and full of goodness." He took a final step toward the older woman, looking down into her face. "So this," indicating the room around them, "-this is OUR fault... yours and mine, Mary."

When Mary made no comment nor any effort to move away, Mr. Hawkins looked up and saw Thane standing there with Emma. He moved toward them.

Emma was surprised to see his clear eyes. They weren't clouded by drink. They were focused on her and full of remorse. The emotion she saw there made her breath catch.

"Emma," Mr. Hawkins took his hat from his head. "I don't have any words to explain ta ya what I've done. In my own way, I thought I was helpin' my boy with no thought of yer wishes at all. Drink clouds yer mind into not seein' the results. I coulda killed ya and fer that I can't forgive myself. And I won't be askin' ya ta forgive me either. But I will thank ya. Thank ya fer makin' my boy happier than I've ever seen him." He lowered his face to stare at his hat for a moment before turning to Thane. "I'm sorry, Thane. I promised yer mama that I'd take real good care of ya. And I never did. Instead, you took care of me. Ya deserved better than that." Something changed in the man's eyes, and he slid his hat back on his head. "Tonight, I'll join in the search fer this missin' girl- to atone for any part I may've had in her disappearance. In the mornin', I'll turn myself in to the sheriff. If you'd still like answers, ya can visit me at the jail, and I'll tell ya anythin' ya'd like to know." With a nod, Nathaniel stepped toward the door.

"I forgive ya." Thane's words rang through the quiet church.

Nathaniel's feet froze.

"I forgive ya fer the drinkin'. You were right. I didn't understand yer meanin' at first, but now I do. *Emma is my home.* Mama was yours. I know I'd feel lost without her. I can't blame ya fer that." Thane watched his father turn back to him. "I can't even imagine how hard that was fer ya. Raisin' a baby on yer own. My heart hurts jest thinkin' about raisin' a baby without Emma there every day. So, I forgive ya."

Nathaniel nodded as tears escaped down his cheeks.

Emma felt tears run down her own cheeks. All the fears she had felt that winter about dying and leaving Thane alone, were there in this man before her. This man who had hurt her and carried her off. All the terrible things he had done, just to give his son the things that he, himself, had lost. She could no longer find any fault in him. "And I forgive ya."

Someone in the room gasped, and murmurs sounded around the room.

"I'm na sayin' what ya did was right. But I canna find it in my heart ta hate ya fer it," Emma wiped the tears from her cheeks. "I'll be givin' ya the forgiveness you do na think ya deserve."

The man stood still.

After a moment more, Thane stepped forward and embraced his father. Emma could see the tears on Thane's cheeks.

"This is all verra nice... but my daughter is still missin'. Are ya riding with us, Mr. Hawkins?"

"Aye." Both men answered, stepping away from their hug.

Thane pulled Emma into a quick hug and whispered against her hair. "Thank ya fer that. I love ya, Emma." He gave her a kiss and followed the menfolk out the door.

Emma watched him leave and then turned to her Da.

Da pulled her into a hug and squeezed her. "I'm sure glad I know where my daughter is on this night. That is fer sure and fer certain." He kissed the top of Emma's head and left.

Emma caught James' eye as he walked past, and he smiled at her. A small, sad smile.

"Thank you, James."

James nodded. Sadness in his eyes.

"How is yer Pa?"

He smiled then. "Better. He wakes up for several minutes at a time. They are worried about the headaches and that he seems ta struggle fer words. Sadie made him a tea for the headaches. Pa says it helps. But it also makes him sleep a lot. The doctor hopes he'll improve as his head heals."

"That's good news. I woulda come ta sit with him but-"

James interrupted her. "But yer baby has ta be comin' soon. You need ta rest." He touched his hat and filed out with the last of the men.

As the door closed behind them, the room was quiet except for the voices of the women around her.

"-I have my suspicions."

"We all do. I mean-"

A pain shot around her back, and she pressed a hand to her side. Holding her breath, she didn't notice Sadie approach.

"Let's get ya sittin' down." Sadie guided her over to a pew.

"Oh, Sadie! My brother said that the deputies had roughed ya up. I was afraid ya'd-"

Sadie shushed Emma. "Never ya mind about all that. It'd take more than a bunch of ill-mannered boys ta keep this ol' gal down. Now... let's get ya sittin'." Helping Emma lower into the pew behind her, Sadie swung Emma's feet up to prop them on the bench beside her. "Let me go make ya some tea."

Nellie came closer. "Here," she said, tucking a coat behind her back to cushion the hard boards. When it was all tucked in, she sat next to Emma.

"Thank you. It's very comfortable."

A moment of silence passed before Nellie spoke again. "I know what ya were thinkin'. How could I accept attention from such a man? I'm not a romantic sort. He wants marriage, and so do I. When he isna desperate, he is respectable." Nellie looked down at her fingers. "Some of us don't get men stealin' us away in the night and fightin' over our hand in marriage. Some of us barely get the man who agrees ta marry us. His gaze flittin' ta anythin' that sparkles or holds a drink."

The girl next to Emma wasn't that much older than her, but the years had not been easy for Nellie. She had been injured when she was a young child, and her arm had not set properly. Emma could see how it had grown crooked. She wondered if that had kept men from wanting to court her. It hadn't kept Nellie from working hard.

But Emma didn't know what to say about Mr. Nash. This man had caused her so much embarrassment. And then his actions had caused Mark to offer to marry another girl. But all he had done was try to secure a wife. Not the right way. But in the end, he had done no worse than Thane's Pa.

"I shouldna have judged ya, Nellie."

That seemed to be enough for her. Smiling her thanks, Nellie stood and moved off to stand with another group of women.

Emma couldn't help but think Nellie deserved someone better than Nash, but her words made sense.

Looking around her, Emma could not see Rachel among the women there. As her eyes swept past the groups of women, many turned their eyes away, but a few offered her a weak smile. *Will we ever know peace, Lord? Or will we always feel like outsiders here?*

Sadie interrupted Emma's thought as she slipped a cup of sweet-smelling tea into her hands. "Sip it and relax."

Emma sipped the tea and sighed. "Thank ya, Sadie. I think I overdid it today. I jest wanted ta clean everythin' in the cabin." With her feet up, the pains were less.

"That's often the way it is. Mamas wantin' ta clean everythin' in their house before they bring their little one into it."

"I remember Abby did the same last fall- jest before little man was born."

"That baby of yours is tellin' ya it's ready."

"I'm na sure I'm ready," Emma stated. "I still have some sewin' ta finish."

"Well," Sadie smiled down at Emma. "Ready or not- your baby is comin'."

Emma's mind raced to all the things she needed to do before the baby arrived and wished she could get back home to finish them. She looked around the church. There was coffee brewed and baked goods sitting on the table. But there was nothing else for them to do. Being nighttime, no one would expect a meal when they came in from searching.

Lydia's face flashed before Emma's eyes. Guilt filled her. *A girl is missing, and all I can think about are my own needs.*

"Everyone will understand if you need to go home," Sadie stated.

Startled, Emma's attention jumped back to the lady next to her. "But I-"

"But you feel like ya need to be here because the last time we were searchin'... we were searchin' fer you?" Sadie raised her eyebrows in question.

"Yes." Emma smiled. *It's like she can read my heart.*

Sadie stood up. "Well, you can come back tomorrow then. Every lady here knows that you should be home restin'." She looked thoughtful for a moment. "Let me find a way ta get you home."

Sadie wandered over to a group of ladies. Emma felt their attention shift to her. Feeling uncomfortable, she focused on the tea she was drinking.

Footsteps approached, and she looked up again. Mrs. Moore stood there with Sadie. "Good evenin', Emma. I have my wagon here in town for me and my girls. Would ya allow me ta drive ya home?"

"I'd be in yer debt."

"No. You're family. Let me get my coat, and we'll get you home. I was wantin' ta check on Rachel anyway. This'll get me a chance."

Watching Rachel's mom walk away, Emma realized how tired she was. The long day of cleaning and the confrontation they had when they arrived in town had taken their toll on her. She knew that she wouldn't be getting any more work done that night.

Sadie took Emma's teacup and helped her rise to her feet. Pulling her coat around her, she started toward the door. With a glance around the room, she paused when she caught sight of Mary. Thane's grandmother sat by herself, facing the alter. Emma could not see her face, but she could see her proud shoulders were wilted somewhat.

"We asked if Mrs. Preston would go home with ya," Sadie said, close by her side. "She said she needed ta spend time in prayer."

With a nod of understanding, Emma allowed Sadie to help her down the stairs and into the wagon. As Mrs. Moore clicked to the team, Emma wondered where Lydia was. She wondered if she was scared. She breathed a prayer for Lydia's safety. As the wheel slipped on the snowy roads, she said another for their own safety.

~Thirty-Three~

May 29, 1859...

Darkness surrounded her when Emma woke. She wasn't sure what woke her. The house was quiet except for the sound of Jade's gentle snore coming from the other room.

Reaching across to Thane's side of the bed, her hand found an empty space. Emma sat up in surprise.

The events from the night before crept in. *They must be still out looking for Lydia,* she realized.

Emma pushed back the covers and pulled her dress over her head, deciding to get some work done since she was awake anyway. She headed to the outhouse before she stoked the fire in the new cookstove. Smiling, she couldn't believe how much easier cooking on the stove was then using the hearth.

While she waited for the water to heat for her tea, she swept the floors again. Emma paused to rub her back. *I think I overdid it yesterday. I need to take it a little slower today.* Putting the broom away, she sat down in her rocker to finish the sleeping gown for the baby.

It wasn't long before Emma grew uncomfortable in the chair. Setting her needlework aside, she got up and walked around the room. Sunlight made the little window by the door light up. Stopping to look out, she saw how beautiful the morning looked. The sun reflecting over the snow.

Emma could never remember getting a snowstorm so late in the spring. She had a feeling it would melt by midday when the sun came out.

A cramp in her round belly made her catch her breath. "Alright, little one. I'll go back and sit," she said with a smile. She settled back in her chair and stitched on the hem along the bottom of the baby garment.

Before long, Emma grew uncomfortable again. She stood and walked the room once more. Seeing the sun spread a hint of color on the horizon, she decided to feed the animals. She slipped on her work coat and grabbed a water bucket.

After two trips to the well to lug water, Emma's stomach tightened again. She didn't want to push herself too hard, so she left the horse's trough for Thane to fill. Rubbing her back, she headed for the house again.

When Emma swung the door open, the wind pushed it out of her grasp and slammed against the wall. As the wind blew through the room, it moved Mary's door. She watched the letters next to her bed scatter on the floor. Quickly closing the door before the wind could scatter anything else, Emma latched it behind her. Lowering herself to the floor, she picked up the envelopes. The last one lay tucked behind Annabel's trunk.

As she tried to squeeze her fingers between the heavy trunk and the wall, her thoughts turned to Annabel. Pieces of her past had been knitting themselves together over the last months. A girl so in love with Nathaniel. A girl brought up to believe in a curse.

Sighing, Emma realized she wouldn't be able to get the envelope with the trunk so close to the wall. She set the letters on the table and pulled at the heavy chest. When it didn't budge, Emma put her back against the bed and tried again. The chest gave way and moved several inches. Reaching for the letter, she put it with the others.

With her task done, Emma remembered the talk about the letter Annabel left her parents. The missing letter. As she saw the envelopes laying there, she couldn't help but wonder where Annabel's envelope had gone.

Wind rattled the window frame.

Emma studied the floor where the papers had fallen. Had the wind blown Annabel's letter off the table all those years ago? Pushing the chest further away from the table, Emma searched for any sign of a paper edge. Leaning forward, she looked down into the cracks between the floorboards until her back started to ache again.

Rubbing her back, Emma rocked back and sat down on the floor again. She felt a little foolish. Why had she thought that she could find a letter that no one else had ever found?

But it has to be somewhere. And it never left this room, she reasoned.

Leaning forward again, she moved her hands over the floorboards. She could not feel anything sticking up from the gaps. With a sigh, she leaned back against the wall and rubbed her stomach. Emma knew she should go lay down. She would need to rest today.

One more look.

Pulling herself to her feet, she walked around Annabel's trunk. She wondered if she could see something different if she looked at it from above, letting the light shine down on the area. She put her hands on the lid and leaned over the edge. From her new view, she could see the gaps in the floor clearly. And there were no paper edges showing.

With another sigh, Emma started to rise but stopped. Inches from her fingers, where the back sloped down toward the hinges, there were metal bands that bound the chest together. Sticking out from the edge of the wide band was a triangle of discolored paper. Slowly, Emma pulled the paper from the crevice.

Staring at the envelope in her hand, she lowered herself to sit on the trunk.

"*Mother & Father,*" it read.

Tears filled Emma's eyes. Annabel's letter had been there all along. She found herself wondering if they would have found the letter, would things have turned out differently for Annabel. Would they have turned out differently for Thane?

A pain tightened around her stomach. Breathing carefully, it lessened. Emma was starting to be a little concerned. She knew it was getting close to the time for her baby to come, but she had figured she would have a couple more weeks. Rubbing her stomach, she tried to think what she should do. If her labor had indeed started, she needed to get the midwife. Without Thane there, she had no way to send for her.

The pain subsided, and she saw the forgotten letter in her hand again. She was curious about it but knew it wasn't hers to read.

Rising, she took the envelope and placed it on the kitchen table. Remembering the wind, she placed the butter crock on the edge to keep it in place. "Can't chance losing it again, now that we have found it."

Better get some water to boilin'. She knew it could be hours before they needed it, but she wasn't sure when someone would come to check on her. *Best to do it while I'm able.* Putting her large pot on the stove, she emptied the last of the water from the bucket into the pot and headed out to the well.

The day warmed up before long, and the snow melted. Emma walked around the yard as she waited for Thane to return. The tightening in her stomach and back became more frequent.

She knew for certain that she was in labor.

The noon meal came and went without Emma cooking anything. Her appetite gone with the pains. She started to wonder if she should try to make it to Da's house. She knew Rachel had not gone to the church the night before but worried she had walked to town with first light.

The sound of horses in the yard brought Emma from her thoughts. She opened the door and stepped out to see Thane and Seth climbing down.

Thane smiled at Emma when he saw her. "We found Lydia and her husband. The deputy's dogs led us right to them. They were already married."

Leaning around his horse's neck, Seth winked at his sister. "Turns out she wasna kidnapped at all. They jest used the storm to cover their trail. Her father didna approve of her poor farmer. So, he'd picked out an older gentleman fer her, from the next town over."

Knowing that her brother liked to tell tall tales, she looked to Thane to clarify.

"Mr. Fender didn't think her young beau- her young husband would be able to provide for her. His concern was for her being well cared for." Thane gave Emma a lopsided smile. "You met the other gentleman last night. Not a gray hair or wrinkle in sight."

"Zeke?" Emma asked, remembering the man who blamed her.

Thane nodded once.

"Maybe I shouldna suggested the deputies join up with the search party," she realized.

"Was no harm in it. If she had been taken away, it would have saved her from harm," Thane assured her.

Emma saw a shadow passed over her husband's face. "What is it?"

Pausing for a moment, Thane seemed reluctant to continue. "The dogs picked up the trail for the runaways on the ride back- just north of the Moore's farm."

Oh no! Emma's mind pictured those vicious dogs chasing after the little slave girl she had found in her barn all those months before. A chill ran through her.

"North of the Moore's? Isna that-?" She couldn't finish.

"Widow Craig's farm."

Emma's eyes flew to Thane's face. "What if they catch them there?"

Emma's stomach tightened down, and she grabbed the stair rail for support. Closing her eyes, she concentrated on her breathing.

"Emma?" Thane's voice was close and filled with concern.

When she opened her eyes again, Thane was standing in front of her. His hands were outstretched, ready to catch her as if he was afraid she would fall over.

Smiling, she straightened. "I think this baby is on its way."

"The baby? I thought we had weeks left?" Thane squinted in concern.

"It appears he doesna want ta wait any longer."

Thane put his hand under her elbow and led her through the door. She sank into a chair. "Do ya want ta go ta Abby's? She offered so you'd be close ta town?"

Emma shook her head.

"Or I can get ya to Da's." Emotions swirled through Thane's eyes.

Shaking her head again, Emma smiled. "I want to stay here. I want our child ta be born here in our home."

He studied her face for a moment before he nodded. A smile curved one side of his mouth. "Our daughter ya mean?"

"Only God will be knowin' that. Until He shows us."

"I'll jest be gettin' the midwife then," Seth stated from the open door.

Emma looked over at her little brother standing in the door. His face was serious. Emma had rarely seen him so serious. "Yes, Maggie would be good. And maybe Rachel."

"I'll see if she's feelin' better." With a nod, Seth left. She heard him ride out of the yard a few moments later.

Another pain shot through her.

"What can I do?"

When she opened her eyes again, Thane had knelt by her side. His eyes so full of worry. Now that he was home, Emma could admit that she felt tired. "Could ya help me get into my nightgown?"

Nodding, he sprang up and hurried from the room, bringing back her nightgown.

Emma smiled at his nervousness. "Maybe I could change in the bedroom."

Soon Emma was in a fresh gown and tucked in the bed. The pains were coming closer together. Knowing that she wasn't alone, she allowed herself to concentrate on breathing through each pain. *Please, Lord, protect this baby.*

Rachel arrived first, but the midwife wasn't far behind. Time was being marked by the pain for Emma. The pains and the moments in between the pains.

Hours passed, and the night with little sleep started to take its toll on Emma. She started resting her eyelids between the pains. At one point, Emma opened her eyes to the midwife encouraging her to keep her eyes open.

Behind the older woman, Thane stood in the doorway. Emma could see the worry in his stormy eyes. Mark and Seth pulled him away from the door, and Da pulled the door closed. Just before it latched, Da paused for one more look at Emma. "We're all prayin', Emma girl."

The door closed and darkness crept in. Exhaustion swept over her.

Everything went quiet.

❧ Thirty-Four ❧

May 30, 1859...

"Emma."

Sleep pulled her back. Her eyelids felt heavy.

"Emma? Please open your eyes."

"She is movin' more. I think she is wakin' up," a voice said.

"Iffen she's this tired, shouldn't we let her sleep?" Rachel's voice echoed in the silence of the room.

"We did let her sleep."

Sleep pulled at the edge of her thoughts. *Why was everyone in her room?*

"Emma. Please?"

The concern in Thane's voice made it gruff.

Struggling against the darkness that pulled her back, Emma tried to talk.

But the exhaustion was strong.

The darkness surrounded her, and everything went quiet again.

~*~*~*~*~*~*~*~*~*~*~*~*~*~*~*~*~*~*~

Sunlight shone through the window. The brightness made Emma wince, and she turned her head away.

"Come on, Emma girl."

Opening her eyes, she saw Da sitting by her bed. "Da?"

Tears filled his eyes as he smiled. "Good mornin' to ya, sleepyhead."

A memory of Da outside her door flashed before her eyes. "Where's Thane?"

Da dropped his eyes to the floor next to the bed. Emma turned a little. There, propped against the wall, was her husband. His hand lying on the pillow by her head.

Concern filled her. Everyone looked at her with guarded eyes. Her hands went to her stomach as a pain shot through her. But her hands met a flatter surface. It wasn't flat. But it was no longer round or hard.

"Where is my baby?" Worry clouded her throat and made her voice crack.

Flashing looks at each other, everyone eventually turned back to her.

"Ya do na remember?" Maggie asked, stepping forward.

Their worried expressions caused Emma's heart to sink. She couldn't speak past the lump in her throat. Eventually, she gave up trying and shook her head.

"You have all the luck." Abby entered the room. "I wish I could forget bringin' little man into this world." With a wink at her friend, Abby stepped closer to the bed.

Da stepped out of the way.

Abby smiled at Emma. "It's time ya met yer little girl." Leaning forward, she settled a bundle next to Emma on the bed. As she stood back, the blanket fell open.

Emma's breath caught. There in the blanket lay the most beautiful baby at peace. Dark curls showed around her face. But when the baby didn't move, her heart beat hard in her chest. *Oh Lord, please-*
.

"Is she alright?" Emma finally managed to ask. "Why is she so quiet?"

Da laughed then. "Yer girl is fine. And likely willna be quiet fer much longer." He tucked the blanket back up by the baby's chin. "I'm afraid this little one takes after her Uncle Seth. She has a mighty hunger."

It took a moment for Emma to realize they were teasing her.

"And a little of my Annabel in her. She definitely knows what she wants." Mary Preston breezed into the room with a stack of fresh sheets. An apron tied around her waist. She paused and looked down into Emma's face with a small smile. "Ya gave us all a scare when you wouldn't wake up."

Emma looked around the room. Every face studied her. No one looked at the baby in her arms. Relief flowed through her. "So, the baby is fine, then?"

"Yes," Thane said, sitting up. He blinked the sleep back from his eyes. "This daughter of ours is a strong one. But you-," he whispered. "You scared me half ta death. I've never prayed so hard in all my days. Not since-." He kissed her head. Tears overflowed down his cheeks.

"Daughter? You were right," Emma whispered with a smile.

Thane's lip raised into his lopsided smile. "Yes. I was right. We have a daughter."

Quiet laughter echoed around the room.

"Of course, Thane was right. I told you he was." Abby gave Emma a wink. "Breakfast is ready for everyone." With another wink, Abby ushered everyone out of the room except Thane.

When the room was empty except for her little family, Thane leaned over the baby and kissed Emma. Emma watched the emotions pass through his stormy gray eyes. "I thought I'd lost ya to this family curse. I prayed that God wouldn't take ya from me." Clearing his throat, he smiled. "Pa and yer Da stayed by me all night, praying too. They kept assurin' me that this sad story had no control over us. But ya wouldn't wake." Tucking a curl behind her ear, he continued. "It reminded me of last fall. When you couldn't wake."

"I slept through everythin'?"

Thane shook his head. "No, they said you were awake until the birth. Ya don't remember?"

"No," Emma gave him a shaky smile.

With a careful study of her face, Thane frowned. "I reckon none of us knew how tired ya really were. I knew ya were workin' hard. I'm thinkin' I didn't really know the full extent."

"I'm sorry I worried ya."

He kissed her again then sat back on his heels. "Have ya thought any ta what name ya want to give this little one?"

Names? "I canna decide. Part of me thinks we could name her after our mamas... Annabel and Lilianna. We could call her Anna or Annie? But I also like the name Ruth- to tell everyone that wherever you are, will be my home too. Because you and this little soul are my home now.

Thane's eyes filled with tears. Coughing, he cleared his throat. "No need to saddle this little one with so much of a name. We know our home lies with each other." Looking down at the baby in his wife's arms, he lowered his voice, "So little Annie... ya've been givin' yer mama a hard time of it. I expect that'll change some now that yer out here where we can hold ya."

"Annie," Emma repeated. Looking at the little face, the name fit perfect.

❧ Thirty-Five ❧

May 31, 1859...

mma woke with the sun on her face. Sensing she would need to feed Annie soon, she tried to sit up. But she was still weak.

A chair creaked. "Here, let me help you." Mary set a teacup next to her bed and propped pillows behind her. "Is that comfortable?"

Nodding, she leaned back into the pillows.

"Emma?" Mary hesitated. "I know this isn't a good time for this, but..." she paused again. "I feel like I caused you to have a rough time bringing this baby into the world. I'm sorry for the trouble I've caused you." She sat back in the chair by Emma's bed. "The Reverend came to me the night of the search. We discussed what the Bible meant when it said the *sins of the father visited upon three generations* verse. And how anger can lead us down a dark path.

"Annabel tried to tell me much the same thing, all those years ago. And I wouldn't listen. I finally feel the weight of that guilt. I should have listened to her. For Annabel's sake. I still believe she deserved better than Nathaniel Hawkins, but my Annabel thought there was no one better." Tears filled the older lady's eyes. "Thank you for finding her letter for me."

Seeing Mary so emotional, Emma's eyes filled with tears. She didn't know what to say, so she simply nodded.

Mary smiled. "I would like you to read the letter." She pulled the yellowed paper out of her apron pocket and laid it in Emma's hand.

The seal was broken, so Emma unfolded the paper.

Dear Mother & Father,

By the time you read this letter, I will be gone. Nathaniel and I asked for your permission to get married, and you refused. You cling to this wish for me to atone for a curse that I did not cause.

Please forgive me, but I cannot honor your wishes. My heart is breaking that it has to be this way. That I need to leave in the night so that I can marry the man I love. But I have nothing else to apologize for. I have no other obligations to you. I was always honorable in courting. I always obeyed your commitments for me. And I was always honest in my intentions. You knew that I would never marry for any other reason than love. Just as my namesake did. But I also promised to give you no reason to question my honor.

Please let go of this curse. It isn't holding on to us. We are holding on to it. Mother, if you could just release the idea that we will all die unless we marry who our fathers pick, then we could feel hope again. Then this ridiculous curse would be gone forever.

Maybe we got it all wrong. Maybe what God really wanted from our family was for the old and the young to honor each other. Maybe that's why He made us all look the same? To remind us that we failed with the last generation. Failed to forgive or even failed to love each other enough to let go. Maybe what God was asking of us was to heal the brokenness. For all of us to find love and forgiveness for each other. Not just in marriage.

I have fallen in love with Nathaniel, and we will be married today. It wasn't what I had *planned. Indeed, I had promised you I would die an old spinster. But this love is something so beautiful to behold that I hope you will someday be able to see it for yourselves. And when you do? I hope you will find it in your hearts to give us your blessing.*

I love you both. And I'm ever so sorry that it had to be this way. Please find it in your heart to forgive me.

Love,
Annabel

Emma's heart broke. Annabel had tried to make everything work. She had begged for her parents to listen. But she hadn't planned on was the letter getting blown over. *Poor Annabel.*

Mary took the letter when Emma held it out. "My Annabel figured out something I never could." Tucking the paper back into her pocket, she wiped her eyes on the corner of the apron. "There is someone else here to see you."

Thane stood in the door, holding Annie. As he settled the baby into her arms, she saw that his pa stood behind him. He stayed back, uncertain.

"You wanted ta see me?"

"I came ta apologize. Proper." He held his hat in his good hand, tapping it against his leg. "I wanted ta make sure you came through this before I turned myself in. Emma- I never intended to steal ya away. That night, I had gone ta town ta get drunk- again. The same way I always did when I couldn't handle seein' Thane upset. The same way I always got drunk whenever I didn't want to face somethin'." He looked down in shame. "I was so angry. Once again, *honor* was gonna ruin my family. Seein' Thane so miserable? It reminded me of my Annie being so upset at defyin' her parents. Then when I found ya- at Annie's house?" Lifting his head, he looked Emma in the eye. "The full impact of what I'd done

289

hit me- once I ran out of drink. And then I ran- ran and left Thane there alone ta deal with the consequences."

Turning toward Thane, he continued. "When you came lookin' fer me and wantin' answers, I ran again. It was only then that I realized my mistake. For the first time? I felt alone- truly alone. I figured it was too late, but I knew I needed ta try and make it right. Turns out, givin' up the drink is harder than I thought. I ended up in a lumberjack camp with the shakes. A young lady named Alejandra nursed me through. When the shakin' had me feelin' sorry for myself, she set me straight. Remindin' me how lucky I'd been ta find love at all. You see? Her marriage was ta repay a debt. There was no love. But she said her mama told her ta stay the course and she would make a home. That road ta home wasn't goin' straight or easy for Alejandra. Yet there she was assurin' an' ol' drunk man that no matter how late I came home, I could always get back on the path ta make it good."

Nodding, he pulled a book out of the bag at his side. "I reckon I'm about twenty years late ta make this family a home fer ya, kid. It only took Emma here about one year. She reminds me of my Annie. But I would like ta try. You came to me lookin' fer answers. I brought ya some. I don't have all the answers myself. But I brought ya the ones I have."

With a hesitant look at the book in his hand, he passed it to Thane. "I expect most of it is too personal fer ya to read. But there's a spot I marked..." The older man's words drifted off as if he didn't know what to say.

Thane took the book from his father and sat next to Emma on the bed. The place that Mr. Hawkins had referred to was marked with a piece of ribbon. A piece that seemed to have been used a lot by the frayed edges.

"That's all that's left of the ribbon I bought Annie. It wasn't much. But she treasured it like it was gold." Emotion made his voice thick, making him sound more gruff than usual.

Emma looked at the man standing before them. Looking down at his hand, at the empty place where his hand should have been.

The sound of a page turning brought her attention back to her husband. He ran his finger down the page to track where he was reading.

"... my parents have still refused to accept Nate. I had hoped that my letter to them would bend their hearts. But that hope is gone. For now. With time they will fall in love with my husband. He is such sweetness. Joy. And he works day and night to get this cabin ready for the weather ahead. I know he worries that he won't get the holes filled in before the snow flies. But I told him we will weather all things together."

Sweetness. Joy. Emma felt her eyes drift back to the man before them. These words did not seem to match him. This man who had kidnapped her in the night. This man who had ridiculed Thane's speech about love.

But yet he stands before you now. Broken.

Nathaniel lifted his head and met Emma's gaze. His eyes churned with emotions. Without the cover of drunkenness, his eyes spoke of pain and sadness.

Clearing her throat, Emma turned back to Annie's diary.

"The chimney fell last night in the storm. I fear it is bad timing because I feel pains. I think this baby is on his way. I do not want to tell Nate. He is already worried because it has been so cold. He will want me to go to town. I'll just bundle up until he has the hole filled in."

"She must've been so cold," Emma didn't realize she had said the words out loud until she heard Nathaniel answer from across the room.

"She was. But she never let on. It took hours for me to clear away the debris so that we could have a good fire goin' again. She even helped me warm the clay I dug up. I never noticed the pains until it was too late ta move her ta town. My Annie never complained that whole day." Nathaniel's voice cracked.

Emma felt Thane look at her. Meeting his eyes, she saw the emotions churning in his gray ones. He leaned in to press his forehead to hers. After a moment, he took a deep breath and turned back to the book.

"My baby was born last night. A more beautiful baby you will never find. I named him Thane after his papa. Nathaniel. My two loves. Nate sat with me all night and helped me bring little Thane into this world. Then he rode out early this morning to get the midwife. He is so worried about me. My mother has always told me I have a cursed life. But how can I be cursed? I am so proud of my husband. And we created the most beautiful little boy. A boy. The first boy to be born into our family in 10 generations. I know when Mama sees that my baby is a boy, she will know that the family curse is broken. She was right to name me Annabel. The first Annabel may have started a curse. But it ends with me. This boy will be raised in love and never hear of the old Douglas curse. I am so glad I followed my heart. God has certainly blessed us."

Thane was slow to turn to the next page. The paper itself had been crumpled and then attempted to be flattened again.

Emma met Nathaniel's eye for a moment before he turned and left the room. In that moment, she knew what could drive a man to drown his sorrow in alcohol for so many years. Her heart hurt for this man who had never shown her anything but trouble. It hurt for a young lady who had loved so completely.

Her attention was brought back when Thane set the book on her lap.

She lifted it, not sure she wanted to read the words.

My dearest Nate,

I can see the truth on the midwife's face. And I know now that my pride has killed me. I should have allowed you to take me to town while you fixed the cabin. Even if my parents didn't want me. But I didn't want to miss one minute by your side.

I know that you are not ready to see the truth yet. And I cannot bear to destroy the hope that is left in your eyes.

But I need you to hear what my heart has to say.

I have loved you, Nathaniel Hawkins, from the moment I saw your eyes smile when I asked you to the town dance. I know you didn't expect me. I know I certainly didn't expect you. But I have wanted no one else since that moment. And I regret nothing. This year of being married to you has contained more joy and love than the entirety of my first 19 years. It has made up for all the heartache that I have had to endure.

Every day of my life, I felt like a disappointment to my father. I was never enough. I never did the right thing. Even to my mama, I was a trial. But in every day with you? I felt like I was exactly who I was supposed to be. Every time you looked at me, I felt like I was your whole world.

I can only hope that I showed you enough love.

My only regret is not being able to wake up every morning by your side and make sure you feel all the love that you deserve. One hand or two, you are the best man I have ever known.

Please tell our Thane how much I love him every day. How much we wanted him. Tell him how much I didn't want to leave him. But I know he will be in the best of hands. The most amazing Pa a boy could ever want. I pray that God will continue to look out for you.

And Thane. Please love your pa every minute of every day for me. I pray that you look like me, so he has a piece of me always.

I am not ready to say good-bye to you both, but I know in my heart that it will be soon. I have never felt more loved than I do at this moment. It has been a good life with you. I cannot ask for more.

I will love you always, Nate.

All my love,

Your Annie."

Tears blurred Emma's eyes. She set the book down to wipe them away. "Thane..." she started. But she didn't know what to say and fell silent.

Thane's head rested in his hands. Slumped forward, Emma couldn't see his face.

"For so many years, I knew he suffered. I knew that is why he drank. But I wanted him ta jest stop. I had no idea what he suffered." He lifted his head up to meet Emma's gaze. "If I had ta say goodbye to you in this moment? I'm not sure I could be any stronger." Thane's voice broke on the last word.

Emma felt herself pulled against her husband's chest. He cradled her, and the baby close. When she felt tears wet her forehead, Emma thought her heart would break.

"But ya won't have ta say good-bye ta yer Emma."

No one had heard Nathaniel come back into the room. Emma turned her head a little so she could see him.

"Ya won't lose yer girl because ya refused ta bring her ta a cabin that was fallin' apart. Ya did the honorable thing by givin' her up so that she could have the best life." Silence filled the room for a few minutes. "But I was angry. It was like the old curse was back. And 'twas gonna ruin my boy's life like it ruined mine. Well, I wasn't about ta sit there and watch my son lose his love like I lost mine." Nathaniel met Emma's eyes. "Anger is an ugly thing. And so is drink. I never meant to hurt ya, Emma. My Annie..." Nathaniel paused to clear his throat. "My Annie would be ashamed of me. Her eyes tellin' me she expected better from me. Her eyes lookin' at me... every time Thane looked at me. She expected me ta be able ta go on without her. But how could I?"

Emma watched tears slide down Nathaniel's cheeks. His eyes looked so much like her husband's, except that the color was different.

"My Annie expected me ta take care of ya. I failed her."

Thane stood up from the bed and crossed to his pa. Pulling him close, they hugged and cried.

Emma watched until her tears blurred them out of sight. She looked down at little Annie in her arms. She couldn't imagine leaving this world and not being able to watch her grow up. And she couldn't imagine how lost Thane would be if he had to do the job of father and mother all on his own. Closing her eyes, she pressed a gentle kiss against her baby's forehead.

When she opened her eyes again, she caught the date on the letter. "January 12, 1838."

Thane pulled away from his father. "What?"

Emma met her husband's gaze. "January 12, 1838. That must be your birthday."

"Actually, his birthday is January 7. His mama lived for 6 days after he was born."

"But ya said ya never kept track," Thane stated.

"I never wanted ta know how long she had been gone," he admitted, "but I could never forget."

Tears slid down Emma's cheeks as she yawned.

"January 7," Thane repeated.

"Isna that the day ya brought Avery home?" Emma asked as she settled lower into her pillows.

Thane stood to help Emma move the extra pillows so she could lie down. Once she was settled, he put the baby close by her side.

"I think Avery came in February. But I started findin' his broken traps right after the new year."

Emma smiled, trying to keep her eyes open. "So, Avery was yer birthday present."

Thane smoothed the hair away from her cheek. He chuckled. "I suppose in a way he is."

"Thane-," Emma was interrupted with another yawn.

Concern crossed Thane's face. "We should go, so ya can sleep."

"Aye, you should," Mary agreed.

Emma had forgotten the other lady remained in the room. Looking around her, she smiled. She never would have guessed she would be content to see the two people who had caused her the most turmoil. Her eyes returned to Thane. "What a day."

"What a day," he agreed. "I love ya, Emma."

"And I love you," she said with another yawn. "Stay with me?"

"Always," he whispered.

Content, Emma let her eyes drift closed. She thought of Annabel having to close her eyes on her husband and baby for her last time, and Emma's eyes opened again. She drank in the sight of Thane's face.

Thane smiled down at her and kissed her forehead. After a pause, he leaned further and kissed her softly on the lips. "Sleep."

Her eyes drifted closed again, and she felt Thane settle on the bed next to her.

"Will you have to be jailed for taking Emma?" Mary asked then.

"I need ta pay fer my crime," Nathaniel answered. After a pause, he continued. "There are also the charges of kidnappin' Clara that I have ta be cleared from."

She listened to them discuss how long the sheriff would keep Nathaniel. The words began to sound muffled to Emma. She heard Clara's name and her own a few times.

Her thoughts returned to Annabel and Nathaniel. *Please Lord, let me wake up tomorrow. Please don't let Thane and Annie have to learn to live without me. But if they do- let me have Annabel's peace- peace knowing that You have everything under control. Let me have faith that everything will work towards Your plan.*

Peace filled Emma.

Then there was silence.

❧ Epilogue ❧

Ashush was on her lips as Thane called her name. As she pushed herself toward being awake, Emma saw the light through the window. Thane continued to shake her awake with a gentleness she recognized as his. "Oh! I didna mean ta sleep so long."

Thane put his finger to his lips, gesturing to the sleeping baby in the corner. Sliding the covers back, he pulled her to the door.

Annie had been an easy baby, but she had been teething for weeks. Neither baby nor mother had slept well in days. Emma could not say she was surprised that she overslept. She was exhausted.

The birds' singing was so peaceful it almost lulled her back to sleep on her feet.

"I think I felt a tooth break through last night. Annie fell asleep soon after that," Emma shared. "Maybe she'll be able to rest better now."

"I hope so. Ya both need it."

She hesitated for a moment when Thane opened the door, and she realized she still wore her nightdress. "I'm na dressed, Thane."

Thane smiled. "I know." He guided her into the yard and pointed up to the sky.

As the sleep cleared from her eyes, she saw the strange color above them. "The sunrise..." but she stopped when Thane interrupted.

"It isn't mornin' yet."

Emma looked back to the sky. "But the sun..."

Thane pointed again.

Looking again, Emma realized the color was across the whole sky but started from the north, not the east like a sunrise. When her eyes focused, she saw the moon was in full view.

"I do na understand."

"When I was a boy, we went trappin' far into the north. The men up there called these northern lights. They were more blues and greens up there. I've never seen the red lights." He circled his hands around Emma's waist and pulled her back to his chest. "And I've never seen them so bright that men and beasts get up ta start their day."

Emma pulled her eyes away from the bright lights on the horizon and looked at the animals. Jade was circling the chicken coop, trying to find a way in. The chickens were busy scratching around in the dirt for worms. She could even hear the pigs moving around in the barn, asking for their food. "They're truly convinced it's mornin' time."

"Yes, they are. I know I should've let you sleep. You need to sleep. But I couldn't let you miss this sight."

Gazing up at the sky, Emma rested against Thane, breathing in the easiness of the moment. The color in the sky was amazing to see. When she looked close, she could see the waves of color move. She knew it was the middle of the night and that she should be sleeping. But at that moment, there were no tasks to complete, and no one needed her to do anything. She felt like she was able to relax and enjoy this moment with her husband. Free from guilt.

Thane had been in the fields for weeks. Whether it was their own fields, or her father's, or even another neighbor's, he had been up before dawn and often home after dark. The night before had been no different. She missed talking to Thane.

"Thank ya fer wakin' me." She pulled Thane's arms closer around her, wanting to remember that moment always. How perfectly happy she was at that early morning hour.

A conversation she had overheard the day before flashed before her eyes. "With Annie bein' so fussy last night, I forgot to ask ya something. The deputies were in town yesterday, arguin' with some men. Ever since they arrested Sadie, it seems like the tension in town is gettin' worse."

"The slaves runnin' to Canada is gettin' worse."

"The deputies said it sounds like they are thinkin' about sendin' more Federal Marshalls after them ta take them home? No one wants ta be forced ta comply with this law anymore."

Thane nodded. "I've seen the same."

She hesitated. "Do ya think it will come ta blows?"

Thane pulled Emma tight against his chest. "I don't think it'll come ta that- but I have no way of knowin'. One thing I'm certain of is how thankful I am that God has given me such a blessed family. Whatever happens? We will face each day of our lives as it comes- together."

Emma pulled her husband's arms closer once more. Turning her gaze back to the beautiful colors of the northern lights in the sky, she smiled. "Together."

❧ about the author ❧

Jules Nelson *grew up in northern Michigan, the middle child of seven. With these siblings, she confidently explored the world around her. She spent her childhood making up stories and writing them down. The characters in her stories so real to her that they seemed to come alive.*

Today, Jules uses her writing, photography, and theatre to bring those stories to life.

At home in rural Michigan, Jules makes the most of every moment with her family.

Visit Jules Nelson's website to follow her current projects!

Julesnelson.net

Jules would love to hear your comments at jules.nelson@ymail.com

Also from Jules Nelson

Shadows

Remember...

The best compliment you can give an author is to leave them a review!

❧ Acknowledgments ❧

I want to personally thank everyone who helped me with the developing of **Road Home**...

Thank you, Chad... for listening to my endless obsessing over plot-lines and plot-holes. For your constant support and patience (...not to mention all the extra meals you cooked...) through this long process. I love you!

Thank you to my kids, Sabrina and Simon, for your patience when dealing with me saying, "Just one more paragraph..." and all the extras you do for me when I live in the "edit" world. I love you both so much!!

Thank you to my Biggest Fans- my parents... Grant and Gail Olmsted. Your support throughout my life means the world to me. I love you both!

Thank you to my siblings... Andy, Tammy, Paul, Dan, David, and Mark... You have been my most precious blessings throughout my lifetime. Even though I only used one of your names, each of your personalities went into the creation of "Mark"... I love each of you like crazy!!

Thank you to my TEAM. Sabrina Nelson (my baby girl), Melanie Olmsted (my personal trainer), Jill Hulsey, Tracy Kutchuk, my own dear Da (Grant Olmsted), Jamie Cowden and especially Cheree Castellanos. These wonderful people took time out of their busy lives to read, edit, advise, encourage and/or criticize this book. Love you all!!

Thank you to everyone who has ever read one of my creations and encouraged me to create another. Without all of your encouragement, I may never have had the persistence to FINISH **Road Home.**

And last... but most importantly... Thank you, God... for the gift of writing and for filling my life with the most amazing people!!

✢ Bible References ✢

John 8:32 NIV

Then you will know the truth, and the truth will set you free.

Luke 2:1-19 KJV

And it came to pass in those days that a decree went out from Caesar Augustus that all the world should be registered. This census first took place while Quirinius was governing Syria. So all went to be registered, everyone to his own city. Joseph also went up from Galilee, out of the city of Nazareth, into Judea, to the city of David, which is called Bethlehem, because he was of the house and lineage of David, to be registered with Mary, his betrothed wife, who was with child. So it was, that while they were there, the days were completed for her to be delivered. And she brought forth her firstborn Son, and wrapped Him in swaddling cloths, and laid Him in a manger because there was no room for them in the inn. Now there were in the same country shepherds living out in the fields, keeping watch over their flock by night. And behold, an angel of the Lord stood before them, and the glory of the Lord shone around them, and they were greatly afraid. Then the angel said to them, "Do not be afraid, for behold, I bring you good tidings of great joy which will be to all people. For there is born to you this day in the city of David a Savior, who is Christ the Lord. And this will be the sign to you: You will find a Babe wrapped in swaddling cloths, lying in a manger."

And suddenly there was with the angel a multitude of the heavenly host praising God and saying:

"Glory to God in the highest, And on earth peace, goodwill toward men!"

So it was, when the angels had gone away from them into heaven, that the shepherds said to one another, "Let us now go to Bethlehem and see this thing that has come to pass, which the Lord has made known to us." And they came with haste and found Mary and Joseph, and the Babe lying in a manger. Now when they had seen Him, they made widely known the saying which was told them concerning this Child. And all those who heard it marveled at those things which were told them by the shepherds. But Mary kept all these things and pondered them in her heart.

1 Corinthians 13:4-8a NIV

Love is patient, love is kind. It does not envy, it does not boast, it is not proud. It does not dishonor others, it is not self-seeking, it is not easily angered, it keeps no record of wrongs. Love does not delight in evil but rejoices with the truth. It always protects, always trusts. Always hopes, always perseveres.
Love never fails.

1 Corinthians 13:13 NIV

And now these three remain: faith, hope, and love. But the greatest of these is love.

Exodus 20:5 KJV

You shall not bow to them or serve them, for I the Lord your God am a jealous God, visiting the iniquity of the fathers on the children to the third and fourth generation of those who hate me,

Deuteronomy 24:16 KJV

The fathers shall not be put to death for the children neither shall the children be put to death for the fathers: every man shall be put to death for his own sin.

1 John 1:9 KJV

If we confess our sins, He is faithful and just to forgive us our sins, and to cleanse us from all unrighteousness.

Jules' Favorite Bible Verses

Luke 2:19

Mary kept all these things and pondered them in her heart.

Jeremiah 29:11

"For I know the plans I have for you," declares the Lord, "Plans to prosper you and not to harm you, plans to give you hope and a future."

Psalms 46:10

"Be still, and know that I am God"